'A remarkable achievement'   Arthur C. Clarke

'Intelligent, humorous . . . deeply moving . . . Morrow is a
lyrical, inventive writer'   Brian Aldiss

'I have not been so moved by an SF novel for a very long
time'   *The Times*

'If Kurt Vonnegut had collaborated with Jonathan Schell on
an antinuclear novel, this might be the result'
                                New York Times Book Review

Also by James Morrow

NOVELS

The Wine of Violence (1981)
The Continent of Lies (1984)
This is the Way the World Ends (1986)
Only Begotten Daughter (1990)
Towing Jehovah (1994)
Blameless in Abaddon (1996)
The Eternal Footman (1999)
The Last Witchfinder (2006)
The Philosopher's Apprentice (2008)
Shambling Towards Hiroshima (2009)

SHORT STORY COLLECTIONS

Swatting at the Cosmos (1990)
Bible Stories for Adults (1996)
The Cat's Pyjamas & Other Stories (2004)

SF MASTERWORKS

This is the Way the World Ends

JAMES MORROW

This edition first published in Great Britain in 2013 by
Gollancz
An imprint of the Orion Publishing Group
Orion House, 5 Upper St Martin's Lane,
London WC2H 9EA
An Hachette UK Company

3 5 7 9 10 8 6 4 2

A CIP catalogue record for this book
is available from the British Library

ISBN 978 0 575 08118 5

Typeset at The Spartan Press Ltd,
Lymington, Hants

Printed in Great Britain by Clays Ltd, St Ives plc

The Orion Publishing Group's policy is to use papers
that are natural, renewable and recyclable products and
made from wood grown in sustainable forests. The logging
and manufacturing processes are expected to conform to
the environmental regulations of the country of origin.

www.orionbooks.co.uk
www.gollancz.co.uk

For my daughter Kathy

Some say the world will end in fire,
Some say in ice.
From what I've tasted of desire
I hold with those who favor fire.
But if it had to perish twice,
I think I know enough of hate
To say that for destruction ice
Is also great
And would suffice.

— Robert Frost

INTRODUCTION

This novel, written in 1986, is reminiscent of Jonathan Swift and Philip K Dick in its satirical seriousness and its biting magical realism. It says much about how perceptions have shifted that now on reading it in 2012 I felt hard-pressed to consider it SF at all, in spite of its fantastical setting and its alternate-reality technology. I think partly this is due to its treatment of the fantastical elements: while the technology is clearly ordinary SF fare, it's a minor feature. Here it is simply a necessary instrument for the design of the story and its outcome, the purpose of which is an effort to make a scathing critique of the notion of Mutually Assured Destruction, both as a principle and as one of many such human rationalisations which serve no one and perpetuate world views in which acts of the most extreme tragedy and cruelty are no more than the necessary logical outcomes of a particular political arena.

The novel feels like it belongs with the literary novelists whose work clearly inspired Morrow: Vonnegut, Heller, Swift – rather than with a more orthodox SF canon, although as I write that I feel that I have elevated literature and downgraded SF, instead of which I would much rather do the other and add another well-deserved kick into the pants of literary snobbery, as Morrow would too. SF should be glad to have Morrow as Morrow is to have SF (and he did say so in an interview in 2000, which makes me like him all the more).

Regardless of who belongs to what genre the inclusion of this book in the SF Masterworks series is justified by its quality of thought and execution. As in several of his other works Morrow is at pains to demonstrate the universality of human folly when it comes to philosophising about difficult situations, and he places the blame at the door of insufficiently evolved human beings; the people who never grew up but who learned enough to manage all the intellectual tools of how to talk yourself out of your responsibilities. What's not to like about that?

Since it was written the boundaries on genres, the scope of general literature and the 'Terreur Du Jour' have changed. The one thing that has most dated is its central focus on the nuclear threat and the Cold War as the most, in fact the only, real extinction event facing humankind. Nowadays this rates relatively low – perhaps too low – on my personal scale of ways for the world to end, although at the time of its composition in 1986 I regularly woke from nightmares about the bomb dropping on some ordinary day in which I was unable to reach those I loved, whether they were separated from me by miles or mere yards – the flash came, the silence descended and those yards were instantly forever. I remember lying awake in bed after, countless times, wondering if it would really happen and how it was that humans could contemplate doing such things to one another. This book, in all its horrific detail, captures exactly those emotions of wonder, fear, denial, hope and horror. It combines them with Carroll's surreal logic of Wonderland and shows the aftermath of destruction as a Through The Looking Glass-world in which the ideas that led to the holocaust must be dealt with directly. Guilt must be felt. Justice must be served. Someone will be held to account and made to pay. It answers my question. That the answer is not a solution is hardly Morrow's fault.

Morrow spares no detail of anguish in going for this jugular but the story is written so that at times its comic absurdity lurches into farce, then back into satire and then into tragedy. As such it could have fallen prey to becoming too much an intellectual exercise or a horror story, but is spared by remaining tied to the human through its central character, George Paxton, and his fanciful notions of repopulating the dying Earth. This stands in a slightly odd contrast to the frame story in which Nostradamus and Leonardo are both portrayed as significant; complicit as witnesses and harbingers, long-dead conspirators of doom.

One of the things that I enjoyed most about this book is its use of these whimsys and devices that toy with prediction and invention, fantastic and realistic, literary allusion and real reference, putting them together in ways that make for a complex satisfaction in that it adds up to something, although what exactly I am unable to articulate. It is like Eliot's poems in this respect – big and odd enough to allow almost an infinity of meaning to be poured into it at times. It is this refusal to become sufficiently simple that is most pleasing and life-affirming about good literature; it recognises and surpasses the limits of single systems of thought or perception and Morrow does this here quite well.

This is the Way . . . also stands in a strong and obvious relation to Eliot's *The Hollow Men*, not only because it takes its title from that poem, but most of its sensibilities too. None of the characters here put on trial for the annihilation of the human race, with the exception of the ordinary George Paxton, have much in the way of personality or redeeming features. In that they perhaps are the best portraits of whom we like to think of as responsible for such unbearable visions – monsters of our own kind who are not amenable to trauma and as such cannot be pulled into compassion. Their lack of neuroticism, imagination and social restraint and their ability to be easily convinced by arguments enable them to commit acts of extinction others would never dream of. Able to blind themselves with causes, reasons and the drama of being important they lose connections to reality, connections that have also been severed in the past by religions or other panoplies of ideas intent on justifying cruelty and explaining away tragedy. The soul's panaceas become the tormentors of the world.

Here, from their own mouths, the reasoning of the accused make them ridiculous in the face of the horror they have unleashed, but Morrow makes them also sympathetic and credible. Ultimately they seem to make George Paxton's simple act of signing up to his complicity in the nuclear war merely trivial, until Morrow makes us face the fact that good men need only do nothing for evil consequences to rule the day. It is Paxton's desperate need to save his daughter that makes him willing to sign, and his disenfranchisement from power that makes him

PROLOGUE

Salon-de-Provence, France, 1554

Doctor Michel de Nostredame, who could see the future, sat in his secret study, looking at how the world would end.

The end of the world was spread across the prophet's writing desk – one hundred images of destruction, each painted on a piece of glass no larger than a Tarot card. With catlike caution he dealt out the brittle masterpieces, putting them in dramatic arrangements. Which should come first? he wondered. The iron whales? The ramparts of flame? The great self-propelled spears?

By late afternoon the paintings were properly sequenced, and Nostradamus made ready to compose the hundred commentaries that would accompany them. He opened the window, siphoned sweet air through his nostrils.

Tulip gardens. Sun-buttered fields of clover. Crisp, white cottages. A finch chirped amid the nectar-gorged blossoms of a cherry tree. Now, thought the prophet, if only a cat would come along and devour the finch alive, I could rise to the task at hand.

He consulted the finch's future. No cats. The bird would die of old age.

He pulled a drape across the window, lit seven candles, dipped his crow quill in a skull filled with ink, and began to write. The gloom, morbid and relentless, inspired him. Like blood from a cut vein, words flowed from Nostradamus's pen; the nib scrabbled across the parchment. Shortly before midnight he completed the final commentary. The painting in question showed a bearded man standing alone on a boundless plain of ice. *And so our hero,* wrote the prophet, *last of the mortals, makes ready to fly into the bosom of our Lord. Such are the true facts of history yet to come.*

The dark oak of the writing desk had turned the painting into a looking glass. Etched in the ice field were the prophet's raven eyes, craggy nose, and black tumble of beard – a face his wife nevertheless loved. Anne is going to enter my study soon, he realized.

3

She will tell me something most troublesome. A pregnant woman waits downstairs for me. The woman is in labor. The woman wants . . .

'The woman wants my help,' said Nostradamus to his wife after she had appeared in the study as predicted.

Anne Pons Gemmelle gave a meandering smile. 'Sarah Mirabeau has come all the way from Tarascon.'

'And her husband—?'

'She has no husband.'

'Reveal to Sarah Mirabeau that I foresee an easy birth, a robust little bastard, and happy destinies for all concerned. Reveal to her also that, if she troubles me further, I foresee myself losing my temper' – the prophet brandished his Malacca cane – 'and tossing her into the street.'

'What do you *really* foresee?'

'It is all rather murky.'

'Sarah Mirabeau did not come to have her fortune told. She came—'

'Because I am a physician? Inform her that a midwife would be more to the point.'

By closing her eyes and biting her tongue, Anne retained her good humor. 'The Tarascon midwives will not attend a Jew,' she said slowly.

'Whereas I shall?'

'I advised the woman that you have not been Jewish in years.'

'Good! Did you show her my record of baptism? No, wait, I foresee you saying that you have—'

'Already done so, and she was—'

'Not convinced. Then you must tell this fornicator that I have never delivered a baby in my life. Tell her that the medicine I practice of late consists in removing creases from the faces of aging gentry.'

'She is not a fornicator. One hundred days ago her husband was—'

'Killed by the plague,' anticipated the prophet.

'The widow believes you could have cured him. "Only the divine Doctor Nostradamus can keep me alive today," she said.

4

"Only the hero of Aix and Lyons can bring me a healthy child."
Yes, she has heard of your victories over the Black Death.'

'But not of my defeats? This Nostradamus she worships is not much of a Catholic, not much of a Jew, and not much of a miracle-maker – tell her that.'

'We must show her Christian charity.'

'We must show her *my* charity, nothing better. Your widow may, for tonight only, take to Madeleine's bed. Madame Hozier, I am given to understand, is a competent midwife, I shall pay her five *écus*. If she objects either to the fee or to your widow's heathenism, tell her that I shall forthwith cast her horoscope, and it will be the grimmest horoscope imaginable, full of poverty and ill health.'

Anne Pons Gemmelle scurried off, but the prophet's privacy did not endure. He foresaw as much: a boy would wander into his secret study.

A boy wandered into his secret study.

'You were about to give your name,' said the prophet.

'I was?' The boy was fourteen, diminutive, olive-skinned, his curly black hair frothing from beneath a cloth cap.

'Yes. Who are you?' said the prophet.

'They call me—'

'Jacob Mirabeau, Your mother is in my daughter's bedroom, giving birth. Tell me, lad, was the invitation that brings you to my private chambers printed on gold-leaf vellum or on ordinary paper?'

'What?'

'That was sarcasm. The coming thing. *Mirabile dictu*, what a reversal Bonaparte will suffer once he reaches Moscow!'

The boy yanked off his cap. 'I know you! You are the one who sees what will happen. My mother collects your almanacs.'

'Does she buy them, or does she merely find them lying around?'

'She buys them.'

'Would you care for a fig?' Nostradamus asked cheerfully.

'*Merci*. My mother places great store in your predictions. She thinks you are God-touched.'

5

'Opinion about me is divided. The Salon rabble think I am a Satanist or, worse, a Huguenot, or, worse still, a Jew.'

'You *are* a Jew.'

'We are quite a pair, lad. I can see your future, you can see my past.'

'I am a Jew as well.' The boy gobbled his fig.

'Do not trumpet it. Being Jewish is not exactly the wave of the future, believe me. The Inquisition has not yet run its course, the Pope would have us in ghettos. Get yourself baptized, that is my counsel to you. Forget this whole enterprise of being a Jew.'

'Can you see some piece of the future right now, Monsieur le Docteur, or must you stare at the constellations first?'

'The stars are unconnected to my powers, little Jew.'

'But you have an astrolabe.'

'Also a brass bowl, a tripod, and a laurel branch. My readers expect a full complement of nonsense.'

'What do you foresee at the moment?' asked the boy, rolling a fig seed between his tongue and teeth.

'You are up too late. Do you realize it is almost midnight?'

'What else do you foresee?'

'Myself. Writing a large book.' Nostradamus wove his crow quill through the air. 'One hundred prophecies, in ill-phrased and leaden verse. Gibberish, every last line, but the mob will love them. From now until the end of the world, booksellers will make fortunes out of vapid and dishonest commentaries on these stanzas. I shall mention the River Hister, and my interpreters will claim that I was referring to Hitler.'

'Who is Hitler?'

'You don't want to know. More bad news for Jews.'

'If your book will be gibberish, why write it?'

'Fun and profit.'

'It would seem that—'

Fear silenced the boy. A nasty black wasp had fumbled past the drapes and looped into the study. It buzzed fatly. The boy sought refuge behind an enormous globe.

'Easy, little Jew. It will not sting you.'

'With all respect, Monsieur' – raising his cap, Jacob stalked forward – 'I have my doubts.'

He swatted the wasp to the floor and stomped it past recognition.

'Why were you certain it would not have stung me?' the boy asked.

'I foresaw you smashing it first.'

Jacob replaced his cap, secured it by stuffing his curls beneath the sweatband. 'Will this baby kill my mother?'

'Your mother will live to see seventy. Furthermore, Truman will defeat Dewey, forecasts to the contrary.'

'You are truly blessed, Monsieur.'

The prophet thought: a likely lad. He appreciates my talent, he does not hide his religion, he is quick with his cap. If my show can astonish a fellow so sharp, it is certain to set the rabble on their oversized ears.

'Tell me, Master Jacob,' said Nostradamus, opening a walnut coffer and removing a contraption of metal and glass, 'would you like to see the future?'

'Very much so.'

Nostradamus carried the machine to his writing desk. The boy's lips quivered. His eyes expanded.

'You are right to be awestruck, for the man who contrived this device is the most wonderful person of our age. Quick, who is the most wonderful person of our age?'

'You, my lord.'

The prophet alternately grinned and scowled. 'The most wonderful person of our age is Leonardo of Vinci, who alone knew what expression each saint wore when dining with Christ.'

'I have heard of Leonardo of Milan.'

'Of Milan, yes. Of Florence, of Rome, of Vinci. But he ended his days in France – Amboise, the manor of Clos-Lucé. I was at his deathbed. With his final breath he bequeathed to me this picture-cannon, as he called it. Monsieur Leonardo loved cannons. He loved all weapons. Happily, this cannon fires no ball.'

Mastering his astonishment, Jacob approached the writing desk. The machine was a tin box with a chimney on top. From

7

one side jutted a tube holding a brass ring in which sat a sparkling crystal disk.

'I was no older than you when the great man summoned me to Amboise. That was in . . . 1518, during my first schooling. Leonardo had heard of my gift. At Avignon they called me the Little Astrologer. I was frightened. Here was he, the illustrious Leonardo – *Premier Peintre, Architecte et Méchanicien du Roi*. And here was I – a boy of fifteen, burdened with peculiar powers. As it turned out, he fell in love with me, but that is another story.

'He showed me some drawings – our world in its final days, shattered by storms and floods. "Is this how God will contrive for His Creation to end?" he asked me. Brother Francesco translated. "No," I replied. "I did not think so," he confessed.

'I told him how our world would end. "It will not be an act of God or Nature," I explained, "but a conflagration of human design." He painted what I described – fireballs hurled from great spears that had in turn been catapulted from the backs of iron whales. The renderings were perfect, as if plucked directly from my brain. He did them on glass.

'Odd – but of the hundred awful scenes I recounted, only four seemed to vex Leonardo. They all involved vultures. "Are you certain that vultures will be part of this war?" he asked again and again. "Quite certain," I always answered. "I was once visited by a vulture," he would say. I could not imagine what he meant.

'The old man had in mind a great public spectacle. He wanted first to exhibit his holocaust paintings in Rome. Then we were to tour the countryside, finally the whole continent – taking the capitals by storm, dazzling rabble and rich men alike, warning them of the terrible future, filling our pockets with their coins.'

The portrait under which Nostradamus stood shimmered with the grace of its subject. Within the gilded frame, a woman smiled subtly.

'The old man never got out of France,' Nostradamus continued wistfully. 'But I shall. Pope Julius himself will marvel at these masterworks – this I vow.' The prophet clapped his hands. 'We need a white wall, boy. Take down this picture here – another gift

8

from Leonardo. In a few centuries it will be worth an unimaginable amount of money. Little good that does me.'

Why a white wall? Jacob wondered. If this wizard means to perform some magic, would not a black wall be more suitable?

The boy removed the smiling woman. Even in the feeble candlelight, the exposed wall was as shockingly white as the winding sheet in which his father had been buried. Perhaps white was good for wizardry after all.

Nostradamus lifted a door in the side of the picture-cannon, revealing a small oil lamp, which he lit. Smoke wandered out of the chimney. 'Believe me, Master Jacob, there is no sorcery in this machine, but only the divine reason with which God filled Leonardo to overflowing. You have heard of the *camera obscura?* Leonardo managed to turn one inside out. This part here – the aperture. Here – the plano-convex lens, ground from purest beryl.' The prophet inserted the first painting. 'This business also requires darkness.'

Jacob snuffed the candles, one by one, and night fell upon the study like a succession of blows. The boy looked at the wall. What he saw made him dizzy and afraid.

'Dear God – it's what Christians call the devil's work!' A vast vision had appeared, many times the size of the smiling woman. Where does it come from? he wondered. Instinctively he turned toward the picture-cannon. 'But the painting you put in there was so small!'

Jacob fixed on the vision. No less stunning than its size was its substance, a swollen, smoking, demon-spawned, self-propelled spear. 'Will it really destroy the world?' he asked.

'Not by itself. There will be thousands like it, in many varieties.' Nostradamus glanced at his parchment script. '*This Satanic lance is a Soviet SS-60 missile,*' he read. '*Land-based. Intercontinental. Multiple warheads.* Do you understand?'

'No.'

The candle in the picture-cannon flickered. Shadows trembled along the shaft of the missile.

Nostradamus projected painting number two. '*This iron fish is a fleet ballistic missile submarine,*' he read. '*The dorsal scales will flip back, and the spears will fly to their targets using inertial guidance.*'

'How can a fish have spears inside it and not die?' asked the boy.

Nostradamus projected painting number three. '*From hell's hearth, a thermonuclear fireball—*'

'Is that Latin?'

'I am confounding you, Jacob. It will be best, I can see, not to begin with the weapons. These pictures need a *tale* to accompany them, am I right?'

'Tell me a tale,' said the boy.

Nostradamus sorted through the paintings, chose one, projected it. A vulture. Hunched, ragged, sallow-eyed, carrion-bloated.

'This is about a vulture, a war, and a man named George Paxton. A common man in many respects, but also perhaps a hero, entrapped in Fortuna's wheel and sent on a series of frightening and fantastic adventures.'

The prophet projected another painting. A bearded man standing by a gravestone.

'Until he saw the three children in white . . .'

BOOK ONE

Those Who Favor Fire

CHAPTER ONE

*In Which Our Hero Is Introduced and Taught the True
Facts Concerning Strategic Doctrine and Civil Defense*

Until he saw the three children in white, George Paxton's life had
gone just about perfectly.

Born in the middle of the twentieth century to generous and
loving parents, people of New England stock so pure it was found
only in northeast Vermont, he came to manhood in the tepid
bosom of the Unitarian Church. It was an unadorned, New
England sort of faith. Unitarians rejected miracles, worshiped
reason, denied the divinity of Jesus Christ, and had serious
doubts about the divinity of God. George grew up believing that
this was the most plausible of all possible worlds.

By the time he was thirty-five he had been blessed with an
adorable daughter, a wife who always looked as if she had just
come from doing something dangerous and lewd, and a cozy
cottage perched on stilts above a lake. He was in good health, and
he knew how to prevent many life-threatening diseases through a
diet predicated on trace metals. George took inordinate pleasure
in ordinary things. Hot coffee gave him fits of rapture. If there was
a good movie on television that night, he would spend the day
whistling.

He had even outmaneuvered the philosophers. A seminal dis-
covery of the twentieth century was that a man could live a life
overflowing with advantages and still be obliquely unhappy.
Despair, the philosophers called it. But the coin of George
Paxton's life had happiness stamped on both sides – no despair

for George. Individuals so fortunate were scarce in those days. You could have sold tickets to George Paxton.

Now it must be allowed that not everyone in his situation would have shared his contentment. Not everyone would have found fulfillment in putting words on cemetery monuments. For George, however, inscribing monuments was a calling, not simply a job. He was in the tomb profession. He kept a scrapbook of the great ones: the sarcophagus of Alexander, the shrine to Mausolus at Halicarnassus, the Medici tomb at San Lorenzo, the pyramid of Cheops. Don't you get depressed being around gravestones all day? people asked him. No, he replied. Gravestones, he knew, were educational media, teaching that life has limits: don't set your sights too high.

Occasionally his wife accused him of laziness. 'I wish you would go out and get yourself some ambition,' Justine would say. But George's world satisfied him – the pace, the simplicity, the muscles he acquired from lifting granite.

And then they came, the three children in white, jumping out of the back of John Frostig's panel truck and sprinting toward the sample stones that spread outward from the foundation of the Crippen Monument Works. The stones were closely spaced, as in a cemetery for dwarves. 'Floor models,' George's boss liked to call them. 'Want to take one out for a spin?' the boss would quip.

Sitting near the smeared and sooty window of the front office, George watched as the white children leapfrogged over the stones. Their suits – trim, one-piece affairs cinched by utility belts and topped with globular helmets – afforded complete mobility. Each child wore a pistol. The leapfrogging boys looked ready for the bottom of the ocean, the inside of a volcano, a Martian sandstorm, a plague of bees, anything.

Briefcase in tow, John climbed out of the driver's seat. A painting of a white suit decorated the side of the truck, accompanied by the words PERPETUAL SECURITY SCOPAS SUITS . . . JOHN FROSTIG, PRESIDENT . . . WILDGROVE, MASSACHUSETTS . . . 555-7043. The president of Perpetual Security Scopas Suits marched toward the office exuding the sort of nervous energy and insatiable ambition that made George feel there are worse things in life than being satisfied with what you have.

Entering, John imposed his rump on a stool, balanced the briefcase on his knees.

'Has someone died?' George asked.

'Died? Nope, sorry, you won't sell me anything today, buddy-buddy.' John's friendship with George had been primarily John's idea. 'No tombs today.'

George swiveled away from the window. A swivel chair, a rolltop desk, a naughty calendar, a patina of dust, the stool on which John sat – these formed the sum total of Arthur Crippen's office. Arthur was not there. He never appeared before noon, rarely before 2 P.M. Just then it was 3:30. Arthur was doubtless at the Lizard Lounge, a bar administering to the broken hopes and failed ambitions of the town's shopkeepers.

'Look out the window, buddy-buddy. What do you see?'

George pivoted. The children had begun a science fiction game, laser-zapping each other with their pistols, using the monuments for cover. 'White children,' he reported.

'Safe children. There's a war coming, George, a bad one. It's inevitable, what with both sides having so many land-based, first-strike ICBMs. Soon we'll all be living in scopas suits. That's S-C-O-P-A-S, as in Self-Contained Post-Attack Survival. Just five weeks I've had this franchise, and already I've sold two dozen units without once leaving the borders of our fair hamlet. The company tells us to operate under any name we like, so I'm Perpetual Security Scopas Suits. I thought that up myself – Perpetual Security Scopas Suits. Like it?'

'I can't see why the Russians would want to bomb Wildgrove,' said George the Unitarian. He was what his church had made him, a naive skeptic.

'You don't know jackshit about strategic doctrine, do you? Ever hear of a counterforce strike? The enemy wants to wipe out America's war-waging capability. Well, Wildgrove is part of that war-waging capability. We've got food, clothing, gasoline, trucks, people – many things of military value. All the apples we grow here could prove decisive during the intra-war period.'

15

'Well, if they ever do drop their bombs, I imagine we'll all die before we know what hit us.'

'That's pretty pessimistic of you, buddy-buddy, and furthermore it's not true. Put on a scopas suit, and you won't be able to *avoid* surviving.'

John opened his briefcase, took out a crisply printed form headed ESCHATOLOGICAL ENTERPRISES – WE DO CIVIL DEFENSE RIGHT. George knew about sales contracts; you could not acquire a stone from the Crippen Monument Works without signing one.

'Eschatological – doesn't sound very Japanese, does it?' said John. 'Don't worry. Right now all the units might come from Osaka, but next month there'll be a plant in Detroit and another in Palo Alto. Hell, talk about being in the right place with the right product at the right time. Greatest thing since the rubber. A smart bunch of bastards, those Eschatological people, a bunch of shrewd—'

'This isn't my kind of thing.'

'The price wouldn't shock you.'

'Sorry, John—'

'Begin simple – that's what I tell everybody. One or two units, expand later. Do the kids first. The smaller the suit, the lower the cost. Your daughter—'

'Holly is four.'

'Wise decision, truly wise. I must tell you, it puts a lump right smack in the middle of my throat. Now, the way I figure it, the warheads won't arrive for two years. Yeah, I know, the world's going to hell in a slant-eyed Honda, but smart money still says two years. So you'll need something that will fit Holly when she's six, right? Normally we'd be talking over seven thousand pictures of George Washington, but for you, buddy-buddy, let's make it sixty-five ninety-five plus tax.'

'That's more than I take home in . . . I don't know, four months. Five. I'll have to say no to this.'

The suit salesman hammered the contract with his extended index finger. 'You think we're talking cash on the barrelhead? We're talking *installments* on the barrelhead, teeny tiny *installments*.' The finger skated across a pocket calculator. 'Figuring a five

16

percent sales tax and an annual interest rate of eighteen percent or one-point-five per month, we can amortize the loan through a constant monthly payment of three hundred and forty-five dollars and seventy-one cents, so in two years you'll own little Holly's unit free and clear. You probably spend that much on beer.'

George took the contract, attempted to read it, but the words refused to resolve into clear meanings. Holly liked to draw. She produced an average of four crayon sketches a day. Their refrigerator displayed one that looked exactly like George – exactly.

On the other hand, if a war occurred of the sort John was predicting, it wouldn't matter how much art schools cost.

'Do you happen to have the kind for a six-year-old with you? I mean . . . I'm just wondering what they look like.'

John's nod was smug. 'When you work for Perpetual Security, George, you're prepared for anything.'

They left the office and wove through the tiny cemetery. Most of the stones embodied a macabre optimism; there was nothing inscribed on them. First came the Protestant district, then the Catholic section, finally the Jewish neighborhood. John opened the back of his truck and hoisted himself into the dark cavity, where several dozen scopas suits of varying sizes hung like commuters packed into a subway. George noticed one suit intended for a dog, another for a baby.

To the casual observer it might have suggested a nineteenth-century body-snatching scene, two men hauling a limp and pallid shape through a graveyard. First George – short, muscular, with rough-hewn features attempting to reclaim themselves from a scrub-brush beard and a jungle of hair. Then John – tall, clean-shaven, aggressively handsome, self-consciously suave. The white children followed them into the office. John and George arranged the little scopas suit on the swivel chair. George struggled to recall the names of the Frostig boys. The youngest was in the same nursery school as Holly and had once murdered the hamsters. Rickie – was that his name? Nathan?

'Mr Paxton wants to see your units,' John announced grandly, lining up his sons like army recruits. 'Gary, show him your cranial gear.'

The fifteen-year-old removed his dinosaur-egg helmet. He had inherited his father's disconcerting good looks. 'Upon sensing the detonation,' Gary recited, 'the phones shut down – hence, no ruptured eardrums from blast overpressures. As for the fireball, the wraparound Lexan screen guards against flashblindness and retinal scorching.'

'Excellent, Gary.'

'Thank you, sir.'

John went to his second son. 'Lance, Mr Paxton wants to know about the fabric.'

When Lance removed his helmet, George recognized the ten-year-old he had once caught spraying WALTERS BITES THE BIG ONE on a headstone Toby Walters had ordered for his dead mother. Lance looked middle-childy – casual, unassuming. He tugged on his front zipper, making a V-shaped part and revealing a sweat shirt emblazoned with the logo of a rock group called Sperm. 'Alternating layers of Winco Synthefill VII, Celanese Fortrel Arcticguard Polyester, and activated charcoal,' he chanted, folding back one flap to display the lining. 'In terms of initial ionizing radiation and subsequent fallout, the protection factor is a big one thousand, shielding you from a cumulative dose of up to two hundred thousand rads. As for . . . as for . . .' The boy twitched and turned red.

'Thermal radiation, son.'

'As for thermal radiation, a scopas suit can deflect over five thousand degrees Fahrenheit. You can be one hundred yards from the hypocenter, and all you'll get is a sunburn.'

Again John consulted his first son. 'Gary, let's hear about blast-wave effects on the human body.'

'Because the material is interlayered with fibrosteel mesh,' said Gary, 'it can withstand dynamic pressures of up to sixty-five pounds per square inch, such as you might experience one mile from ground zero. Flying slivers of glass – a significant hazard in any thermonuclear exchange – cannot penetrate. Finally, even though the overpressures could catch you in a cyclonic wind and hurl you nearly three hundred feet, the padding in your nuke suit guarantees that you'll walk away without a bruise.'

'They aren't "nuke suits," lad,' the salesman corrected cheerfully. 'What are they?'

'They're Perpetual Security scopas suits, sir.'

'You probably think the Eschatological people forgot about Mother Nature,' said John, rapping on George's shoulder with his index finger. 'No way. Each unit gives you a built-in commode – the Leonardo Porta-Potty.'

Now it was the little one's turn. 'Nickie, show Mr Paxton your utilities.'

Nickie – ah, yes, that was his name – unbuckled his sashlike belt, removed his helmet. His hamster-killer's face was swarthy and firm. 'Let's see . . . here I have an indiv— , indiv—'

'Individual.'

'Individual radiation . . . doze . . . er, doze-matter.'

'Dosimeter, Nickie. Say *dosimeter*.'

'Dosimeter. Then I've got a Swiss Army knife, a canteen, vitamins, and my' – joy flooded through the child – 'my Colt Mark IV forty-five caliber automatic pistol!'

'Way to go, Nick!'

With a clumsy flourish the boy flipped the gun out of its holster. George pulled his hands in front of his face and said Jesus' name.

'Note your Pachmayr grips,' said the suit salesman, 'your King-Tappan fixed combat sights, your—'

'Is that real?' George asked.

'She's not loaded. Safety first.'

'We have target practice in the basement,' Nickie explained, waving the pistol around in a manner that made George say *not loaded* to himself several times. 'We shoot paper Communists.'

John strutted behind the line of boys, patting them on their sleek, narrow backpacks. 'Last but not least, you have your survival gear. The bottom compartment is an oxygen tank – those warheads could touch off a conflagration or two, and that means smoke and toxic gases. You also get a primus stove, a portable water purifier, and a vacuum-packed can of vegetable seeds, including soybeans, barley, and other species resistant to ultraviolet light. In the medical kit you'll find penicillin-G tablets, tetanus toxoid, hydrocortisone, and a bottle of nitrous oxide for anesthesia. And, of course, each pack includes an item from your basic assortment of survival guns. Gary is carrying a disassembled Armalite AR-180 light assault rifle. She fires – tell the man, Gary.'

'The standard US military five-point-five-six-millimeter round. Effective range – four hundred and fifty yards.'

'Right you are. Now Lance here is toting all the parts for a Remington 870 twelve-gauge shotgun. Most useful of all' – John caressed Nickie's pack – 'is the Heckler and Koch HK 91 heavy assault rifle with collapsible stock. That's the piece you'll get with Holly's suit. Effective range – one thousand yards.'

George had to admit that thermonuclear exchange worries crossed his mind occasionally, and that he did not know where to seek reassurance. It would be wonderful to lose this anxiety, which erupted at odd moments. Assuming they could squeeze another hundred dollars a month from Justine's paycheck, there was every reason to put this thing under the Christmas tree.

'If I give you the first installment today, can I take it home?'

An elaborate smile appeared on John's face. 'Sure, you can take it home. Hell, next you'll order a suit for your pretty wife, then one for yourself, and then you'll both sleep a lot better. Any more kids in the works?'

'We've been talking about it. Yeah.'

'Go for it.'

George took out his checkbook. John fondled the contract.

'It's like the fable of the grasshopper and the ant,' said the suit salesman. 'Mr Grasshopper wastes the whole summer singing and playing and having a ripsnorting time – sort of like that lushy boss of yours – while Mr Ant works his abdomen off saving up food. So when winter comes, Mr Grasshopper, he wants a piece of Mr Ant's larder. Naturally Mr Ant tells Mr Grasshopper to piss off. Now, if you ask me, old Aesop was really writing about atomic wars. He got one thing wrong, though. Know what he should have called it?'

'What?'

'*The Fable of the Grasshopper and the Cockroach.*'

And so it was that George Paxton became the happy owner of a Self-Contained Post-Attack Survival suit.

CHAPTER TWO

*In Which Our Hero's Daughter Is Shielded
from the True Facts Concerning Seagulls*

As it turned out, George could not have picked a worse day for buying a scopas suit. That very morning, his wife was fired for breaking a tarantula.

Justine had never liked her situation at Raining Cats and Dogs, a franchised pet store located in the Wildgrove Mall. The job entailed most of the disadvantages of working for an orphanage and few of the rewards. It seemed to her that a given kitten or puppy never ended up with an appropriate owner; indeed, Justine mistrusted the motives of *anyone* who would patronize Raining Cats and Dogs when there were so many psychologically healthier, albeit less convenient, places from which to obtain a pet: a farm, a kennel, an alley. And, of course, there were those animals who did not find homes at all, every week growing older and conspicuously less adorable, their lives circumscribed by the glass-walled cages (which the chain's owners called habitats), until the day came when Harry Sweetser would ship them back to headquarters, where God knew what fate awaited. These unadoptable pets were a continual temptation to Justine, but George would have no more animals in a house where the nonhuman population already stood at six.

The fat boy wanted the tarantula, really wanted it, and his mother seemed far less repulsed by the idea than most mothers would have been. Justine sensed that here, for once, were customers with proper credentials. Normally she took a dim view of those parts of the inventory that had too few or too many legs –

the pythons, indigo snakes, scorpions, crabs, and spiders – not because they frightened her (they did not), but because they were gimmicks, bought by the wrong people for the wrong reasons. To look at this boy, however, a loser by all odds – homely, awkward, and shy – was to realize how much he needed the tarantula, and how much the tarantula needed him.

And so Justine undertook a mission that she saw as, among other things, a test of her acting talent. More than anything else, George's wife wanted to act. She was no dreamer, though; no visions of Hollywood danced in her head. Her sober and plausible ambition was to be the clown who gave out balloons at children's parties, the radio voice that told you where to purchase a new sofa, or the pretty lady at the local cable television station who explained why you should patronize the Wildgrove Hardware Store or Sandy's Sandwich Shop (or, for that matter, Raining Cats and Dogs).

'What's *your* name?' she asked the boy, making *your* light up.

'Andy.'

'Well, Andy, this spider will make you the envy of your friends. You have my guarantee.'

'I've heard that they can kill you,' said his mother, winking humorfully. Without this particular mother, Justine decided, Andy would never survive.

'Treat a tarantula badly and, oh yes, it'll bite. Rather like a dog.' Justine unwrapped a stick of spearmint gum and with a histrionic gesture placed it in her mouth. 'The venom is unpleasant but never lethal. In fact, far from being savage beasts, tarantulas are quite delicate.'

'Aren't they kind of boring?' asked the mother.

'Not when they're injecting you with venom, no,' said Justine, and the mother laughed.

'Can you play with it?' Andy wanted to know.

'Sure you can play with it.' Justine removed the tarantula from its cage and set its fuzzy body on her shoulder. 'See?' As the animal strutted down her arm, Andy's face gave off equal amounts of light and heat.

'Wow!' he concluded.

When a tarantula is dropped, the result is always the same. It blows up. Justine was never sure why the spider panicked and jumped from her forearm, although the disaster occurred simultaneously with, and might very well have been caused by, Harry Sweetser's sudden, boisterous arrival. 'Arrgh!' he screamed as the forty-dollar spider exploded.

'Jesus, I'm sorry, Harry.' Pity and remorse swept through Justine. 'Poor bugger.'

'Women should never try to handle these things.' Harry was a balding little fussbudget with a double paunch. 'You're too squeamish.'

'Well, as a matter of fact,' said Justine, 'it only fell because you came over.'

'New rule,' said Harry. 'Anyone who can't touch the arachnids without panicking has to leave them alone.'

'Why don't you go snort a toad, Harry?' she snapped. She thought about the remark, felt astonishingly good, and flashed her teeth theatrically.

Harry ordered her to clean up the tarantula's remains. 'And then I want to see you in my office,' he announced, giving each word an ominous spin.

The mother looked at the mess on the floor and said, 'I guess we're not all that interested in tarantulas today.' She steered her bewildered son out of the store.

Entering Harry's office, Justine noted with mild surprise that he was not at his desk. He stood in the middle of the rug, thumbs hooked in his belt. 'So anyway, I think maybe Raining Cats and Dogs isn't the place for you, right?' he said. 'I'll mention one thing, though – you were always a pleasure to look at in the morning.' Advancing, he groped toward her face. 'You have an inspirational way of feeding the fish.' He stroked her cheek. 'In fact, Justine, everything about you is inspirational.'

She backed off. If I ever stoop to this, she thought, it will be in the name of landing a major role in a cable TV commercial. Harry's countermove consisted of crossing to the door, closing it, and maneuvering her into a corner.

'With a little encouragement I could be persuaded to give you your job back.' He placed a practiced, unequivocal hand on her left buttock. 'Why don't we swing by the Lizard Lounge this afternoon for a drink?'

'You know, Harry' – she slipped out from under his palm and started for the door – 'there's something special about you that you may not be aware of.'

'What?'

'You're an absolutely astounding scuzz-bucket.'

Harry then informed Justine that she was fired.

And so when George came home that evening proudly displaying the scopas suit, Justine's reaction approximated that of the mother in *Jack and the Beanstalk* learning that Jack had bartered away the family cow for some magic seeds.

'Six thousand five hundred and ninety-five dollars?' she gasped. 'For *what?*'

'For civil defense against thermonuclear attack. For Holly's future. We pay three hundred and forty-five dollars and seventy-one cents a month – that's including the tax – and after two years it's ours. It's from Japan.'

Justine listened morosely as George jabbered about individual radiation dosimeters, primus stoves, Lexan screens, and Winco Synthefill. He placed the suit on the sofa and took off his work shirt, showering the floor with granite flakes and aluminum-oxide bits, the detritus of his trade; their cottage was highly tactile: granite, aluminum-oxide, sand, pet hair, pieces of mail too important to throw away yet too trivial to file, clothes that quit their hangers on their own initiative, all subsumed in the endless onrush of Holly's toys. The Irish setter loped over and sniffed the suit. Lucius the cat jumped on it, curled into himself, and took a nap.

Justine's horror of the scopas suit was nonverbal and intuitive, the horror of a mother hen seeing a hawk shadow glide across the barnyard. She could find no flaw in the garment's design, no error in its execution, no fallacy in its purpose. And yet she knew that Holly must never own one.

'I think Santa Claus should bring it,' said George, eagerly

caressing his purchase, which rested on the sofa like a boy king lying in state. 'She'll be more likely to wear it if she believes it came from him.'

'George, I lost my job.'

'You what?'

'Harry Sweetser fired me. I blew up a tarantula.'

'Nuts.'

'I'm glad. Not about the tarantula – but I really couldn't have faced another day at that place.' She inserted a stick of spearmint gum between her lips like a cigarette, puffed on it. 'Noah Webster College has a drama department, I hear.'

'I thought we were talking about having another kid. This your way of changing your mind?'

'I'll take evening courses. By day I'll be a mother, by night you'll be a father. Life works out.'

'Our plumbing is rotten, our car has cancer, we can't afford life insurance, we're trying to have a baby, and *you* want to join the circus!'

'Not the circus, the drama department!' The gum entered her mouth like a log entering a sawmill.

'You have no sense of reality!'

'You have no sense of anything else!' Justine's anger had thrown her hair across her face, and now she pushed it aside; curtains parted on large brown eyes, high cheeks, abundant lips, a sensual over-bite – to wit, a face that one might easily imagine on the talent side of a cable television camera, a face that was, by all but the most banal criteria, beautiful. 'With training I can bring in twice what I was making at Cats and Dogs.'

'Let's be honest, Justine. Money isn't something you and I will ever understand. If it grew on trees, we'd be raising chickens.'

'You're worried about money?' She chomped violently on her spearmint stick. 'Then stop going around spending seven thousand dollars like it belonged to somebody else.'

A fight followed. There was some screaming. Fists were pounded. Resentments emerged like bits of an ancient civilization tossed up by an earthquake. The fight encompassed George's tendency to assume that the pets were solely Justine's responsibility, and it included Justine's tendency to treat her parents shabbily, always forgetting their birthdays. It touched on whether they could really cope with another child, money worries or not, and eventually it even embraced thermonuclear war and strategic doctrine. George believed that the bombs were normally dropped from airplanes. Justine was certain that they would arrive via guided missiles. Whenever the fight began to lull, George demonstrated some additional virtue of the suit.

'What the hell good are *those* going to do anybody?' Justine demanded after George showed her the vacuum-packed seeds. 'Do you know how long it will take for those to grow?'

'They're resistant to ultraviolet light.'

'Yeah? What does that mean?'

'It's like the grasshopper and the ant.'

'It's like *what?*'

'A bad move that was, Justine, getting fired. Truly dumb. This suit will give us peace of mind. You'll just have to ask Harry for your job back.'

'There's one thing I forgot to tell you, darling,' said Justine with a tilted smile. 'Today Harry grabbed my ass.'

The moment John Frostig saw George standing in the doorway with the little scopas suit under his arm, he knew that he had lost the sale. Taking the contract and the $345.71 check from his briefcase, he rolled them into a tube and thrust it toward George's belly as if knifing him. He spoke in grim whispers.

'I'm going to explicate a few things now, buddy-buddy,' He curled his arm in a yoke around George's neck and led him into the house. 'Right now we're friends, my dear grasshopper, but when the warheads reach their targets, I'm going to be looking out for me and mine and nobody else. That's the way with us ants.'

Scopas suits cluttered John's living room, sprawling on the floor, resting on the couches, relaxing on the chairs. One suit was watching a football game on television. Another played the piano. The house looked like a meeting place for an extraterrestrial chapter of the Ku Klux Klan.

'In short,' John continued softly, 'anybody who hears that us ants have a few extra suits stored up . . . anybody who drops by our larders looking to borrow one of those suits . . . such a person – even if he's an old buddy – such a person is asking to get his brains dredged out with a Remington 870.'

Alice Frostig glanced up from her sewing machine – she was repairing a scopas suit glove – and moved her bulbous and balding head with an amen sort of nod. Among other pitiable things, she was the female equivalent of a cuckold. More than once George had seen John approach a vulnerable housewife in the Lizard Lounge and convince her to accept his hospitality at the Wildgrove Motel.

'Justine lost her job,' said George. 'She's going to take acting lessons. We can't afford the suit any more.'

'Tell that to the Soviets,' said the suit salesman.

'There probably won't even be a war,' said George.

Throughout his entire life, George had never discovered a pleasure more complete than reading to his daughter. Food did not go beyond taste and satiation, sex lacked intellectual rewards, but Holly's bed-time had everything. There was, first of all, the sheer physical enjoyment of swaddling oneself in blankets. Then, too, the process brought out Holly's adorable side, suppressing the whiny beast that lived in four-year-olds and fed on parental exasperation. And frequently the books themselves were pithy and provocative, the sorts of things an advertising executive might have written in a fit of scruple.

Father and daughter were huddled together, orienting Holly's selection for the evening – a bad selection as it happened, a vapidity called *Carrie of Cape Cod*. A kitten scampered amid the blanketed terrain. Holly's menagerie of stuffed animals went about their soft habits. George began reading: Outside the cottage harsh winds whipped the lake, giving it whitecaps and a tide. Canadian geese splashed down, squonking loudly.

Carrie of Cape Cod slogged on. Near summer's end, Carrie saw a seagull pick up a clam and drop it on a rock. The shell shattered, and the bird ate what was inside.

'How did the seagull know the clam was dead?' Holly asked.

I must get her a scopas suit, thought George. I'll break into Frostig's truck and steal one.

'I know!' said Holly. Freckles were sprinkled on her face. Her skin seemed lit from within. 'If the clam is alive, he opens his eyes, and then the seagull knows not to eat him!'

'Yes,' said George. 'That's the answer.'

She pondered for a moment. 'But then how does the clam get a new shell, Daddy?'

If George could have one wish, he would remake the world as Holly saw it. This Utopia would consist largely of cuddly ducks, happy ponies, and seagulls who spared live clams. 'I don't know how the clam gets a new shell,' he said. Maybe he puts on a scopas suit instead, he thought.

At the climax Carrie walked the nocturnal beach, gazing toward heaven and identifying the constellations. One of them was the Big Dipper. 'Why is it called that?' Holly asked.

'It looks like a dipper.' George was always careful to speak in complete, grammatical sentences around Holly. 'Do you know what a dipper is?'

'What's a dipper?'

Instantly George was off to the kitchen. He returned bearing a small saucepan that more or less resembled an ancient Greek dipper. He believed it was for melting butter.

'I wish *I* could see the Big Dipper,' Holly said.

'One night soon we'll go out and look for it.'

'Daddy, I have something important to say. This is important. Could we go out and look for it now?'

'You don't have any shoes on.'

'Could you carry me?'

He seriously considered doing so. 'It's pretty cloudy tonight. I don't think we could find it.'

'Let's try. Please.'

'No, honey, it's late,' he said, extricating himself from her little finger. 'We'll look for it some other night. I'll tell you a story instead.'

'Goody.'

He started out with the grasshopper and the ant, then suddenly realized he didn't like the ending, and so he ad-libbed his way through the chronicle of a clumsy bunny who wanted, more than anything, to be able to ride a two-wheeler bicycle. The bunny tried and tried and kept falling off, covering his fragile body with little bunny bruises. (The wind could hurl you three hundred feet, young Gary Frostig had said.) Then one day the rabbit hutch caught on fire. The determined bunny leaped on his two-wheeler, raced to the fire department, and saved the day.

'I wish *I* could ride a two-wheeler,' said Holly.

'You'll learn,' said George.

'I *know* that,' said Holly, slightly annoyed. She closed the book. 'It's going to be a long world.'

CHAPTER THREE

In Which the United States of America Is Transformed into a Safe, White Country

Halloween was coming, the pumpkins were off their diets, and the little cemetery where George worked had acquired a ghost.

When he first glimpsed the specter, she was contemplating him through the front window of the Crippen Monument Works. Inside the office, barrel-bellied Jake Swann perused a sales contract – a big order set in motion on Columbus Day when Jake's uncle had come home and shot all of his immediate family dead – and as the customer reached for the pen to write his signature, George looked up.

Spider webs and arabesques were scribbled on the window in frost. A blood-red October leaf was pasted to one pane. George and the specter locked eyes. While he sincerely doubted that the old woman was in fact a ghost – Unitarians did not believe in ghosts – her every aspect suggested a netherworld address. She wore a mourning ensemble, loose-fitting as a shroud: black cloth, black gloves, and black veil – raised. Her complexion had the greenish pallor of mold. Her frame displayed the jagged profile of a dead tree. When she smiled at him, jack-o'-lantern teeth appeared, and one of her eyelids collapsed in a wink.

Ice formed in George's gut. His throat tightened like a sphincter.

'You got the sniffles?' asked Jake Swarm, a phlegmatic man who had not been noticeably affected by the prodigal loss of kin.

George took the contract, knitting his brow in a manner he

thought appropriate to a tomb professional. Furtively, he glanced out the window. The specter was gone.

But later, as George was leaving the office, she reappeared, kneeling amid the sample stones. Mud spattered her mourning dress; the veil was down. He ducked behind Design No. 3295. The old woman stared at a wordless headstone for several minutes, as if reading an epitaph written in a medium only ghosts could perceive, then reached forward with black velvet fingers and stroked the granite surface of Design No. 6247, the one with the praying Saint Catherine on top. George considered speaking, but the remarks that suggested themselves – 'That one has real value,' 'We also offer it in Oklahoma pink,' 'For whom are you in mourning?' – seemed inappropriate.

Evening pressed softly on the Crippen Monument Works. The woman uncrooked her back, hobbled forward. 'I have a task for you,' she said. A spry voice inhabited her antique body. 'You'll learn of it soon.'

'Have we met?' he asked.

'I have always been with you,' she said, smiling, 'waiting to get in,' and then she vanished into the dusk.

As the week progressed, George noticed her a dozen more times – peering through the window, bending over a sample memorial, standing outside the decaying picket fence that enclosed the little cemetery.

Waiting to get in . . . ?

On Halloween afternoon she watched from the weed-corrupted field on the other side of Hawthorne Street. She sat on the ground, a basket of apples in her lap. Her dark dress was covered with leaves; she appeared to be stuffed with them. Her weak and decimated teeth had to fight their way into each apple. George wondered why she had selected such an ambitious lunch. Some early trick-or-treaters came past: a witch, a devil, a cat, a preschooler from Venus, a ghoul. When the woman offered the children an apple, they shrieked gleefully and ran off, laughing all the way down Hawthorne Street. At the corner they stopped laughing but kept going, faster now, panting, sweating, trembling with terror, to the far end of Blackberry Avenue and beyond.

Fade-in on a man seated at a desk. He wears a business suit and is flanked by American flags. During his speech the camera dollies forward and a subtitle tells us that this is Robert Wengernook, Assistant Secretary of Defense for International Security Affairs.

WENGERNOOK: As one of the officials charged with implementing America's defense strategy, I know where our security lies. We must prove to the Soviets that they can never succeed in their ugly schemes for winning a nuclear war . . . The key to our security is deterrence. The key to our deterrence is civil defense. And the key to our civil defense is a technology developed by Eschatological Enterprises . . . If you've already bought that scopas suit – wear it. If you haven't – well, don't you think you owe it to yourself and to your country's future? Remember, deterrence is only as good as the people it protects.

Fade-out.

In the screening room of Unlimited, Ltd., Phil Murcheson of Eschatological Enterprises blew cigarette smoke into Robert Wengernook's projected face.

'He looks nervous,' said Murcheson as the tail leader of the thirty-second spot rolled out of the film gate and began flapping around on the take-up reel.

'Intense, we thought.' Dave Valentine, Creative Associate at Unlimited, Ltd., shut off the projector. 'He looked intense to us.'

'Nervous.'

'He needed a cigarette,' said Valentine.

'You'll notice a big difference when it's transferred to tape,' said Lou Marquand, Assistant Creative Associate. 'Film is high resolution, right? It's not his medium. Wengernook is definitely low-res iconography.'

'Nervous as a cat,' said Murcheson. 'This is not a man I would want leading me into battle, and our customers won't want him either.'

'I hate to fail you like this, Phil,' said Valentine. 'I can't tell you the pain I'm experiencing right now.'

Murcheson lit a fresh Pall Mall. 'Look, what you did is okay for the six o'clock news, the *Rise and Shine* show, the Sunday morning evangelists. No problem. But this country has a Super Bowl coming up in a couple of months. This is not a Super Bowl presence you're giving me here, Dave.'

Valentine began jumping up and down. 'Hold on, Phil! Concept time! Hold on! Here comes the egg . . . now the sperm . . . direct hit! Insemination! You'll love this. It has action, a medieval knight, and a sex-role reversal.'

'I like the knight. Sex-role reversal?'

'We're on top of it. Eighty-five percent of male viewers enjoy sex-role reversals, as long as you keep the threat factor in harness.'

'Okay. But life is short – need I remind you? The Super Bowl, Dave.'

'Phil, you'll have it in time for the goddamn Army-Navy game.'

Robert Wengernook proved a far more persuasive scopas suit salesman than anyone at Eschatological Enterprises had anticipated. Seven seconds after the commercial was aired for the first time, John Frostig's phone rang. It was the chairman of the Wildgrove Board of Selectmen; he wanted two adult units and three child-size ones. No sooner had John replaced the receiver when the phone jangled again. The principal of Wildgrove High School required seven suits.

By Thanksgiving, John had supplemented his panel truck with a factory showroom, the Civil Defense Stop, open every night till nine.

America was becoming a safe, white country. From sea to shining sea, citizens began wearing their civil defenses as a matter of daily routine. Cheerfully they mastered the arts of eating, sleeping, working, and playing in perpetual preparedness for warheads. Not only did the suits promise survival in times of nuclear exchange, they also discouraged muggings and rapes.

Spin-off industries flourished. Rare was the entrepreneur who could not turn a profit from dry-cleaning scopas suits or adorning them with sashes, plumes, jewels, and decorative inlays. Little girls placing orders with Santa Claus commonly requested scaled-down scopas suits for their dolls. Patches bloomed everywhere, woven from fireproof thread: TRACY LIVES HERE . . . WHICH

Fade-in on a village somewhere in medieval Europe. A gang of fat, bearded brigands is running amuck, setting the peasants' huts on fire. Women and children flee in panic. Men are cut down by the brigands' spears, axes, and swords.

NARRATOR (voice-over): The threat. It's always been there. It always will be. Wherever you find freedom, you find forces seeking to destroy it.

A helmeted knight enters the village on a white charger. His armor catches the glow of the burning huts. He dismounts, draws his sword, and falls upon the brigands. Their weapons prove useless against breastplate and mail.

NARRATOR: But for every threat, there is a defense. In ancient times, body armor deflected swords. Today, scopas suits deflect blast, heat, and fallout.

As the victorious knight removes his helmet, his armor is magically transformed into a particularly svelte scopas suit. Surprise: the knight is a woman. She swirls her head, sending luscious blond hair in all directions. The background dissolves. A suburban living room emerges in its place. The woman's husband rushes over, children trailing behind.

DAD: Marge, you did it! You saw our Eschatological representative!

MOM: Deterrence is only as good as the people it protects, Stan.

DAD: I'm so glad we had that talk.

Fade-out.

When Justine Paxton saw the thirty-second spot during the Army-Navy game, she concluded that she could have done a better Mom than the woman who played the part.

Her acting teacher agreed.

One bitter December morning, as George sat at his work table putting the final cuts in a stencil, he was enveloped by a sense of well-being. The feeling seemed to originate from outside his body. He turned.

The specter stood in the middle of the shop, veil up, smiling. A handbag dangled from her black-shrouded arm. She glanced longingly at Design No. 7034, rendered in South African granite.

34

The granite was blacker than her eyes, the blackest of the black, as Arthur Crippen called it.

'My name is Nadine Covington,' she said. How smooth her voice, how young.

'Why have you been spying on me?'

'Not spying. Appreciating. You are a good man, George Paxton, a saint in a business swarming with ghouls.' Although she had no trace of a foreign accent, she spoke as if English were an unfamiliar language. 'I am honored to meet you.'

Sensations of peace and contentment continued to flow from the specter to George. 'This is a service business,' he said. 'The product comes second. We must be as sensitive as any funeral parlor director – it's amazing what people have on their minds when they come in here. The idea is to make the customer feel good about his choice, even if it's the cheapest.'

'You're skillful at that.' Nadine went to an electric heater and began massaging the winter out of her finger bones.

'No memorial will take away grief, ma'am, but it can help.' George had not drawn such pleasure from the sheer act of talking since he was three. 'I'll tell you what gets me upset, though. It's when people buy, er, you know' – what to call them? – 'guilt stones.' (That sounded right.) 'I'm thinking of . . . well, I won't say his name, but he treated that kid of his like junk. And then, after the boy drowns, what does this guy do? Has us order a four thousand dollar model of the Taj Mahal.'

'I must give you your task,' said Nadine. 'An ordinary commission – not a guilt stone. I need an epitaph, and something to put it on.'

'Is this a pre-need?' he asked.

'A what?'

'Do you want the stone for yourself?'

'No. Some people very close to me are dying . . . my parents.'

'I'm sorry.' Good God – how old were her parents?

'The stone must endure,' she said.

'We carry the best bonded granites.'

'I fancy this material.' Nadine caressed the South African

sample, which was polished to a mirror brilliance. 'I can see my face in it.'

'Our stones have extreme density – they can take the most detailed carving. Also low porosity – no moisture gets inside, ever. The guarantee is unconditional, valid to you, your heirs, and your assignees. If a crack appears, even a hairline, you get a new monument, free.'

'I have no heirs or assignees. My real concern is the epitaph. I want . . . eloquence.'

'Eloquence?' said George lightly. 'Really? But why, ma'am? I mean, it's not like it's going to be carved in *stone* or anything . . . That's a little joke we have around here.' He reached into the shelves above his work table and pulled out a plastic binder containing twenty sample epitaphs, typed, double spaced. It began with Number One, IN OUR HEARTS YOU LIVE FOREVER, followed by ASLEEP IN THE ARMS OF JESUS, then I AM THE RESURRECTION AND THE LIFE, all the way through Number Twenty, GOD IS LOVE. He handed the epitaphs to the old woman, who studied them with pursed lips.

'No, no,' she insisted, tapping the paper. 'There's no honesty here. I want *you* to write it.'

'I don't write epitaphs, ma'am, I inscribe them.'

'Show me how,' said Nadine, lifting the utility knife off the work table.

As George took the knife from her, her thumb strayed across the blade. At first he thought she was unharmed – but no, her ancient flesh had split. Violently he sucked in a mouthful of air, and then she expired with equal vigor. For several seconds they continued to co-breathe in this manner, George neglecting to exhale, Nadine to inhale.

The old woman's blood was black. Black as her eyes. Black as South African granite. It had a sulphurous smell.

'Would you like a bandage?' he asked.

'Please.' She sucked her thumb.

His nervous fingers returned to the shelves where the epitaphs were kept and procured a tin box. He punished himself by biting

36

his inner cheeks. Way to go, George. Always be sure to draw blood – best way to firm up a sale.

Ripping the tabs from the bandage, Nadine wrapped it around her black, burning wound.

A rubber stencil spanned George's work table. He sliced some final touches into the inscription. IN LOVING MEMORY OF GRACE LOQUATCH . . . THE HAMMER GROWS SILENT. Grace Loquatch's birth and death dates followed. She had been a carpenter. The epitaph was her sister's inspiration.

Black blood? What awful disease had Mrs Covington contracted?

He affixed the stencil to Grace Loquatch's monument, Design No. 4306 on Vermont blue-gray. Using a hoist-and-chain he transported it across the shop, a job that if necessary he could have accomplished with his bare hands. Grace Loquatch's immortality moved past three droning electric heaters, the mounted pencil drafts awaiting customer approval, and several shipping crates filled with uninscribed stones from the great quarries of Canada and Vermont.

'Then we have your self-hatred stones,' he said. (Self-hatred stones? Yes, that wasn't a bad term for them.) 'The customer uses them to take revenge on himself for never having gotten around to being alive, know what I'm saying? Yesterday we buried . . . a woman. She came here as soon as the doctor told her about the lung tumors. "For once I want to do something really nice for myself," she said. So we worked up this special thing, all sorts of flowers and birds. Angels. Job took twice as long as usual, but I didn't want to charge extra, she had enough problems. I brought the pencil draft into her hospital room. She said, "It's beautiful." Then she said, "I don't deserve it." '

George maneuvered the stone inside the chamber of the ABC Electric Automatic Sandblaster, closed the door, and turned on the motor. Sharp splinters of noise filled the air. Nadine watched in fascination as the jet of aluminum oxide gushed down the hose and spewed forth. The abrasive grains ricocheted off the rubber stencil; others slipped through the incisions, hitting the granite and biting deep. Corundum dust engulfed the stone like fog.

'A person would not last long in there,' Nadine observed after George shut the sandblaster down. 'You'd be turned to bone.'

'Unless you were wearing a scopas suit.' He entered the chamber and peeled away the stencil. Now and forever the stone said, GRACE LOQUATCH . . . THE HAMMER GROWS SILENT. He ran his fingers along the excellent dry wounds.

'You and I may be the only people in Wildgrove not wearing scopas suits, George.'

'My wife and kid don't have any either.' He hauled the monument out of the chamber. 'For some of us, seven thousand dollars is a lot of money. I sure wish Holly had a suit. She's in nursery school.'

'The Sunflower Nursery School,' said Nadine. 'I go over there sometimes. It's my hobby, you might say – watching children play. Holly is very bright, isn't she? And decent. Yesterday the class painted rocks. Holly helped the children who didn't know how.'

'Really? I wish I'd been there. Do you ever baby-sit, Mrs Covington?'

'I would be happy and grateful to baby-sit for your daughter. Are you certain you want her to have a scopas suit?'

'Of course.'

'I'll strike a bargain with you. Do this task – write an epitaph for my parents – and I'll see to it that Holly gets a scopas suit, free of charge.'

'Free?'

'Free.'

'I don't even know your parents.'

'Pretend they are your parents, not mine.'

'My parents are dead.'

'What does it say on their headstones?'

'Nothing. Names and dates. I'm a Unitarian.'

'What should it say?'

'I don't know.'

'Let's begin with your mother.'

'Huh?'

'Your mother. What was she like?'

38

'You want me to tell you about my mother?'

'Please.'

'My mother,' George began. 'Well . . . certainly my mother should have been happier. She was always running herself down, always trumpeting her faults – kind of an inverse boaster, I guess. She had diabetes, but I think it was the high standards that killed her.' Had he been storing up these ideas, waiting for Mrs Covington's questions? 'I loved her very much. She was better than she knew, and—'

' "Better than she knew," ' Nadine intoned. 'There, you've done it – that fits my mother exactly! "She was better than she knew." I love it.'

'For an *epitaph*?'

'Let's discuss your father.'

'A simpler person than my mother. Very likely he was the most unselfish man on earth.'

'Tell me more.'

'I think of him as always smiling. He smiled even when he was unhappy. They should have paid him a lot of money for being so nice. His job was pointless. He never found out what he was doing here. His car didn't run right.'

' "Never found out what he was doing here . . .' My, my, that's quite perfect – Dad is just like that. Your epitaph-writing talents are extraordinary, young man. You've earned that suit twice over. So, how much for the finished stone?'

'Seven hundred and fifty dollars plus tax. We usually ask for half-payment down and the balance when your monument is ready.'

Nadine opened her handbag and drew out a roll of withered bills. 'I don't want change,' she said, depositing nine hundred dollars in George's palm. She squeezed his hand. Her skin was vital and warm, not at all the clammy membrane of a ghost. 'And I don't want a sales contract, either. We must trust each other.'

'Come back on Monday and you can approve the pencil draft. We should select a lettering style now, though.' I do trust her, George thought.

'Any style you like will be fine. It's the *message* that must be right. At the top, simply, "She was better than she knew." '

'No name?'

'I'll know who's buried there. At the bottom, "He never found out—" '

' "He never found out what he was doing here." '

'Precisely.'

'What about dates?'

'We needn't trouble ourselves with dates.'

From her handbag Nadine produced a large, tattered map, unfolding it atop Grace Loquatch's stone. George recognized the waterfront district of Boston – full color, fine detail, all the key buildings illustrated in overhead views. The paper was disintegrating along the creases. Entire warehouses had fallen into the holes.

'This particular scopas suit store isn't easy to find,' she said. 'And today your average cartographer doesn't even bother with some of these little streets.' She pointed to a vacant space on Moonburn Alley. 'Here's your destination – Theophilus Carter's establishment, the Mad Tea Party he calls it. I'll tell him to expect you this Saturday. Professor Carter is a tailor, a hatter, a furrier . . . an inventor. He makes extraordinary things for human bodies.'

She started to leave, paused, and scurried up to George, kissing him softly on the cheek. 'I'm so pleased you're the way you are,' she whispered. 'It was lovely talking with you.'

'I enjoyed it too, ma'am, most assuredly.'

'Fare thee well, George.'

'Good-bye.'

On her way out of the shop, Nadine hesitated by the South African monument. 'She was better than she knew,' she mumbled, evidently projecting the words onto the granite. When the black gleam caught her eyes, George was certain he saw tears.

CHAPTER FOUR

In Which Our Hero Is Asked to Sign
a Most Unusual Sales Contract

Saturday. The big day. George the small-town artisan had little affection for Boston, with its self-importance and its arrogantly unlabeled streets, their plan evidently derived from a fallen wad of spaghetti. He trusted that Mrs Covington's map would see him through the worst of it.

'I'm going to the waterfront today,' he told Justine. Husband and wife were snuggled together, basking in the afterglow. The chatter of cartoon squirrels and the giggles of animated elves blared into the bedroom. Working in cosmopolitan and distant Los Angeles, were the creators of these virginal diversions, George wondered, aware of the enormous quantity of screwing that their products brought about in the hinterlands of Massachusetts? 'There's a new memorial on Snape's Hill. Arthur asked me to check it out. We might order one for the showroom.'

One-third truth, two-thirds lie. The Snape's Hill Burial Grounds had indeed erected a remarkable memorial that month, a replica of a prehistoric megalith commissioned by an eccentric young man named Nathan Brown for his recently departed and allegedly Druid uncle. Arthur had not asked George to look at it, however, and the Crippen Monument Works would almost certainly not be ordering one.

He kissed her. They had not used contraception. If a girl: Aubrey. If a boy: Derek. They had been taking the necessary lack of precautions for the last ten weeks. Everything would work out.

He wanted another girl, had instructed his sperm accordingly. Aubrey Paxton.

'Is Arthur paying you to run around like this?' asked Justine sneeringly. 'Can't *he* look at the damn rock?'

'He's busy today.'

'Busy hauling Scotch bottles. Busy lifting shot glasses. It's supposed to snow, you know.'

'It won't snow that much.'

But it did snow that much. Even before George had gotten their terminal-case Volkswagen van to the end of Pond Road, the first storm of December was under way. The heater fan groaned and squeaked as it shunted inadequate amounts of warmth toward his frigid toes. The wiper motors dragged frozen rubber across the windshield. Flakes came down everywhere, a billion soft collisions a second.

He turned left onto Main Street, steered the skittish vehicle past the post office, the Lizard Lounge, and the Wildgrove Mall, home of Raining Cats and Dogs. (Damn you, Harry Sweetser. I hope one of your tarantulas bites you on the ass.) A happier sight now, Sandy's Sandwich Shop, where on Tuesday and Thursday nights, while Justine learned to act, he and Holly shared a pizza and something he was not embarrassed to call conversation; it was a tribute to children that whatever you discussed with them seemed important. A mechanical horse stood outside the shop. GIANT RIDE, the sign said. 25 CENTS, QUARTERS ONLY. INSERT COIN HERE. Holly always asked her daddy for an extra ride. The chances of her not getting one were equal to those of the sun not coming up the next day.

After the Arbor Road turn, the van rattled past John Frostig's house. The Perpetual Security panel truck sat in the driveway, jam-packed with deterrence. George recalled his old fantasy of breaking into the truck and stealing a scopas suit for Holly. How wonderful it was not to be burdened with this temptation, to be bound instead for the Mad Tea Party and its free merchandise. Spying through the picture window, he saw little Nickie, clad in a scopas suit, watching TV. On the screen a mouse unleashed a bomb from a World War One fighter plane. As it detonated, a wave of well-being hit George.

Shoulders heaped with snow, a crooked figure was walking up the Frostig driveway. He recognized her handbag, shuddered to see her bent, defenseless frame. She should have a coat on, he thought, a sweater, a scopas suit, something besides that black dress.

Rosehaven Cemetery rushed by. Grace Loquatch's stone – THE HAMMER GROWS SILENT – was now in place. White drifts engulfed black South African obelisks. Marble saints grinned stoically as the blizzard whipped their faces and stuck to their sides. Should I have offered Mrs Covington my down jacket? he wondered. Old ladies get cold . . . especially those with her kind of blood.

George switched on the car radio. The North Atlantic Treaty Organization was deploying a hundred and fifty additional ground-launched Raven cruise missiles in Belgium to offset the Soviet deployment of three hundred intermediate-range SS-90 missiles in Poland. The snow slackened. George hummed along with Brahms's String Quintet No. 2 in G Major. The van sailed into the white city.

He parked in a lot – five dollars, paid in advance, but who cares when you're about to get a free scopas suit? – and, securing Nadine's map under his arm, set off. The storm was over. Snow crunched beneath his boots. White sculpted mounds clung to everything, cars, fire hydrants, litter receptacles, subway entrances, all lying half-interred, vast pieces of quiet. Scopas-suited Christmas shoppers appeared on the frosted streets. George saw a Santa Claus, then an other, and another. Their scopas suits were blood red. Beards were glued to their helmets. The white strands vibrated in the wind. When the Santa Clauses rang their bells, the sound was lost in the fast bitter air.

George hurried on. He pitied the shoppers, sealed in their suits, unable to sense the magical white silence. Walking here was like being on a deep-sea dive into the heart of winter. He wore a wool cap, wool mittens, and a down jacket, but they were not enough – the wind still pinched his nose, stung his cheeks. Curling his fingers into self-warming fists, the epicure of everyday pleasures wished for hot coffee.

By the time he reached Snapes Hill, he had started doubting the wisdom of his trip. A free scopas suit? Just for making up a couple of silly epitaphs? More likely the black-blooded old woman was playing some senile joke. ('I have always been with you . . .' Nut talk.) He looked at the prehistoric megalith. Crude, humorless, and stern, it towered over stones of more conventional design. Here at the Snapes Hill Burial Grounds a canny observer could witness the entire evolution of a technology. In one section rose the limestone memorials, names, dates, and fond remembrances smeared away by decades of Boston weather. In an adjacent area leaned markers of slate, a sturdier proposition, inscriptions soft and worn but still readable. And finally, of course, the precincts of immortal granite, more permanent than anything a Pharaoh had ever demanded.

He left the graveyard, walked on, and suddenly it appeared, the coffee shop of his humble dream, the Holistic Donut. He went inside, treated himself to coffee with actual cream plus two donuts filled with a wondrous white goo. The waitress's breasts flowed lushly against her scopas suit.

Had he and Justine conceived an Aubrey Paxton that morning? George began to whistle. Daddies could sense these things. Father's intuition.

Still whistling, he stepped out of the Holistic Donut. He consulted Nadine's map, charted his course. He turned left, went down an obscure street called Gooseberry Place, turned right, followed something called Pitchblende Lane, turned left, entered Moonburn Alley. It was a twisted, cobblestoned passageway pinched between rows of shops – cheese shop, rare coins shop, used books shop, clock repair shop – each snug and quaint, crescents of snow resting in their windows. Golden light spilled through the panes, marking the ground with shapes that George decided were elf shadows. Tonight, he thought, I'll tell Holly a story about an elf who casts a golden shadow.

The sign advertising Theophilus Carter's establishment was a hearty slab of oak bearing a painted teapot captioned THE MAD

TEA PARTY – REMARKABLE THINGS FOR HUMAN BODIES. Under that, PROFESSOR THEOPHILUS CARTER – TAILOR, HATTER, FURRIER, INVENTOR, PROPRIETOR. Across the front of the Mad Tea Party ran a bellied, multi-paned window displaying a definitive collection of hats: beaver, homburg, derby, tricorne, fedora, slouch, bowler, fez, stovepipe, even a king's bejeweled crown.

A frail carillon from three tin bells announced George's entrance. The Mad Tea Party was dark and musty. It was also, he surmised, extremely popular – customers jammed the shop to the walls – but then he realized that this impression owed entirely to the several dozen mannequins stationed about, their reflections inhabiting a multitude of full-length mirrors. Like the hats in the front window, the mannequins' clothing was extraordinarily varied, with no fashion or era neglected. George moved through a tangled mass of gowns, togas, kimonos, doublets, jerkins, sarongs, crinolines, tunics, and shining armor. Could these all be scopas suits? he wondered. Had Theophilus Carter figured out how to combine deterrence with style?

'So tell me, my good man, why is a raven like a writing desk?' A British accent, precise, aristocratic.

George stumbled free of the congested clothing like a jungle explorer breaking into a clearing. 'What?'

Behind the counter sat the most disturbingly comic person he had ever seen. The salesman was beetle-browed, sharp-nosed, rabbit-toothed, and small. Polka dots speckled his large four-in-hand tie. Wild red hair escaped from beneath his top hat.

'Why is a raven like a writing desk?' the salesman said again. He rushed forward, rubbing his hands together as if lathering a bar of soap. He was on the downward side of middle age, yet his voice and movements had a robust, rat-a-tat quality. 'A vulture then.' He issued a chuckle that might have come from a jack-in-the-box. 'Why is a vulture like a writing desk?'

'I'm not here for riddles.'

'I can tell you why a vulture is like a raven, but the answer is distasteful, involving carrion and bad table manners.' The squeal of automobile brakes suddenly penetrated the shop from Moonburn Alley, conjuring up images of narrowly averted death. 'The human body is an egg. "Humpty-Dumpty sat on a wall: Humpty-Dumpty had a great fall. All the King's horses and—" Now why in the world would anybody expect *horses* to be able to put an egg back together? People were naive in those days.'

'I'm looking for Professor Carter.'

The salesman pulled off his top hat, and his hair spilled out like released champagne. 'Also known as the Tailor of Thermonuclear Terror. Also known as the Sartor of the Second Strike. Also known as the MAD Hatter.'

Now we're getting somewhere, George told himself, although he sensed that this situation would not endure.

'But if I am the Mutual Assured Destruction Hatter,' Theophilus trilled, 'then where is the Mutual Assured Destruction Tea Party? In Geneva, of course. Entry number three in the Strategic, Tactical, and Anti-Ballistic Limitation and Equalization talks – STABLE III to you. The Soviets and the Americans sit down at the STABLE table, and the Soviets say, "We don't like that MAD Hatter you've got sitting over there. Nobody mutually assures Mother Russia's destruction." And the Americans reply, "Then meet the MARCH Hare, named for our new war-fighting strategy, Modulated Attacks in Response to Counterforce Hostilities. MARCH puts the fun back in nuclear war – you can actually *do* MARCH."'

'I really don't want to hear about this, Professor Carter.'

'Quiet, sir! So the MARCH Hare comes bounding in, and Alice says, "Now that Russia's forces are the same as America's, both sides will make reductions." And the Hare says, "Russia's forces are not the same as America's, they are equivalent, which means you'll get reductions when Frosty the Snowman conquers hell."'

'Professor Carter, I am losing patience,' George snapped.

'Hold your tongue, sir! "And don't forget," says the Hare, "they are equivalent because the Soviets began matching the American buildup necessitated by the early sixties missile gap that did not exist."'

'I am George Paxton,' the tomb inscriber stated calmly, deliberately, 'and I would appreciate it if you would let me speak.

46

Nadine Covington said you have a scopas suit for my daughter. If she was mistaken, then—'

'Mistaken? No, I'm the one who's mistaken. It's the mercury we use to cure our felt. Makes me mistaken. Crazy as well. The doctors say there's no cure, because I've used it on the felt, but I *feel* cured, I really do, never cured more felt or felt more cured. Mrs Covington, did you say? Oh, yes, a sterling woman, sterling. You could serve tea off her. The old girl and I have a lot in common. One nose. Two eyes. Black blood. We have always been with you, waiting to get in. Of *course* I have a suit for you, George. Let me dig it out. Meanwhile, have some wine.'

'I don't see any wine.'

'There isn't any.'

The MAD Hatter vanished behind velvet drapes, returning almost instantaneously with a child-size scopas suit, one unlike any George had ever seen.

The material was golden, silky, and phosphorescent, bathing the shop in a bright, boiling-butter glow. The boots and gloves suggested vulcanized jade. George pulled off his mitten and touched a sleeve. Warm milk.

'This is the only one I shall ever make,' said the Hatter. 'I raised the caterpillars myself – fed them on vitriol and metal shavings so they'd put out tough silk. It takes a hefty fabric to get through a thermonuclear exchange, George. They were marvelous caterpillars. They smoked hookahs and sat on mushroom clouds.'

When Theophilus flopped the luminous invention on the counter, George thought he saw golden sparks.

'Is it as good as an Eschatological?' he asked warily.

'Better. It actually works.'

'Then why don't you make more?'

'That will be obvious once you read the contract.'

'I thought it was free!'

'If you want the suit, you must sign the sales contract.' The Hatter reached behind the counter, drawing out a crisp, rattly sheaf of printed paper and a fountain pen. 'Here,' he said, sliding the paper toward George. 'Put your John Hancock, or the founding father of your choice, on the line.'

Sales Contract

BY AFFIXING MY NAME to this agreement, which entitles me to receive one scopas suit free of charge, I hereby confess to my complicity in the nuclear arms race.

I, THE SIGNATORY, AM FULLY AWARE that the prevalence of these suits emboldens our society's leaders to pursue a policy of nuclear brinksmanship.

I AM FURTHERMORE AWARE that these suits are a public opiate, numbing our society to the dangers inherent in the following: the failure of the STABLE agreements to constrain meaningfully the arsenals of the superpowers; the ongoing refinement of the MARCH Plan for waging a limited nuclear war; the refusal of the current administration to adopt a no-first-use policy regarding theater nuclear forces; and the continued deployment by the United States and the Soviet Union of first-strike intercontinental ballistic missiles with multiple warheads.

Signed:_____

'I don't understand this,' said George.

'Just sign it.'

' "Complicity." That means . . . ?'

'Partnership in wrongdoing.'

'Sounds like I could go to *jail*.'

'Well, you might go to jail anyway. I mean, suppose you woke up tomorrow morning and murdered somebody. They'd surely put you in jail.'

'STABLE agreements. You said they were the Strategic, Tactical, and . . . Anti-something.'

'Anti-Ballistic Limitation and Equalization. Hey, George, if you don't want the suit, I'll give it to somebody who does.'

'MARCH Plan. Moderate Attacks—'

'*Modulated* Attacks in Response to Counterforce Hostilities. Just

48

another war-winning strategy. Old wine in new bottles. Don't worry about it. Sign.'

' "No-first-use," it says.'

'As opposed to no-second-use, no-third-use, no-seventeenth-use . . . Have you forgotten how to write your name?'

George picked up the pen. When Holly was born, the first words out of his mouth were, 'I don't ever want anything bad to happen to her.' He signed. The minors recorded his deed. The mannequins fixed him with their plasticine stares, whispering among themselves.

He took the warm, soft suit in his arms. He felt as if he were hugging Holly. Her incandescence poured through him.

'This is her Christmas present,' he said.

The Hatter picked up the sales contract with a carefulness he might have accorded a china figurine. Taking off his top hat, he stuffed the paper inside.

'I hope that your daughter enjoys many years of not using her Christmas present,' he said, complementing his rabbit teeth with a smile that George did not find entirely benign.

'Thank you.'

George shoved the precious garment under his arm, plowed through the crowded shop, and yanked the door open. He waited for the bells to settle down.

'Holly is safe now,' he asserted quietly to the mannequins, and he was off.

CHAPTER FIVE

*In Which the Limitations of Civil Defense Are Explicated
in a Manner Some Readers May Find Distressing*

Complicity. Partnership in wrongdoing. Am I a wrongdoer? wondered George as his van chugged away from the snow-muffled city. He glanced at the fabulous suit, which he had carefully strapped into the infant car seat. It fit perfectly. The golden helmet seemed to smile. You did it, Paxton. You brought it off. Merry Christmas, Holly.

But then his palms grew damp, and his bowels tightened. All the way up Route 2A, he studied his rear-view mirror for police cruisers. The traffic lights became eyes on the lookout for signers of scopas suit sales contracts. At each red light, he half-expected some jackbooted commandant to open the van door and arrest him.

He turned on the radio. Things were terrible in Indonesia. Malaysia was doomed. George glanced in the rear-view mirror. In Costa Rica terror was the norm. In Libya people's tongues were being removed without their permission. George checked the mirror. Assistant Defense Secretary Wengernook, of scopas suit commercial fame, gave an interview taped earlier that day. He was asked whether, because the new Soviet ICBM deployments could reach the American heartland in eighteen and a half minutes, the Strategic Air Command was now putting its own long-range missiles on a so-called hair trigger. Security and flexibility go hand in hand, Wengernook replied.

Bundled in snow, pine trees and stone fences coasted by, George clutched his seatbelt strap, checked the mirror. Holly was going to get a Mary Merlin doll for Christmas. She would find it standing under the tree, right next to her civil defenses. George had bought the Mary Merlin in October – on the very day Holly had seen the magazine advertisement and asked whether the doll was something to which Santa Claus had access. Bitter experience had taught George not to leave doll purchases to the last minute. Between the Mary Merlin in his closet and the scopas suit riding next to him, he felt astonishingly secure.

He looked at the road – the solid, reliable open road with its recently plowed surface and shoulders of spangly snow. Not far ahead, an old wooden bridge reached across the Wiskatonic River. A sign sailed past: WILDGROVE CENTER – THREE MILES. Next to the sign, a talented and macabre-minded sculptor had fashioned a snowman whose head was a skull. The van rumbled over the Wildgrove Bridge, which for an antique seemed to George remarkably sturdy.

Mary Merlin dolls were modeled to suggest precocious female babies. They came in three races. Mary Merlin could be made to perform a repertoire of magic tricks, such as pulling scarves from a cardboard tube and causing a coin to disappear from—

Something extraordinary happened . . . Something far more astonishing than a scarf materializing in a cardboard tube . . . Something that the United States and the Soviet Union had been spending large amounts of diligence and money to bring about. What happened was that the winter, which would be officially recognized by the calendar in a mere three days, and which only that morning had smothered southern New England with snow, went away.

It went away in a brilliant burst. The light hit George from the direction of his hometown, the brightest experience a human being could have in those days, a searing supernatural blaze, dazzling, hot, as if a vast array of flashbulbs were being fired at some cosmic wedding celebration. The sky hissed. The snowman perished, vaporized. Static leaped from the radio. The van motor expired with a whine. George thought the sun had crashed to earth.

Jesus Lord God!

The light bleached his retinas, making his vision a luminous void. His face became an unbroken first-degree burn, the pain reminiscent of a severe sunburn. The blind, dead van glided forward. Staring into the horrible, endless, sunny hole, George applied the brakes and bailed out through the passenger door. Had he lingered – instant death, for among the many quick, loud, and evil events that follow the detonation of a one-megaton thermonuclear warhead is a wave of pressurized air that transforms automobile windshields into barrages of glass bullets.

Jesus Lord God in Heaven!

The blast built to a crescendo, pummeling the van and lifting him off the ground. Briefly he flew. He hit the Wiskatonic, skimming across its surface like a tossed pebble. The water soothed his face, but he did not notice. Relief was agony, north was south, odd was even, fair was foul. Afloat on his back, he became driftwood. Blind. Eyeless, The wind hated him, meting out this ill-proportioned punishment for his signature, and the sky hated him, and the trees, and the moon, and the MAD Hatter, and Harry Sweetser, and John Frostig. The river hated him, and so it sent him smashing into a log, crack, everything knocked from his head, *no, God, please—*

He awoke on a mattress of silt – an hour lost? a day? – silt everywhere, silt to eat, to breathe. He flipped over, realized that his stunned retinas were recovering. A dead leaf lay several inches from his nose. An ant crawled on it. Ant. . . grasshopper . . . Aesop . . . roach. Eyes back, thank you, God. He looked up. No birds, no sun, millions of black specks awhirl like insects, smoke weaving through the sky, what sky, no sky, the sky had fallen, Chicken Little lay boiling in a forgotten pot. He stood up, knee deep in the river, spitting wads of silt from his mouth. His face ached. Dust clogged the air, each mote acrid and black. The trees had become roaring masses of flame. Whatever had happened, he was certain that it was important enough to be on the evening news that night; people would be talking about this for a long time. He looked toward where the fireball had been. A vast ring of pink smoke attacked the clouds, frothing atop a ten-mile-high column of gas and windblown dirt. In the late twentieth century such shapes had come to symbolize madness, but the effect on George of this particular celestial mushroom was to yank him fully into sanity. ICBM deployments. Counterforce strike. The Russians wanted Wildgrove's apples. I am not to blame.

His terror was glue, he could not budge. The Wiskatonic seeped into his boots and through his socks. From somewhere far away a voice cried, over and over, 'Find Justine! Find Holly!' For nearly thirty minutes George could focus on nothing but those cries, which he did not realize came from himself.

Pieces of Wildgrove protruded from the silt – chairs, tables, lamps, bureaus, television sets. A smoke detector lay buzzing on a rock. George was fairly certain he saw Emily McCarthy's birdbath and Clarence Weatherbee's ceramic Negro. He would have to tell his neighbors where these belongings were.

A logjam of corpses spanned the Wiskatonic. Their scopas suits were in a dreadful state. The material was mutilated, Winco Synthefill VII leaking through split seams. Most of the helmets were shattered, so that the corpses wore jagged fiberglass clown-collars.

Townspeople marched down to the river – fractured helmets, mangled fabric, torn backpacks – walking stiffly, arms out-stretched to lessen the weight of their burned hands. Many lacked hair and eyelashes. Synthefill bits were fused to their skin. A white lava of melted eye tissue dripped from their heads; they appeared to be crying their own eyes. Driven as lemmings, grace-less as zombies, the marchers tumbled over the banks and splashed into the water, rising to the surface as buoyant, lifeless hunks of local citizenry. All about, the upheaved earth was settling – dust, dirt, ashes by the ton – a radioactive rain on the final parade: the drum majors were skeletons; the baton twirlers tossed human bones. Vomitus and diarrhea gushed from most of the marchers. George, who not long ago had felt hated, now felt hatred instead. He hated these survivors with their worthless suits, their unsanitary behavior, their junk strewn across creation, their agony. They really made him mad.

The van sat under the bridge. A lunatic had gone after it with a large can opener. Mud slopped out of the shaggy metallic wounds. Thrown from the infant car seat, the golden suit lay loose-limbed against the front bumper like a marionette awaiting animation.

The Hatter's masterwork! Holly's Christmas present! The one suit in the world that would work! George's paralysis ended. Hobbling forward, he recalled some points from John Frostig's sales pitch: fire, poison fumes, fallout. . . If I get the suit home, he thought, she'll be able to leave this mess by any route she wants, walking through flames if need be, crossing fields of deadly vapor, free as a bird.

Golden suit draped across his arms, George started for town. The terrain was like some enormous gas stove, its countless burners turned up high. In the soot-soaked heavens, the mushroom cloud had become a wide gray canopy.

A mass of shocked and rubble-pounded refugees wove among the fires, improvising roads. George moved against the tide. Was Justine in this retreat? Holly? *Find my family, God!* (There are no Unitarians in thermonuclear holocausts.) *Please, God! Justine! Holly!* No. Nobody but ambulatory cadavers ruined by unbelievable burns and implausible wounds. *This cannot be happening, this cannot be happening, this cannot* . . . He saw torsos more cratered than the surface of the moon. Skin fell away like leaves of decayed wet lettuce, spirals of flesh dangled like black tinsel. He got angrier and angrier, he really couldn't forgive these people for having ended up so badly. What had they been doing, fooling around with his sandblaster? Fragments of the refugees' possessions – metal, wood, glass – had been driven into them like nails. One woman lacked a lower jaw. An old man held his left eyeball in his cupped hands. *Damn them – how dare they come out in public like this?* Tearful parents carried dead children. The sound of mass weeping engulfed him like a horrible odor. And still another variety of suffering – thirst. Acute, cruel, infinite, radiation-induced thirst. Cries for water rose above the sobbing and the shrieks and the bellowing fires. *Damn them all to hell.*

The roads belonged to the walking wounded. The rest of Wildgrove belonged to the immobiles. *Keep going. Don't stop for anything.*

A six-year-old girl lay in a ditch, clutching a teddy bear and whimpering, 'I'll be good.'

A fat man sat on an overturned federal mail deposit box, gripping a stack of Christmas cards. He kept trying to pull back the lid, but it was melted shut.

A seeing-eye dog, its scopas suit and fur seared away, licked the face of its dead master. 'Somebody put the fur back on that dog!' George shouted.

A middle-aged plumber held his wrench toward the sky and made twisting motions, as if trying to stop the dust leaks.

At the base of a charred, blasted tree, a boy of about two snuggled against his dead father and pressed a candy cane to the corpse's lips. 'Daddy, food?' he asked.

Several children gathered around a man whose tattered scopas suit was in the Santa Claus style. The man sang snatches of 'Rudolph the Red-Nosed Reindeer.' One little girl was telling Santa Claus to find her parents. Another was saying she wanted a sled. A boy with a mangled hand was asking Santa Claus for a thumb.

Why wasn't anybody helping these people? Somebody should be *doing* something!

A horse blocked George's path. Once it had sat outside Sandy's Sandwich Shop. GIANT RIDE. 25 CENTS. QUARTERS ONLY. INSERT COIN HERE. The chances of Holly not getting an extra ride were equal to those of the sun not . . . Previously the horse had lacked an ear. Now it lacked both ears, its left front leg, and its hindquarters. The horse's name, according to Holly, was Buttercup.

The third-degree burn victims lay on their sides, backs, and stomachs, quivering piles of excruciation, daring not to move, naked beyond flesh. A cyclone made of screams moved across the land. As the mobile survivors passed by, the third-degree burn victims begged to be shot to death with scopas suit pistols, their own hands (weeping, pulpy rubble) being useless to the task. 'Somebody please kill me,' the third-degree burn victims gasped with curious politeness.

God, make this stop. Help them, God.

George began to run, desperate to reach a place, any place, where indecent death was not. He dodged fires, circumvented walls of smoke, leaped over corpses. Large sections of Wildgrove had become beaches of broken glass; it would take a thousand years to put the town together again. He went past burning houses, pulverized automobiles, stray toilets, lost sinks, fallen traffic lights, smashed STOP signs, wayward CHILDREN – DRIVE CAREFULLY signs, severed water mains, uprooted fire hydrants, and telephone wires lying on the ground like dead pythons.

The stones of Rosehaven Cemetery had survived the disaster splendidly. Most had been torn from the earth, but George could find no gouges or fissures. A familiar place. A place to get one's bearings. Granite is truly forever, he thought.

Dead Wildgrovians were sprawled on the grave sites as if seeking admittance. To George's left lay old Mrs Mulligan's stone, Design No. 2115 in Oklahoma pink. He remembered inscribing ASLEEP IN THE ARMS OF JESUS on it. To his right was a memorial to the Prescotts, Louis and Barbara. ERECTED IN LOVING MEMORY BY THEIR CHILDREN, the stone said. (In truth, only their daughter Kathy had erected the stone; their deplorable son Kevin, who had wanted little to do with his parents while they were alive, wanted even less to do with them dead.) The blast had opened a ravine from one end of Rosehaven Cemetery to the other. Several previously interred Wildgrovians had fallen into it; they were mainly bones. Such was the extent of observable resurrection.

George faced north, the direction of the post office, but the intervening smoke and dust were opaque. He saw the post office anyway, saw it in his thoughts, and beyond the post office he saw the lake, and on the shore he saw his cottage, and inside his cottage he saw Justine and Holly packing their suitcases, feeding the pets, waiting for Daddy. He merely had to go there. Giving the golden suit a quick little hug, he started off.

The most convenient route home took George across acres of black dirt and directly into a crater. Cautiously he clambered down the pulpy walls, from which cut cables and broken pipes protruded like diced earthworms in a newly dug grave. Poisoned by radioisotopes, drained by their wounds, hundreds of disoriented refugees had died crossing the pit. He picked his way through a mottle of white corpses.

The center. Ashes, stench, dead refugees, another survivor. The man was naked but for his utility belt, a few hunks of scopas suit, and a cracked, Humpty-Dumpty helmet. He negotiated the rubble methodically. Now and then he would kneel down, unzip a corpse's suit, and study with scientific intensity the dead flesh beneath. Approaching, George recognized the survivor, who was examining the corpse of a child.

'Tsk, tsk,' the survivor muttered. 'Tsk, tsk, tsk.'

The attack had wrecked John Frostig's good looks. Much of his nose was gone, and all of one ear. His brow was a swamp of blood and perspiration.

'John?'

'Afternoon, buddy-buddy.' The blaze in John's eyes, the cackle in his voice, would have made Theophilus Carter seem by comparison as rational as a grammarian. 'Looks like we've got a failure-to-meet-specifications problem here, eh? Of course, with the fallout still trickling down, it's too early to say how they'll handle the cumulative doses, but obviously we should beef up thermal shielding and overpressure protection by at least twenty percent, at *least* twenty percent, wouldn't you say? All these holes in the fabric – shoddy workmanship, plain and simple. Those jackasses in quality control are going to hear from me, you'd better believe it, they're going to *hear* from John Frostig. They're going to hear from Alice and Lance and Gary – shit, George, have you ever seen so many dead people? Gives me the berries, I don't mind telling you. They're going to hear from Gary, too. And Lance and Gary and . . . and—' The scopas suit salesman, who had probably not wept since the doctor swatted his rump to prime his lungs, was weeping now, torrents of stored tears.

George said, 'Your showroom used to be around here, didn't it?'

'Fucking Cossacks!'

'It's amazing you aren't dead.'

'I was at the Lizard . . . a quick drink, that's all, and a minute of talk with . . . a lady, nothing wrong with that, two minutes of talk, because my boy . . . Nickie – you just asked about him, didn't you? – well, he's off sledding at the Barlows with this nice old person we use for a baby-sitter, the Covington lady, though I can't even *find* the Barlows, which is where my boy is, with Mrs Covington, who's a good baby-sitter, we can definitely recommend her, so I'm sure he's alive, I mean, the units can't *all* have been defective, just the Palo Alto line, probably – the Osaka ones must be okay, especially Nickie's, who was sledding at the Barlows – right? – broken suit or no.' The salesman groaned, and a viscous mix of water and pink solids poured from his mouth. 'The point is, I'm not having my company associated with a cheapjack product, people will lose faith. The customer is always right – you probably learned that at the tomb works, eh, buddy-buddy? If we don't get a better performance out of these units next time, why, the whole industry will go down the toilet. What's that *gold* thing?'

'Scopas suit.'

'Never saw a gold one before.'

'It's special. Custom-made.'

'Kind of small.'

'It's for Holly – her Christmas present. She's going to get this *and* a Mary Merlin doll.'

'You're mistaken,' said John, who had drawn the Colt .45 from his utility belt and was now aiming it at George. 'It's for Nickie. He's sledding with Mrs Covington. Damn good baby-sitter.'

George vomited. 'Forget it, John,' he said, wiping his mouth.

The pistol was ugly. It did not waver. Is this where the bomb had come from? No, too small. An airplane had brought it, or a missile. Was there any hope? Yes, there was, lying in the holster of Holly's suit . . .

'I'll bet it doesn't even *work*,' said the salesman. 'It's not an Eschatological.'

George made a swift, calculated grab toward the utility belt. He heard a sound like a firecracker exploding.

The bullet rammed through the left glove of Holly's suit and entered his stomach, throwing him to the ground. The suit embraced him. He felt nauseated, terrified. A burning poker had spitted him, drilling his bowels. It hurt more than anything possibly could, and yet it did not hurt enough, did not punish him sufficiently for failing to bring her salvation home.

'Oh, shit, I'm sorry, George. I didn't mean to do that. I don't even *want* that stupid suit. You shouldn't have moved. I hope I haven't killed you. Nickie's off sledding. Jesus, what a horrible day this has been. Have I killed you? I *told* you not to move!'

John slid the Colt .45 muzzle between his lips. He moved it back and forth as if operating a bicycle pump, licked the metal, pushed it tight against the roof of his mouth. Odd behavior, George thought, for a man who has just survived a thermonuclear war. There was a pop. Something coral-colored and soggy flew out of the back of John's head, and he fell.

George looked heavenward. A bloated, bellied shape wheeled across the scorched sky. It had a scraggy neck and a beak like the jaws of a steam shovel. Its eyes were yellow, glowing, crosshatched by veins. The beating of its wings, loud and violent as a stampede, raised a wind that stirred the ashes in the pit and heaped them on George's body.

He named the creature. Vulture. The mightiest vulture in the world, big as a pterodactyl. It had come to pick his bones.

CHAPTER SIX

*In Which a Sea Captain, a General, a Therapist,
and a Man of God Enter the Tale*

Lieutenant Commander Olaf Sverre, who could see beyond the horizon, stood in the periscope room of his strategic submarine, watching the Commonwealth of Massachusetts burn down.

'God help them,' he mumbled, pressing his good eye against Periscope Number One. Each town's flames had a distinctive tint. Stockbridge burned orange, Worcester violet, Wellesley gold, Newton vermillion.

The periscope was a wondrous blend of mysticism and know-how. Its lenses were made of beryl, the very substance from which Roger Bacon, the thirteenth-century wizard, had fashioned a looking glass that enabled him to observe events occurring a hundred miles away. When Sugar Brook National Laboratory, working under a cost-plus contract from the United States Department of Defense, had aligned these fabulous glass disks according to doodles found in the notebooks of Leonardo da Vinci and then linked them to an array of geostationary satellites, the result was a periscope of infinite range. The US Congress had recently bought the American people forty-two such devices, one for every *Philadelphia*-class fleet ballistic missile submarine in the Navy. The people were for the most part surprised and delighted by these gifts, and pleased to learn that the people of the Soviet Union did not have any yet.

Sverre narrowed the focal length, bringing the glowing mass of Boston into view. Confused sea gulls soared through the skies above the harbor. They were on fire. He closed his right eye and opened his left, which was made of gutta-percha. There, that was better, no burning gulls. Each evening Sverre would remove his rubber eye, soak it in gin, and replace it, whereupon the alcohol would seep into his brain, giving him a unique and copacetic high. In these troubled times, it was the only way he could get to sleep.

Although Sverre could monitor places as remote as India and Argentina, he could not see what was happening on his own ship. For this he relied on his executive officer. 'Mister Grass,' he growled into the intercom, 'bring me a status report.'

It would take Lieutenant Grass several minutes to reach the periscope room. Time for a drink. Time for two. Sverre yanked a bottle from his claw-hammer coat, poured gin into a Styrofoam cup. Black fur thrived on the sides of his stovepipe hat. Dark, silky hairs sprouted along his cheeks, rushing down his jaw and coming together in great torrents of beard.

A stanza of poetry jumped spontaneously into his mind. Grabbing a booklet called *The MK-49 Torpedo: Repairs and Servicing*, he turned it over and scribbled:

> Midgard's serpent now unfurled
> Its circuit round the mortal world.
> When Jormungandr shakes its coils
> The slimy ocean swirls and boils.

Lieutenant Grass came in, brass buttons sparkling, white uniform croaking softly with starch. His freckles looked newly polished. He loved the Navy.

Sverre crossed out the stanza. 'Can we leave this ghastly place?'

'They pulled the man free an hour ago,' said the exec. 'He's in surgery.'

'Surgery? Hell. I'm not delivering any corpses, that's not how my orders read. Prognosis?'

'Fair. The bullet probably would have finished him, but it went through some kid's scopas suit first. He's a strong fellow – carved tombstones for a living.'

'Tombstones?'

'Yeah.'

'What do they want with *him*?'

'Beats me, Captain.'

'Contaminated?'

'Over two hundred and fifty rads, the needle said.'

'Got any more bad news, as long as you're here? Tell me the ward can't handle another case.'

'Well, they're still treating Wengernook and Tarmac, but even after Paxton's admitted they won't be near capacity. This is a fine boat they gave you, sir.'

Sverre contacted the control room and ordered the diving officer to bring them around. 'Take her down, Mister Sparks. Two hundred feet.'

'I'm curious, sir,' said Lieutenant Grass. 'When they picked up Paxton, he was at ground zero – right in the crater. A crazy place to be, wouldn't you say? What do you suppose he was doing there?'

Turning his good eye to the periscope, the captain watched the red, boiling waters of Boston Harbor splash across the deck. 'He was doing what we're doing,' said Sverre. 'Trying to get home.'

'Facts,' a woman said. 'You need facts, Mr Paxton. Facts will steady your mind.'

George became conscious of several varieties of pain. He concluded, with mixed emotions, that he was still alive. Despite the bullet from John Frostig, the thermonuclear bomb, and his keen desire to be dead, he had evidently not yet left the world – unless, of course, the blurry creature standing near him was an angel.

'Facts. You are in the radiation ward aboard US Navy submarine SSBN 713 *City of New York*, out of McMurdo Station. Displacement – thirty-four thousand tons submerged. Draft – sixty-five feet. Delivery system – thirty-six tubes loaded with Multiprong missiles. Warheads – W-76 reentry vehicles, eight per bus, five hundred kilotons each.'

Fever coursed through George's body. His brow oozed sweat. His bowels ached. His stomach churned sour milk. Barbed wire flossed his brain.

'There is a document,' she said. 'The McMurdo Sound Agreement. Six names appear in it. You are all being evacuated to the Ross Ice Shelf.'

George suddenly realized why the angel was so fuzzy. He was inside a plastic tent. She was outside.

'Aurhgh,' George responded. Two marbles seemed to be lodged in his throat. As if to diagnose the problem, he inserted his fingers. The back of his hand was covered with purple spots. His gums were bleeding.

'Your benefactor is Operation Erebus. When they rescued you, there was a bullet in your stomach and a scopas suit in your arms. The bullet came out last week. The suit is now in the cabin you will occupy if and when your convalescence begins.'

Why is my head so cold? George wondered. Your head is cold because you are hairless, his fingertips revealed. You are as bald as a slab of South African granite.

'Final fact. For the last six days you have been unconscious, during which interval you passed from the prodromal phase of radiation sickness through the latency phase and into the life-or-death phase. And that's your situation. I'm sorry it's not better.'

Beyond his physical pains lay additional anguish, emotions that rested on him like the stones with which his New England ancestors had pressed witches to death. There was a stone for loss, a stone for fear, a stone for Holly, a stone for—

'I have a wife,' he said. Four words, four swallows of acid. A coughing fit possessed him, and he expectorated onto the pillow case. Dots of blood were suspended in the sputum. 'And a daughter,' he rasped. 'I'm supposed to tell her a story about an elf who casts a golden shadow.' He struggled to sit up, collapsed in a heap of pain and fatigue. 'Ice shelf? Submarine? You mean – under the water? Why are there purple spots on my hands? What's in my throat?'

'The spots indicate intradermal bleeding. The things in your throat are infected tonsils. My name is Morning Valcourt. I'm a psychotherapist, and I intend to help you.'

George coughed, less severely than before. He vibrated with fever. His lungs felt as bloated as unmilked udders.

After strapping a surgical mask over her face, Dr Valcourt pushed back a corner of the tent and entered.

One glance was enough to disprove George's angel theory. A silk kimono enveloped a body that was decidedly secular. The woman's eyes were a saturated blue-green, her hair thick and red like the coils in the electric heaters back at the Crippen Monument Works. Six days unconscious, is that what she said? Then he had missed his Monday appointment with Mrs Covington.

'What you must realize . . . just after you were evacuated, another warhead found its target. Direct hit.' She came closer, her mask pulsing with her breaths. 'Nobody except you got out of Wildgrove. Do you understand?'

His dislike of Dr Valcourt was not far from disgust. How did she know whether anybody got out? What right had she to speak of such things?

She pulled away and stepped backward, so that the plastic veil parted and then dropped, walling them off from each other once again.

'Please kill me,' he said, quoting the Wildgrove burn victims as calmly as if asking for a glass of water.

Dr Valcourt paced behind the milky tent. She seemed to emanate from an unfocused movie projector. 'My job is not to kill you, but to cure you.'

'Of radiation sickness?'

'Of shame. Survivor's guilt, it's called. To live through a disaster like this, where so many died – it's a terrible burden on your psyche.'

'Where are we going?'

'Home.'

'Wildgrove?'

'Antarctica.'

'Please leave me alone.'

'Here's a straight opinion for you, Mr Paxton. That's something you won't often get from a psychotherapist – especially from a survivor's guilt specialist – so listen carefully. I think you have a duty to learn why your name is in the McMurdo Sound Agreement. After you have found out – do what you will. Eat, drink, and be merry – or curse God, and die. I don't especially care which.'

There were footsteps, and the distasteful psychotherapist melted away . . .

Curse God, and die. In the Book of Job, the Lord's most pious follower is subjected to a kind of wager between God and Satan. With God's sponsorship, Satan inflicts on Job everything short of a thermonuclear warhead. Job loses his oxen, sheep, camels, she-asses, servants, sons, and health.

'Curse God, and die,' his wife advises. Job is sitting on ashes at the time.

'My bowels boil, and rest not,' complains Job, who does not have the proverbial patience of Job. 'I am a brother to jackals, and a companion to ostriches. My skin is black, and falleth from me, and my bones are burned with the heat. Therefore is my harp turned to mourning, and my pipe into the voice of them that weep.'

Curse God, and die. To George it seemed like remarkably sage and relevant advice.

If one had to say something good about acute radiation sickness, it would be this: either it kills you or it doesn't. Knowing that success was a distinct possibility, the medical staff of the *City of New York* got busy. They cultured George's mucus, blood, and stool, then loaded him up with appropriate antibiotics. They stuck a tube in his arm and gave him a new set of white blood cells. They bathed him in antiseptic solutions every twelve hours, shampooed him with chlorhexidine gluconate every twenty-four hours, and trimmed his fingernails and toenails every other day.

To the end of his life, George would be haunted by the notion that the onslaught of gamma rays had planted the seeds of God-knew-what diseases, but the United States Navy was still within its rights when they pronounced him well. His fever broke, his hair grew back, his purple spots vanished, his tonsils shrank, his lungs drained, his gums stopped bleeding, his platelet and white cell counts became exemplary. The paramedics assured him that he had inhaled very little fallout and that, thanks to his precipitous departure from ground zero via Operation Erebus, his cumulative dose had been well under three hundred rads.

'More like two hundred and eighty rads, if you want my opinion,' said the medical officer, a lieutenant senior-grade named Brust. 'You're in great shape, believe me. There's only one thing we couldn't fix.'

'Oh?' said George.

'Your secondary spermatocytes are failing to become spermatids.' Dr Brust was a small, tubby man with a face so incongruously gaunt it seemed to be on its own separate diet. 'Blame the radiation.'

'What are you talking about?' George asked.

'You're sterile,' said Dr Brust evenly.

'Sterile?'

'Sterile as a mule.' Black stains covered Brust's surgical gown. 'I can't imagine that it would make much difference to you at this point.'

'My wife and I were planning . . .' George closed his eyes.

'Didn't they tell you about your wife?'

'Yes.' When he opened his eyes, he saw only his tears.

'I wouldn't worry about my gonads if I were you,' said Dr Brust. 'You're lucky to be alive.'

They moved George out of the radiation unit into an ordinary sick bay.

'You in the McMurdo Sound Agreement?' asked the patient in the next bed, a long, nervous, weasel-bodied man with an expression so intense George could not look at it without squinting.

'Yes. George Paxton. You in it too?'

'At the top of the list. Love to lean over and shake your hand, friend, but I've got this tube up my silo.'

'Me too.'

'Ever hear of Robert Wengernook?'

'Haven't I seen you on television?'

'Ah, another one of *those*,' said Wengernook with mock distress. 'Here I am in the goddamn D-O-D, and everybody thinks of me as the guy who does the scopas suit commercials. For my hobby,

66

I'm the Assistant Secretary of Defense for International Security Affairs.'

'My wife always wanted to be in a scopas suit commercial. The one with the lady knight.'

'Really? Your wife was in that? Small world.'

'No, she *wanted* to be. She would have been right for it too, because Justine was very pretty, everybody thought so. They say a warhead got her.'

'You've got to believe me, George, I really thought the suits were good.' Wengernook's twitchy fingers knitted themselves into elaborate sculptures. His tongue, which was remarkably long, darted in and out like a chameleon's. 'I guess it's Japan's way of getting back at us.'

'For Hiroshima?'

'I was thinking more of import quotas.' He lit a cigarette, puffed. 'God, this is all so awful. You might suppose that on a submarine there wouldn't be much to remind a man of his family, but that's not true. I'll see some fire extinguisher, and that gets me picturing the one I gave Janet last Christmas. You wouldn't think a fire extinguisher would have such emotionalism attached to it.'

'I'd like to talk about something else.'

'Same here.'

But the tomb inscriber and the Assistant Secretary of Defense for International Security Affairs had nothing more to say to each other.

At the end of the week they transferred George to a cabin more suggestive of a civilian ocean liner than of a military vessel. The luxury suffocated him. He wanted Justine to be there, making fun of the kitschy floral wallpaper and reveling in the cornucopia that was the *City of New York*'s galley – eggs Benedict breakfasts, steamer clam lunches, lobster dinners – all served up by cheerful, redfaced enlisted men who seemed to be auditioning for jobs in some unimaginably swank hotel. He wanted Holly to be there, delighting in the tank of live sea horses and giving them her favorite names, the ones she had already bestowed on dozens of dolls and stuffed animals. These names, for some reason, were Jennifer, Suzy, Jeremiah, Alfred, and Margaret.

And so, despite posh surroundings and great food, George still felt himself a brother to jackals. His pipe was still turned into the voice of them that weep. Sometimes he smashed things until his knuckles bled. The Navy sent a seaman third-class around to clean up the mess. At other times he contemplated his closet, where Holly's golden scopas suit and its shattered glove hung as if on a gibbet. He stared at the suit for hours at a time.

It would have saved her life, he told himself, although he suspected this was not true.

'I should have tried harder,' he moaned aloud at odd moments.

A small bubble of consolation occasionally drifted into his thoughts. If death were as final and anesthetic as he had been taught, then his family had at least been granted the salvation of nothingness. Justine could not now be mourning the death of her daughter. Holly could not now be wondering whether all this chaos somehow precluded her getting a Mary Merlin doll for Christmas. Thank God for oblivion, ran his Unitarian prayer.

The knock on George's door had the brisk, impatient cadence of a person accustomed to getting his way.

'It's open.' George sat on a plush divan reading the Book of Job for the third time that week. Once again he was finding the drama cruel and absurd.

A military man entered. His uniform, curiously, was of the United States Air Force. His presence on a Navy submarine entailed the incongruity of a rabbi in a cathedral.

'You're evacuee Paxton, aren't you?'

George closed the Bible and said yes. The Air Force refugee approached, arm poised for a mandatory handshake. He was constructed of massive shoulders, a rough rock-like head, a formidable trunk, and limbs of simian length. A flurry of decorations and service ribbons hung from his breast opposite a nameplate that read TARMAC.

'Major General Roger "Brat" Tarmac,' the refugee said in a large, wholesome voice. Shaking hands with Brat Tarmac was a workout. 'Deputy Chief of Staff for Retargeting, Strategic Air Command. I was in downtown Omaha when the Cossacks came.

Had to do my Christmas shopping some time, right? So there I am, buying my sister's kid this *clown*, when quick-as-shit a warhead goes off behind me, and the next thing I know I'm in the *Navy*. It's all so crazy. The clown needed batteries – that was going to be my next stop. I keep telling myself, "Brat, face facts. You'll never see those people again – your sister's a casualty." I say that, and I don't believe it. She was a pilot. Like me. Flew strategic interceptors. Jesus. Incredible.'

George had never taken so immediate a liking to anyone before. Brat Tarmac was the sort of handsome, athletic soldier ten-year-old boys wanted for fathers, a fantasy to which George, at age thirty-five, was not entirely immune.

'Coffee?' George offered.

'Affirmative,' said the general.

Obtaining coffee aboard the *City of New York* was a simple matter of walking up to your cabin's vending machine and pushing some buttons. 'Cream and sugar?'

'Black. In a dirty mug, eh? No frills for us bomber jockeys.'

A Styrofoam cup caught the stream. George's hand made a spider over the rim, and he carried the coffee to his guest.

'So far I've managed to locate all the Erebus personnel but that evangelist, Sparrow.' Brat sucked coffee across his leathery lips. 'We'll be working with a pretty broad spectrum of talent. Wengernook is—'

'I met him in the sick bay.'

'Impressive guy, huh?'

'Nervous.'

'Intense. He should quit smoking. Then we've got Brian Overwhite of the Arms Control and Disarmament Agency, and you'll never guess who they stuck in the cabin next to yours.'

'Who?'

'William Randstable. Remember when he beat that Cossack at chess? He was only seven or something.'

'I don't follow chess.'

'It was a big propaganda thing for us. The kid worked at one of those think tanks for a while, then they put him on missile accuracy over at Sugar Brook or someplace. All in all it's a pretty classy act our President's putting together down in Antarctica. In a few days they'll be calling the whole team together – after they run us through this survivor's guilt crap – so we can chart out our options. God, I hope they've got a crisis relocation effort going. I can't bear to think of this turning into a high civilian-casualty thing.'

'Why Antarctica?'

'A big chunk of real estate, right? Hence, a high warhead-exhaustion factor. Excellent place for a command-and-control center. Looks like the Joint Chiefs thought of everything – I'm a good man with an ICBM, Wengernook knows what we should commit to the European theater, Randstable can probably maintain a decent R and D effort throughout, and Reverend Sparrow will do wonders for our morale. All right, all right, I'll admit it. We should all just *admit* it, right? We're scared. We've never done this before. The cheerleader and the quarterback. You must be dousing your drawers, what with your MARCH Plan on the line and everything. I'm a big supporter of MARCH, you know. Over at SAC they called me the MARCH Hare.'

'*My* plan? I don't have anything to do with the MARCH Plan, General Tarmac. I'd never heard of it until Professor Carter—'

'Modulated Attacks in Response to Counterforce Hostilities – that's not your baby?'

'No.'

'The SPASM, then. You're one of the geniuses behind the SPASM.'

'The SPASM?'

'Single Plan for Aligning the Services of the Mili . . . er, what exactly are you *doing* on this team, Paxton?'

'Wish I knew. Two weeks ago I signed a really strange scopas suit contract.'

'Scopas suits? Hell, they don't work. We ran tests.'

'I have one that works. In my closet. It didn't get. . . where it was supposed to go.'

'You aren't in the defense community? You aren't at Sugar Brook or Lumen or anything?'

'I inscribe tombstones.'

'Tombstones?'

'Lately I've been writing the epitaphs.'

'Epitaphs? I hate to say this, Paxton, but they sure made a mistake evacuating *you*.'

'I don't want to be on the team. I just want to be dead.'

The MARCH Hare could think of no adequate response to this. 'Dead?' he said. He rubbed his hand across his hair, each strand of which was as straight and rigid as a sewing needle. 'Dead?' he said again. His waist was encircled by a utility belt from which hung an object that looked like a skyrocket. 'Nice cabin you got here. Mine's not bad, either. But then, the Navy always *did* have a sweet tooth, eh? I understand this boat hauls thirty-six E4 Multiprongs, all gassed up and loaded for Russian bear.'

George looked at the sea horse tank, studied the antics of Jennifer, Suzy, Jeremiah, Alfred, and Margaret. The previous day some babies had appeared. He could imagine Holly discovering them. The hallucinated sound of her ooooooh's and ahhhhh's was like a jagged bronze bell implanted in his skull.

Brat got himself a second cup of coffee, drained it instantly, went for a third. 'Epitaphs, you said? Hmmm, maybe they expect this fight to last so long we'll all be needing a few well-chosen words over our heads. In any event, welcome to the show. We've got some tough decisions to make. Started your therapy?'

'No. You?'

'I suppose so. Mostly we just sit in Dr Valcourt's cabin and palaver, for which the Navy evidently pays her the going rate. I tell her the main guilt I've got comes from not being at SAC when we retaliated.' He grinned, forced a laugh. 'Don't let anybody kid you – our air-launched Javelin missiles are the finest a federal deficit can buy.' His grin suddenly degenerated. He grabbed his mouth as if to forestall vomit. 'Hell, I'm scared, Paxton.'

'I don't like Dr Valcourt.'

Brat took a deep breath. 'Yeah, I know, kind of an ice cube, but I do enjoy our sessions. Maybe I'll end up on the fun side of her pants some day.' He crushed his Styrofoam cup. Coffee erupted over his fist. 'Shit, wouldn't you think they'd give us a few scenarios to mull over? You can be sure the *Cossack* generals aren't sitting around in some goddamn submarine.'

Jeremiah Sea Horse and Margaret Sea Horse were kissing. 'Have you ever noticed that when a four-year-old draws a human face, it's always smiling?' George asked. 'At least, my four-year-old's faces were always smiling. Her name was Holly.'

'I'm sorry. War is hell, huh?' Brat removed the skyrocket from its holster. 'Jesus Christ – it's really happening! Just about the most tragical thing a person can conceive of, and it's . . . happening! The point is, after you get into one of these failed-deterrence situations, you can't let the enemy call the shots. In quite a few scenarios – more than you'd think – the victor is the guy who gets off the last strike.' Brat waved his weapon. 'It's small, but it packs a wallop. David and Goliath.'

'A hand grenade?'

'Nah, come on, we're in the age of microtech, Paxton. The Navy may get to piss in gold cups, but turn to your Air Force for the state of the art. This is a one-kiloton man-portable thermo-nuclear device complete with delivery system. Looks just like—'

'A toy,' said George, edging toward the back of his cabin. Indeed, the missile was so toylike that, had Holly been there, she would have used it to send a teddy bear to the moon. 'I would like you to leave now,' he said. 'I feel an attack of survivor's guilt coming on.'

George spent the next four days in his canopied bed, under silk sheets, wishing for death. He cursed God, but he did not die. His mind wanted no dealings with whatever remained of the world, but his body declined to cooperate. His heart, unmindful of Justine's fate, kept beating. His kidneys, indifferent to Holly's absence, continued to filter. His mouth got dry, and he drank. His stomach growled, and was fed. George Paxton cursed God, and he cursed the false adage that time heals all wounds.

The only exercise he got that week came from walking in his sleep.

'Well, well, who have we *here*?'

He was being shaken so vigorously that all his bones seemed

about to disconnect. He opened his eyes. Six ensigns filled his field of vision. They became four. The vibrations stopped. Two ensigns – moon-faced, pudgy, not notably distinguishable from each other.

'To begin with, you should salute us,' said the first ensign.

'Quite so,' said the second.

'Salute who?'

'Ensign Cobb,' said the first.

'And his cousin, Ensign Peach,' said the second.

'Mister Peach, I do believe we are in the presence of George Paxton,' said Ensign Cobb.

'Do tell, Mister Cobb. Are you referring to George Paxton of the McMurdo Sound Agreement?' said Ensign Peach.

'One and the same,' said Ensign Cobb.

Ensign Peach lifted a stray thread from the Navy insignia on George's silk pajamas. 'Some say we should build slow, inaccurate, invulnerable missiles,' he said with a sly grin.

'Thereby allaying Soviet fears that we intend to strike first,' continued Ensign Cobb.

'Whereas others say that a force of fast and accurate missiles—'

'Is a more credible deterrent,' said Ensign Cobb.

'Because it does not imply mutual suicide,' said Ensign Peach.

'Contrariwise, some say the enemy command-and-control structure must be spared.'

'So that the war can be brought to a negotiated end.'

'Whereas others say you must hit command-and-control right away—'

'So that the enemy will be decapitated and unable to retaliate.'

'Contrariwise, if it was so, it might be.'

'And if it were so, it would be.'

'But as it isn't, it ain't.'

'That's strategic doctrine.'

'Salute us, Mister Paxton.'

George fired off an uncertain salute.

'Sorry,' said Ensign Peach. 'Not good enough.'

George saluted again.

'*Still* not right,' said Ensign Cobb. 'Looks like we'll have to put you in a torpedo tube after all.'

'In what?' asked George.

'Don't worry. You won't be there for long,' said Ensign Peach.

'A minute at most,' said Ensign Cobb.

'And then – zowee, powee – off you go into the wild blue Atlantic!'

'That's the one with all the salt in it.'

'Can you swim?'

'Can you breathe water?'

Two facts entered George's disorganized brain. He was afraid of these cousins. And they were dragging him down a corridor. He struggled. His muscles pulled in contradictory directions. Steam ducts and neon lights bounced by. He tried telling his captors they had no right to treat an Erebus evacuee this way, whereupon he discovered that Ensign Cobb's sweaty hand was sealing his mouth.

The torpedo room was green and pocked with rivets. Muzak oozed through the air, countless strings performing 'Anchors Aweigh.' The ensigns hauled him up to Tube One, opened the little door. The chamber beyond, which reeked of brine and motor oil, suggested a womb in which man-portable thermo-nuclear devices were gestated.

Ensign Cobb held a copy of the McMurdo Sound Agreement before George's uncoordinated eyes. It was a document of several hundred pages, bound with a spiral of barbed wire. He opened it and thrust Appendix C toward George. Appendix C was headed *Scopas Suit Sales Contract*.

'That's your signature, isn't it?' said Ensign Cobb.

'Yes, but—'

'Look, Mister Peach, he signed it!'

'And with his own name, too!'

'I'm a friend of General Tarmac's,' asserted George.

'The MARCH Hare?' said Ensign Cobb.

'Right.'

'Any friend of General Tarmac's is an enemy of mine,' said Ensign Peach.

'Don't forget to close your mouth,' said Ensign Cobb.

'Don't forget to hold your nose.'

'Don't forget to write.'

'We have always been with you—'

'Waiting to get in.'

George swung at Cobb's jaw. The connection was firm and noisy. Peach retaliated, planting a fist in the tomb inscriber's stomach, thus awakening the dormant agony of his bullet wound.

I can take this, George said to himself after they had shoved him into Tube One and closed the door. I will not scream, Oblivion is what I wanted all along, and now here it is, oblivion, my good Unitarian friend.

The chill seeped into his flesh. His breaths echoed off the cylindrical walls. He decided that this was how his customers felt, snug in their caskets. Were they soothed knowing that a seven hundred and fifty dollar chunk of bonded granite sat overhead? He screamed. The reverberations knifed his eardrums.

He thought of the damage he had just inflicted on Peach. Had he seen correctly? Could it be? When he split the ensign's lip, had black blood rushed out?

George wet his pajamas. The warmth was at once terrible and comforting. They had said this would take only a minute. Black blood. Just like Mrs Covington. An effect of the radiation? No, her visit to the Crippen Monument Works was before the war, wasn't it? His wet pajamas grew cold.

Movies had always been fun, especially with Justine. Post-marital dates were the best kind. You could relax, and if there was no butter for the popcorn the world did not end. You sat there, bathed in conditioned air, waiting for the movie to start – any movie, it didn't matter – like an astronaut in zero gravity, nothing pulling at you, no obligations . . .

The tube door opened. Someone grabbed his ankles and yanked him backward. The torpedo room smelled like burning hair, something he had not noticed before. The syrupy strings were now playing 'Over There.' George flexed his knees and stood up. Pain screwed through his shoulder bones.

A thirtyish man, handsome and stocky, dressed in an immaculate three-piece suit, grinned at him with what seemed like a surplus of teeth. His hair was auburn and abundant, like a well-nourished orangutan's coat.

'What happened to those ensigns?' George asked. He stepped forward, scissoring his legs so as to hide his soggy crotch.

'They had to go off watch, George,' said his rescuer amiably. 'I believe they just wanted to scare you.'

'Whatever made them think that threatening to launch me into the ocean would scare me?' The tomb inscriber laughed. His rescuer did not. George had never before met such a clean-shaven individual. It was as if all the man's whisker follicles had been cauterized.

'My grandfather was in the Navy,' said the rescuer. His voice was like gourmet coffee, silky, layered. 'Evidently it's changed a lot since those days. These sailors have not received the Holy Spirit.'

George looked at his knuckles. They were speckled with a substance resembling tar. 'Their blood is black.'

'I'm not surprised,' said the rescuer.

'You in the Navy, too?'

'Ever watch Christian television?'

'Not a great deal.'

'Last year *Countdown to God's Wrath* – you've never caught it? – we had a consistently better rating than *Gospel Sing-Along*. We get two and a half tons of mail a week. The Lord is doing so many wonderful things.'

'My wife always wanted to be on television.'

The evangelist extended a soft, pliant hand. 'Reverend Peter Sparrow,' he said. Taking Sparrow's hand, George felt sustenance and comfort radiate from each finger. This was a very fine evacuee indeed.

'Television is becoming God's chosen medium these days, just the way Gutenberg's press used to be,' said the evangelist. 'We've been running a lot of old movies on *Countdown* lately, to build up our audience, follow what I'm saying? You've got to start where people are at. Sure, maybe *Ben-Hur* isn't such a great picture – I mean, leprosy doesn't really look like that, it's quite a bit worse – but then you can move them toward the better stuff, *The Robe* and *Quo Vadis* and so on.'

George coughed. The torpedo tube had probably contained several infectious diseases. 'So we're all going to Antarctica.'

'Isn't it wonderful how nuclear exchanges cannot touch Christians?' said Sparrow. 'I knew the Perfect Exile would be a time of joy, but I hadn't realized how rapturous the joy would be. I'm about to see my family.'

'They're in Antarctica?'

'They're in the sky with Jesus.'

George glanced up.

'May I ask you something?' The evangelist touched George's spotted knuckles. 'Are you saved?'

'Yes, you just saved me. I'm most grateful to you. If your program was still on, I'd watch it.'

'I'm talking about your relationship with—'

'My family died when the Russians blew up Wildgrove. Or so I'm told.'

Reverend Sparrow frowned. 'The Hebrew prophets – Ezekiel, Jeremiah – they're all batting a thousand, understand? The Perfect Exile, the Terrible Trial, the destruction of the temple at Jerusalem – they saw everything, right? You're saved, George, or you wouldn't be on this trip.'

'I'm a Unitarian.'

'I'm going to pray for you,' said Reverend Sparrow firmly.

'I appreciate it,' said George, and he did.

CHAPTER SEVEN

In Which Our Hero Makes a Strategic Decision and
Acquires a Reason Not to Curse God and Die

In the days that followed, George's grief took on a New England quality, becoming not so much an emotion as a job to do.

He tried to remember all those times when fatherhood had seemed a crushing burden. Moments when Holly's screeching or stubbornness had brought him to the brink of child beating, moments when he felt as if his life had been stolen and replaced by a talkative iron ball chained to his ankle. But only cloying memories came. Holly putting her dollies to bed. Trying to feed the sick cat before it died. Singing to herself. Struggling to grasp the point of a knock-knock joke. She had never understood that proper knock-knock jokes are puns. Knock-knock, she would say. Who's there? a four-year-old friend would ask. Jennifer (or Suzy or Jeremiah or Alfred or Margaret), Holly would reply.

Jennifer who?

Jennifer Poopie Diapers Stupid Dumb Face!

And then she and her friend would dissolve in giggles, overwhelmed by preschool social satire.

Knock-knock.

'Who's there?' George didn't really need to ask. The knock was as characteristic as a fingerprint. 'It's open, Brat.'

The MARCH Hare pushed boisterously into the cabin – a one-man infantry charge. Accompanying him was a fiftyish man with a dark razoring stare and a marionette's gangly frame.

'Meet Dr William Randstable,' said Brat. 'The whiz kid of Sugar Brook Lab and, it is rumored, a certifiable genius.' The general had lost some weight, and the bags under his eyes looked like change purses. 'William, this is George Paxton – the poet laureate of Wildgrove, Massachusetts.'

'I'm not really a whiz kid any more,' said Randstable. His suit was several sizes too large. 'More of a whiz middle-aged man.'

'I hear you once beat the Russian chess champion,' said George.

'I made the next-to-the-last mistake,' said Randstable modestly.

Brat patted his man-portable thermonuclear device. 'Well, men, looks as if some more fat is about to enter the fire.' His words fought past a trembling throat and clenched teeth. 'They're planning to knock over the remaining enemy missile fields at fourteen hundred hours. If we hurry to the launch control room, we can catch thirty-six Multiprongs go galloping off like Grant took Richmond.'

'Sugar Brook did the technical support for Multiprong guidance and control,' said Randstable with a quick chuckle. He removed his horn-rimmed eyeglasses and began chewing on the ear piece. 'I always wondered how I'd feel on the day they actually left the nest.'

'Pretty upset, I guess,' said George. An understatement, he concluded from what came out of Randstable's chest, a conglomeration of sighs and uncontrolled wheezing.

After moving down a narrow passageway crowded with pipes, ducts, ladders, and stopcocks, the three evacuees came upon a hatch labeled RECREATION AREA: AUTHORIZED PERSONNEL ONLY. Brat decided they were authorized personnel. Crossing over, they entered a throbbing undersea metropolis, each facility scaled to the constraints of submarine space. They started along a corridor named Entertainment Lane. George noted a compact skating rink, a slightly abbreviated bowling alley, a miniature golf course where every hazard entailed placing the ball in one orifice or other of a plaster mermaid, and a pair of succinct indoor swimming pools. The enlisted men's pool was eight feet deep, the officers' ten. A waking nightmare seized George – Peach and Cobb wrapping his body in chains and throwing him into the officers' pool. Or perhaps they would favor the bowling alley. They would tie him up and leave him behind the pins.

A movie marquee blazed outside a small theater. SERGEI BONDARCHUK'S 'WAR AND PEACE,' the marquee shouted. Several blue-suited sailors were lined up at the box office; Peach and Cobb were not among them. Opposite the theater, the little Silver Dollar Casino dazzled George with its hurlyburly of lights and its promises of instant fortune. Through the swinging doors he noticed a seaman second-class dealing blackjack. The clacks and gongs of slot machines ricocheted into the corridor.

Passing through a bulkhead labeled DETERRENCE AREA: AUTH-ORIZED PERSONNEL ONLY, the evacuees found themselves before an open doorway to the missile compartment. Enlisted men streamed back and forth. Brat accosted the first officer he could find, a freckle-faced lieutenant named Grass.

'Mister Grass, I thought you were due to launch at fourteen hundred hours.'

The young officer neglected to return Brat's salute. 'The reentry vehicles aren't ready,' he said.

'Not ready? What kind of operation are you running here, Mister? Sverre will have your pips on a plate.'

Now Grass did salute. He used the wrong hand. Marching up to George, he presented a conspiratorial wink. 'Aren't you the one they tried to blow into the water last week? Pretty funny.'

They followed Grass into the cavernous, echo-laden room.

'I nearly suffocated,' said George.

'I believe that was the point,' said Grass.

Overbearing in their size, dazzling in their metallic sheen, the thirty-six launch tubes rose toward the ceiling like rows of ancient Egyptian pillars. Indeed, the missile compartment suggested noth-ing so much as a technological incarnation of the Temple of Karnak. George advanced at a stoop, cowed by the overbearing majesty of national security. There were worshipers in the temple. Perched on scaffolding, sailors swarmed up and down the tubes, unbolting the access plates and lowering them to the deck via steel cables.

'Why are they opening the tubes, Mister?' Brat demanded.

'To get at the nosecone shrouds,' Grass replied.

'Why get at the shrouds?'

'To reach the bombs.'

'Why?'

'To uncover the arming systems.'

'Why?'

'To smash them to pieces.'

Brat stuck a finger in his ear and swizzled it around. 'Excuse me, Mister, but the EMP from that Omaha explosion must have shorted out my hearing. Sounds like you're defusing the warheads.'

'Those things are dangerous, General. If one detonates during launch, somebody could get hurt.'

A cluster of bomb-carrying reentry vehicles was visible at the top of the nearest tube. Each vehicle looked like a witch's hat: black, conical, smeared with strange oils.

'You're shooting off unarmed missiles?' said Randstable, eyebrows arching with curiosity. 'Some part of your strategy is eluding me, Lieutenant.'

'As you no doubt know, Dr Randstable, on a submarine every cubic inch carries a premium.' Grass smiled boyishly. 'Once I clear out all these boosters and payloads, I'll be free to use the tubes for cultivating orange trees.' He winked. 'Project Citrus.'

'Orange trees!' Brat's voice echoed through the great glimmering temple. 'Orange trees, my left nut!'

The sailors stopped working. They stared down from on high.

'As you might imagine, General, fresh oranges are difficult to come by at the bottom of the Atlantic Ocean,' said Grass. 'If you ask me, fruit tree conversion is the wave of the future.'

The sailors went back to their disarmament duties, busy as ants on a Popsicle.

Lieutenant Commander Olaf Sverre had an apocalypse collection. His hobby was the end of the world. When not stunned by gin or engaged in naval activities, he would ransack the ship's library for a new vision of doomsday, and, finding one, write a bad epic poem about it. Fire, ice, famine, flood, drought, pollution, war – Sverre had collected them all. In his *Noah and Naamah* the captain had written of the forty-day flood in which earth's sinners drowned, of Noah sending out a white raven to seek dry land, of the snowy bird finding instead a floating corpse and feasting on it, since which time all its feathers have been black. For *Yima Victorious* Sverre had written of a fierce endless winter, of Yima receiving instructions from the Zoroastrian God of Light, of the great enclosure into which the hero brought the seeds of men and animals. No humpbacks' seeds, the God of Light, an early eugenicist, had counseled Yima. No impotents, lunatics, lepers, or jealous lovers.

Sverre sat down at his writing desk and, after thrusting his quill pen into a skull-shaped ink pot, attacked the paper with bold flourishes. Noah's raven peered at him – an alabaster knickknack, white as a scopas suit. The captain wrote of the sea monster Jormungandr, hidden in the icy depths, a serpent so long it girded the mortal world, Midgard. The Norse god Thor had once hunted the Midgard serpent using a chain baited with the head of an ox. Jormungandr bit. Thor hauled the serpent from the sea, raised his hammer for the deathblow. The chain snapped. But Thor and the serpent were destined to meet again, at Ragnarok, World's End, and this time—

A pounding halted Sverre's progress of the *Saga of Thor*. He inserted his pen in the raven's mouth, swallowed some gin, staggered across his cabin.

'These evacuees insisted on seeing you,' grunted Lieutenant Grass as Sverre yanked open the door.

Brat offered a hostile salute. 'Captain Sverre, an activity that could seriously erode our security – evidently it goes by the code name Citrus – is presently under way in your missile compartment.'

'You may leave, Mister Grass,' said the captain in a foreign accent that refused to declare itself.

Certain that nothing good was about to transpire between Brat and Sverre, George attempted to absent himself by surveying the captain's elegantly anachronistic cabin – dark wood walls, plush carpets, puffy sofas, antique globe. Perched on the writing desk was an alabaster raven that Holly would have liked.

'I see you fancy my pet, Mr Paxton,' said Sverre. 'His name is Edgar Allan Poe.'

'Somebody once asked me a riddle,' said George. 'Why is a raven like a writing desk?'

'I've heard that one,' said Sverre. 'It has no answer.'

'I'll go to work on it,' said Randstable, happily perplexed.

'You'll be wasting your time,' said Sverre. 'Now here's one that does have an answer – when is a first strike not a first strike?'

'When?' asked Randstable.

'When it is an anticipatory retaliation,' said Sverre.

'Hmm . . .' said Randstable, sucking on his eyeglasses frames. 'Right. Good.'

Brat's face had acquired the color and proportions of a ripe tomato. 'I am told that this Project Citrus carries your authorization, sir,' he hissed, rapping loudly on the launching pad of his man-portable thermonuclear device, 'and I wish to register the strongest possible objection!'

A smile stole out from Sverre's black beard. 'Those Multi-prongs just slow us down, and the sooner Grass replaces them with a hydroponic orchard, the better.' His eyes were glittery black discs. His nose, a noble pyramid, threw a quarter of his countenance into shadow. 'What's the matter, General, don't you like oranges? The fact is, this war doesn't interest me much any more, and neither does the United States Navy. Anyone want a drink? We serve gin around here.'

Brat twisted his mouth into the quintessence of contempt. 'I know your breed, Sverre. You're one of those renegades, aren't you? You've got your emergency-action message, you're supposed to take out some targets, and now you're getting all philosophical or something.'

The captain set out four Styrofoam cups on his writing desk and procured a grungy bottle from his claw-hammer coat. 'The Brazilian Indians foresaw all this,' he slurred as he poured. 'They believed the earth was suspended over a fire, like a chicken on a spit.' He served the gin, then gestured his three guests onto a sofa with scrolled arms and a rosette that put George in mind of tombstone Design No. 8591. As Brat seethed, Sverre wandered back to his desk and took down a slide projector. 'Before you start leading a mutiny, General' – the oak paneling on a bulkhead parted to reveal a screen – 'I want you to see some damage assessments.'

Flicking a switch, Sverre brought utter darkness to a room that had never seen the sun. He turned on the projector, and a bright wedge of light shot forward, hitting the screen. No specks hovered in the beam; the *City of New York* was a world without dust. Sverre stood before the rectangle of light, his silhouette gesturing broadly. 'The transmissions we monitored from the National Command Authority suggest that the Soviet Union started the war. The first evidence reached NORAD via airborne look-down radar. A flurry of Russian Spitball cruise missiles was flying over Canada on a trajectory for Washington. Grounds for preemption, the Joint Chiefs argued. And so a surgical counterforce strike was launched against a few selected Soviet ICBM fields and bomber bases. And so the enemy . . . shot back.'

The captain went to his desk and, swallowing a mouthful of gin, dropped the first slide into place. 'These pictures were taken through Periscope Number One's geosynchronous satellite array.'

'We worked on that rig,' said Randstable.

'Like any global conflict,' said Sverre, 'World War Three included many exciting and memorable battles.' A blur lit the screen. Sverre twisted the projector lens, and a charred crevasse appeared. 'The Battle of Joplin, Missouri,' he narrated. He changed slides. A burning field, automobiles lying on their roofs like flipped turtles. 'The Battle of Dearborn, Michigan,' said Sverre. New slide. A prairie covered with dark scars. 'The Battle of Dodge City, Kansas,' the captain explained. New slide. A stand of blistered trees rising from a swamp. 'The Battle of Winter Haven, Florida.' New slide. An ocean of ashes. 'The Battle of Twin Falls, Idaho.'

Now the images came in rapid fire. Racine: Amarillo. Hagerstown. Bowling Green. Chattanooga. Bangor. Within half an hour

Sverre had spun through four circular trays, each holding a hundred and twenty slides.

He shut off the bulb, and the fall of Troy, New York, dissolved into nothingness. The evacuees sat in the thick darkness, drinking. Randstable made a sound like a dog having a nightmare. Brat alternated snorts with coughs. For five minutes not a word was spoken.

'Just how reliable are these damage assessments?' an invisible Brat said at last.

'No doubt there are pockets of survivors,' said Sverre, 'and I'm fairly confident that ten or fifteen towns were overlooked.' The lights came on. 'But on the whole the post-exchange environment is accurately reflected here.'

'Yeah? Well, that's absurd,' said Brat. 'The MARCH Plan was chock full of escalation controls.'

'Oh, dear,' said Randstable. 'Oh, God. Oh, dear.' The former whiz kid pulled a small magnetic chess set from his jacket. 'Quick! Does anybody know a good chess problem? Give me a problem, please, somebody!'

Sverre said, 'Put eight queens on the board in such a way that none can take another.'

'Not enough queens,' wheezed Randstable. 'Doesn't matter. I've solved it already.'

'All right. Use all four bishops to—' Sverre cut himself off, having noticed that Brat's man-portable thermonuclear device was out of its holster and firmly fixed in the general's right hand.

'Captain Sverre, should you disobey my command, I shall exercise my option to fire this missile, thereby airbursting a one-kiloton warhead within ten inches of your body.' Brat aimed the weapon at Sverre's stomach. 'I hereby order you to terminate Project Citrus. I further order you to feed the following strategic enemy targets into your fire-control computers.' He removed a small key from around his neck and stuck it in the launching pad. 'The ICBM complex at Novosibirsk, the ICBM complex at Kirensk, the Strategic Rocket Forces headquarters at Kharkov, the warhead factory at Minsk, the central command post at Gorky, the alternate—'

'We have always been with you,' interrupted Sverre, his smile ever-growing, his eyes hot and pulsing like those of the vulture George had seen at ground zero, 'waiting to get in.'

'I don't know what school *you* went to, Captain,' said Brat, 'but at the Air Force Academy they teach that winning is better than losing.'

'Oh, dear,' said Randstable as he set up his chess pieces. 'Oh, God.'

Sverre placed a bony, weathered hand on George's shoulder. 'I think we'll leave the key strategic decision with Mr Paxton here. Say the word, George, and I'll send all thirty-six of my Multi-prongs, fully armed, against the enemy. A grand-scale one hundred and forty-four megaton retaliatory strike.'

'You want *me* to decide?' said George.

'Yes,' said Sverre.

'Me?'

'Correct.'

'Why me?'

'I'm curious to see what will happen.'

George did not think it right for the fate of the Union of Soviet Socialist Republics to be in his hands.

'I'm not really qualified for this,' he said.

'You've fought as many nuclear wars as the rest of us,' said Sverre.

A mile-high tombstone appeared in George's mind, Design No. 1067 in Vermont blue-gray. A million names were inscribed in the granite. DULUTH. DODGE CITY. SAN FRANCISCO. PHILADELPHIA. CHRYSLERS. CBS. XEROX CORPORATION. THE SUPER BOWL.

What had Sverre called it? A retaliatory strike? A fair and reasonable notion. They sandblasted us. We must do the same to them.

And yet . . .

'Tell me if I've got this straight, Brat,' said George. 'You want to blow up Russia, correct?'

'I want to kill the Soviets' reserve ICBMs and prevent their being salvoed in subsequent attacks,' Brat replied.

'Why?' asked George.

'What did you say?'

'I said, why?'

'National defense, that's why.'

'Yes, yes, I can understand that,' said George. 'Sure. However, if we're going to have national defense, Brat, don't we also need, well . . . you know . . .'

'What?' said Brat.

'A nation.'

'It's a necessary condition,' said Randstable, whose left cerebral hemisphere was preparing to play chess with his right. 'Please put that thing away before you get us all killed.'

'If we don't take out their reserves,' Brat insisted, 'the Soviets will use them to hunt down the survivors.'

'Painful as it may be, I think we must conclude that MARCH is no longer the operative strategy here,' said Randstable, staring blankly at the chessboard. 'We've even gone past the SPASM, I'd say – the motive matrix is completely different now.' He turned suddenly toward Sverre, his fingers splayed and wriggling. 'But then why this Antarctica business?'

'Your job for the present,' said the captain, 'is to work with Dr Valcourt on conquering your survivor's guilt.'

Brat perspired and trembled, as if gripped by a high fever. 'You want a motive, William? I've got a motive. Vengeance may not be a pretty word, but it's what's expected of us.'

'Right!' said Sverre. 'We owe it to all those millions of dead people to make more millions of dead people. Be careful how you rewrite strategic doctrine, General, or you'll come out of this war without a single medal. Mr Paxton, I need your answer.'

XEROX CORPORATION. THE SUPER BOWL. MAXWELL HOUSE COFFEE. HERSHEY BARS. THE WORLD SERIES. CHEERIOS. AUNT ISABEL. COUSIN WILLIE. NICKIE FROSTIG. JUSTINE PAXTON. HOLLY PAXTON.

Vengeance. George pictured the word in his mind. Obviously Brat felt strongly about it. Still, the strategic decision is mine, he thought – mine and mine alone. An epitaph materialized at the bottom of the mile-high tombstone. A ONE HUNDRED AND

FORTY-FOUR MEGATON RETALIATORY STRIKE WILL NOT BRING US BACK, it said.

That settled the matter.

'I believe I would like to start having fresh orange juice with my breakfast,' said George. 'Keeps away the scurvy, I hear.'

'Lousy decision, Paxton,' fumed Brat. 'Really bad.'

'I'm sorry,' George said softly.

The general's forehead threw off hot droplets. 'Ten seconds, Captain. That's all you've got, and then David fires his slingshot. Nine . . . eight . . . seven . . .'

'He's bluffing,' said Randstable, who still hadn't made an opening move. 'I'll give you a hundred to one odds he won't do it.'

Sverre went to his writing desk and continued the *Saga of Thor*. Brat retargeted the missile.

'Six . . . five . . . four . . .'

'I don't believe I have any,' said Randstable.

'Any what?' asked Sverre.

'Three . . .'

'Survivor's guilt,' said Randstable.

'Two . . .'

'We can fix that,' said Sverre.

An uncanny noise issued from the MARCH Hare. George thought of the cackling piped into the funhouse at the Wildgrove Apple Blossom Fair. Brat's now flaccid fingers uncurled, and the little missile clattered impotently to the floor. Lying on the rug, it looked more toylike than ever.

'I've never seen one of those before,' said Sverre, pointing to Brat's defenses with his quill pen.

The MARCH Hare collapsed on the sofa, guzzled some gin, and began mourning his dead country through hyperventilation and high-pitched wails.

Sverre left his desk, picked up the weapon. 'What kind of guidance?'

'Inertial navigation,' muttered Randstable, 'updated by terrain contour matching.'

'Propulsion?'

'Air breathing F-218 turbofan engine.'

'Throw-weight?'

'Nine pounds.'

Later that day, after the three Erebus evacuees were gone, Sverre ordered his officers and men to their main battle stations. The launch tubes were pressurized to match the outside ocean. The hatches opened. A small rocket in the rail of each Multiprong missile began to burn, boiling pools of water in the tubes. Steam built up, hurling the missiles to the surface, whereupon the main motors ignited. The stages fell away. Within fifteen minutes the warhead buses had scattered their sterile payloads across the Gulf of Mexico, from the Florida Keys to the vanished city of New Orleans.

Like all *Philadelphia*-class fleet ballistic missile submarines, SSBN 713 *City of New York* held within its lowest decks a labyrinth of forgotten passageways and unmarked corridors. Leaving Sverre's cabin, George realized that he and Brat were for the moment not on speaking terms – he could tell by the general's sour face, his aloof gait – and so he ran ahead, soon finding himself in the submarine equivalent of a back alley. Naked light bulbs swung on brown cords like phosphorescent spiders. The air was murky and still. He became aware of the boat's sound, a fitful hum. Under other conditions, getting lost this way would have upset him, but he was still feeling extraordinarily good about his strategic decision. Thanks to him, the men, women, and children of the Soviet Union had been spared a retaliatory strike – my monument to Holly, he thought, as glorious and firm as any block of granite.

He pounded on doors. The echoes traveled up and down the empty corridor. He tested the latches. Every cabin was sealed as tight as the cottage-like tomb that the Sweetser family owned back in Rosehaven Cemetery. Fear weaved through his chest and bowels – a creeping conviction that Peach and Cobb would soon appear and inflict some new torture on him. Hell, anybody would have signed that ridiculous sales contract. Anybody. Black blood. Just like Mrs Covington. Certain facts should not be thought about too much. I shall think about something else. Holly saved Russia . . .

Beneath a nearby door, an orange glow advanced and retreated like surf. George approached, knocked.

'Come in.'

A female voice. Entering, he saw a monster. He stopped dead and thought, yes, they're on the loose again, trying to intimidate me . . .

It looked like a gigantic winged shark. The eyes shot blood, the nostrils flamed and smoked like the vents of a volcano.

He had seen this species before.

'Hello, George.'

In the center of the cabin an old woman stood hunched over the sort of antique machine that, as he knew from taking Holly to the Boston Children's Museum, was called a magic lantern. A cone of smoke-filled light spread toward the projected vulture. Shadows hovered above the woman's nose and cheeks. She removed the vulture, slipped it under a stack of similar glass paintings.

'Mrs Covington! I never expected to meet *you* here.'

'It's good to see you again, George.'

'I did those pencil drafts we talked about.' As usual, Mrs Covington's presence filled him with well-being. ' "She was better than she knew," remember? "He never found out what he was doing here." They looked pretty good. Design seven-oh-three-four. I guess they got burned up.'

'We mustn't dwell on Wildgrove,' said Nadine. 'I loved that town. The children. Nickie Frostig died in my arms. Blast wound.' She gestured toward the glass slides. 'Some people say these paintings show the future.' Her raincoat looked wet and slimy, as if made of live eels. 'Do you believe in prophecy?'

'I'm a Unitarian, ma'am.'

'They've been in my family for centuries – painted by Leonardo da Vinci during his last days. The seer Nostradamus – that brilliant, courageous, plague-fighting Renaissance scholar – dictated their content. Want to see the future, George?'

She inserted a new slide. A short, muscular, bearded man stood alone on a boundless plain of ice.

'My goodness, I guess I really *am* going to Antarctica,' he said.

She changed slides. George saw himself in the Silver Dollar Casino, playing poker with Randstable and Wengernook.

As the show continued, it proved far more varied and perplexing than the other such presentation he had seen that afternoon. Slide: George sitting at a banquet table, eating ham. Slide: Captain Sverre slashing his own forearm with a knife. Slide: the vulture again, devouring a dead penguin.

A happy family burst upon the wall – husband, wife, young child. They were dressed in scopas suits. The child's suit was gold. Their various arms and torsos had fused in a complex hug. Their smiles threw back twice the brightness that the lantern flame provided.

No visual image, painted, photographed, or dreamed, had ever moved George so much as that adroitly rendered Leonardo. The child was Holly. Compared with this truth, his realization that the man was himself and that the woman was Dr Morning Valcourt seemed almost dull.

'I know the man,' said Nadine. 'And I've seen the woman around here. But the child—'

'It's Holly!' The future! Some people said these paintings showed the future!

'Nobody except you got out of Wildgrove. Dr Valcourt told you that.'

'But it *looks* like Holly.'

'Exactly like her?'

'Yes. Exactly. Perhaps not *exactly*. But . . . if it's not Holly, then . . .'

Aubrey?

'The sister we were going to give Holly?' he asked.

'Nobody except you got out of—'

All right. Not her sister. Who then? He studied Dr Valcourt's glowing, flickering face. Though ill-equipped for smiling – he remembered her chilly persona, her brisk manner – she was doing an excellent job of it.

'Holly's stepsister? Dr Valcourt and I will marry and then have a baby girl?'

'A reasonable interpretation.'

'I'll call her Aubrey.'

'Lovely name. Do you *like* Dr Valcourt?'

'Not at all.' The wrong thing to say, he decided. 'I'll *learn* to like her.' His bullet wound throbbed with excitement. 'I'll do anything to get Aubrey. Marry a snake.'

Nadine yanked the family portrait off the screen. 'Evidently you will become a father again.'

He envisioned the Giant Ride mechanical horse from Sandy's Sandwich Shop. Aubrey sat bouncing in the saddle, giggling, trilling. Horse. Donkey. Mule. Infertility . . . 'No, that can't be right either,' he said. 'I'm sterile as a mule. That's what Dr Brust told me. My secondary spermatocytes . . . the radiation.'

Nadine projected a new slide. A man approached the gates of a fabulous white city. Its marble ramparts glowed beneath a skull-faced moon.

George saw that the pilgrim was himself.

'Even in this age of chaos,' said Nadine, 'there are places one can go to have one's fertility restored. The earth has its marble cities.'

After swaddling the glass slides in a US Navy bath towel, Nadine slipped them into the pocket of her raincoat. She opened the side of the magic lantern, blew out the flame, and lowered the hot device into a canvas duffel bag.

'Let me help you with that,' he said.

She seemed not to hear. Slinging the bundle over her shoulder, she hobbled into the corridor. He followed her up a long spiral staircase. So great was his obsession with the thought of Holly's reincarnation – Aubrey Paxton, predicted by Nostradamus, painted by Leonardo da Vinci, fathered by George Paxton, borne by Morning Valcourt – that he was taken aback upon seeing that Nadine had led him to the deck of the surfaced submarine. The air was choked with puffs of dark vapor. Waves detonated along the speeding prow. The wind stung his cheeks; it tugged his hair like a comb in the hands of a vindictive parent. God! So cold!

An open sailboat bobbed beside the hull, Nadine sitting in the stern. After hoisting the sail, she reached into her raincoat and pulled out a magic lantern slide, placing her gloved hand over the painted surface to protect it from spray. George took it like a starving man receiving bread.

'How can I find that city?' he called.

'I have no idea,' she replied, casting off.

'Was this Nostradamus any good?'

'He was on to something.'

A great, ever-expanding wedge of ocean and air grew between them. George looked at his Leonardo – the detail was astonishing, like the circuits on a computer chip, and he was especially impressed by the firm, crisp contours of Aubrey's beautiful face. The wind quickened. Sea water began dripping from his hair. He moved the painting away before it got wet, tucked it under his shirt. When he glanced toward the horizon, Nadine Covington's sailboat had become a firm white sliver beating its way south toward the horse latitudes.

CHAPTER EIGHT

*In Which Our Hero Witnesses Some of the Many
Surprising Effects of Nuclear War, Including Sundeath,
Timefolds, and Unadmittance*

'I had a happy childhood,' said George at the beginning of his first treatment session.

'Happy childhoods are overrated,' his therapist replied.

When George first met her, he had found Morning Valcourt vaguely attractive, but now he saw that the surgical mask she wore during their encounter in the radiation unit had been covering cheeks littered with scab-like freckles, a nose that seemed always to be experiencing a stench, and a mouth perpetually poised on the brink of a snarl. Yet Leonardo had given her a warm smile . . . obviously an artist of formidable imagination.

'I'll be honest,' she said. 'Survivor's guilt threatens its victims with sudden mental collapse. To prevent this, we must tear certain facts from the shadowland of denial, thrusting them into the daylight of consciousness.'

Could this pompous woman really be Aubrey's mother? When would the warm smiling start?

'Any trouble sleeping lately?' she asked.

'I used to suffer from somnambulism. A couple of ensigns cured me of that.'

'What ensigns?'

'Peach and Cobb. They said they've always been with me, waiting to get in.'

'But you're sleeping through the night?'

'Yes.'

'Losing weight?'

'No.'

'Bowels okay?'

'Fine.' It would take considerable ambition to fall in love with this woman.

'I've been prescribing a lot of sedatives lately,' she said, 'but in your case I'd rather not. They found you clutching a golden scopas suit.'

'I got it from an inventor. Professor Theophilus Carter. He made me sign a sales contract.'

'I know. A confession of complicity. I don't approve of such things. Tell me what happened after you left Carter's shop.'

George sucked air across his teeth, making the roots ache. He spoke of searing light and a mushroom cloud, of fires, wounds, black dust, and cries for water, of people needing burn wards that no longer existed. A desperate pause followed each image, so that the hour was nearly up by the time he got to the smashed Giant Ride horse. 'She loved that stupid thing,' he said. Scar tissue grew in his throat.

'It's unendurable, isn't it?'

The tenderness in Morning's voice caught him by surprise. 'Unendurable,' he repeated.

'Chicago winters got awfully cold,' she continued softly, 'but I had lots of books in the apartment, shelves floor to ceiling, so we were quite snug, me and the cats. I used to put all the warm authors on the windward side – Emily Dickinson, Scott Fitzgerald. Henry James gives off his own draft. I lived a block from my little sister – a Methodist minister and in her own way a better therapist than I. We called Linda the white sheep of the family. All I want is to be able to bury her.' Leonardo was right: Morning could smile. This was not the joyful smile of the mother in the portrait, however, but the brave, taut smile of someone fighting tears. 'Linda was the best person I ever knew.'

'That would make a good epitaph. I keep wondering how they feel about being dead.'

'Your wife and daughter?'

'Yes, And the others.'

'You wonder how they feel—?'

'About being dead. That's crazy, isn't it?'

'Do you think it's crazy?'

'They're dead. They don't feel anything about it . . . Sverre said there are pockets of survivors.'

'No doubt.'

'You don't suppose—?'

'No, I don't.'

'I just thought—'

'You entered the bomb crater, right? And then your neighbor shot you?'

George chomped on his lower lip. 'I ended up on the ground. Next thing I knew, a vulture was hovering over me.'

'A what?'

'A vulture. A large black vulture – big as one of those flying dinosaurs, you know, the pterodactyls.'

'The pterodactyls were not dinosaurs.' She issued a succinct, intellectual frown. 'Close enough. This is not the first time a vulture has entered the annals of psychotherapy. The species once haunted the great Leonardo.'

'Leonardo da Vinci?' George asked.

'Yes.'

'I have one of his paintings.'

'You believe that you own an original Leonardo?'

'I *do* own one. I keep it in my cabin.'

She gave her eyes a quick toss to the left, as if to say, *Well, we have our work cut out for us, don't we, you lunatic*, and stood up. Her stiff and forbidding gray suit was like a whole-body chastity belt.

She walked to a bookcase stuffed with volumes on brain diseases. Her office reconciled the rational and the primal – an anatomy chart, a Navaho tapestry, a ceramic brain, a Hindu god, a biofeedback rig, an obsidian knife that had last seen employment in a human sacrifice. She removed a slender volume, flashed the title – Sigmund Freud's *Leonardo da Vinci: A Study in Psychosexuality* – opened it. 'When Leonardo was a baby,' she said, 'a vulture swooped down to his cradle and massaged his lips with its tail. Or so he believed. Did your vulture do that?'

'My vulture?'

'The one that appeared at ground zero.'

'Are you saying it was a hallucination?'

'Do you think it was a hallucination?'

'I don't know.' George was not forming a very positive first impression of psychotherapy. 'My vulture did not massage my lips,' he reported.

'Leonardo, it seems, was illegitimate. He and his mother had an intense relationship – much kissing and pampering.' She hugged a phantom baby. 'You must understand that, in ancient times, maternity cults commonly centered on vultures. The Egyptians believed it was a species without males, inseminated by the winds. Through the vulture fantasy, Leonardo was confessing to a sexually charged relationship with his mother – or so Freud theorized. The tail prying open the lips. The insertion.'

'I thought we were going to talk about *my* problems,' said George.

She slammed the book shut with the suddenness of a steel trap being sprung. 'On Monday your immersion in death begins,' she announced evenly.

George took out his wallet and removed a rectangle from its blurry plastic envelope. 'Do me a favor? Hide this where I can't find it.' He set the rectangle on the desk. 'I keep looking at it.'

The therapist picked up Holly's picture – her official class photograph from the Sunflower Nursery School – and placed it in her top desk drawer.

While Holly's nursery school picture had been a wellspring of grief – 'unendurable' was his therapist's word, the perfect word, for his loss – the portrait of himself, Aubrey, and Morning was another matter entirely. He looked at it whenever he could, testing it under different kinds of light, memorizing each brush stroke. On Saturday afternoon he looked at it for so long that he lost track of time, consequently arriving several minutes late for the screening of Sergei Bondarchuk's lengthy film adaptation of *War and Peace*.

Pierre Bezukhov and Prince Andrei Bolkonsky were walking through the woods. 'If evil men can work together to get what they want,' said the narrator, 'then so can good men, to get what they want.'

George enjoyed the battles of Schoengraben and Austerlitz. The lines of infantrymen stretched on and on, far beyond the reach of the camera's lens.

When the lights came up for the first intermission, he saw that the only people in the little theater were himself, an enlisted man, Randstable, and – shifting now in the row ahead, turning to face George – an older gentleman who, with his bushy beard and substantial abdomen, might have found employment as Santa Claus's stunt double.

'Hello, friend.' When Santa Claus smiled, his beard expanded like a peacock's tail.

'Are you an Erebus evacuee?' George asked.

'Brian Overwhite,' said Santa, nodding. 'US Arms Control and Disarmament Agency.'

'I'd heard you were aboard.'

'My ticket for Geneva had just arrived – we were about to begin the STABLE III talks – when this war . . . incredible, isn't it? The mind isn't built for such things. Nuclear exchanges. Failed deterrence. STABLE III would have put tough limits on missile throw-weight and anti-satellite weapons – that was my hope, anyway.'

'I'm George Paxton.' He went to shake Overwhite's hand. A sling cradled the negotiator's right arm. 'Were you in one of the battles?'

'No – two unreasonable ensigns came after me. Cousins.'

'I know who you mean.'

'They said, "You've spent your life controlling other people's arms, and now we're going to control yours!" So they broke it. Snapped the damn ulna. I reported the incident to Lieutenant Grass. Now get this – the man laughed at me. That's right. He *laughed*.'

'There seems to be some kind of resentment against us,' said George. 'Take me, for example. I was placed in a torpedo tube.'

'Resentment? Yeah, I guess that's the word for it.' Overwhite scratched his cast, as if trying to relieve an itch. 'Tell me, George, which do you fear more, the gamma rays or the betas?'

'What?'

'The gammas go shooting right through you, zip, zip, but the betas ride in on the food you eat and the air you breathe.' Overwhite reached under his beard and caressed his throat. 'The buildup in the thyroid is what you've got to watch for. The betas go for the thyroid, especially with the children. It's a terrible thing when they won't even let you negotiate a simple goddamn arms control agreement.'

George wished that *War and Peace* would start again. 'Good movie, huh?'

'I can see your viewpoint. Eight hours of mongrel film technique in the service of murky Soviet propaganda, and yet there's much to admire – the energetic grandeur, the meticulous Tolstoyan ambience.' Overwhite massaged his elbow. 'Cancer almost never forms in the elbows.'

'Not much of a turnout,' said George.

'These enlisted men, all they want is Clint Eastwood and tits.' Overwhite interlaced his fingers. 'Cancer doesn't bother with the fingers, either, not as a rule.' He rubbed his chest. 'In general, we needn't worry about breast cancer.'

Later that afternoon, the Russians fled from the Battle of Borodino, Andrei died of his wounds, the Grand Army occupied Moscow, Napoleon suffered his calamitous retreat, and Pierre ended up with the vital and appealing Natasha Rostov.

Morning Valcourt is probably quite vital and appealing, George decided, once you get to know her.

From the perspective of the average consumer, psychotherapists in the second half of the twentieth century were an overpaid population. A hundred dollars an hour seemed a high price for the privilege of being listened to. What people don't realize, Morning thought, is that I never stop working, night or day. When I'm having lunch, I'm working. I dream about my patients.

She sat down in the middle of the periscope room and arranged her lunch. A thermos of skim milk, a cucumber sandwich. She

99

wanted to lose five pounds by the end of the voyage. Her Defense Department patient came to mind. Wengernook. All those feelings – he actually saw his wife die of radiation sickness – and no vocabulary for them. He talks about ballistic missile defenses. And Randstable, rambling on about inertial guidance and his old 'think tank.' He confuses systems analysis with thought. And the arms controller. Poor Overwhite, riddled with nonexistent tumors. Repression . . .

She finished her lunch, stuffed the refuse into the garbage scoop.

And Paxton. Why does he look at me that way? It's not sex, not entirely. He wants something else from me.

The door hissed open.

George knew that, as a Unitarian, he was not competent to deal with metaphysical commodities, including prophetic glass paintings. He had decided to approach the situation on the theory that his Leonardo did not spell out an inevitable fate but, rather, a possible future, something that he could make happen through diligence and creativity. I shall not let Leonardo and Nostradamus and Holly's stepsister down, he had resolved. I shall woo Morning Valcourt, make myself fascinating to her, fall in love with her, convince her to become my wife.

'You and I have a lot in common,' he said, entering the periscope room. 'Did you know that selling tombstones is quite similar to psychotherapy? I would talk to people about their troubles.'

'We're the talking cure,' she said tonelessly.

'For example, we had guilt stones. Also self-hatred stones.'

'Oh.'

He saw that he had been misinterpreting her face. The odd tilt of her mouth came not from snarling but from speaking so much truth, while the sharp flare of her nostrils traced to sensitivity rather than snobbery. He twisted his wedding ring. Forgive me, Justine.

'I want you to see a fire,' she said.

'A fire? I got enough of that at Wildgrove.' All business, this woman.

'Wildgrove was nothing.' She led him toward Periscope Number One. 'Odessa had the distinction of being the last city to receive a warhead. It was attacked five days ago by the strategic submarine *Atlanta*. It's still burning.'

'Odessa? You mean . . . they hit Russia's cities after all? They didn't just go for the missile bases?'

'Basic nuclear strategy. We took out their fixed silos, but they thought we were after their cities, so they went after our cities, and . . . *quid pro quo.*'

George pressed his eyes against the soft rubber viewfinder. A frantic orange haze appeared. He adjusted the focus. Odessa vibrated with flames. Inky smoke filled the heavens. 'Fabrics, insulation, oil stores, polymers – there's plenty to keep it going,' Morning narrated. 'The survivors must inhale a demon's breath of dioxins and furans.'

'You know so much, Dr Valcourt,' he said in what he hoped was a seductive tone. The periscope room, he decided, was a lousy environment for making romance bloom. He would have to take her on a date. Would the movies be best? The bowling alley? The casino?

She pulled on the periscope handle, aiming the device at the continent where the United States of America had once been located. Fires. Back to the Soviet Union. Fires. America. City fires. Oil well fires. Coal seam fires. Grassland fires. Peat marsh fires. Forest fires. A pall of mist hung in the air, black as the blood of Nadine Covington and Ensign Peach. The Northern Hemisphere was wrapped in soot.

That night – Monday night – George dreamed he was made of smoke. His smoke legs would not let him walk. He could hold nothing in his smoke hands.

Then came Tuesday. The periscope room again.

'Can you tell me what day it is, George?' she asked.

Was it his imagination, or were her questions getting increasingly pointless? 'The tenth of January. I've been aboard three weeks.'

'Good. But out there it's the beginning of July.'

'Out where?'

'In the world.'

'What?'

'Time is ruined, George – one of the many effects of nuclear war that nobody quite anticipated. All those fundamental particles being annihilated – time gets twisted and folded. A minute passes in here, but out there it might be an hour, a day, or a week.'

'Folded?'

'Like a Chinese screen. Post-exchange physics – something even Einstein didn't foresee. In local regions of the quantum-dynamics fabric, space is taking on the role of time, and vice versa. According to our best evidence, there are only two places where the old ways of counting time still work. This ship is one of them. Antarctica is the other. Are you upset?'

He recalled the book he used to read Holly, *Carrie of Cape Cod*, full of clams and hermit crabs. I am a hermit crab, he decided. Place a blowtorch against my shell, I won't feel it. Scratch me – no pain. 'If time is crinkled, then time is crinkled,' he said. 'We hermit crabs can take anything.'

'You what crabs?'

'Hermit crabs.'

'Yes. Hermit crabs. Good,' Morning said. 'Hermit crabs seek out shells because they want to survive,' she added thoughtfully. 'Hermit crabs believe in the future,' his therapist concluded.

She's starting to care about me, he thought. Should I show her my Leonardo? (Look, Dr Valcourt – you and I are destined to marry and have babies!) No. Not yet – she won't understand. It might come across as a joke, or a symptom of survivor's guilt, or a weird seduction attempt.

'Jocotepec, Mexico,' she said.

He leaned toward the eyepiece, twisted the focus knob.

'Today,' she said, 'we're going to deal with ice.'

A crowd of peasants stood on a frozen lake. Soot walled over the sky. Cold rain fell. The survivors' teeth vibrated, plumes of breath gushed out. They wore rags. Many went barefoot – blue ankles, missing toes. Faithlessly they huddled around a limp and sputtering fire.

'I thought you said July.'

'July. High noon. Those people are freezing to death. Blame the urban conflagrations. There's so much smoke in the air that ordinary sunlight is being absorbed. Right now the average worldwide temperature is minus twenty degrees Fahrenheit. The soot cap migrates with the climate. In April it crossed the equator, sending ice storms through the Amazon basin. Photosynthesis has been shut down, the earth's vegetation mantle is crumbling. For many years, this was an unanticipated effect of nuclear holocaust. Then, shortly before the war, certain scientists foresaw it. Sundeath syndrome.'

She tugged on the periscope handle. Rigid corpses littered the planet like the outpourings of some crazed taxidermist. Unable to penetrate the ice-sealed rivers and ponds, many wanderers were dying of thirst. Under bruise-purple skies a starving French farmer clawed at the iron ground with bloody fingers, seeking to exhume the potato he knew was there. At last he lifted the precious object from the dirt, staring at it stupidly. George rejoiced at the humble victory. Now eat it! The farmer fainted and toppled over, soon becoming as stiff as the stone angel that George used to sell under the name Design No. 4335.

Wednesday.

'Fourteen months have passed,' said Morning. 'It is September. The strategic submarines have put to port. The soot has settled. Light can get through. Sundeath syndrome has run its course.'

'Thank God.'

'Don't thank anybody. This light is malignant.' Morning closed her eyes. 'The high-yield airbursts created oxides of nitrogen that have shredded the earth's ozone buffer. Ultraviolet sunshine is gushing down. What does it all mean?' Her sigh was shrill, piercing. 'Famine,' she said.

George hated being difficult at this point in their courtship, but he couldn't help asking, 'Is this really the way to cure me?'

'Yes,' she said, as if that settled the matter. 'Last year's harvest was a disaster. The frozen ground could not receive seeds – those few crops that were planted emerged into a spring laden with smog and acid showers. This year's harvest will be worse – roots reaching into eroded soil, leaves seared by the ultraviolet. And there is another enemy . . .'

The locusts rolled across the Iowa corn fields in a vast insatiable carpet, stripping the crop to its vegetal bones, devouring the botanic carrion.

'The post-exchange environment is utopia for insects. Their enemies the birds have succumbed to radiation. Stores of carbaryl and malathion have been destroyed. The omnipresent corpses are perfect breeding places. So what will our hungry survivors do? Forage? Nuts and berries are fast disappearing. Dig shellfish? Radioactive rainouts have contaminated coastal waters. Hunt? Not if the game is dying out . . .'

She pivoted the periscope. A rabbit pelt hung on a mass of rabbit bones. The pelt took a hop and collapsed.

'Not if the tiny creatures that underwrite the earth's food chains were killed when the ultraviolet hit the marshes and seas . . .'

Can a walrus, paragon of things fat and full, look emaciated? This one did. Its eyes were sunken. Its ribs pushed against taut, sallow flesh that had been feeding on itself and now could feed no more.

'Not if thousands of species are at risk because the ultraviolet has scarred their corneas . . .'

A blind deer moved through the organic rubble that had been the woods of central Pennsylvania, pacing in crazed parabolas of misery and hunger. Poor deerie, George could hear Holly saying.

'You know what comes next, don't you? You know what people eat when they can no longer gather berries, hunt game, or harvest the seas?'

Out in the timefolds, Italian office workers ate human corpses. Belgian mathematics professors murdered their colleagues and devoured their internal organs. Dave Valentine of Unlimited, Ltd, the agency that had produced the scopas suit commercials, stumbled through the ruins of Glen Cove, Long Island, with cannibalistic intent.

The famine session left George quaking on the floor.

Thursday.

'Five years have passed,' said Morning. 'And yet, in another sense, time has turned around. The modern and pristine city of Billings, Montana, has devolved into fourteenth-century London.'

She worked the focus knob.

'It's time we dealt with pestilence,' she said.

No, no, he thought, it's time we dealt with my magic lantern slide. It's time we made wedding plans.

A brawny survivor in combat fatigues squatted near the entrance of a bomb shelter. He wore a surprisingly intact scopas suit and a fractured grin. A Heckler and Koch assault rifle rested on his camouflage-dappled knees. In the background, neatly stacked corpses formed a bulwark against intruders. George sensed that nuclear war was the best thing that had ever happened to this man.

'His shelter contains an elaborate collection of canned soups,' Morning explained. 'He is hoping someone will try to steal it, so that he can shoot them. Before the war, bubonic plague was endemic among the rats of eleven states in the western United States.'

The lymph nodes in the survivor's neck looked like subcutaneous golf balls. Morning pivoted the periscope. Montana trembled with rats. The roads were paved with unburied corpses.

'If you were a disease – viral gastroenteritis or infectious hepatitis or amoebic dysentery – you could not ask for better conditions than planet Earth after nuclear war. The ultraviolet has suppressed your hosts' immune systems. The omnipresent insects are carrying you far and wide. No pasteurized milk, no food refrigeration, no waste treatment, no inoculation programs – all these circumstances bode well.'

At each point of the compass, a new microorganism flourished. No death happened in the abstract. A particular Nigerian child died of cholera, sprawled across his mother's lap in a brutal and unholy pietà. A particular Romanian machinist died of meningococcal meningitis, a particular Iranian school teacher of louseborne typhus . . .

Friday.

'Infertility,' said Morning.

The word sounded neutral, clinical, non-threatening. Then he looked into the timefolds.

A Cambodian man and his wife sat in a village square and wept. 'The radiation,' Morning explained. 'They'll never have children.'

They should find the city with marble walls, George thought. Nostradamus foresaw this problem.

A Polish mother suffered a miscarriage. The specter of still-birth visited a family in Pakistan and another in Bolivia. The live births were worse. It was an era when thousands of children were required to face the world without such selective advantages as arms, legs, and cerebral cortices. 'Mate an irradiated chromosome with another irradiated chromosome,' Morning noted, 'and no good will come of it.'

'You must tell me something,' said George, reeling with nausea. 'Who will treat *your* survivor's guilt?'

The therapist smoothed a wrinkle from her gray skirt and, in the weakest voice he had ever heard from her, said, 'I don't know.'

For moral reasons, the young Reverend Peter Sparrow declined to join the Saturday night gatherings of the Erebus Poker Club. Gambling, he knew, was Satan's third favorite pastime, after sex and ecumenicalism. Lacking such convictions, the other evacuees gathered around the green felt table in the rattling, flashing heart of the Silver Dollar Casino.

Unsealing the deck, Brat Tarmac weeded out the jokers. He was down another five pounds, easily. 'Ante up. This game is seven-card stud.' The cards rippled through his hands. 'Deuces wild.'

George said, 'Today through the periscope I saw—'

'You *saw*, you *saw*,' said Brat, sneering. 'Jack bets.'

'One dollar,' said Overwhite.

'I'm out,' said Wengernook.

'Raise,' said Randstable.

George said, 'Morning showed me—'

'We'll take a vote,' said Brat. 'How many of us want to hear what Paxton saw through the periscope today?'

No one spoke. Brat dealt another round of up cards. 'Ace bets.'

'We saw it *too*,' said Wengernook, quivering like an overbred dog. 'Jesus.'

'Sugar Brook built that scope,' said Randstable, who had managed to make six poker chips stand on edge. 'Not my department, though – the command-and-control guys.'

'Three dollars,' said Overwhite, reaching under his sling and checking himself for armpit tumors.

'I have a question.' George picked up the jokers, rubbed them together like a razor and strop. 'If America and Russia knew about this sundeath syndrome, why did they work out plans for different kinds of attacks and so on?'

'Well, you see, sundeath theory was based on incomplete models of the atmosphere,' said Brat, clenching his teeth as if in great pain. 'It all depends on dust particle size, the height of the smoke plumes, rainfall, factors like that.'

'You have to take sundeath with a grain of salt,' said Wengernook, pulling cigarettes and a risqué matchbook from his shirt. 'It's a pretty far-fetched idea.'

'But it happened,' said George. 'Right on our planet.'

'That's just one particular case,' said Wengernook. He struck a match. 'In another sort of war, urban-industrial targets would not have been hit. You'd have fewer fires, less soot, no sundeath, and, and . . .' He tried to make the flame connect with the end of his cigarette, could not manage it.

'First ace bets,' said Brat.

'And a much more desirable outcome,' said Wengernook.

'I've got it!' said Randstable. He grabbed one of the jokers from George and set it atop the six vertical chips.

'Got what?' asked George.

'The solution!' said Randstable.

'To the war?' asked George.

'To the riddle.' The joker shivered on its plastic pylons.

'What riddle?'

'Sverre's riddle – why is a raven like a writing desk?'

'Why?'

'A raven is like a writing desk,' said the ex-Wunderkind as his little bridge collapsed, 'because Poe wrote on both.'

To and fro, warp and weft, the young black woman paced the shores of her private tropical paradise. The beach sparkled brilliantly, as if its sands were destined to become fine crystal goblets. Spiky pieces of sunlight shone in the tide pools. The surrounding sea was a blue liquid gem.

She was about thirty. She wore no clothes. Her excellent skin had the color and vibrancy of boiling fudge. When she stopped and sucked in a large helping of air, her splendid breasts floated upward like helium balloons released in celebration of some great athletic or political victory. George thought she was the most desirable woman he had ever seen.

A length of rope was embedded in the beach near a banyan tree. The beachcomber tore it free. Sunstruck grains showered down like sparks. The woman manipulated the rope, sculpting a grim shape from it. A noose emerged in her clever and despairing hands.

George tried to pull away from the periscope, but he could not break his own grip.

The last woman on earth walked up to the tree, tossed the rope over a branch, and, as the waves rolled in and the sun danced amid the tide pools, hanged herself by the neck. Her oscillating shadow was shaped like a star.

George sat down beneath the periscope and panted. 'We're through?' he said, half inquiring, half asserting.

'At this irrevocable point in history,' said Morning, 'not one human being exists anywhere – with the frail and tentative exception of this boat.'

The hermit crab had left his shell. He was a shivering mass of tender protoplasm. 'Nobody can ride a mechanical horse.'

'True.'

'Or see the Big Dipper.'

'Correct.'

'Or take acting lessons.'

He was weeping now, copiously, and he could not tell whether his tears were for Justine, Holly, the Frenchman who had clawed the potato out of the ground, the Iranian school teacher who had died of louse-borne typhus, the last woman on earth . . .

Morning knelt beside the hurt man. She hugged him and dried his tears.

He returned her embrace. His bullet wound throbbed like a castanet grafted to his stomach. As if to stop the spasms, he reached into his shirt. His fingers touched glass, and slowly he withdrew his Leonardo.

'Look at this,' he said, licking his tears. 'It's you. And me. And our child.'

'I don't understand. Are you an artist?'

'I told you about it before. The painter was Leonardo da Vinci. You know – the man with the vulture complex.'

'A forgery, right?'

'An original Leonardo – inspired by the brilliant prophet Nostradamus. It predicts the future. See? Holly's stepsister is coming. You'll be the mother.'

She took the slide. Light ascended from the glass and ignited her blue-green eyes. 'It really does look like me. Spooky.'

'It's you.'

'And the child . . . ?'

'If Justine had gotten pregnant again, we would have named the baby Aubrey. Have you ever had a child?'

'No.'

'They do all these amazing things.'

'I've never been married. Aubrey?'

'Aubrey Paxton.'

'Pretty name.'

'And there will be others. Aubrey's brothers and sisters. Holly always wanted a sister.'

'Why would anybody want to bring children into—?'

'Into *this* world? I may not know about psychology or sundeath, Dr Valcourt, but I did learn something at the Crippen Monument Works. Our children will take whatever world they can get.'

'You're sterile.'

'I have reason to believe the condition is not permanent.'

'Next you'll be saying we have the power to restore the race.'

Justine Paxton had frequently accused her husband of lacking ambition. She should hear what I'm about to say, he thought. 'Maybe we do.' (Maybe they did!) 'Maybe it's one of those unexpected effects of nuclear war you're always talking about. Your own fertility is . . . ?'

'No problems that I know about.' She hefted the slide, ran her fingertips over the tiny bumps and furrows of paint. 'Where did you get this thing?'

'A civilian passenger. Nadine Covington. Her blood is black.'

'Black?'

'Like ink.'

'I doubt that she can be trusted.'

'I trust her.'

Without unlocking arms, they stood up. Again they embraced. George took his Leonardo back and departed with the words 'restore the race' ringing in his ears. There, you see, my poor, extinct Justine? You did not marry a lazy man after all.

Lieutenant Commander Olaf Sverre
of
SSBN 713 *City of New York*
United States Navy
Cordially Invites
GEORGE PAXTON
to a
Celebration Banquet
2000 Hours, 29 January
Main Mess Hall

The extinction of one's own species is an event not easily comprehended. Only by using Periscope Number One privately, over and over, did George begin to grasp the contours of the event. He studied his planet for hours on end, rubbing his nose in oblivion. He even looked at the stars. Nothing. Nothing save the burned land, the poisoned water, the harsh stillness, the rare clam, the occasional roach, the intermittent swatch of grass, the clusters of salt-pickled corpses floating in the South Atlantic timefolds like barges of flesh.

Brian Overwhite was wrong. The human mind can accommodate anything. Some parents beat their children. Auschwitz. Sundeath. It's just blood, the mind says. It's only pain. It's merely putting people into ovens. It's simply the end of the world . . .

Long ago, George's grandfather had died on the last day of June, an event that had plunged the family into a quandary. Should they hold the usual Fourth of July picnic? George's grandfather loved the Fourth of July. He always built cherry-bomb-tipped skyrockets for the occasion, deploying them against a balsa wood model of Fort McHenry. During the battle, the family would sing 'The Star-Spangled Banner' while toy frigates shot marbles at the ramparts and the cherry bombs detonated around a tattered little American flag.

The solution to the dilemma came from George's Aunt Isabel. 'Daddy would want us to celebrate,' she asserted. 'Daddy would be angry at us if we didn't have a good time,' she insisted.

The picnic happened, and with a vengeance. Horseshoes flew, beer flowed, banjos sang, chickens vanished without a trace, blueberry pies were reported missing in action, and rockets glared redly over Fort McHenry. Everyone agreed that Aunt Isabel had made the right decision.

And so it was that whenever Chief Petty Officer Rush brought the dinner menu around, George always checked off the most opulent and sauce-laden dishes. He began frequenting the Silver Dollar Casino, making wild, Scotch-inspired bets at the blackjack table. The invitation to Captain Sverre's banquet sent waves of joyous anticipation – food! coffee! dessert! – through his body.

'Your species would want you to celebrate,' he told himself. 'Your species would be angry at you if you didn't have a good time,' he decided.

Swathed in velvet drapes, lit by crystal chandeliers, the main mess hall of the *City of New York* proved just how tasteful and sophisticated defense spending could be. The banquet itself, by contrast, followed the gaudy lines of Imperial Rome, with an eye to

Babylon and a nod to Gomorrah – gold plates, bejeweled goblets. The tablecloth was thick enough to blot a liter of priceless wine without leaving a drop. The serving staff – a dozen seamen and noncorns – patrolled the borders in their dress blues, pushing carts brimming with slabs of ham, planks of beef, heaps of bread, cauldrons of soup, and pots of satiny black coffee.

Ceramic dolphins held the place cards. George ended up between Overwhite and Reverend Sparrow – in the crossfire of a debate over the STABLE II treaty. (Evidently one of Sparrow's broadcasts had figured decisively in the US Senate's decision not to ratify this agreement.) Sadness and confusion enveloped his friends like gray scopas suits – the human extinction was not sitting well with them. Wengernook sucked on an unlit cigarette. Randstable built strange perpetual-motion devices out of the silverware and then knocked them over. Brat was down to about a hundred and thirty pounds. Overwhite's beard looked mangy. Sparrow's voluminous smile had wilted. They should all go see Mrs Covington, George decided. They should find out about their futures.

At the far end of the table Captain Sverre spoke with a civilian, a small, raffish fellow who managed to look youthful and eminent at the same time. Between remarks they stuffed themselves in gluttonous rivalry, Sverre favoring ham, the young man specializing in roast beef. Sverre's gin bottle sat faithfully at his elbow. Gravy stains bloomed on the young man's dark suit.

Brat was saying, 'Personally, I think this race-loss business has been exaggerated. Psychotherapists like to be dramatic.'

Wengernook nodded in agreement. 'The earth is really much more resilient than those periscope views suggest.'

The serving staff was well-meaning but graceless, dumping food on the table as if shoveling coal into the furnace of a tramp steamer. Champagne came forth in torrents. George drank enough to put music in the air and a pleasant buzz between his ears.

He had to admit it – Morning had not taken to the Aubrey Paxton idea with great enthusiasm. Just remember, he told himself, it's a big step for a woman, having a kid, restarting a species. You must let the idea grow on her.

'They don't run very good movies on this ship,' said Reverend Sparrow. '*War and Peace*, what a boring mess.'

'What should they run, your old TV shows?' sneered Overwhite.

'Ever see *King of Kings*?' said Sparrow. 'It's wonderful the way Orson Welles pronounces the T in "apostles."' He placed George's shoulder in a warm grip. 'I'm still praying for you.'

'That's nice,' said George.

As soon as dessert arrived – the evacuees could corrupt themselves with either German chocolate cake or lemon meringue pie – Sverre drew a carving knife from a ham and clanked it against his water glass. All eyes shot toward him. The serving staff scurried out of the hall.

'Antarctica,' whispered Randstable. 'He's going to tell us about Antarctica.'

'Tonight's banquet was advertised as a celebration,' the captain began. 'Dr Valcourt reports that, when we dock at McMurdo Station, six rational and competent survivors will disembark. We are here to rejoice in your cure. You have looked extinction in the face and lived. Operation Erebus will succeed.'

He set the carving knife on a linen napkin, poured gin into a gold goblet, drank.

'Extinction. Such a sterile word, so Latin. What does it mean? When you kill a species, good guests, you do not simply kill its current members, you also kill the generation that lies dormant in its germ cells – and, thus, the generation that the descendants of those germ cells would have made, and the next generation, and the next. Extinction is an endless crime, quietly slaughtering all the lives that would have been. The human birth canal is the only way into human existence, gentlemen. There is no other port of entry.'

'What is this guy, one of those warrior intellectuals?' whispered Wengernook.

'Lawrence of Arabia joins the Navy,' said Brat.

Sverre took off his claw-hammer coat, tossed it on the floor, and rolled up his shirt sleeve.

'At a certain moment in the great nuclear arms race, it became common knowledge that an extinction was in the offing. The universe trembled with the news. Your species mattered, gentlemen – more than you knew. The planets reeled, the trees wept, the rocks cried out. But from which place did the greatest anger issue? From the place that keeps my kind. We have always been with you, waiting to get in . . . and now the door has been shut.'

'That keeps his *what*?' said Brat.

'His kind,' said Overwhite.

'Oh God,' said Randstable.

'Shut,' repeated Sverre.

George's bullet wound began to throb. Waiting to get in . . .

'So great was our anger that, shortly before the war, we achieved a tenuous hold on life,' said Sverre. 'We even managed to insert ourselves into your affairs.'

'Do any of you know what he's talking about?' said Brat.

'Oh, dear, I think so,' said Randstable. 'Oh, God.'

Sverre picked up the knife, which was long and shiny with fat. What happened next would visit George's dreams for many nights to come. Slowly, wincingly, Sverre opened his arm. Arteries came asunder. Muscles perished. A lustrous black liquid spurted from the wound, as if someone had drilled for, and found, oil in his flesh. A sulphurous odor rushed out. Once on the tablecloth, the blood did not die, but collected itself into a viscous lump. The lump became a small, screaming, human head with a face that bore a disquieting resemblance to Sverre's.

'We are the inheritors who can never take title,' said the bleeding captain. 'We are the darkblood multitudes whose ancestors were exterminated before they could sire us,' asserted the pilot of the *City of New York*.

He sat down, pressed a napkin against his wound, and anesthetized himself with gin. The blood-head dissolved into a puddle.

'We are the unadmitted,' said Lieutenant Commander Olaf Sverre of the United States Navy.

Nuclear war entails many surprising effects. George had learned this from his therapist. The unadmitted . . .

Overwhite's lips encircled words he could not voice. Brat

looked dredged in flour. Wengernook tore the unlit cigarette from his mouth and eviscerated it. An aura of wrath surrounded Reverend Sparrow. 'Foul wizard!' he cried. ' "But the abominable and sorcerers shall have their part in the lake that burneth with fire!" ' he quoted.

'Mercy! A discontinuity!' gasped Randstable, pulling a pocket calculator from his vest.

'You mean it's a trick?' said George.

'Trick? No – a quantum aberration.' Randstable stroked the little keyboard. 'Normally such things happen only at the sub-atomic level, when your pions and antineutrinos and so on burst out of nothing as vacuum fluctuations.' A string of zeros appeared on the display screen. 'In the macroworld, where you have your people and so on, the expected frequency of such an event is very, very low – just shy of zero, in fact.'

The captain told of his locked-out race. He took his guests back to the time of the materializations, bade them see the Antarctic glaciers gestate men, women, and children, each scheduled to gain the continent at the high point of his would-be life, the time of greatest fulfillment and promise.

'Watch us rise through the ice, crack into the frigid dawn, rub the snow from our eyes, stretch our hypothetical limbs. My parents were killed in the Battle of Washington exactly two weeks before they would have conceived me. I would have gone to Annapolis. I would have served my country with honor and distinction. I would have—'

Bypassing the goblet, Sverre drank directly from the bottle.

'Do you know what our outrage was worth? A year. A year is nothing, gentlemen. Half my life is already gone. I can tell you how many hours I have left. How many minutes.'

Faces jumped into George's brain. Nadine Covington. Theophilus Carter. Ensign Peach. Darkbloods all.

Morning Valcourt.

Was she one of them? Was Aubrey's mother a woman from the future?

'If unadmitted, you must use your sojourn well,' said Sverre. 'A year is nothing.'

First priority – get warm. And so you become pirates, plundering the scopas suit barges on their transpacific crossings.

'Such attire is excellent for keeping out the cold,' the captain explained.

A year. Nothing. You cannot raise a family in a year. You cannot forge a great republic. But you can, with luck, after making appropriate political arrangements, track down certain key individuals and call them to account. So you build a courthouse. Judge's bench. Witness stand. Prisoner's dock. A Multiprong submarine lies at the bottom of McMurdo Sound. Unadmitted Navy frogmen bring her up. You set sail. You snatch six men from the jaws of the holocaust. You want more – President Orlaff, Senator Krogh, the Secretary of the Navy, the National Security Advisor – but they are already dead.

'Courthouse?' Brat tried to eat a forkful of German chocolate cake, failed. 'Is that what he said?'

'Courthouse,' muttered Randstable.

'We want admittance,' said Sverre. 'Instead we must settle for knowledge. You will tell us why this war was necessary. Consider how fortunate you are. We could have left you to the flames, as we elected to do with *them*. The others. Their gimcrack Party, their bankrupt Marxism, their outrageous pretensions – all blessedly extinct. You, by contrast, are ambiguous. You don't add up. It was your ambiguousness that saved you, that alone.'

George had never thought of himself as being ambiguous.

'Surely you don't presume to lay this tragedy at *our* feet,' grumbled Overwhite. 'We did everything in our power to prevent—'

'Er, wait a minute, Brian,' said Randstable. 'Surely they *do* presume to lay this tragedy at our feet. I mean, when you consider that the alternative is . . . you know. The extinction loop.'

'You have no jurisdiction over us,' said Wengernook. 'Zero. None. *Nada*.'

A new voice said, 'I'm afraid that's not true.'

Sverre's table companion was standing. 'The McMurdo Sound Agreement charters an International Military and Civilian Tribunal,' asserted the young man as he devoured a glob of lemon meringue pie. 'The first appendix lists the counts against you.

116

Have no fear – we shall challenge the competence of the court as soon as the trial begins.'

George's appetite for dessert, a primary drive not long ago, was completely gone. Counts against us? Trial? All because of some ridiculous sales contract?

'Who the hell are you?' demanded Brat.

'Your advocate. Martin Bonenfant, unadmitted counsel for the defense. My staff and I have been hired to argue your case before the judges. I strongly recommend that you retain us.'

'We don't *need* a goddamn lawyer,' asserted Wengernook.

Bonenfant raked his fingers through his glossy black hair. 'Yes, you do – though your case is much better than you might suppose. We've been researching your enemy's morals, as well as the many imaginative ways you sought to prevent mutual destruction. Do you realize that the Soviets violated the spirit and at times the letter of both STABLE agreements?' He devoured more lemon meringue pie. 'And if all else fails, I've got a rabbit or two in my hat. I believe we should go for acquittals, count by count.'

He's so young, George thought. They sent a child to defend us.

'Yes, an acquittal strategy is certainly the way to play this one,' muttered Randstable. Turning, he solicited his co-defendants with large, clumsy gestures. 'Let me put it this way. A photon that doesn't exist can borrow energy from the uncertainty relation to make a real positron-electron pair, which annihilates to produce the photon that created it in the first place.'

'Sounds like witchcraft,' said Sparrow.

'No,' said Randstable. 'Physics.'

Slowly, anxiously, Bonenfant licked lemon muck from his lips. For the unadmitted, evidently, there was urgency in every pleasure. He explained that, if let upon the earth, he would have been a civil liberties lawyer living in Philadelphia. He would have defended child murderers and neo-Nazis.

George stood up. 'I would like to assert here and now that I am—'

The event that kept him from saying 'innocent,' stopping his tongue as abruptly as an arrow stops a bird in flight, was the sudden arrival of the *City of New York*'s officers and men. Lieutenant

Grass, Ensign Peach, Ensign Cobb, Lieutenant Brust, Chief Petty Officer Rush – and over two hundred others. Down the spiral staircase they came, straight into the main mess hall, a roiling mob.

Snatching steak knives from the banquet table, the front-line officers slashed themselves, then passed the knives to the waiting sailors. Chandelier light sparkled in the black rivers. Clouds of burning sulphur rolled through the mess hall. Unadmitted blood filled the wine glasses and frosted the desserts; it speckled Wengernook's brow, splattered Sparrow's hair, rushed down Randstable's cheeks, matted Overwhite's beard, stuck to Brat's hands, pooled in George's lap.

'Admit us!' cried the nullified descendants. 'Let us in!'

A swamp of blood collected in the center of the table. It swirled and bubbled, spitting out ashes. As Peach and Cobb gestured toward the vortex, something took form – an ebony sculpture rising awkwardly from the ghostly tissues.

A model scaffold. A miniature noose. A little hanging corpse – a doll two feet long, its face a blob, its tongue lolling on black lips. Slowly, drippingly, like a reverse-motion film of a melting figurine, features emerged, eyes, nose, mouth.

George reached into his pocket and drew out his Leonardo. This family is mine, he told himself. No canceled generations can take it from me.

'Count One – Crimes Against Peace!' screamed Peach.

'Count Two – War Crimes!' screamed Cobb.

'Count Three – Crimes Against Humanity!'

'Count Four – Crimes Against the Future!'

The sculpted corpse had acquired Wengernook's face. It wept tears of ink.

The cousins blew on the scaffold. The black oozy face transmogrified. Now Randstable was being executed for war crimes. Now Sparrow. Overwhite. Brat.

'They're just trying to scare us,' said the general.

'They're succeeding,' said Randstable.

'All they want is an explanation,' said Overwhite.

George pressed his lips to the painting, kissed Holly's stepsister. He looked at the doll, saw what he knew was coming, a relentless transformation of the Brat-face into a George-face. He had always wished his nose was smaller. There will be a birth, he vowed. For unto us an Aubrey Paxton will be born. Nostradamus was on to something. I am innocent. Aubrey will be admitted to the good, resilient earth.

CHAPTER NINE

*In Which by Taking a Step Backward the
City of New York Brings Our Hero a Step Forward*

Morning finished reading the last chapter of Merribell Braddock's *Scarlet Passions*, closed the book, and, without particularly meaning to, sighed.

Before her career was cut short by the end of the world, Merribell Braddock had single-handedly contributed over three hundred titles to the genre of romantic fiction. *Scarlet Passions* was as false as Olaf Sverre's left eye, and yet, because it described the love of a woman for a man, Morning was touched. Poor extinct Merribell had reached right into Morning's throat and raised a lump. The guileful author was making her see that her feelings for George – for his rough body and deceptively simple personality – definitely qualified as romantic.

'You're one of them, aren't you?' he said to her as he entered the office.

'Them?'

'The unadmitted. I love a shadow.'

'I'm human,' she said. 'I'm human, and you love your dead wife, and I'm not her.'

George released a sharp, explosive moan. Why bring up Justine? Wasn't it their duty to focus on the future? 'You're asking me to believe there were no unadmitted therapists in Antarctica? They had to go outside their race?'

'The McMurdo framers failed to anticipate the survivor's guilt problem. When they went to Chicago to kidnap Randstable, I offered my services. I was given an audience with Sverre. He hired me. No pay – but I would get to live out my life, such as it is.'

She removed the sacrificial knife from the wall and rested the blade against her wrist.

'My blood is as red as yours, George. It's as red as the blood of the innocents whose hearts were excised by this knife.'

He thought of her coming pain, winced. 'Don't. I've seen enough blood lately.'

She was human.

Human . . . and something of a whore.

'How can you work for these . . . discontinuities?'

'I owe them my survival. So do you.'

'I hate them.'

'They come to see me. They are, as you might imagine, troubled. An intolerable case load. I try my best. I listen to them, but I can't give them what they want.'

'They want—?'

'Memories. Real memories, with a bite. They tell me of their lovers, friends, careers, obsessions, but it all happened to some-body else. Seaman Sparks wants me to teach him what music was like, good music – jazz, baroque, not the treacle they pump through the intercom. He would have played the flute. Then there's Lieutenant Grass. He's trying to recall his brother – fishing trips, touch football. It's rare for relatives actually to find each other. Not enough time, too big a continent, and if they do connect the ages are usually wrong. Old women run across their pre-adolescent husbands. Newlyweds stumble into their middle-aged children.'

'Are they always sad?' George asked.

'They have their flashes – moments you and I would call satisfaction, even joy. But most of the time, life is something they read about in a book. Yesterday Seaman Raskin said to me, "Imagine sittings in a gray, still, empty room, taking an endless true-or-false test, getting each question right, and realizing you'll never experience anything else."' She nicked her desk with the sacrificial knife. 'Don't ever confuse unadmittance with living, George.'

'I still hate them. Anybody would have signed that sales contract.'

'Let me guess. You're feeling . . . betrayed? Framed? Manipulated?'

'All those things.'

'Manipulated by your therapist? By the darkbloods?'

'Both. You never cared about me.'

'Don't say what you know isn't true.'

'You just wanted to patch me together so I'd be fit to stand trial.'

With the sacrificial knife she began flipping back pages of *Scarlet Passions*. 'Give me your Leonardo.'

'What makes you think I have it?'

'Give it to me.'

He pulled the painting from his shirt. She received it respectfully, holding it by the edges.

'I don't know what to make of this.' Morning touched her unconceived daughter's hair. 'But I like what it shows. I like everything about it. Your hand is almost on my breast.'

She's starting to get it right, he thought. Love. Marriage. Sex. Children. Species regeneration. 'I must find a city with marble walls. They cure infertility there.'

'It could be a hoax, of course,' she said. 'Nadine Covington's bid for revenge.'

'I believe the painting. So do you.' Love. Marriage. Sex. But not necessarily in that order. 'Tonight we'll have a drink together in the Silver Dollar Casino.'

'No.'

'If we're going to marry and raise a family, we should get to know each other.'

'I cannot have a drink with you.' She returned the Leonardo. 'The darkbloods are here, George. They have gained the continent. Do you truly understand your situation? If the judges find against you, nothing we want – a wedding, Aubrey, her siblings – none of it will happen.' Leaning toward him, she spoke in a frantic whisper. 'From now on, we must never be seen together. We can't let anyone claim that I lack objectivity. "Dr Valcourt? Oh, she's his ex-therapist, nothing more." I'm coming to your trial, friend. Morning Valcourt, witness for the defense. I know something that will help your case.'

'I won't just walk away from you. I won't.'

Her conspiratorial voice dropped even lower. 'You will. Until the hour of my testimony, I'll be gone from your life. Do you understand? Gone. Searching for me will prove futile. No one can master the back passageways here, the dead ends.'

'What do you know that will help my case?'

'I know that I care deeply about you.'

They parted not by kissing, not by hugging, but by discreetly brushing their fingertips together. For George it was one of the most fleshly and impassioned experiences of his life. The sensation lingered in his hands. The pleasure stayed in his memory, waiting to be called up whenever he wanted to feel it.

Captain Sverre was right. A year is nothing. So far, at age thirty-five, George had known twelve thousand days full of physical sensations, many of them astonishingly wonderful – drinking coffee, reading to his daughter, touching fingertips with Morning Valcourt. But a year is nothing. No wonder the unadmitted wanted to hang him.

The Erebus Poker Club did not accomplish much poker that weekend. Brat kept forgetting what beat a straight. Whenever it was Wengernook's deal, he couldn't remember which cards should go up and which down. Overwhite got the chips confused, insisting that he was betting five dollars when he was really betting one.

'These damn zombies,' said Brat. 'They just don't seem real to me, know what I mean? I wouldn't be surprised to hear this whole business was being cooked up in Moscow.' Not a single aspect of the general – posture, visage, tone of voice – suggested that he believed himself. The unadmitted were here. They had gained the continent. They were as real as South African granite.

'Provided that the conservation of electric charge and the balance between particles and antiparticles are obeyed,' said Randstable, 'there is nothing to stop a lot of molecules, even organic molecules, from materializing and then combining into lifeforms . . . er, assuming that the discrepancy is never noticed, of course.'

'And if the discrepancy is noticed?' asked Wengernook.

'The molecules disappear, naturally,' said Randstable.

'But we *did* notice,' said Brat. 'And the zombies are still around.'

'That's got me stumped too,"' said Randstable.

'Know what I think, William?' said Wengernook. 'I think you don't know what the hell you're talking about.'

'I wonder if we'll get a fair trial,' said George.

'I wonder if wishes are horses,' said Brat. He tried to shuffle, made a mess of it. 'Believe me, fellas, the whole thing is a sham, like those show trials of Stalin's. Our best chance would be a prison break.'

'My father was a lawyer,' said Wengernook. 'All those counts against us – it's what you call a retroactive indictment. We didn't violate any laws, so they had to go out and invent some, *ex post facto*. If Bonenfant knows his stuff, he'll get the case dismissed for lack of precedents.'

'Maybe we *should* testify,' said Overwhite. He checked himself for jaw tumors. 'I see their point of view, more or less.'

'Hell, Brian, they're a bunch of hanging judges,' said Brat. 'This is vigilante vengeance. Don't you understand?'

'I think we owe them something,' said Overwhite.

'We owe them nothing,' said Brat.

'We owe them an explanation,' insisted Overwhite.

'We're innocent,' said Wengernook.

'They're *more* innocent,' said Overwhite.

'If I was in their shoes,' said George, 'I'd be curious about a lot of things too.'

She was not in her office. She was not in the skating rink. The bowling alley held no trace of her. The movie theater was empty.

He stayed for the feature, *Panic in the Year Zero*. In this low-budget melodrama from American International, Ray Milland survived a thermonuclear holocaust by driving into the country in a car full of groceries.

He went to the library. Morning was not there. He found a college biology text, leafed through it. The section on the male reproductive system was surprisingly detailed and frank. A gonad appeared in cross-section. Explicit drawings depicted the *seminiferous tubules*, the *spermatids*, the *spermatogonia*, and the *spermatocytes*. 'Your secondary spermatocytes are failing to become spermatids,' Dr Brust had told him. He closed the book and smiled with satisfaction. When I get to the marble city, he thought, I'll be able to tell them exactly what needs doing . . .

He decided to try Lieutenant Grass's hydroponic orange grove. Perhaps she liked oranges.

A fruity scent throbbed through the missile compartment as he slipped into Tube Sixteen. The tree looked vigorous and fecund. He grabbed an orange, tore it from the branch. Succulent. Perfect. Were oranges now extinct? Had unadmitted orange trees been permitted a fleeting tenure on the earth?

He left Tube Sixteen and, sitting down on the cold steel deck, began his vigil. In his mind the portrait of his latent family multiplied into an entire museum. He saw himself walking along a bright corridor, sun-washed windows on one side, paintings on the other. He paused before Morning in a wedding dress – at least, it was probably Morning, though it also looked a bit like Justine. The signature was Leonardo's. Next he inspected a mental painting of himself and Morning making love, brewing the next generation. Oh, how he missed sex, how he hated subsisting on onanism. (We must never be seen together . . . I'll be gone from your life.)

International Military and Civilian Tribunal: phooey. International Kangaroo Court. Yes, Brat had his faults, he was too hasty with his man-portable thermonuclear device, and he hadn't understood that a nation that doesn't exist doesn't need to defend itself, but this 'crimes against the future' stuff was really stretching it. Overwhite? A windbag, sure, but not a dangerous man. Randstable? He could barely walk across a room. Wengernook? He cheated at poker, but that was about it. Reverend Sparrow?

Come off it. No, not one of George's new friends deserved to be in this jam.

A hideous odor cut into his thoughts. He stood up, peered around Tube Sixteen. A young civilian reminiscent of Martin Bonenfant, but with blond hair and a baby-pink complexion, crouched in the middle of the compartment, opening a hatch in the floor. He wore a business suit. The stench evidently traced to the duffel bag on his shoulder.

The intruder disappeared through the hatch. Creeping forward, George followed him down.

A dark, mucosal passageway lay under the missile compartment. It might have been tunneled out by a large earthworm. (Were there unadmitted worms in the world?) The young man stepped into an alcove bathed in a sallow light of uncertain origin. Rusty iron rods went floor to ceiling, turning the alcove into a cage. Inside, a trapped bird the size of a pterodactyl snorted and squirmed.

George thought perhaps he was again seeing Mrs Covington's magic lantern show. But no, this vulture – *his* vulture, as Morning would have it – was alive, as alive as eaters of the dead ever get. It looked exactly as it had at ground zero – tattered wings, rancid eyes, steam-shovel beak, broken posture. And Morning had assumed it was a hallucination. Hah . . .

The vulture's young keeper pulled a penguin carcass from the bag. He looked foolish standing there in his business suit, holding carrion. He pushed the penguin between the bars. The vulture pinned it against the floor with its claw, tore it to pieces, feasted noisily. The keeper winced and gagged, unable to constrain his disgust.

Sneaking back down the passageway, George began to tremble. My family is dead, my planet is dead, my gonads are dead, I'm a prisoner of the murdered future, I'm going to be hanged for a crime I didn't commit, there's a vulture on the submarine, a real vulture, a huge crazy real vulture . . . He climbed to the missile deck. A species without males – that's what the ancient Egyptians believed, according to Morning. Inseminated by the winds.

*

It occurred to him that he knew nothing about Morning's religious convictions. On Sunday he went to church, hoping she might show up.

The *City of New York*'s chapel was an all-purpose facility, with missals and icons suited to almost any sacramental need a sailor in the US Navy might have. George sat in the back pew along with the Presbyterian Brat, the Lutheran Wengernook, and three noncommissioned officers of indeterminate denomination. Ship's Chaplain was a lieutenant named Owen Soapstone. George felt at home in Soapstone's flock, for had the chaplain been born, he would have followed up his navy stint with a long career as a Unitarian minister. He mounted the pulpit and opened an Unadmitted Bible. A respectful hush settled over the congregation.

'In the end Humankind destroyed the heaven and the earth,' Soapstone began.

'Oh, boy,' said Brat.

'One-track minds,' said Wengernook.

'And Humankind said, "Let there be security," and there was security. And Humankind tested the security, that it would detonate. And Humankind divided the U-235 from the U-238. And the evening and the morning were the first strike.' Soapstone looked up from the book. 'Some commentators feel that the author should have inserted, "And Humankind saw the security, that it was evil." Others point out that such a view was not universally shared.'

'I didn't come to hear this crap,' Wengernook announced, rising.

A tremor passed through the chapel. The bulkheads moaned. As Wengernook stalked out, a lily-filled vase fell over and shattered.

Casting his eyes heavenward, Soapstone continued. 'And Humankind said, "Let there be a holocaust in the midst of the dry land." And Humankind poisoned the aquifers that were below the dry land and scorched the ozone that was above the dry land. And the evening and the morning were the second strike.' Soapstone closed the Bible on his hand, a bookmark of flesh. 'Many commentators reject the author's use of the term "Humankind" as bombastic and sentimental, arguing that blame should be affixed more selectively. Other commentators—'

The chapel was on the move, pitching and rolling. Altar candles took to the air like twigs in a gale. Rivets detached themselves from the ceiling and rained into the aisles. Twisting in their seats, the panicked churchgoers grabbed the backs of their pews and hung on like people who had lives.

George decided that he could not cope with another unexpected effect of nuclear war.

Round and round went the room, ever rising, as if traveling up the surface of an enormous corkscrew. The ride seemed to unleash some latent fundamentalism in Soapstone. He embraced his pulpit, binding himself to it like a helmsman lashed to a ship's wheel. The chaplain's reading became a fire-and-brimstone sermon, his eyes spinning, his tongue spiraling, each word a scream.

'And Humankind said, "Let the ultraviolet light destroy the food chains that bring forth the moving creature!" And the evening and the morning—'

A candlestick clipped Soapstone's nose, releasing black blood. His Bible flew up as if being juggled by a poltergeist, then crashed through a stained-glass window. The congregation tumbled into the aisles, George sputtering, Brat cursing prolifically. Still hugging the pulpit, Soapstone continued from memory.

'And Humankind said, "Let there be rays in the firmament to fall upon the survivors!" And Humankind made two great rays, the greater gamma radiation to give penetrating whole-body doses, and the lesser beta radiation to burn the plants and the bowels of animals! And Humankind sterilized each living creature, saying, "Be fruitless, and barren, and cease to—" '

George sailed into the outstretched arms of Saint Sebastian. As he and the statue collided, skullbone against marble, he experienced sensations reminiscent of being shot by John Frostig, but when he looked up he did not see his vulture. Of course – it's under the missile deck, he thought. It's in a cage. It can't come for me this time . . .

*

He awoke in his bunk, staring at dead sea horses. Jennifer, Suzy, Jeremiah, Alfred, and Margaret were now pulpy blobs floating near the top of the tank. He had nurtured them as best he could, raising the new generation, maintaining the old, talking to them, but his efforts were not equal to their death wish. Bits of Soapstone's sermon drifted through his brain. And Humankind said, Be fruitless, and barren . . .

'We hit rough water,' said a voice from nowhere.

George blinked. The MARCH Hare's emaciated form stood over him, proffering a Styrofoam cup filled with coffee. His face showed abundant evidence of the recent chaos: bruises, bandages, clotting cuts.

'Worse than rough,' Brat continued. 'A maelstrom.'

George's head felt as if it had been recently employed as the ball in some violent team sport. He fingered his scalp. The major lump was surrounded by tender foothills. He slurped down coffee. 'Maelstrom?'

'Big fat one.' With unrestrained glee Brat described the whirlpool – a latter-day Charybdis sucking in a hundred tons of water every second, chewing her way across the sea, feasting on archipelagoes, washing them down with vast areas of the South Atlantic. 'Now, here's the sweet part. The thing pitched us right out of the water. Believe it or not, we're on God's dry land.'

George stumbled from his bunk and, after securing the necessary material from the bathroom, began wrapping the little equine corpses in toilet paper shrouds. 'Land? You mean Antarctica?'

'Antarctica is a thousand miles away. We're beached on an island off the Cape of Good Hope. Saw it through the periscope. Tide's going out. Tomorrow it will return and raise us up.' Brat's eyes expanded with crazed joy. 'I've got a question for you, Paxton, and if the answer is yes, then God is surely in His heaven. You brought a scopas suit on board – right?'

George silently recited an epitaph for Jeremiah Sea Horse – HE WAS A GOOD FATHER – and nodded.

'Could I see it?' Brat asked.

The tomb inscriber went to his closet and took down Holly's undelivered Christmas present. Brat pounced on it, ripping the

Colt .45 from the utility belt and sticking it in his man-portable thermonuclear device holster.

'That happens to be my gun, Brat. Or, to be precise, my daughter's gun.'

'You're welcome to join me.'

'Where are you going?'

'Through the amidships hatch.'

'You mean – an escape?'

'If the natives prove unfriendly, we can build a raft and sail to the mainland. We'll find the pockets of civilization, help them clean the shit off the fan blades. We'll put it all together. The world is our oyster, Paxton.'

'Our dead oyster.' He wrapped up Suzy, composed her epitaph: A FINE SWIMMER.

'What's the matter, don't you trust your survival instincts?' asked the general. 'Got a dishonorable discharge from the Boy Scouts?'

'This strikes me as a foolish idea, Brat.'

'There must be lots of untargeted towns out there.'

'It's the back of the moon out there.'

'That's what you think. I've been telling you all along this extinction stuff was a lot of horse manure. There's a city on this very island, a whole city, not a crack anywhere.'

'A city?'

'I saw it.'

'What kind of city?'

'It's . . . I don't know. A city.'

'Does it have white walls?'

'Yeah. White walls. Like marble. How did you know that?'

CHAPTER TEN

*In Which Our Hero Learns that Extinction Is
as Unkind to the Past as It Is to the Future*

Holly's pistol proved unnecessary. No sailors were on watch outside George's cabin or in the corridors beyond. The flight to the amidships hatch was accomplished without spilling a single drop of black blood.

They popped the hatch, leaped up. George underwent a succession of pleasant shocks – technological hum to whispering surf, chilly submarine to warm night, canned oxygen to sweet air. Formless tufts of decaying jungle growth reached out and smothered the grounded prow. A full moon looked down, its brilliant whites and harsh blacks forming a luminous celestial skull.

The fugitives raced between the rows of missile doors – steel cables girded the walkway – climbed out on a rear diving plane, and dropped into the shallows. George followed Brat's moonlit form wading to shore.

Beyond the beach stretched a tidal marsh, a miasma of malodorous silt and terminally ill grasses. The fugitives slogged through the mud, George moving with a vitality acquired from his years of hauling granite. The swamp belched fierce gases; the air heaved with the sticky residue of the vanished sun. High above, beyond the hot sky, the stars of the southern hemisphere welded themselves into grotesque and pornographic constellations.

The clay ground became soft, then hard, kiln-fired. Threaded by mist, great stone slabs grew from the plain. They were riddled with holes – missing gobbets of slate and marble suggesting that some rock-eating vulture had feasted here. Moonlight splashed against the slabs, darkening the plain with perforated shadows.

The ground folded, hills bellied up. Trees broke from the bottom of the ravine like immense black hands. They bore not fruit but violence – thorns that were spikes, seed pods that were the heads of medieval maces. The moon took on a deathly pallor, becoming in George's mind the corpse of his planet's sun, sun-death syndrome leaving behind something to bury.

At the base of each tree, rings of mushrooms went round and round. For species living in the post-exchange environment, their abundance and variety were astonishing. George and Brat ran past mushrooms shaped like elf hats and others shaped like horns of plenty. There were trumpet mushrooms, umbrella mushrooms, candlestick mushrooms, phallus mushrooms, pig-snout mush-rooms, toadstools, toadchairs, toadtables, and toadhammocks. Spiraling out of the forest, the island's vast fungus population spread across dead meadows and desiccated fields like an army of maggots, right up to the gates of the city.

The city. It was as Brat had promised, whole, impounded by blast wave, unburned by thermal pulse. The marble walls glowed like phosphorous, the marble towers sweated in the torrid night. Fat vines slithered up and down the parapets. Gray, withered leaves, each the size and complexion of a shroud, lolled on the vines, embracing the ramparts as petals embrace the organs of a flower, so that the city seemed a kind of plant sprung from some mutant, war-irradiated spore. At one point the ramparts divided to receive a thick, tumid river. The main gate was open and unattended, the guard towers deserted. The fugitives entered freely.

A bent city. Twisted alleys, fractured sidewalks, crooked courts, each lamp post curved like the spinal column of a hunchback. Tall marble buildings leaned over the cobblestone thoroughfares, in certain places touching, fusing to create tunnels and high walk-ways. The fog, fat and milky, floated through the city like a cataract lifted from the eye of a giant. Dank vapors escaped from the well shafts and sewer gratings. As the river advanced it became the city's prisoner, chained by bridges of stone, bound by levees of concrete, forced to feed a labyrinth of canals.

On the coiled and buckled streets, figures moved in a shadowy parade.

'There – what did I tell you?' said the MARCH Hare. 'This extinction has been blown all out of proportion. We're a tough breed, Paxton. Who knows? Maybe one of these survivors is that fertility expert you want.'

George paused beside a wrought iron gate and caught his breath. Had the war completely bypassed this island? Or had a faction of darkbloods emigrated from Antarctica and set up a colony off the tip of Africa? Closer observation suggested that the marchers were not unadmitted – certainly they bore little resemblance to Olaf Sverre's cynical and irreverent Navy. They were like their city, palsied, broken, lost. Something pathological had visited these people – if not the war, then an equivalent catastrophe. They stepped to the beat of a convulsing drummer. They gasped like beached fish. Their clothing, a potpourri of styles and eras, was in worse shape than a scopas suit wardrobe after a thermonuclear exchange – rends, gashes, holes, with bare flesh beneath, yellow flesh, white, brown, cracked and gelatinous, here and there melting to bone.

'Quite a show they put on, huh?' said Brat. 'Folk festival, I guess.'

Whenever he tried speaking with one of the marchers, the best he got was a blank look, more often a moan transmitting stenches and despair.

'They don't understand English,' the general concluded.

The defendants moved down the sultry, glutted streets, jostling through the parade but in no way joining it. They came upon a plaza. Bricks glowed beneath the death's-head moon. A defunct fountain lay in a web of fog. Across the way, a bright shop beamed through the night like a huge kerosene lantern.

The paunchy window was filled with hats. George gulped. How had it managed to survive the Battle of Boston? How had it gotten here? Even the sign was intact: THE MAD TEA PARTY – REMARKABLE THINGS FOR HUMAN BODIES, followed by

PROFESSOR THEOPHILUS CARTER — TAILOR, HATTER, FURRIER, INVENTOR, PROPRIETOR.

'Looks like my best shot is to buy a costume and disappear into this Mardi Gras thing until the tide takes Sverre away,' said Brat. 'Are you really determined to get your balls back in order?'

'Yes.'

'I imagine I've got some pretty fantastic adventures ahead. I could use a man like you on my team, somebody who's smart, strong . . . a little pig-headed.'

'Sorry, Brat. A cure, then Antarctica, then a family – I've seen it all.'

The bells tinkled mournfully as the defendants entered. Gushing sweat, they wove through the vast collection of costumed mannequins. World War Three had not been kind to Carter's inventory. The disintegrating tweeds of Edwardian gentlemen dusted the broken armor of Japanese knights. Eighteenth-century waistcoats rubbed tattered shoulders with nineteenth-century gowns.

'Do you need lodgings?' a voice called out in a British accent. 'Several funerals are happening upstairs. Would you like a room with a viewing?'

The MAD Hatter had aged, not by the decades that had elapsed outside the darkblood realms, but enough to push him past the mortal side of sixty – eyes receding, red hair fading toward pink, brow stippled with liver spots. His top hat appeared to have contracted eczema.

'I was sorry to hear of your species's death,' he said. 'I meant to send a sympathy card. They don't make belated sympathy cards, do they? "So sorry I missed your mother's bout with cancer." '

For the first time since the celebration banquet, George's bullet wound began to throb. 'I'm in a lot of trouble because of you, Professor.'

'Trouble?' said the Hatter.

'I'm on trial for ending the world.'

'Just remember, it could be worse. You could *not* be on trial for ending the world. You could be the *corpus delicti* instead. Signing that sales contract was the smartest thing you ever did.'

'Hey, you *know* this bird?' Brat asked of George.

Theophilus pulled off his hat. 'Bird? The raven is a bird, also the vulture, but not I. You're not a bird either, General Tarmac, though we'd all be better off if you were. Say, George, did you ever find out why a raven is like a writing desk?'

'Right now I'm trying to find out about fertility. My secondary spermatocytes are failing to become spermatids.'

The Hatter's sigh was long and musical. 'There just isn't much reproduction going on in the world any more, is there? What with the extinction and everything. These post-exchange environments have little to recommend them.'

'Extinction?' said Brat. 'Nonsense, the streets are teeming with your customers. You must do a pretty good business around carnival time.'

Spontaneously – no one knew who was leading and who following – the three men went to the window. The parade crawled across the plaza like some huge organism, flagella and antennae lashing in all directions.

'Welcome to the City of the Invalidated Past,' said the Hatter, 'or, if you prefer, the Necropolis of History, or, if you don't prefer, the City of the Invalidated Past. It's your kind of town, George. Yours too, General.' He jabbed his index finger toward the window. 'Look, there's a guard from the court of Harun al-Rashid in eighth-century Baghdad. And a Roman civil engineer who built a water mill in 143 BC. A merchant responsible for bringing improved plow designs to Flanders in 1074. A bishop who participated in the Council of Trent. A worker on Henry Ford's original assembly line . . . Think about it! These people actually lived!' Theophilus held his top hat in front of his heart. 'They got up each morning. They breathed, argued, screwed, moved their bowels. They saw the sun. They had opinions about cats. Listen, do you hear it? Do you hear their sorrow? Their sobs and wails? They're sad because they've been invalidated. When you turn the human race into garbage, you also turn history into garbage. "Why did we bother to invent writing?" they ask. "Or spinning jennies? Why did we trouble ourselves with the cathedrals?" '

They followed the Hatter's short beckoning arm as he led them

135

back to the counter, behind the velvet drapes, and into a hot, squalid room suggesting a laboratory from which nothing beneficial ever issued. Detached human heads were suspended over steaming vats of what looked like liquid flesh. Disconnected limbs swam in tanks of purple fluid. Skeletons dangled from the ceiling as if waiting to make their entrances in some demented marionette show. George felt that he was about as far from a fertility clinic as he could get.

'This is where Victor Frankenstein did his post-graduate work,' said Theophilus. Rusty surgical instruments and corroded technological bric-a-brac filled a dozen cabinets. 'This is where Thomas Edison invented the burned-out light bulb.'

The Hatter, George decided, had lost his mind. Was it possible for a lunatic to go mad?

Tea things overran a linen-swathed table. Hungry and thirsty from their dash across the island, the fugitives sat down and indulged themselves, gulping hot tea, gobbling their way through a heap of stale rolls and crumpets. The Hatter joined them.

'Every night, corpses float through the city,' he explained merrily, smearing butter on a bran muffin.

'War victims?' A silly question, George thought. Of course they were war victims.

'No, they died long before the war, *centuries* before in some cases. I pull them from the river. I dress them. I perform surgery. No problem finding spare parts. The whole world is made of spare parts now. Out go the shriveled organs and the dehydrated blood. In go the relays, motors, microprocessors, voice synthesizers, and spark plugs. But does that do it? Of course not. What is history without hopes, ideals, neuroses, illusions? Hence – my Z-1000 computer over there. Isn't it wonderful what a man can do with a little technology and some free time?'

'Oh, I get it – they're robots!' said Brat. 'It's like Walt Disney.'

'If admitted,' said Theophilus, 'I would have lived in the early twenty-first century, turning out automatons as efficiently as a cobbler turns out shoes.' He went to his work table and began transferring eyeballs from one glass jar to another, tossing the rejects into a teacup.

'This can't be the shop you had back in Boston,' said George. How far the Hatter had sunk – from designing scopas suits to desecrating war victims.

'My humble establishment is like the submarine from which you escaped,' Theophilus explained. 'It flits about from place to place. More twenty-first century know-how.'

'I must say, Carter, you've got an impressive project under way here,' said Brat. 'My hat goes off to you.'

'First I have to sell you one.'

'Probably not the best way to keep civilization afloat, but still ingenious.' The MARCH Hare grabbed a crumpet, slammed it into his tea.

'Brat, those aren't *people* in that parade!' said George. 'Don't you understand?'

The Hatter cackled.

Brat ate the soggy crumpet. 'In any event, it's this flying shop of yours that really interests me. I'm trying to hook up with the other survivors. Can you run me over to the mainland?'

'Most ambitious, General,' said Theophilus. 'You can't make deals with extinction, but you can make deals with me. To wit – help us with tonight's labors, and I shall fly you wherever you want.'

A hospital gurney displayed the topography of a sheeted female corpse. Approaching, the Hatter uncovered her. She was Oriental and, considering her water-logged condition, quite beautiful.

'Born in the twelfth century. Southeast Asia, the Khmer Empire. These eyes once beheld the Angkor Wat temple complex for the royal phallic cult. Imagine – a royal phallic cult once existed in medieval Cambodia!'

'Have you no respect for the dead?' snapped George, restoring the sheet.

'I have nothing but respect for the dead,' said the Hatter. 'Why do you think I work so hard on the parade? Night and day – my monument to the invalidated past. *You* know about monuments.'

'This is lunatic's business!' said George. He made a fist but could not decide what to do with it. 'Disgusting! She isn't from the twelfth century, she's just another victim of radiation or hunger or—'

'Actually, I find the whole thing rather sane,' said Brat.

'Sane? Sane? Call me sane, will you?' screamed the Hatter. 'They called the Joint Chiefs of Staff sane! They called the National Security Council sane!'

He went to his Z-1000 computer, arching his fingers over the keyboard as if playing a concerto.

'Mostly it's the supporting cast of history who wash up here, but sometimes we get a star. On Sunday I found Nostradamus, that brilliant, courageous, plague-fighting scholar of the Renaissance. What I wouldn't give for Hitler. I can change the past, you see – I can improve it. Last night Joan of Arc burned ten priests at the stake. If I had Hitler, I'd make him Jewish. Spermatids, George? Was that your wish? Little baby sperm? You've come to the right place.'

'I have to see a fertility expert.'

'I am one. I can make you as fertile as an alley cat.'

The Hatter dashed into a dark alcove, its entrance flanked by two dressmaker's dummies, headless and skinny. Seconds later he emerged holding a crumbling, mossy hunk of bark. A white mushroom – robust, symmetrical, and shaped like a church bell – clung to the wood. 'Behold your friend and mine, *Agaricus cameroonis.*'

'Toadstools can be poison, I hear,' said George.

'Thermonuclear mushrooms cause sterility, Cameroon mushrooms cure it. Or, to be technical, Cameroon mushrooms promote spermatid production in irradiated seminiferous tubules. This fact has been known since 2015 AD.'

'I don't believe you.'

'Have you a choice?'

George's bullet wound was thumping crazily now. Why couldn't Mrs Covington's magic lantern show have been more explicit on this matter? A simple slide of him devouring a Cameroon mushroom – was that too much to ask? Why did the post-exchange environment involve so damn many decisions?

'Walk through our forest on a moonlit night,' said the Hatter, 'and with luck you'll spot *Agaricus cameroonis* lifting his wan head through the crevice in a rotting log. But don't expect to see him there the next day, for at the first blush of dawn he slips back into his palace of decay and hides. You're looking at a rare one, George, a collector's item. You aren't going to find this fellow in your local drug store.'

'All right. I'll eat it.'

'Nope. Sorry. Bad idea.' Theophilus thrust the *Agaricus cameroonis* under his morning coat. 'You don't *really* want children. They make a lot of noise, they spill their milk, they leave their crayons all over the place.'

'Please . . .'

'First you must answer the question.' He rubbed the concealed fungus.

'What question?'

'Ah – what question? Good question.'

'Maybe he means the question about the raven and the writing desk,' said Brat.

'Yes! That's it!' said the Hatter. 'Nobody has figured that one out!'

Nobody except Dr William Randstable, thought George, struggling to avoid a grin.

'Beyond their expertise in spermatid production,' said the Hatter, 'Cameroon mushrooms make marvelous soup and terrific—'

'A raven is like a writing desk,' said George, 'because Poe wrote on both.'

'What did you say?'

'I said a raven is like a writing desk' – he paused for dramatic effect – 'because Poe wrote on both.'

The Hatter huffed and puffed like Rumpelstiltskin hearing the miller's daughter say, 'Is your name Rumpelstiltskin?' He did a manic little dance, smashing his high-button shoes into the floor.

'You must promise to name all the children after me,' he said as he pulled the *Agaricus cameroonis* from his coat.

'All but the first,' said George.

He tore the mushroom from its bark, thrust it in his mouth. The meat trembled on his tongue, and he chewed. It tasted like what it was, mushroom flesh, tangy, succulent, damp. A soft buzz traveled from his stomach to his gonads. As he closed his eyes, his mind overflowed with his psychic museum – pictures of his forthcoming family thriving in the timefolds. Aubrey and her siblings romped through a tropical paradise. Glow-faced boys devoured uncontaminated fruit. Lithe girls swam in clean waves.

Nostradamus was on to something, Mrs Covington had said.

'Is that it?' George asked. 'Am I fertile now?'

'No,' said the Hatter.

'But soon – right?'

'Nope. Sorry.'

'You said I'd be an alley cat.'

'Spermatids do you no good until they enter your epididymis, where they can mature, grow tails, acquire motility, and learn the facts of life. Unfortunately, your Spermatids will be too feeble for that.'

'Too feeble?'

'Weak as newborn babes.'

'Can I help them?'

'Perhaps.'

'How?'

'The South Pole.'

'The what?'

'The magnetic forces at the South Pole have been known to steer spermatids on their proper course.'

'The South Pole – in Antarctica?'

'This sounds like bushwa to me,' said Brat. 'I'd be careful if I were you, Paxton.'

'Stand on the exact endpoint of the earth's axis for one full minute,' said Theophilus with the imperial confidence of a contract bridge champion sitting down to a game of go fish, 'and the next day you'll be able to book passage for four hundred million sperm at a time.'

*

'Paxton just ate a mushroom,' said Sverre, squinting into Periscope Number One.

'Why?' asked Morning.

'To cure his sterility,' said Sverre. 'State of the art medicine, circa 2015.'

'He's been wanting a family.'

'If there's justice in this world, he'll get a noose.'

'I believe he's innocent.'

'You love him, don't you?'

'No.' She nudged Sverre away from the eyepiece and focused on her beloved.

He was crossing the plaza, Brat on one side, the MAD Hatter on the other. They cut through the spastic parade and approached the river, its dark surface swept by moonbeams and wisps of fog.

'I seem to recall that sex was something quite special,' said Sverre. 'Had I lived, I would have been a devotee of sex.'

'Sex was something quite special,' Morning confirmed. How perfect George looked as he moved down the concrete steps and jumped onto the Hatter's barge – how right was the sweat on his brow, how correct the cords of his muscles.

Sverre noted her wistful smile. 'What is it like, Dr Valcourt?'

'It?'

'Having red blood. Living.'

'Ambiguous.'

The captain pointed to the long black scab on his forearm. 'Then it is in every way better than unadmittance.'

Removing his stovepipe hat, he blew on the fur and watched it tremble. A memory dragged itself forward like a dying animal. He clutched at it. Intimations of mortality. A blur. Something to do with love. Love for a parent? A child? Sharper now. A wife. He would have been married. Christine? No, Kristin ... Kristin who? He couldn't recall her last name. Kristin the pretty ensign. She would have been crazy about amusement parks. He saw her on a merry-go-round. Kristin, lovely Kristin, astride a wooden horse, going merrily around, singing, laughing.

Dissolving ...

He reached out with his spindly fingers, stroked Morning's cheek. 'You are a woman of great passion. I felt that when I hired you.' A tear formed in his right eye, a drop of gin in his left, and he pulled away. 'Don't worry, I won't call you to my bed. I am more honorable than that.'

And less potent, he thought.

The bottle had wrecked him. His Number One Periscope did not go up.

'You must understand – Paxton is my patient,' said Morning, tightening her grip on the scope handle. 'I cured him. Naturally I want him to have ambitions.'

Pacing furiously around the room, Sverre attempted to coax additional Kristin images out of his brain – a fruitless enterprise, as he knew it would be – then returned to Morning and asked, 'Where are they now?'

'On a barge,' she reported. 'They're collecting war dead. The Hatter is frustrated. He wants all of history in his parade, and he's afraid that it will always be . . .'

'Incomplete!' wailed the Hatter. 'Lord knows I try, but there's a limit to what one man can do.'

The fugitives crouched in the stem and surveyed the night's catch. Theophilus had made them fishers of men; under the influence of George's muscled arms, four corpses had risen from the river. Droplets speckled their brine-cured flesh. Grave robbing, George realized – whether the violated medium was earth or water – was a damning, unholy enterprise, blasphemous even by Unitarian standards.

'A fine haul, no doubt about it,' said the Hatter, misreading George's dazed look. 'Still, we have a long way to go.'

According to Theophilus, they had retrieved a former patient of Sigmund Freud's, a gladiator whose highly entertaining death had occurred in 56 BC, a clerk employed by the Bank of Amsterdam from 1610 to 1629, and a Viking.

A resurrected galley slave poled the barge forward. Blind marble houses glided by. Bridges passed overhead, dark arching shapes that put George in mind of his vulture.

'Do you realize I don't have a single subject of the Pharaoh Akhnaton? Not one.' Bubbles of sweat dotted the Hatter's forehead. 'The Arabian Caliphate and Abu Bakr? Nobody. The Gupta Court of fourth-century India? Zero!' Lunging forward, he grabbed George's shirt, bunching the material in his fists. 'And victims? Don't remind me! There's a severe victim shortage in this city, I can tell you. Yes, I've got Napoleon covered, and the Trojan War, but what about the Young Turk Revolution of 1908? The Opium Wars of 1839 to 1842? The Crusades, for Christ's sake! Don't even talk to me about the Crusades!'

The Hatter took the tiller and steered them toward a concrete pier. The moonstruck water threw bright, dancing sine waves on the steps leading up to the street.

'This is where you get off,' he announced as the galley slave moored the barge.

'You promised to take me to the mainland!' Brat protested.

A fearsome drumming echoed through the marble city, as if a rain made of shrapnel and bones were felling on its streets.

'I lied,' said the Hatter.

'You *what*?' screamed Brat.

'Something wrong with your hearing, General? I've got a root back at the shop that cures deafness. I lied. Folks around here don't like the idea of your war crimes going unpunished. They're coming, gentlemen. I wouldn't want to guess what they'll do when they arrive, but it's certain to include tearing you limb from limb. You'll wish you'd taken your chances with the court.'

'I *was* going to take my chances with the court!' said George. The drumming grew louder. Footfalls, he concluded – the clogs, galoshes, pumps, sandals, and buskins of Professor Carter's citizens. 'I'm innocent!'

'Innocent, eh? Then why is the world over?'

'You gave me spermatids, and now you're going to have me killed?' asked George.

Theophilus jumped onto the pier. 'It's the post-exchange environment. Nobody behaves rationally any more.'

As the mob rumbled forward, Brat drew Holly's pistol and

aimed it at the Hatter's chest. 'Call off your dogs, Carter! Call them off, or I'll shoot!'

'There's a logic to what you're saying,' said Theophilus, 'but, being insane, I cannot grasp it.'

Whereupon George, out of motives he would never fully comprehend, snatched the pistol from Brat and hurled it toward the front of the barge. The weapon glanced off the gladiator's head, plopping into the dark gray river and vanishing instantly.

'What's happening?' Morning asked.

'Your lover just saved the Hatter's life,' Sverre replied, leaning away from the eyepiece. 'Oh, and something else.'

'Yes?'

'They're in a lot of trouble with history.'

Up and down the crippled, dawn-lit avenues the bewildered defendants ran, Theophilus's citizens in frantic pursuit, a booming cloud of invalidated peasants, princes, beggars, scholars, scientists, farmers, clerics, and soldiers. Every time George looked back, he noticed a different category of pre-nuclear weapon. The macabre rattle of spears, swords, muskets, and battle axes filled his ears, mixing with the mob's computer-generated howls. These things are just puppets, he reminded himself – they cannot harm me. He could understand the post-exchange environment being horrible and depressing, but did it also have to be ludicrous?

As the defendants reached the main gate, a fat citizen with teeth like barbed wire popped out of a turret and, ever beholden to the Z-1000, cried, 'I am not garbage!'

Stomping mushrooms under their boots, George and Brat ran beyond the walls, through the ravine, across the field of megaliths. Marsh gases hit them like a fist. Spears flew past. As the defendants charged into the muck, tiny fireballs began choking the sky. George glanced over his shoulder. The citizens had deployed a weapon of singular malevolence. Puppets, he recited again. Puppets, they're just puppets. The flaming arrows fell everywhere, hissing against the silt, setting the dead grass on fire. The air thickened with a smell akin to unadmitted blood. A brawny officer from Genghis Khan's army, dressed in what looked like the plating of some particularly vile and stupid dinosaur, sent a fireball sizzling over George's scalp.

Directly ahead lay the submarine, wallowing in the rising tide. George rejoiced to see that the amidships hatch was still ajar. Or am I hallucinating? he wondered. No, it really looked open. There was definitely a chance they would succeed in getting themselves recaptured by Operation Erebus.

But the swamp, George learned, was in conspiracy with the invalidated past. It seized his boots, holding him fast with its dark paste. Brat, he saw, was also stuck, rooted to the island like a tree, writhing and raging. The clockwork mob slogged forward, spears poised, swords waving, flesh slipping from their faces like ill-fitting masks, so that each citizen soon wore a skull's persistent smile.

Craning his jeopardized neck, George fixed on the hull, and it was at this critical moment in his fortunes, when death-by-history seemed a foregone conclusion, that all eighteen port-side missile doors suddenly flew open, their oil-soaked hinges making no sound. Instantly the ship took on the appearance of a medieval parapet. Olaf Sverre's navy, armed with scopas suit guns, came streaming out of the hatches, Peach and Cobb in the lead, their chubby faces split by smirks. Oh, brave, splendid men, thought George, you will all receive medals for this. Taking cover behind the battlements, the unadmitted sailors aimed their lovely Colt .45 pistols, their beautiful twelve-gauge shotguns, and their gorgeous HK 91 assault rifles.

Sverre stood atop the sail, his frame tall and sharp against the reddening sky, his stovepipe hat cocked toward the sunrise. A loud, unintelligible noise came from his mouth, a sound that George hoped and prayed was an order to open fire.

Targeted by hands that had been alive for barely two hundred and fifty days, the bullets flew in all directions, but even so random a salvo was enough to drop half the citizens. Relays and motors spurted from busted flesh. Bodies hit the swamp, flopping, wriggling, plastering themselves with silt. A broken samurai rolled up to George's knees. Its cries evoked a phonograph needle skidding along the surface of a record.

The surviving citizens retaliated. Spears smashed uselessly into the hull, sling-tossed rocks bounced off the missile doors like hail encountering a tin roof. Sverre – oh, excellent soldier, glorious hero – ordered a second salvo. Fifty more died, but history had not yet learned the meaning of defeat. The citizens kept coming. Burning arrows suffused the swamp with smoke and otherworldly light. George felt a trembling in his recently resuscitated . . .

Gonads, thought Sverre. This fight is doing something to my gonads. (Keep it going, men! Let's get more smoke over there to the left, more chaos to the right, bring up the heavy artillery – I want trumpets, drums, banners, flying earth, explosions of many colors!) When he once again called for fire, he realized that remembered passions were now coursing through his ducts and veins, as if they had been waiting for the proper stimuli. How subtle were the uses of pitched battle! In his mind he left the field, the better to savor the rare and precious images.

Yes, it was all quite clear. He would have invited Kristin the pretty ensign to Barbados, and they would have made love in the open water – a steamy night, smooth breezes, insects and birds surrounding them with primordial jazz. (Did he propose to her that same weekend? Yes, most likely.) Excited by the fabulous souvenir, Sverre's penis now assumed heroic proportions, pushing against his trousers, eager to get into the world. Oh, how he wished his life had happened, the Caribbean part if nothing else. Unadmittance was so unfair. No wonder he drank.

He ordered a fourth round. Among many others, a Renaissance soldier fell, a young man who had fought side by side with Pope Julius II at the siege of Ferrara. The skull-faced soldier struggled to his feet, drew his sword, and rushed toward the mired defendants.

'Fire!' shouted Sverre.

The bullets came in a great slashing volley, dissecting the soldier like so many scalpels, turning him into a heap of rubber and plastic. The defendants laughed with astonishment and relief. And then, suddenly, Sverre saw that it was over, saw that like a nuclear strategist he had run out of targets, and a short while later his fine, impossible erection went away.

*

After his exec had taken the Erebus defendants from the field and returned them to the ship, Sverre climbed down the hull and, gin bottle at the ready, waded through the biotechnical carnage. He inspected the shattered torsos, the dismembered limbs, the severed pieces of muddy flesh. He was exhilarated and sickened – exhilarated by the slaughter, sickened by his exhilaration.

War, he had learned, was fun. Massacre, when accomplished efficiently and successfully, entails profound emotional fulfillment. Ordering sailors to open fire will, under certain conditions, make a man's blood sing – admitted blood, unadmitted blood, no difference. Ah, but he would sleep well that night, no need for an eye filled with gin! He stared at the mess and wept. By what right do we accuse the Erebus Six? How are we better than they? The tribunal is a fraud. I shall deliver my prisoners – *here they are, learned judges, every one of them healthy and intact, mission accomplished* – but I shall not dance at their execution.

Half an hour went by. Eighteen hundred seconds that, despite the care he normally took to squeeze every drop from his sojourn, Sverre would never be able to recall. Lieutenant Grass arrived. Paxton and Tarmac were in their cabins, the exec reported. Guards posted, double locks on the doors.

'Are we cleared for sea, Mister Grass?' Sverre asked.

'Cleared for sea – yes, sir.'

'Then we'd better get on with it.'

'Take her out?'

'Take her out.'

'All engines ahead full?'

'All engines ahead full.'

'Set course for McMurdo Station?'

'Set course for McMurdo Station.'

Harsh winds descended. The morning grew dark. The shadowed ship heaved up and down, back and forth, eager for the open South Atlantic. Sverre crossed the swamp at a funereal pace, drinking, coughing, shuddering from the cold in his rubber eye, cautiously picking his way through the invalidated past.

ENTR'ACTE

Salon-de-Provence, France, 1554

'. . . cautiously picking his way through the invalidated past.'

Nostradamus's gloved fingers removed the hot glass painting of Olaf Sverre crossing the swamp. The projected flame bounced off the wall and washed the study in white-gold light.

Jacob Mirabeau's face was indecipherable, a stone etched with hieroglyphics. But then a yawn of astonishing dimensions appeared.

'You are bored,' groaned the prophet. Nocturnal winds troubled the curtains.

'No, Monsieur – tired,' said the boy. 'I would be asleep by now were this show of yours not so terrifying. I fear to dream. Nightmares would stalk me, worse than when the plague came.'

'Terrifying, did you say?' Nostradamus clapped his hands. 'Nightmares? Splendid!' The night air swelled with flower scent and cricket music. 'Everybody loves a good fright.'

'Will George get his sterility back?'

'His *fertility*. When the medical officer checked him out, his seminiferous tubules had definitely begun spermatid production.'

'I remember – spermatids are baby sperm. That's what the Hatter said.'

'Very good, Master Jacob.'

'What are sperm?'

'People won't know about them until Leeuwenhoek's microscope studies in 1677. If you've been following the plot, you understand that George needs to steer his spermatids into his epididymis, so that they can achieve motility and enter his *vas deferens*.'

'I liked the battle.'

'I assumed you would.'

'Captain Sverre reminds me a bit of you.'

'Yes. I can see that. He's rather noble, don't you think?'

'Oh, yes.'

Cries came, jagged shapes of pain cutting through the floor

from below. The boy shuddered, hugged himself, began breathing in frog gulps.

Nostradamus stretched out his hand, and Jacob's shoulder rose to meet it. The boy grew calm under the prophet's gnarled touch.

'Why does God make it so painful?' Jacob asked. 'Why does He punish all women for the sin of Eve?'

'God is not the problem. The babies are the problem – their big heads. Ah, but they must be that big to hold our brains. Look here – the next painting. It will take your mind off your mother.'

The wall exploded in silver glaciers advancing between snow-cloaked mountains.

'To appreciate the rest of the tale, Jacob, you must know something of its setting. Antarctica comprises—'

'I've been meaning to ask you – what is this Antarctica everybody keeps talking about?'

'A continent. The English explorer James Cook will discover the first evidence of it in 1772. Might I assume you've run out of interruptions?'

'Sorry, Monsieur.'

'The continent of Antarctica comprises . . .'

BOOK TWO

For Destruction Ice Is Also Great

CHAPTER ELEVEN

*In Which Our Hero Is Treated like a Common
Criminal and Endures an Uncommon Torture*

The continent of Antarctica comprises five million square miles of ice heaped atop a grim and frigid bedrock. It is, on the whole, a useless place. When the world had countries, even the most enterprising of them could not profitably contrive to extract the continent's oil, gas, copper, iron, or coal. Antarctica is ten degrees below zero on a hot day. The Soviet Union once recorded a temperature at Vostok Station of minus 126.9 degrees Fahrenheit.

Near the middle of the twentieth century, the love of peace reached such a fever pitch among the nations of the earth that they signed an agreement declaring that they would not go to war over this depressing and inconvenient pile of nothing. Thirteen sovereign states agreed to put aside their conflicting territorial claims. You would not need a passport to visit the ice block.

Near the end of that same century, almost four decades after the 1959 Antarctica Treaty was signed, a caravan of six Sno-Cats began a journey along the western edge of the Ross Ice Shelf, from McMurdo Sound to the Nimrod Glacier. To George Paxton, who sat in the back of the lead Cat, the vehicles suggested Sherman tanks designed by Unitarians: treads, metal plating, slotted windows, no guns. Clumsy and slow, the Cats traversed the shelf like giant armadillos waddling across a white desert.

Staring toward the Transantarctic Mountain Range, George felt his newborn spermatids thrash about in his seminiferous tubules. 'It's a miracle!' Dr Brust had declared upon examining him. 'But am I fertile?' George wanted to know. 'Fertile?' said the medical officer. 'Not by a long shot. Spermatids as feeble as these, they haven't got any future. Hey, Paxton, don't you know there's been an extinction? The world has no use for human chromosomes.'

A sign bounced past: ICE LIMBO 414 – FIVE KILOMETERS. 'Just wait, my little friends,' he muttered in the direction of his spermatids. 'Somehow I shall get you to the endpoint of the earth's axis.' He turned from the window. A narrow-eyed young woman guarded him with a Remington twelve-gauge shotgun. Her name-plate said GILA GUIZOT, and her scopas suit – 'excellent for keeping out the cold,' as Sverre had explained on the boat – displayed the Bleeding Hand insignia of the Antarctic National Police. On meeting George, the first thing Gila Guizot had done was kick him in his resuscitated gonads.

The transfer of George's person from US Navy custody to the International Military and Civilian Tribunal had occurred in one of McMurdo Station's many corrugated-steel huts, a morbid place guarded by the national police and lit by whale-oil lamps. George sat on a wooden stool. His recently issued scopas suit was riddled with holes, so that sadistic little streams of Antarctic air flogged him whenever the door opened. Every half-hour a liaison from some unadmitted faction or other would enter the hut, taking a seat behind a snow hummock carved to resemble a desk. Scribes recorded George's deposition. Name? Birthplace? Religious convictions? Political affiliations? Were New Orleans restaurants as good as I remember them? Was California really warm and sunny most of the time? King *Lear* – that was a truly fine night in the theater, wasn't it? Bach was brilliant, if memory serves. Could you hum me a Bach tune, Mr Paxton? Bach would have moved me to tears, I think.

His ally throughout these interrogations was Dennie Howe, an agonizingly attractive young darkblood with sharp turquoise eyes and a double-decker smile. As soon as George entered the hut, she identified herself as Bonenfant's chief assistant and explained that she would be using her several degrees in international law to keep George's inquisitors at bay. My client does not have to answer that question. My client is not obliged to initial that extradition paper. My client is entitled to a cup of . . .

Coffee, thought George as the caravan entered Ice Limbo 414. I would do anything for a cup of coffee right now. They rumbled down the main street of the community. Police officers patrolled the sidewalks, keeping the demonstrators in line. Boos and hisses wafted into the Cat, making George's bullet wound ache and his spermatids cringe. The passing signs and banners were lettered with dried black blood. NO ACQUITTALS FOR WAR CRIMINALS . . . HANG THE ABORTIONISTS OF THE HUMAN RACE . . . AND HITLER BEGAT WENGERNOOK . . . MAKE RANDSTABLE EXTINCT . . . ADMIT US. George noticed a few dissenters. FREE THE ARMAGED-DON SIX . . . NO VIGILANTE VENGEANCE . . . LET THEM EXPLAIN THEMSELVES . . . PAXTON WAS FRAMED. An embarrassed thrill passed through him, as when the *Wildgrove Eagle* had published his letter protesting the plan to turn part of Rosehaven Cemetery into a golf course.

He looked beyond the sidewalks. For many darkbloods, time was too precious to spend on activism. In the side yard of Barrack F a mother and her daughter tossed a snow basketball back and forth. Next door an elderly man with rippling white sideburns stood on a hummock and pretended to conduct an orchestra, while behind Barrack W an adolescent boy attempted to make a Weddell seal jump through a hoop.

Eggs sailed out of the crowd, splattering the sides of the Cat. Thick wads of embryonic penguin seeped down George's window. A rock flew from the scopas-gloved hand of an angry young Oriental woman, thunked into the windshield, and left a starburst.

'That does it!' shouted Dimitri Eliopoulos, a fat bespectacled man of volatile enthusiasms and potential Greek ancestry. He slapped the steering wheel with his palm. 'From now on we stay clear of the population centers!'

The caravan got through Ice Limbo 414 without further incident.

'We have ninety percent of the world's ice here,' said Dimitri later that afternoon, 'See that glacier? Mulock. My place of birth.'

'Birth?' said George.

'It was a birth to *me*, Paxton. Being dust and then suddenly getting a body and thoughts and cracking out of the ice, well, maybe it wasn't snuggly blankets and my own private tit, but, by damn, it was something.'

On the outskirts of Ice Limbo 415 a scopas-suited Bulgarian ballerina danced. Despite her attire she was quite graceful, and her face displayed the sort of intellectual frown that George had so often seen and admired on Morning Valcourt. Morning is doing something at this very moment, he realized. Something ordinary? Sleeping? Eating? More likely – something profound. She is musing profoundly about Leonardo's vulture fantasy . . .

Between Limbos 416 and 417 a Norwegian man with a fishing pole and a hacksaw tried to cut a hole in the ice. A flock of penguins ambled into view. Antarctica, Dimitri explained, held the planet's one remaining ecosystem, a dystopia of birds and aquatic mammals awaiting the inevitable hour. George was endlessly saddened by the penguins' trusting faces, their stuffed-animal cuteness, their utter obliviousness to the imminence of the bird who is like a writing desk.

'Hey, Paxton, maybe you can settle an argument,' said Dimitri. 'I would have been Greek, okay? That means I would have hated all other Greeks, right?'

'Oh, for pity's sake,' laughed Gila Guizot. 'That's completely backwards. You would have hated non-Greeks.'

'That doesn't make any sense,' said Dimitri.

'Take me, I would have been French,' said Gila. 'Also a Catholic.'

'And proud of it,' explained George.

'Proud of French Catholics?' asked Dimitri.

'Proud to *be* a French Catholic,' George answered patiently.

'There, you see?' said Gila. 'I was right.'

'What did she have to do to become a French Catholic?' asked Dimitri.

'Her parents would have been French Catholics,' said George.

'I seem to recall something about Protestants,' said Dimitri. 'She would have been proud of Protestants, too, right?'

'She would have been proud to *be* a Protestant,' said George. 'If she had been one, that is.'

'She would have been just a Catholic? Not a Protestant too?'

'You were never both!'

'Why not?'

'You just weren't,' said George.

'Too bad – she could have been even prouder,' said Dimitri.

'If she was both, I think she would have been less proud.'

'Don't mock me, Paxton.'

'What are you?' asked Gila.

'A Unitarian,' said George.

'You were the ones who hated Jews – did I remember that right?' asked Gila.

'No,' said George.

'Muslims?'

'No.'

'Paxton is proud of *everybody*,' said Dimitri knowingly.

Night came but not darkness, only the perpetual gloom of the late Antarctic summer. George dreamed of spermatids reaching epididymides and growing fine, strong tails.

At dawn the caravan began crossing the foot of the Nimrod Glacier, a river of ice gushing motionlessly from the interior plateau to the shelf. The warped and crevassed surface of the glacial tongue spread toward a promontory called Mount Christ-church, at the bottom of which sat a building made of the forever-frozen material known locally as Antarctic steel.

'The Ice Palace of Justice,' said Gila, pointing. It was a soaring, gaudy structure whose various intricacies – buttressed walls, bas-relief towers, decorous gates – seemed to disguise a sinister agenda, like the peppermint trim on a witch's house. 'Your new home.'

'I'm hoping to see the South Pole,' said George.

'This place is *much* more interesting than the South Pole,' said Dimitri.

'I need to get there.'

'The South Pole is over five hundred miles from here. Between the lack of public transportation and the fact that we intend to hang you soon, you'll have to settle for the Ice Palace of Justice.'

The caravan slithered into the central courtyard. Dimitri twisted the ignition key; the Cat's engine sputtered and died. As Gila dragged George into the frigid air, the wind tore nails of ice from the palace walls and flung them against his suit. The demonstrators waved their signs and brandished their frozen eggs. George and his co-defendants came together in a shivering, forlorn huddle. Wengernook glowered. Randstable hugged his magnetic chess set. Overwhite examined himself for neck tumors. Reverend Sparrow spoke with God. Even the bulk of his scopas suit could not keep Brat from looking pathologically underweight.

Police officers held back the demonstrators. The ground vibrated with angry shouts and the pounding of banner poles. NO MERCY FOR SPECIES KILLERS. George had never seen that one before. EXTINGUISH THE EXTINCTIONISTS. Nor that one. He longed for the witness stand – longed for it, feared it. Anybody would have signed that contract.

A rock-hard little man came forward brandishing a copy of the McMurdo Sound Agreement. The emblem on his scopas suit declared that he was a captain in the Antarctic Corps of Guards, and his nameplate said JUAN RAMOS. Silence settled, as if the lights were dimming in a crowded concert hall.

A conversation drifted into George's ear.

'. . . people who ended the world,' a man was saying.

'Bad people?' a small boy asked.

'Must be,' said the man.

'Father . . . ?'

'Yes, son?'

'How soon before we die?'

'Two months.'

'Is that long?'

'Oh, yes, son. Very long. Very, very long. Be quiet now.'

'As Chief Jailor of the Antarctic National Dungeon,' Juan Ramos began, 'my first duty is to read you Article Sixteen of the Charter of the International Military and Civilian Tribunal.'

'Dungeon? I don't like the sound of that!' bellowed Brat. 'There are *rules* in this world for treating war prisoners!'

Someone hurled a scopas suit glove filled with seal dung. It struck Brat's helmet and erupted.

' "Article Sixteen – Procedures for Ensuring the Defendants a Fair Trial." ' Juan Ramos's mustache flared from each side of his upper lip like the hind legs of a tarantula. ' "Section A – The indictment shall specify in detail the charges against the accused, and, furthermore, a copy of the indictment, translated into a language that he understands, shall be furnished to each defendant." ' Gulls and skuas spiraled gracefully around the palace towers. ' "Section B – Each defendant shall have the right, through himself or through counsel, to present evidence at the trial in support of his case." ' Ramos climbed atop a five-foot pressure ridge. The wind wriggled his mustache; it seemed about to scurry away. 'My second duty is to announce that your collective bail has been set in the amount of three hundred and sixty-two billion dollars, which, as it happens, is equal to last year's United States Defense Department budget.' He paused, grinned. 'If by any chance you have this sum among you, I shall immediately contact your advocate on the matter of your release.'

A stairwell dropped from the courtyard into the white, cold interior of the glacier. Gila Guizot's assault rifle steered George down the steps and then through several hundred feet of rising and falling, twisting and turning passageways. Seal-oil lamps sputtered along the dungeon walls. Guards streamed back and forth, their faces evincing anger, hatred, sadness, and badly developed consciences.

CELL 6 – PAXTON said the sign on the iron door. Stepping inside, George was shocked to see muted February sunlight spreading everywhere. He looked up. A transparent slab of ice roofed his cell. Gray, ugly clouds clogged the sky.

The place had been thoroughly suicide-proofed. The ice ceiling offered no purchase for a noose, and the edges of the furniture – bed, chairs, writing desk, commode – had been sanded into blunt little knolls. For some reason they let him keep his Leonardo, though he might easily have shattered it and then opened his wrist with a fragment. Why this privilege? One day a clue appeared, etched in the transparent ceiling. It was a quote from Fyodor Dostoevsky: 'The end of the world will be marked by acts of unfathomable compassion.'

And so George settled into prison life. He expected a repetition of his recent solitary confinement aboard the submarine, boredom without end. And for the first seventy-two hours, boredom is exactly what the dungeon delivered. Nothing happened there, not even the passage of the sun, the continent being in the twilight of its six-month day. George lay on his ice bed, sleeping, not sleeping, brooding, reading the indictment, visiting his psychic museum – Morning in her wedding dress, Morning suckling Aubrey.

Then the tortures began. Contrary to Brat's fears, the genre of excruciation practiced at the Antarctic National Dungeon fell well within the definition of civilized behavior prescribed by the Geneva Protocols.

The prisoners' torture was this: they were given whatever they wanted. They had only to name a pleasure, and it was theirs. Food? At six o'clock each evening Ramos's underlings would serve a dinner that regarded every human taste bud as an erogenous zone; several bestselling cookbooks could have been derived from the secrets of preparing Adélie penguin en brochette and sea lion flambée. Drink? The milk of the Weddell seal displayed extraordinarily un-milklike properties when fermented. Sex? What the local prostitutes lacked in experience they made up for in eagerness. Intellectual stimulation? Antarctica's population included a large supply of hypothetical Pulitzer Prize recipients.

Above each cell, lively little mobs gathered, and as the prisoners indulged themselves, the darkbloods stared down through the transparent roof. Eyes filled the heavens like dying stars. The spectators clapped, whistled, stomped their feet, and chanted, 'Let us in!' It was a sport of ever-growing popularity. People brought lunch.

The first time George was offered a mug of coffee under these conditions, he swallowed it with equanimity. The second time, he took the mug to a corner and faced the walls, drinking in small, furtive sips. The third time, he let the coffee grow cold.

A prostitute named Trudy came calling. She had gained the continent in her physical prime. 'Sorry it isn't more private,' she said, fiddling with George's Velcro. 'Just pretend they aren't there.'

He glanced up. A young man with a Göttingen University patch on his scopas suit returned his gaze. 'I would like you to go,' said George.

'Go?' said Trudy.

'You are very pretty,' said George. 'Please leave.'

'Okay . . . but I want you to answer me a question.'

'Yes?'

'I'll bet you can imagine what my question is.'

'No, I can't.'

'Imagine.'

'I can't.'

'My question is, why the fuck did you end the world?'

Although the large central cell was intended for exercise, the defendants preferred using it for poker, which was permitted once an evening for ninety minutes. They bet food. Whenever a game ended, Juan Ramos appropriated most of the winnings and ate them on the spot. 'We are not good,' he explained. 'Merely innocent.'

On the night before the trial was to begin, George returned from the poker game to find two lawyers in his cell. Gorgeous Dennie Howe he remembered from his inquisition at McMurdo Station. (Oh, the hearts she would have shattered . . .) Her companion, who introduced himself as Parkman Cleave, looked even more callow than the rest of the defense team. George offered his visitors ice chairs. Children, he thought, always they send children. I'm being defended by a goddamn kindergarten.

'We've just come from the Documents Division,' said Dennie. 'It's like a monastery over there – papers culled from every corner of the United States and Western Europe, scribes copying page after page by candlelight.'

'They arrived on a barge,' said Parkman. His smile was as flashy as the clasps on his briefcase. 'The *Spirit of the Law.*'

'First, the good news,' said Dennie. 'Out of twenty tons of cargo, the entire case against you consists of one scopas suit sales contract.'

'I know,' said George.

'Anything to drink around here?' Parkman asked.

'Cocoa. Coffee.'

The lawyers smiled in unison, ordered cocoa. George began heating water on a whale-oil stove.

'Now, the bad news,' said Dennie.

'The chief prosecutor is Alexander Aquinas,' said Parkman.

'Never heard of him,' said George.

'Really? Oh – of course not,' said Parkman. A smile pushed aside his cheeks, which were as smooth and pink as buffered Oklahoma granite. 'If you've got Alexander Aquinas around, you can put away your steel traps.'

'His books would have dealt mortal blows to plea bargaining and the insanity defense,' Dennie explained with an admiration George thought might have been a touch more reluctant. 'Alexander Aquinas would have gotten judges to hang their mothers.'

George spooned brown powder into two mugs, added hot water, served the sweet-smelling results.

'You're not having any?' Parkman asked. Chocolate steam rolled through the cell.

'No.'

'We want to tell you how to plead,' said Dennie.

'Not guilty,' said George.

'That's almost right,' said Parkman.

'You must say, "Not guilty in the sense of the indictment,"' said Dennie.

'Why?' said George.

'Because you're not guilty,' said Parkman.

'In the sense of the indictment,' said Dennie. 'That's how the Nazi war criminals pleaded,' she added merrily.

'We also want to teach you some tactics,' said Parkman. 'You must make a good impression on the judges.'

'Keep your suit clean,' said Dennie.

'When the barber comes around, avail yourself of his services,' said Parkman. 'Let's go for less hair, a neater beard, right?'

'When you're on the stand, it's okay if you look nervous,' said Dennie.

'*Try* to look nervous, in fact,' said Parkman. 'We want to avoid that cold-blooded nuclear warrior image.'

'Pretty child,' said Dennie, lifting the Leonardo from the nightstand. 'Your daughter?'

'Bonenfant thinks he can get us off,' said George, snatching away the priceless painting. 'He said there's a rabbit or two in his hat.'

'It all depends on whether we find a vulture expert,' said Parkman.

'A what?' said George.

'Vulture expert,' said Dennie.

'Ever hear of the *Teratornis?*' asked Parkman.

'No,' said George.

'A species of vulture,' said Dennie.

'Obviously you're not a vulture expert,' said Parkman. Vultures.

A shock of recognition surged through George. He had seen Parkman Cleave before . . . on the submarine . . . wearing a business suit. . . holding a bag of carrion. 'I know you! You're the one who takes care of my vulture!'

'*Your* vulture?' said Parkman.

'Dr Valcourt calls it my vulture. It's not really mine. I first ran into it at ground zero, then again on the boat, when you fed it.' George returned his family to the nightstand. 'Dr Valcourt told me that vultures can reproduce without males. They're inseminated by the winds – that's what people used to believe. Do you keep it as a charm? Perhaps it will bring your race good luck. It's certainly big enough.'

'Nothing can bring our race good luck,' said Parkman.

'No animals are inseminated by the winds,' said Dennie.

'Not even teratorns,' said Parkman.

'When you're defending the men accused of ending the world,' Dennie explained, 'you try everything you can think of.'

CHAPTER TWELVE

*In Which It Is Shown that the End of the World Was
More Necessary than Previously Supposed*

Across the interior plateau, down the great static swells of the Nimrod Glacier came the legions, shoulder to shoulder, bound for the trial of the millennium. The tromp of their boots sent fissures shooting across the continent's ice fields and brought waves to its lakes and bays. Rushing from the Transantarctic Mountain Range, unadmitted tributaries flowed together in an endless torrent: male, female, young, old, Negro, Nordic, Alpine, Oriental, Pygmy, Eskimo. The pilgrims moved with exuberance and purpose, dodging nunataks, circumventing crevasses. Many of them whistled. A few skipped. Their signs and banners swayed in joyful arcs. Songs warmed the frigid air. For the first time since the darkbloods' arrival, their future crackled with promise: at last they were to receive their due measure of cosmic knowledge, at last they would learn why it had been necessary to end the world.

The sight of the Ice Palace of Justice sent their buoyant spirits even higher. This was the final great construction project undertaken on earth, Antarctica's omega to ancient Giza's alpha, and its white towers, glittery parapets, frisky pennants, and Gothic windows made the pilgrims stop and gape. The drawbridge trembled under the first wave of darkbloods, the lucky ones who would get seats. The throngs left outside cast their eyes on the great ice tablets that formed the eastern face of Mount Christchurch. DEFENDANTS TO BE ARRAIGNED TODAY, the news sculptors had carved in the slopes in letters three feet high. TRIBUNAL WILL HEAR OPENING ARGUMENTS.

The courtroom was as solemn and self-important as the nave of a cathedral. End-of-summer sunlight streamed through the gut-covered windows, suffusing the air with ghostly cheer. Drooping from the balustrades and beams, a thousand melting icicles ticked away. The bulletproof glass booth in the center of the room had been intended to protect high-roller crap games aboard the *City of New York*; now it protected the Erebus Six. George sat between Brat and Wengernook, the latter sucking violently on an unlit cigarette and tying his fingers in knots. Reverend Sparrow pored over a small Bible. Overwhite napped after a sleepless night induced by darkblood tortures. Randstable worked on converting his suit's primus stove into a device for keeping his cocoa at a constant temperature.

Peering through the frost, George scrutinized the mob in the gallery, face after face, hundreds of them. That woman could almost be Morning – a stronger chin was required. And that one had the red hair for it – if only her mouth were thinner. A pimply boy held up a sign that said, NUKE THEM IN THE EAR.

When the court usher, who bore a detailed resemblance to a rabbit, raised his halberd and rammed it against the floor, everyone rose. From a side door came four judges, dark robes trailing from their helmetless scopas suits. The president of the court, Shawna Queen Jefferson, was a spry little black woman who, as the Mount Christchurch news sculptors had recently revealed, would have become THE MOST CONTROVERSIAL SUPREME COURT JUSTICE IN AMERICAN HISTORY. Kamo Yoshinobu's locked-out intellect had been destined to transform the World Court from a joke into the most respected forum on the planet, an accomplishment that would have brought him the first Nobel Peace Prize ever given to a Japanese citizen. Jan Wojciechowski would have one day exploited the shadowed courtrooms of Cracow to expose the travesty that was Soviet justice. The extinction had robbed Theresa Gioberti of the international acclaim that would have accrued to her even-handed trial of a papal assassin.

'The tribunal will hear the indictment,' said Justice Jefferson upon assuming the bench. Hers was a musical sort of English, vibrant with theoretical experience.

At the translator's table a small army of darkbloods leaned toward an array of battery-powered microphones appropriated from the submarine and rendered the judge's decree into fifty languages.

George glanced at the prosecution table. Alexander Aquinas's staff tormented the tomb inscriber with their manifest maturity. Like a hot air balloon cut free of its moorings, a rotund deputy prosecutor gradually left her chair, indictment at the ready. She attempted no theatrics, just smooth inflections, clean, clear, even a bit diffident.

THE UNADMITTED PEOPLES OF ANTARCTICA

– AGAINST –

ROBERT WENGERNOOK, BRIAN OVERWHITE, MAJOR GENERAL ROGER TARMAC, DR WILLIAM RANDSTABLE, REVEREND PETER SPARROW, GEORGE PAXTON, individually and as members of the following groups and organizations to which they respectively belonged, namely:

The United States Department of Defense, The United States Arms Control and Disarmament Agency, The Joint Chiefs of Staff, The United States Air Force, The Strategic Air Command, The National Security Council, Lumen Corporation, Sugar Brook National Laboratory, The Committee on the Incipient Evil.

Defendants.

THE UNADMITTED PEOPLES OF ANTARCTICA, by the undersigned Alexander Aquinas and staff, duly appointed to represent them in the investigation of the charges herein set forth, pursuant to the McMurdo Sound Agreement and the Charter of this Tribunal, **DO ACCUSE THE ABOVE-NAMED DEFENDANTS** of the following crimes.

Count One. Crimes Against Peace: planning and preparing for a war of aggression, whether or not in violation of the domestic laws of a defendant's country of citizenship.

Count Two. War Crimes: deploying weapons explicitly designed for the wanton destruction of cities, for the slaughter of civilian populations, and for other violations of the laws and customs of war.

Count Three. Crimes Against Humanity: namely, biosphere mutilation, radiation poisoning, superfluous injury, unnecessary suffering, and other cruel and barbaric acts.

Count Four. Crimes Against the Future: namely, planning and preparing for a war of extinction against the human species.

'None of that is true,' George whispered toward his new spermatids. A vulture expert. Everything would be fine as long as the defense could locate a vulture expert.

'The tribunal will arraign the defendants,' said Justice Wojciechowski. 'Robert Wengernook, will you please come before the bench?'

Locking his face in a sneer, the assistant defense secretary did as instructed.

'How do you plead to the charges and specifications set forth in the indictment against you – guilty or not guilty?'

'Not guilty in the sense of the indictment,' asserted Wengernook with a credibility George feared he would be unable to match.

So it went, down the line. Only Reverend Sparrow departed from the script, asserting that he was 'a sinful man, guilty as Adam and Eve, but soon to be redeemed by the Son of Man.'

'A plea of "not guilty" will be entered,' said Justice Wojciechowski. 'George Paxton, will you please come before the bench?'

Ten thousand unadmitted eyes drilled into George as he left the booth and walked across the courtroom.

'How do you plead to the charges and specifications set forth in the indictment against you – guilty or not guilty?'

'Not guilty in the sense of the indictment.' The vaulted ceiling replayed his words, filling his ears with the oddly-timbred, public version of his voice.

There was a flurry of activity at the defense table. Martin Bonenfant, looking younger than ever, leaped up. 'Your Honors, at this juncture we are compelled to challenge the competence of the tribunal.' He waved a document in quick little spirals. 'We request that you accept our petition to have this case immediately severed.' Marching forward, he slapped the document on the frozen bench.

'On what grounds?' asked Justice Jefferson.

'We submit that the deterrence measures specified in the McMurdo Sound Agreement were not recognized as crimes under any statutes, national or international, passed prior to the war. Hence, this tribunal violates the most fundamental principle of justice – *nullum crimen sine lege previa*, no crime without preexisting law. It is an *ex post facto* instrument, organized solely to convict. The six men in the dock are not defendants, they are scapegoats. We further submit that, because your Honors are yourselves unadmitted, you are not qualified to pass judgment on men for whom that race bears an instinctual hatred.'

The president of the court smiled, and the effect was of someone flipping back the dust cover on a piano. She removed her whalebone-framed glasses. 'If you have truly forgotten the legal traditions underlying the trial, Mr Bonenfant, then I commend to your attention the document from which our indictment takes its wording – namely the 1945 London Agreement empowering an international court to prosecute Nazi war criminals in Nuremberg, Germany. As for your second argument, I concede that the loss of the human race stirs every judge on this bench, and that the evidence is likely to arouse our abhorrence. But our professional duty is to restrain such feelings, listening with an impartial ear, and this duty we shall honor.' Justice Jefferson tapped her glasses against the icy bench. 'Petition for severance denied,' she announced in a tone suggesting that, in her canceled life, she had denied many a severance petition.

'The same to your cat, Judge,' muttered Brat.

'All they want is an explanation,' said Overwhite.

'All they want is our ass,' said Wengernook.

'The prosecution will make its opening address,' declared Justice Jefferson.

When Alexander Aquinas stood up, George saw that the forces arrayed against them were formidable indeed. The chief prosecutor was well over six feet tall. His head looked like a sculpture of itself – rough-hewn, bleak, larger than life. His shaggy gray hair and thick neck suggested that he owned lion genes. Slowly he walked to the bench, turned, and stared toward the gallery with the intensity of a man having a private audience with an angel. He smiled.

'That this is the most important legal proceeding of all time cannot be doubted. The great precedents – Jerusalem and the trial of Adolf Eichmann, Nuremberg and the trial of Hermann Goering, Rudolf Hess, and others – will in the early days guide us like beacons set along a storm-lashed shore, but then we must head for open sea, with only our remembered humanity to guide us.'

'He thinks like a girl,' said Brat.

'Shut up,' said Overwhite.

'It is a strange proceeding,' continued Aquinas. 'It is both a war crimes trial and a peace crimes trial, with the peace crimes perhaps being more damnable – certainly more incomprehensible – than the war crimes.' Spinning around, he fired a long, accusing finger toward the glass booth. His eyes trembled in his great skull like poached eggs. 'For these men *knew* what the fusion bomb could do. They *knew* that deterrence through terror, which they misnamed "defense," could not last forever. Indeed, they were often among the loudest, though rarely among the most eloquent, critics of the doctrine of mutual assured destruction.'

George reminded his spermatids that he and his five friends were innocent.

'And yet, in place of mutual assured destruction, they offered nothing. No – worse than nothing. They offered their infatuation with nuclear weapons – an infatuation they expressed in elaborate plans for winning nuclear wars . . . even if winning meant, and I quote from a speech by the defendant Wengernook, "that no enemy are left alive, but two Americans, male and female, have survived to start the race up again." '

'Can't you use a goddamn metaphor any more without being dragged into court?' asked Wengernook.

'Do you really think one man and woman could start everything up again?' asked George.

'Of course,' said Wengernook. 'Assuming they got along.'

A calculated rage was building in Aquinas. 'And the people said, "You must not do this!" And the defendants said, "You cannot stop us!"

'And the people said, "We want to live!" And the defendants said, "The weapons are here to stay!"

'And the people said, "We want grandchildren!" And the defendants said, "Don't be so idealistic!" '

A gallows grew in George's mind, the blood-sculpture that Sverre's navy had fashioned at the celebration banquet. His dark, wet body dripped from the noose. He wondered what it was like to hang. He imagined himself at the moment of release, reaching up, grabbing the rope, hoisting himself back to life with a great muscled arm . . .

'The fusion bomb was a costly mistress. Consider, your Honors. In 1979 this planet celebrated the International Year of the Child. Of the one hundred and twenty-two million children born that year, one of every ten was dead by 1982, and most died for lack of inexpensive food and vaccines. Yet in 1982 the world spent one trillion dollars on weapons. *One trillion dollars!*'

George's arm slipped. The noose tightened.

'Lays it on with a trowel,' said Brat.

'Two trowels,' said Wengernook.

'Let us jump ahead,' said Aquinas. 'In the year of the holocaust, the price of one new missile-carrying submarine equaled the combined education budgets of twenty-three developing countries . . .'

For the next half-hour the chief prosecutor reeled off similar statistics, most of them including the word 'children.'

'Nuclear weapons were the *cheap* defense,' Wengernook explained to his co-defendants. 'Can't anybody get that straight?'

When Aquinas went back to his table, an associate prosecutor gave him hot cocoa while a deputy prosecutor delivered a computer printout.

'At 7:34 on a Saturday morning,' said Aquinas, 'Eastern Standard Time, early warning systems detected the launch of ten Spitball cruise missiles from Soviet long-range manned bombers in a holding pattern near the Arctic Circle. NORAD computers inside Cheyenne Mountain, Colorado, calculated the missiles' trajectories, naming Washington, DC, as their target and giving 9:06 as the estimated time of detonation. A preemptive strike was evidently under way, with decapitation of the American command-and-control infrastructure as its primary objective.'

Aquinas presented the printout to Justice Jefferson, who put on her whalebone glasses and studied it with morbid curiosity.

'At 7:40 all strategic forces were placed on full alert,' the chief prosecutor continued. 'At 7:52 satellite views confirmed that the detection was not due to an anomalous phenomenon. At 8:07 the NORAD computers and the SAC computers began debating their options. At 8:08 the debate ended when the computers voted to recommend anticipatory retaliation against Soviet ICBM fields as per the MARCH Plan. At 8:25 the President was taken from the White House by helicopter to Andrews Air Force Base, where he was subsequently spirited away by an airborne command post and never heard from again . . .

'And so the world went to thermonuclear war. First strike, second strike, third, fourth. Keep it clean. Keep it surgical. Go for the other side's war-waging capability, that's all.' Aquinas gave a small, quick smile. 'Ah, but what if that war-waging capability embraces civilian population centers? There is a breezy little term for this particular brand of nuclear strategy. The term, learned judges, is city-busting.' He hurled his mug across the courtroom, cocoa trailing behind like rocket exhaust. 'But wait!' he screamed as the mug shattered. 'Could not the leaders of the superpowers see that they were dragging the human species into extinction? Of course they could. The leaders of the superpowers, however, were not beholden to the human species, but only to their respective sovereign states. How were they to explain the loss of so much for *nothing?* The destruction of a few cities was not a reason to quit, it was a reason to *risk the rest.*'

Returning to the prosecution table, Aquinas picked up a copy of the McMurdo Sound Agreement.

'Thus were the Major Attack Options implemented,' he said matter-of-factly. 'Thus did the world follow the maps of hell so diligently drawn by Robert Wengernook, Brian Overwhite, Major General Roger Tarmac, Dr William Randstable, Reverend Peter Sparrow, and George Paxton.'

The prosecutor caressed the barbed-wire binding of the agreement. A pearl of black blood appeared on his index finger. He moved the finger across the cover, drawing an X in blood.

'If faced with the unenviable task of defending these six men, I would perhaps argue that they had no choice. Their adversary was piling weapon upon weapon, and their only option was to do likewise. But that is a false argument. It *was* possible to rid the planet of the nuclear threat. Not by organizing a world government or bringing heaven to earth, but by diplomatic measures fully within the defendants' knowledge and capabilities. As the case for the prosecution unfolds, you judges will learn exactly what this solution was. The gravamen of the charges against these men lies in their deliberate refusal to consider it. In short, the prosecution is prepared to prove criminal negligence on a scale the world has never seen before – and will never see again!'

Aquinas sat down and accepted handshakes from his assistants.

Although George's worst fear – that the courtroom would erupt in thunderous applause – was not realized, he did see smiles lighting the faces of almost everyone in the gallery. Many spectators, including several of the Mount Christchurch reporters, pantomimed the act of clapping. A young woman, manifestly gripped by a variety of romantic fantasies involving Aquinas, trembled and wept.

'This guy's full of yams,' said Brat.

'Diplomatic measures – hah,' said Overwhite.

'No doubt he leaves a note to the tooth fairy whenever his dentures fall apart,' said Wengernook.

'I never drew a map of hell,' said George.

'The tribunal will recess for lunch,' said Justice Jefferson.

SEVERANCE PETITION DENIED, proclaimed the slopes of Mount Christchurch. AQUINAS MAKES MAGNIFICENT OPENING ADDRESS.

Slowly, Martin Bonenfant approached the bench. His stride was a kind of ambulatory Rorschach test. One could project anything one fancied into it anxiety hiding behind a facade of confidence, confidence hiding behind a facade of anxiety, anxiety and confidence in dynamic equilibrium.

'Learned judges, citizens of Antarctica, friends.' Bonenfant's words rolled hesitantly from between lips set in the slightest of smiles. 'This morning the prosecution addressed us in the language of passion. I cannot condemn his ploy, for atomic weaponry is an invention worthy of no other emotion save horror. Your verdict, however, will be a judgment not on nuclear war but on policies designed to avert, control, and mitigate nuclear war. This case must be decided on the basis of facts, not feelings.

'The first fact, one you will repeatedly be asked to appreciate in the coming weeks, is the extreme improbability of the recent extinction.' His voice was stronger now, his inflections lilting and smooth. 'If I may use a crude analogy, for I lack Mr Aquinas's way with words, it would be this – the chances of the war unfolding as it did, with such a regrettable outcome, were about the same as those of a woman who takes contraceptive pills getting pregnant by her infertile lover.'

Of the four judges, only Theresa Gioberti seemed offended. The others beat down smiles.

An unlikely extinction, thought George. That's an excellent point, he decided.

'The second fact is that my clients, far from wishing to fight World War Three, devoted their professional lives to its prevention. Look toward the dock. You will see not war planners but patriots. If these men are guilty, your Honors, then their crime is limited to a count not listed in the McMurdo Sound Agreement, a count called "Love of Peace." '

'He's good,' said Wengernook.

'He's very good,' said Brat.

'The only game in town is not necessarily crooked,' said Randstable.

'Which brings us to the third fact,' said Bonenfant. 'The threat to peace. Right before Mr Aquinas gave his address, I bet my two assistants that he would get through it without once mentioning the Russian Communist Empire by name. He never did. Twice he used the word "Soviet," once the word "adversary."'

'Your Honors, do you know what nation, prior to the war, was engaged in the largest military buildup of all time?' The advocate's glossy black hair had taken on a life of its own, slapping his forehead, flying skyward. 'Do you know what nation violated virtually every arms control agreement it ever signed? Slaughtered millions of its own citizens in the name of collectivizing agriculture? Employed illegal chemical and biological weapons in Southeast Asia? Persecuted more Jews than anyone since Adolf Hitler? Routinely imprisoned its pacifists and dissidents in psychiatric hospitals?'

In George's mind the blood-gallows had melted completely away. By God, he thought, we do have a case. We're innocent after all.

'Spreading outward since the October revolution, the cancer of Russian Communism engulfed country after country. Azerbaijan. Armenia. The Ukraine. Estonia. Latvia. Lithuania. Poland. Rumania. East Germany. Hungary. Czechoslovakia. Item – in 1983, a Prague grocery clerk was sentenced to five years at hard labor for possessing an unregistered mimeograph machine. Item – reliable observers report that, as part of its campaign of terror in Afghanistan, the Soviet army air-dropped toys into the villages for the little boys and girls of the tribes. Each toy was equipped with explosives that detonated when picked up, commonly blowing off a child's arm . . .'

Bonenfant had a hundred more items ready. The frigid afternoon disappeared, replaced by a bottomless pit of betrayal and atrocity. Whenever George blinked he saw a little Afghan girl picking up a doll. He could not bring himself to visualize the explosion.

'Why are there no Soviet defendants in this courtroom? Where is the Secretary General of the Communist Party? The Commander in Chief of the Warsaw Pact? The Minister of Defense? Their absence speaks volumes. The framers of the McMurdo Sound Agreement *knew* there was no point in putting Soviets on trial, so manifestly guilty was Moscow of turning the world into an armory and ruining the peace that was my clients' daily dream.'

We're going to win, George told his spermatids.

'Following a mandate from the electorate, acting with the consent of the governed, the men in the dock sought to check the expanding Soviet tumor using whatever technologies were available. Mr Aquinas has questioned the wisdom of defending freedom with thermonuclear weapons. Permit me to enumerate the successes of this doctrine.

'The Berlin airlift. The end of the Korean War. The honorable resolution of the Cuban missile crisis. Analysts have linked all of these triumphs – and more – to US nuclear capabilities. If history teaches us anything, it's that tyrants are tempted by weakness and tempered by displays of strength. Does anyone here seriously doubt that, above all else, the Soviet Union respected military might?'

I certainly don't doubt it, George thought.

'For nearly half a century, peace reigned in Western Europe. Why? NATO's theater nuclear forces. During those same decades, the planet suffered no global-scale wars. Why? America's strategic nuclear forces. This is an astonishing record. Indeed, it is fair to say that, between the Second and Third World Wars, these weapons saved more human lives than penicillin.'

Before hurling out his final sentences, Bonenfant rose to full height. To George, the advocate had never looked more mature.

'And so I ask – who among your Honors, who among the prosecutors, who among the spectators in this courtroom would have dared renounce such a sturdy doctrine, leaping into the awesome uncertainties of a non-nuclear world? Who here would have dared do that? Who?'

As Bonenfant settled behind the defense table, Parkman gave him cocoa capped by two marshmallows. He took a long, leisurely swallow.

Delighted chatter floated through the glass booth. Overwhite remarked that Bonenfant knew his stuff. Wengernook noted that the cancer metaphor was 'unexpectedly rich.' Sparrow complained that the advocate had 'said nothing about their atheism.' Brat asserted that they had 'won the opening round, hands down.' His friends' happiness gave George a satisfaction he had not known since Mrs Covington had unveiled his forthcoming family.

He studied the bench. The faces of Justices Yoshinobu and Gioberti had lost the dark flush of unadmitted blood. Eyes shut, mouth drooping, Justice Wojciechowski looked like a man praying to a god in whom he did not believe.

'The tribunal will recess until nine o'clock tomorrow morning,' said Shawna Queen Jefferson in a hoarse and troubled voice.

'Fellas,' said Randstable, 'I think we've got ourselves a game.'

CHAPTER THIRTEEN

*In Which the Prosecution's Case
Is Said to Be a Grin without a Cat*

Like white paper stalagmites, stacks of documents grew from every flat surface in the courtroom. The documents flowed down the aisles and splashed across the judge's bench. Day after day, each passing with the speed of a snail navigating glue, Aquinas's staff read aloud articles from *Strategic Doctrine Quarterly* by Brat Tarmac. Grim-lipped stenographers scribbled down arms control agreements negotiated by Brian Overwhite. Weary translators repeated descriptions of blueprints bearing William Randstable's name. The tribunal heard speeches by Robert Wengernook, entire bestselling books by Reverend Sparrow, and a scopas suit sales contract signed by George Paxton. Memoranda, monographs, reports, resolutions, directives, letters, field manuals, and Republican Party platforms gradually entered the record.

'The judges are growing restive,' observed Randstable.

'Bored out of their trees,' said Brat.

'Mr Aquinas,' said Justice Jefferson, pushing documents aside with a windshield-wiper sweep of her arm, 'the court believes it is time you examined your first witness.'

Aquinas pulled a deposition from his scopas suit and smoothed it out on the prosecution table.

'In the McMurdo Sound Agreement,' he said, rising, 'a date is written, a date so notorious that few of us are willing to speak its name. On this date the Third World War began. According to another calendar, however – the calendar by which we would all have been admitted – something else happened, would have happened, on this date. On this date certain American citizens would have begun to see a way out of the nuclear miasma. Subsequent days would have found them talking among themselves, and then to their children. The children would have grown up . . . The prosecution calls Brigadier General Quentin Flood, United States Army.'

The witness entered the courtroom at the head of an invisible parade. Assuming the stand, he exuded an aura that George was inclined to call gallantry. He seemed chipped from the Tarmac stone – sturdy, handsome, flamboyant. His scopas suit displayed a mass of ribbons and medals.

'Who could this jerk be?' said Wengernook.

'Leave it to the Army to give the world another asshole,' said Brat.

The rabbity little court usher scurried over, pulled a Bible from his unzipped suit, and asked the witness whether he intended to speak the pure truth. 'I do,' said Flood.

'At what age did you gain the continent?' asked Aquinas.

'Forty-two.'

'According to your memories, would you have founded an organization called Generals Against Nuclear Arms?'

'Correct.'

'Forty-two. That's young for a brigadier general.'

'Mine was a new breed.' Flood had a melodious southern drawl. 'Spoilers, they called us.'

'What did you spoil?'

'Nuclear strategy.'

'As defined by Secretary Wengernook and General Tarmac?'

Bats leave hell more slowly than Bonenfant got up. 'Objection!'

'Try another question, Mr Aquinas,' said Justice Jefferson.

The chief prosecutor grimaced and asked, 'Where did you first encounter traditional nuclear strategy?'

'In articles from *Strategic Doctrine Quarterly*,' answered Flood. 'One was "After Deterrence: Options for the Infra-War Period" by Secretary Wengernook over there. Another was "Our Achilles Leg: Triad Theory and Land-Based Defenses" by Major General Roger Tarmac.'

'What was the philosophy of Generals Against Nuclear Arms?'

'That weapons having absolutely no military utility are unfit to be the centerpiece of a great democracy's defensive posture.'

'It must have been hard converting your elders in the Pentagon to this view.'

'Ever try stuffing a melted marshmallow up a wildcat's ass? It can be done, but you have to like your job.'

Strolling over to the prosecution table, Aquinas snatched up the witness's deposition. 'A famous and influential book you would have written – *Weapons for What?* – would have ended with the statement, quote, "Thus do our nuclear forces corrupt us. They debase and dispirit the ancient and honorable profession of soldiering. They are unpatriotic. We must try to—"'

'Objection!' Bonenfant rose fumingly. 'Your Honors, the defense does not find these glib opinions and unsubstantiated assertions very instructive.'

'Yes – might we hear more of the witness's actual experiences?' Justice Jefferson asked of Aquinas.

'He has no actual experiences.' The chief prosecutor turned toward the bench. 'He's one of—'

'You know what I mean,' admonished Justice Jefferson.

Aquinas made an awkward about-face, grabbing the stand for support. 'I see from your deposition that your group endorsed the Einstein VI Treaty. Generals do not normally sponsor arms control agreements.'

Flood said, 'We had concluded that strategic nuclear weapons, particularly the first-strike arsenals favored by Wengernook and Tarmac, make a nation weaker, not stronger.'

'Because they continually pressure the other side to preempt?'

'Right. The guy who goes first goes best – you can't escape that terrible truth.'

'The guy who goes first goes best,' Aquinas repeated slowly. 'Thank you, General. The witness is yours, Mr Bonenfant.'

As Aquinas returned to his team, the chief counsel ambled forward and offered Flood a good-natured grin.

'Let's get a little blood on the floor, Bonenfant,' said Wengernook.

'You can't play nice with the Army,' said Brat.

'Yeah,' said George.

Bonenfant pointed to the witness's chest. 'Handsome medals you've got there.'

'Thank you,' said Flood.

'I imagine they tell of your meteoric rise to the rank of brigadier general.'

'Some of them would have come after that.'

'Oh? Might any of these medals testify to your talents as a commander in the field?'

Flood tapped a metal sunburst. 'I was awarded this one after Skovorodino.'

'Some of us may not be up on our unadmitted history.'

'Skovorodino would have been a major battle of the Greco-Russian War.'

'Which occurred after the Einstein VI arms control agreement went into effect?'

'Yes.'

'Evidently this treaty you're so fond of permitted further Soviet expansionism.'

'Bull's eye, Bonenfant,' said Wengernook.

'Kid does his homework,' said Brat.

Flood's mouth was as straight and rigid as a chisel mark in a granite tombstone. 'That's hard to say.'

'Would many Americans have died in the Greco-Russian War?' asked Bonenfant.

'Almost two hundred thousand,' said Flood.

'Almost two hundred thousand,' Bonenfant echoed. 'You have much on your conscience, General . . . Now, a little while ago I heard you claim that nuclear weapons have no military utility. Suppose that, as a field commander, you had been charged with repelling an attack on West Germany by the Eighth Soviet Shock Army. Wouldn't a few enhanced-radiation charges be pretty useful to you?'

'West Germany doesn't exist.'

'Just answer the question.'

The general's mouth melted into a frown. 'Battlefield nuclear weapons might have been useful in the immediate crisis. But after that—'

'Useful, did you say?'

'Useful in the—'

'One final question. Exactly how many Soviet officers belonged to this organization of yours?'

'There were no Soviet military officers in Generals Against Nuclear Arms. However, we did—'

'*How* many Soviet officers?'

'None,' grunted the witness.

'Thank you, General Flood.' Bonenfant strutted away from the stand, a smile strung between his bulging cheeks like a hammock.

'We blew him out of the water, don't you think?' said Brat.

'Definitely our inning,' said Wengernook.

'Definitely,' said George.

After lunch Aquinas called to the stand a rosy, elfin woman dressed in a black scopas suit with an inverted collar. She was roly-poly and roly again.

'A lady?' said Brat. 'They're using a lady against us?'

'They're getting desperate,' noted Wengernook.

The witness was sworn in on a Douay Bible, giving her name as Mother Mary Catherine.

'If admitted, would you have been a Catholic priest?' asked Aquinas.

'Yes.'

'Female Catholic priests used to be a rare commodity.'

'Times change.'

'Were you also a Vice President of the United States?'

'I would have been, yes.'

'And did you leave office before serving out your term?'

'When I accepted the second spot on the ticket, I had a secret in my heart.' Mother Mary Catherine's high, scratchy voice suggested an early Hollywood sound film. 'I knew that, shortly after being elected, I would resign over my President's defense policies.'

'And who would that President have been?'

'He's over there in the dock – Reverend Peter Sparrow.'

George glanced at the defendant in question. Flabbergasted by the news of his would-be election, Sparrow alternately smiled and grimaced.

Mother Mary Catherine turned to the bench, winked impishly, and said, 'Be sure to convict that chucklehead. He thinks a country's Christianity is measured by the size of its thermonuclear arsenal.'

Sparrow now wore the look of a boy engaged in wetting his pants.

'Objection!' shouted Bonenfant, rising. 'The witness is giving slander, not testimony!'

As Justice Jefferson instructed the stenographers to delete Mary Catherine's last remark, a glimmer of chagrin crossed the prosecutor's face. He denied his distress with a smile and said, 'Before resigning, you would have used your office in an unorthodox manner.'

'Let's face it, Mr Aquinas, I was a cut-up.'

'Some of your activities—'

'Stunts. They were stunts.'

'Didn't you propose a rather strange arms control agreement?'

'I tried to start something called SWAP – the Strategic Weapons Adjustment Plan.' Mary Catherine folded her hands and placed them on her lap in a neat little bundle. 'The idea was to let the superpowers build any sort of crazy arsenals they wanted, but with the stipulation that they would trade once finished. No quicker way to get the warheads defused, I figured.'

'You also wanted to set up Genocide Prevention Centers.'

'Telephone hotlines staffed twenty-four hours a day. Whenever a missile engineer got the urge to design some fiendish new weapon system, he would call his nearest Genocide Prevention Center and somebody would try talking him out of it.'

'Tell us about the Preschooler Empowerment Act.'

'If adopted, it would have prevented the Pentagon from contracting for a new type of bomber or missile until its pros and cons had been explained to a four-year-old chosen at random from any nursery school in Washington, DC. Whatever the four-year-old decided, that was the weapon's fate.'

A dozen spectators held up a huge banner. WE LOVE YOU, MOTHER MARY CATHERINE, it said.

'I would like the tribunal to know about your National Day of Shame,' said Aquinas.

'My husband's idea, really. We called for everyone involved with thermonuclear weapons – technicians, politicians, professors – to stay out of work for a day. We said that the next morning they should bring in notes from their mothers.'

'Notes saying. . .'

' "My child was absent yesterday because he was sick of being up to his neck in excrement." '

'Nuclear weapons make you mad, don't they, Mother Mary?'

'Mad as a hornet.'

'No further questions.'

In the gallery a second banner was unfurled: MOTHER MARY CATHERINE FOR SAINTHOOD.

'Well, men, what do you think?' said Brat.

'She said nothing we haven't all heard before,' Sparrow replied.

'Except the stuff about your being elected President,' said Wengernook.

'There's no telling what a Christian will be called upon to do,' said Sparrow.

'Congratulations,' said George.

'You would have gotten my vote,' said Brat.

Eyes flashing, mouth set in a formidable smile, Bonenfant charged up to the stand.

'He'd better go easy,' said Wengernook. 'Everybody likes a nun.'

'She's a priest,' said Randstable.

'She's heading for hell,' said Sparrow.

'She's unadmitted,' said Overwhite. 'She's in hell.'

The chief counsel began, 'Miss Catherine – these various antics of yours, how do you suppose they went over in Moscow?'

'I have no idea.'

'The old men in the Kremlin must have been delighted knowing that an American Vice President was calling for SWAP talks and so on.'

'I've never visited the Kremlin.'

'Evidently not. Now, when you first proposed the Soviet Day of Shame, was the plan to hold it simultaneously with the American one? Or did you perhaps neglect to call for a Soviet Day of Shame?'

'My goal was to educate the American public concerning the absurdities of—'

'Just answer the question, please. Did you or did you not call for a Soviet Day of Shame?'

'I did not.'

'He's got her on the run,' said Brat cheerfully.

'Nuns don't hold up over the long haul,' said Wengernook.

'She's a priest,' said Randstable.

'You realize, I am sure,' said Bonenfant, 'that these pacifist ideas of yours go against the Catholic Church's doctrine of just war.' He illustrated the word *pacifist* with a smirk. 'Don't you think perhaps you should have been born a Quaker?'

'I think perhaps I should have been *born*.'

'Did you really *resign* your office, Miss Catherine, or did President Sparrow ask you to step down?'

'I resigned. I announced that I could no longer be part of an administration that slept with genocidal weapons.'

George was impressed by the way Reverend Sparrow managed to confine his fury within a broad, loving smile.

'I imagine the Soviets were sorry to see you out of power,' said Bonenfant. 'No further questions.'

'We used to run into her type around Washington,' said Wengernook. 'Always yelling for peace, as if we were at war. You can't be logical with nuns.'

'She's a priest,' said Randstable.

'Jefferson's becoming fed up, don't you think?' said Wengernook.

'The whole damn *bench* is becoming fed up,' said Brat.

George breathed an elaborate sigh of relief. As a Unitarian, he had always found Catholics frightening and vaguely extraterrestrial, all that blood squirting from Jesus' palms. It could have been much worse.

*

187

The following morning a deputy prosecutor told the tribunal that his team would now be introducing a 'new category of evidence.' They wanted the judges to see 'models of the very instruments through which the defendants had committed the extinction.'

'The court cautions you to keep things moving,' said Justice Gioberti. 'We haven't the luxury of a flexible calendar.'

'Nothing to worry about, your Honors,' replied the deputy prosecutor, a tubby man whose stomach kept billowing out of splits in his scopas suit. 'We have taken steps to guarantee that the presentation will be swift, lucid, and even, if I may be so bold' – he blew on a tin whistle – 'entertaining.'

A quick drum roll drew George's attention to the press box, where the reporters had been evicted in favor of a dance band. The cymbal sounded, the trumpets answered with a salacious fanfare, and then all the musicians launched into an uptempo rendition of 'Swanee River.' A line of attractive female associate prosecutors wearing top hats and spangled scopas suits began parading through the courtroom, each carrying an item from America's pre-war deterrent. Rapidly an ice arsenal accumulated before the bench, dozens of intricately carved replicas. Little frozen missiles piled up, labeled with cardboard tags. Short-range, medium-range, inter-continental. Air-launched, ground-launched, sea-launched. 'Such as Gloria's security, Exhibit G here, a solid propellant, medium-range missile intended for the European theater,' said the deputy prosecutor. 'Exhibit H, currently defending our friend Kimberly, represents America's force of Tomahawk sea-to-surface cruise missiles armed with two-hundred-and-fifty-kiloton . . .'

Warheads appeared. Low-yield, high-yield, enhanced-radiation. 'Exhibit M being an MK-12 reentry vehicle from the Guardian Angel II ICBM. And now the court will please observe Dolores and her Exhibit N, one of the Navy's twenty-kiloton nuclear . . .'

Sea mines were paraded through the courtroom. Nuclear land mines, nuclear torpedos, nuclear free-fall bombs.

After lunch the prosecution unveiled a new branch of the ice arsenal, nuclear-capable and nuclear-armed aircraft. 'Including Shirley's deterrent, Exhibit T, a Macho Mike helicopter equipped with two nuclear depth charges. We now present the category of nuclear-capable and . . .'

Nuclear-armed ships arrived. Carriers, cruisers, destroyers, submarines. 'Such as SSBN 688 *Lyndon Johnson*, a high-speed attack submarine armed with Harpoon missiles. Our final weapon, your Honors, Exhibit W, is being fielded by young Wendy. You will observe that it is not made of ice.'

As the band played 'Camptown Races,' Wendy carried Brat's man-portable thermonuclear device to the bench and set it before Justice Yoshinobu.

'This isn't likely to explode or anything, is it?' asked the judge, hefting the weapon.

'Oh, no,' said the deputy prosecutor. 'The firing procedure involves a twelve-digit code and a little brass key. As we all know from personal experience, your Honors, nuclear weapons are one of the safest technologies ever invented.'

'Place looks like a goddamn toy store,' said Wengernook.

'They're pissed by all this clutter, you can tell,' said Brat.

'Really pissed,' said George. 'Toy store,' he added, fighting tears.

At the end of the second week the prosecution called a silver-haired and aristocratic gentleman named Victor Seabird. He was handsome in the way that only advancing age can be, the handsomeness of a deep-rooted tree or an antique clock.

'Mr Seabird, according to your recollections would you have been the principal American negotiator of the so-called Einstein Treaties?' Aquinas asked.

'That is correct,' said the witness.

Waves of well-being surged through George, as if he were in the presence of Nadine Covington.

'At the time of the holocaust,' said Aquinas, 'nuclear weapons control was the exclusive province of STABLE, the Strategic, Tactical, and Anti-Ballistic Limitation and Equalization talks engineered by the defendant Overwhite. Would the Einstein process have continued his initiatives?'

'We broke completely with the STABLE approach,' answered Seabird. 'It was for shit,' he added brightly.

'That's his opinion,' muttered Overwhite.

'Einstein I outlawed anti-satellite technologies,' said Seabird. 'Einstein II was a comprehensive test ban. Einstein III extended the 1968 nonproliferation treaty. Einstein IV was a moratorium on warhead assembly and land-based missile deployment. Einstein V halted production of weapons-grade material. Einstein VI mandated the destruction of all nuclear stockpiles. Our basic goal, you see, was to—'

'Wait a minute,' interrupted Justice Gioberti. 'Are you saying you would have abolished nuclear weapons?'

'Uh-huh,' said Seabird.

The four judges leaned forward in spontaneous but perfect synchronization.

'That must have been a hard treaty to negotiate,' said Justice Wojciechowski.

'A bear,' said Seabird.

'Did it help when you got that funding increase?' asked Aquinas.

'The budget of the US Arms Control and Disarmament Agency has traditionally been one ten-thousandth the size of the Defense Department's,' said Seabird. 'When we went into Einstein VI, however, we were nearly as big as the Post Office.'

'Some of us on the bench are surprised that the Soviets signed Einstein VI,' said Justice Wojciechowski.

'Their motives, I believe, were economic. Totalitarian socialism is a foolish enough way to run a country without throwing in an arms race.'

For the next four hours Seabird outlined the details of the abolition regime. Nations included . . . technologies banned . . . timetables . . . verification . . .

'Verification,' said Aquinas. 'I imagine that took several barrels of midnight oil to work out.'

'God, yes. Don't remind me.' When Seabird smiled, another well-being wave hit George. 'Of course, with an abolition regime, verification is easier than with a more limited agreement, in that a single sighting of a banned weapon is sufficient to prove a violation.'

'Still, no verification system is perfect,' said Justice Gioberti.

'That's where the space forts came in,' said Seabird. 'Orbiting platforms armed with charged-particle beams that could kill enemy missiles during the boost phase. Einstein VI encouraged the nuclear powers to pursue this technology, along with unarmed interceptor-rockets and ground-based laser defenses.'

'America would have taken the lead here, as I recall,' said Aquinas.

'When the Soviet space forts proved unreliable, we saw no alternative but to ship them a few of our prototypes.'

'Let me get this straight,' said Justice Gioberti. 'You *gave* this technology to the Soviets?'

'As you might imagine, your Honors, it's frightfully de-stabilizing for only one nuclear power to be building effective ballistic missile defenses.'

'Do space forts render civilian populations invulnerable?' Aquinas asked.

'In an all-out attack, many cities would still have been lost. The forts were essentially a hedge against cheating.'

'So space-based defenses make little sense in the absence of disarmament?'

'Without Einstein VI, it's a fair guess – I'm certain of it really, when I look at history – a fair guess that the space forts would have carried the traditional arms race into whole new realms of psychosis.' Seabird indicated the frozen missiles piled up before the bench. 'The nuclear powers would have sought to overwhelm each other's forts with huge offensive deployments.'

'Were there any other hedges against cheating?'

'The treaty allowed its signers to build fallout shelters to a fare-thee-well, and even to adopt those weird crisis relocation schemes – you know, where they take everybody out into the country? It also permitted extensive modernization of conventional forces in Europe. After all, this was the real world we were talking about.'

George wondered exactly how Bonenfant was going to rip

apart Einstein VI. Why would Bonenfant want to rip apart Einstein VI? asked his spermatids. To help our case, he replied.

'It must have been a great day when this agreement went into effect,' said Aquinas.

'Two intermediate-range missiles kicked off the regime,' said Seabird. 'The UN brought them here to Antarctica. I watched the whole thing on television. My family and me, my grandchildren. I'll never forget. Who could forget? High noon, Greenwich Mean Time. Ross Island, Antarctica. The ceremony began with a team of scientists removing the fissionable material from the warheads and turning it over to the Nuclear Regulatory Commission, which later diluted it with uranium-238 and burned it up in a Brazilian nuclear power plant.'

'So the missiles were now disarmed . . .'

'An American MacArthur III and a Soviet SS-90. The Army Corps of Engineers carried them to the top of the Mount Erebus volcano and suspended them on chains. And then all these teen-agers, about a dozen high-school students from different countries, they started cranking the windlass and lowering the missiles into the crater. First the one with the American flag on its side – the kids melted it. Then the one with the hammer and sickle—'

As when a shower rushes on an unsuspecting picnic, Victor Seabird began suddenly to cry. His sobs echoed off the slick white walls of the Ice Palace. Aquinas comforted the negotiator with an unembarrassed hand on his shoulder.

'These are painful memories,' said the prosecutor.

'A few minutes later the celebrations started.' Seabird removed tears from his cheeks with little flicks of his index finger. 'It was like . . . I don't know. Like when your team wins the World Series on a ninth-inning homer or something.' The witness's voice became a rasp as he described how people celebrated Einstein VI – how they honked their car horns, blew factory whistles, drank toasts, closed schools, took the afternoon off, observed moments of silence, threw parties, went to church, smiled at strangers . . . 'Stevie went marching around the house. He was three. He had this little American flag. "Granddaddy got rid of the bombs!"

he kept shouting. "Granddaddy got—" ' Despair jammed the negotiator's throat.

The silence was long and thick. George's bullet wound throbbed. All he could imagine was Holly marching through Victor Seabird's house, waving the Stars and Stripes. He saw her doing a silly dance with Stevie.

We're sunk, aren't we? his spermatids asked. Not if a vulture expert shows up, he replied.

Slowly, grandly, Aquinas said, 'No further questions.'

And then it came. The applause. It shook the gallery and laid siege to the glass booth. Overwhite pushed his gloved hands against his ears. When the tumult finally subsided, Justice Jefferson invited Bonenfant to cross-examine.

'There are all kinds of problems with that abolition proposal,' said Overwhite, lowering his hands.

'If Bonenfant is any good, he'll eat it for breakfast,' said Wengernook.

'Remember when they tried to get rid of booze in the twenties?' said Brat. 'A disaster.'

George admitted to his spermatids that he was very confused.

'Mr Seabird,' said Bonenfant, closing for combat, 'I fail to see any ultimate merit in your Einstein VI treaty. Like all such utopian schemes, it depended on trusting a country that had lied about its missile installations in Cuba, had shot down a defenseless Korean airliner . . . the list is endless.'

'Well, the pre-abolition world entailed quite a bit of trust, too, don't you think?' said Seabird. 'Every day, those defendants over there trusted the Soviets not to try a preemptive strike. They trusted them to construct failsafe launch-control devices . . . Utopian? Well, I wouldn't call it that, not when you consider all the renegotiating we did. We had a Standing Consultative Commission on Einstein VI Violations, and I don't think a week went by without a squawk from one side or the other.'

'So you admit that the whole thing would have eventually broken down?'

'We believed that the worst possible situation was the one that had existed – fifty thousand bombs held in check by terror and luck. Vice President Mother Mary Catherine had convinced us that nuclear arsenals were the great evil of the twentieth century, just as slavery had been the great evil of the nineteenth century. The weapons had to be banished.'

'Sheer fantasy. People would always know how to create nuclear arms.'

'People would always know how to create slaves, too.'

'Russia was a huge country. What if the Soviets had squirreled away a few hundred bombs before Einstein VI was signed? Suppose they secretly developed a delivery system capable of penetrating your space forts? They could have demolished America with a bolt from the blue.'

'Yes, but they would have assumed appalling risks.'

'I don't see any risks.'

'Under Einstein VI, deterrence remained in effect.'

Bonenfant made a great show of stifling a grin. 'Deterrence? Without weapons?'

Deterrence? thought George. Without weapons?

'Yes. That's what we called it, in fact. Weaponless deterrence.'

'Now we've really gone through the looking glass.'

'It's like this. One day we said, "Isn't there a significant difference between a nation that has never been a nuclear power and a nation that was once a nuclear power and is now disarmed?" And we answered, "Yes, there is. The second nation still has a deterrent. The deterrent is the capacity to rearm."'

Deep ruts appeared in Justice Jefferson's brow. 'That sounds like a pretty flimsy deterrent to us, Mr Seabird.'

'Not really a deterrent at all,' said Justice Yoshinobu.

The witness raised his hands in a braking gesture. 'Under Einstein VI every side maintained hardened, well-defended factories for the purpose of building new arsenals should an adversary be caught cheating. If I remember right, a typical lead time was four weeks to the production of eighty warheads plus cruise missiles to deliver them.'

In the tone of a teenager dealing with a naive little brother, Bonenfant said, 'So the Soviets wipe out your cities and then sit around drinking vodka for four weeks, waiting for you to rearm and fight back?'

'With weaponless deterrence, the Soviets do not attack in the first place. Given the space forts, the civil defense programs, the possibility of reciprocal cheating, the limited size of Russia's clandestine arsenal, and America's latent potential to retaliate, there are too many uncertainties.'

'Sounds like the same old stalemate,' said Justice Wojciechowski.

'This was a new kind of stalemate. It had the advantage of not occurring on the edge of an infinite abyss.'

'Your regime was really just a method of buying time, wasn't it?' asked Justice Jefferson.

'Time,' echoed Seabird softly. 'Good old time,' he muttered.

'Rather like the policies of my clients,' said Bonenfant smoothly. 'No further questions.'

Justice Jefferson removed her whalebone glasses and stared into blurry space. Her eyes darted rapidly, powered by agitated thoughts.

'Is that abolition stuff really true?' asked George.

'It's a load of camel dung,' answered Brat.

'He's making it all up,' asserted Wengernook.

'The Scriptures say nothing about it,' noted Sparrow.

'If they'd given me the goddamn Post Office's budget,' said Overwhite, 'I might have brought off a few miracles too.'

AQUINAS TO CALL FINAL WITNESS TOMORROW, Mount Christchurch proclaimed.

Hearing his name, Jared Seldin, a small, thin boy with hair suggesting some futuristic strain of wheat, wandered into the courtroom. When he grasped the Bible to be sworn in, its weight nearly knocked him flat. The witness's face was as dark and vibrant as polished oak. He gave his age as eight.

Eight, thought George. Too old to believe in Santa Claus, old enough to ride a two-wheeler.

Aquinas approached the stand cautiously, as if trying to get a better view of a fawn. 'What century would you have been born in, Jared?'

'Let's see, 2134 . . . that's the twenty-second century.'

'And where would you have lived?'

'Habitat-Seven.'

'Is that a country?'

'A what?'

'A country.'

'What's a country?' asked the boy.

'Hard to explain . . . Now, how would you describe Habitat-Seven?'

'Kind of an asteroid, I guess, all hollow inside, with a ramjet. It could go at speeds close to light, 'cause we had this big funnel in front that scooped up hydrogen atoms and sent them into this fusion engine, and then the atoms go *whoosh* out the back. We had plans to visit a star.'

'What star?'

'I forget. It had a planet.'

'Did you *like* Habitat-Seven, as far as you can remember?'

'It was a lot nicer than Antarctica.'

'Yes, Jared, it must have been.'

'I would have had a puppy. His name would have been Ralph. Why does everything have to be so sad, Mr Aquinas?'

'I don't know. Tell me, Jared, did the people in Habitat-Seven ever get into a war?'

'Is that like a country?'

'It's . . . you know. A war.'

'A war?'

'A war.'

'I don't understand, Mr Aquinas.'

Bonenfant rose, his eyes hurling freshly sharpened daggers in Aquinas's direction. 'Your Honors, I move that all of this witness's testimony be stricken. He possesses no expertise concerning nuclear weapons.'

'Mr Aquinas, are you planning to take up a more relevant line of questioning?' asked Justice Jefferson.

'Jared Seldin's testimony serves to underscore the defendants' lack of vision,' said Aquinas.

'Lack of vision is not a crime, sir,' said Justice Jefferson.

'Negligence then,' said the prosecutor. 'Criminal negligence.'

'The decision on this motion is mine, Mr Aquinas, not yours,' said Justice Jefferson, 'and I am now ruling that Jared Seldin's testimony be removed from the record in *toto*.'

Brat and Wengernook toasted each other with cocoa mugs.

'That concludes the case for the prosecution,' said Aquinas in a small, gelded voice.

'Case?' said Brat. 'What case?'

'I didn't hear any case,' said Wengernook.

The chief prosecutor returned to his table wearing an inverted smile, as if fishhooks were tugging at the corners of his mouth.

'The part about eliminating the weapons was interesting, don't you think?' said George.

'Weaponless deterrence is like bodiless sex,' said Wengernook. 'It gets you nowhere.'

'A grin without a cat,' said Randstable.

'Smoke,' said Brat.

'Particularly when your agency is inadequately funded,' said Overwhite.

If Holly had lived, wondered George, would she have traveled to Mars?

CHAPTER FOURTEEN

In Which the Nuclear Warriors
Have Their Day in Court

On the seventeenth of March, as the long polar night crept across the continent, creating glaciers of coal and bergs of pitch, Martin Bonenfant opened the case for the defense.

Throughout the courtroom lampwicks flared, fed by oil from killer whales and Weddell seals. Jagged shadows slithered around the glass booth. Bonenfant's young face glowed orange, as if a candle burned inside his skull.

'Call Major General Roger Tarmac.'

Fearlessly, Brat rose.

'You're gonna be great,' said Wengernook.

'Break a leg,' said Randstable, who was setting up his little magnetic chess set.

'Good luck,' said George, whose mind was crowded with images of high-school students lowering intermediate-range missiles into a volcano.

Prompted by Bonenfant, Brat offered a rousing account of his Indiana boyhood, from which the tribunal learned that he had on two different occasions prevented school chums from drowning in the Muscatatuck River. Then came the Air Force Academy, a juggernaut progression through the ranks, and a brilliant career as a target nominator for the Strategic Air Command in the former city of Omaha.

'Several days ago,' said Bonenfant, 'your name was mentioned during the testimony of Quentin Flood, founder of an organization called Generals Against Nuclear Arms.'

Brat polished his Distinguished Service Medal with his scopas glove. 'He took exception to one of my articles, "Our Achilles Leg: Triad Theory and Land-Based Defenses." '

'That article identified a problem with your country's Guardian Angel missiles,' said Bonenfant.

'America's security has traditionally stood on three legs – the Triad. First, you had your submarine-launched ICBMs. Then you had your manned bombers. And the third force, which I called our Achilles Leg – that was the Guardian Angel land-based missiles.'

'Why had they become an Achilles Leg?'

'Because of the SS-6o – four hundred and thirty highly accurate Soviet ICBMs designed to remove our Guardian Angels in a first strike.'

'A frightening development.'

'After such an attack, an American President would have only two options – he could surrender, or he could retaliate against Soviet cities.' Brat chopped the air with his hand. 'But that would naturally bring reciprocal measures, and then he's *really* in thick shit.'

'And your solution was . . . ?'

'Missile Omega.'

'The Omegas were effective against the new Soviet missiles?'

'Such targets place a premium on response time. Omega is a fast mother. She also has terrific accuracy, long range, and ten high-yield warheads on her business end.'

'Did you ever hear the argument that without a survivable basing mode' – Bonenfant fixed his mouth in a condescending curve – 'Omega had little retaliatory potential and was thus a so-called "first-strike weapon"?'

'We've never given up on the basing problem.'

'What modes have you studied?'

The general splayed his fingers and began ticking them off. 'So far we've considered basing the missiles in blimps, underwater canisters, circular trenches, coal mines, and barges on the Mississippi River.'

'You should have based them up your ass!' a young woman

called from the gallery. It took Justice Jefferson a full minute of gavel pounding to quell the laughter.

'You had an unusual nickname around SAC,' said Bonenfant.

'I was the MARCH Hare,' replied Brat. 'Modulated Attacks in Response to Counterforce Hostilities.'

'Some people have accused the MARCH Plan of being a war-winning scenario disguised as a deterrent.'

'The very best way to prevent a nuclear war is to show that you believe you can win one.'

'The court may have trouble—'

'Forces that cannot win cannot deter. Is *that* clear?'

'It's certainly clear to me. No further questions.' Bonenfant walked away from the stand with the self-satisfied air of a cat bringing a mouse to the back stoop.

Justice Jefferson invited the chief prosecutor to cross-examine.

'He was swell, don't you think?' said Randstable, concentrating on the chessboard, where he was about to launch a king-side attack against himself.

'A real pro,' said Wengernook.

'He certainly gave them the sort of data they're looking for,' said Overwhite.

Forces that cannot win cannot deter. George thought about this particular truth as hard as he could.

'General Tarmac,' said Aquinas, sidling up to the stand, 'I'm bewildered by your Achilles Leg notion. Weren't America's land-based missiles kept in concrete silos?'

'The new Soviet SS-6os had a hard-target kill capacity,' Brat explained patiently.

'Hard target?'

'An ICBM silo is a hard target.'

'As opposed to a soft target?'

'Right. We worked long hours on silo hardness, but there are limits – two thousand pounds per square inch or so.'

'In other words, this whole arms race can be traced to a lot of men trying to get it hard enough?'

'You can joke about it, Prosecutor, but a vulnerable land-based force is no laughing matter.'

Aquinas assumed a posture of dismay. 'But didn't the Triad, being so redundant, allow for vulnerabilities to emerge from time to time?'

'We had a serious parity problem when it came to land-based missiles,' answered Brat. 'We needed the Omegas.'

'Are you saying that the Triad was ill-conceived, and America should have been mimicking Communist strategy instead?'

'No, I'm saying that the Russians had more land-based missiles than we did. Why is that so hard to understand?'

'And you really believed they were about to take out your own fixed ICBMs in a nuclear Pearl Harbor?'

'This was on the low end of the probability curve, but we were still worried.'

'And, before the Omega program, the Soviets could have expected to get away with such an attack?'

'Right.'

'After which you would have to surrender?'

Brat gulped down his annoyance. 'Yes.'

'Why?' asked Aquinas.

'We would have been disarmed.'

'Couldn't the American President have used the two surviving legs to disarm the Soviets in turn?'

'Be logical. If the SS-60s have already hit us, then their silos are empty.'

'So you have to surrender?'

'Yes.'

'Why?'

'I just explained that. We've been disarmed.'

'So have the Soviets. You just explained that, too.'

'They've probably kept a reserve force,' Brat noted.

'Then you *could* retaliate,' Aquinas replied.

'No. The enemy would protect the reserve.'

'How?'

'By launching it.'

'So you have to surrender?'

'Yes!'

'Why?'

'How many times do I have to say it?' Brat snapped an icicle off the stand and crushed it. 'We've been disarmed! Can't you grasp the most elementary piece of strategic doctrine?'

'Suppose that, instead of surrendering, the President ordered the strategic submarine fleet to destroy Soviet society?'

'No President would answer a surgical strike with an all-out attack. That's jumping far too many rungs on the escalation ladder.'

'How many American civilians would have been killed in this surgical strike?'

'Worst-case scenario is twenty-five million.'

'Might not a President mistake such slaughter for an all-out attack?'

'Not if he was willing to calm down for a minute and look at *how* those casualties occurred.'

The interview continued in this manner for over an hour, interrupted by a recess for a box lunch of hardboiled penguin eggs and blubber sandwiches, until Aquinas suddenly asked, 'Wasn't Omega in fact a first-strike weapon, General Tarmac?'

'No,' Brat replied.

'What was it?'

'It was a functional and credible second-strike retaliatory deterrent.'

'A sure-fire deterrent?'

'A functional and credible second-strike—'

'No further questions,' grunted the chief prosecutor, lurching away from the stand in a spasm of exasperation.

Brat rose, folding his arms across his chest. The interview seemed to have bestowed about twenty pounds on him. He sauntered back to the booth and asked, 'So – how'd I do?'

'Academy Award time,' said Wengernook.

'Hope I come off half as well,' said Randstable, putting himself in check.

'I hadn't realized that forces that cannot win cannot deter,' said George.

Overwhite was next on the stand. The oil lamps sprinkled flecks of bronze onto his snowy beard as he narrated his life's story

– the Foreign Service, the Diplomatic Corps, the State Department, and, finally, the Arms Control and Disarmament Agency. To George, Overwhite still seemed like a windbag, but he was obviously a resourceful and intelligent one, a windbag woven of the finest material.

'Two treaties that you helped negotiate have been read into the record by the prosecution,' said Bonenfant. 'Evidently my learned opponent feels that your efforts did not go far enough.'

'I can see Mr Aquinas's point of view,' replied Overwhite, examining himself for jaw tumors. 'However, let me remind the tribunal that general and complete disarmament was always the stated goal of my agency. Unfortunately, the massive Soviet buildup made this impossible in our time.'

'But your achievements were still impressive.'

'Any man would be proud to have on his tombstone, "He negotiated STABLE I and STABLE II." '

Design No. 4015, thought George. Vermont blue-gray.

After reviewing the details of both STABLE agreements, Bonenfant concluded that, 'We might well have introduced them as exhibits for the defense.'

Overwhite agreed.

Bonenfant said, 'Critics have charged that the STABLE treaties allowed the US military too much latitude with multiple warheads and cruise missiles.'

'I can understand that sentiment,' said Overwhite. 'However, you should always remember that new systems become bargaining chips when you sit down at the negotiating table. They force the Soviets to get serious about reductions.'

'Excuse me,' said Justice Wojciechowski. 'You seem to be saying that by declining to regulate particular weapons, you were serving the cause of arms control.'

'My point is that technical innovation has diplomatic as well as military benefits.'

Bonenfant asked, 'In retrospect, Mr Overwhite, could your agency have done anything more to prevent the recent war?'

'If we knew for a fact that it was coming – yes, we would probably have pressed for certain confidence-building measures.

For example, the hotline between Washington and Moscow badly needed upgrading.'

'Well, nobody can blame you for not owning a crystal ball.'

'I would have trouble empathizing with such an attitude.'

'No further questions.' Returning to the defense table, Bonenfant sniffed emphatically, as if his nose could barely accommodate all the victory it sensed in the sub-zero air.

'Why does not regulating weapons serve the cause of arms control?' George asked Brat.

'Brian just explained that,' the general replied.

'This trial must be pretty boring for a guy like you,' said Wengernook.

'I'm not bored,' said George.

The chief prosecutor approached the stand carrying a slab of ice under his arm. 'Mr Overwhite, if complete disarmament was so dear to your agency's heart, why didn't you ever propose an abolition treaty?'

'Well, as soon as you entertain radical proposals, you run into horrendous problems deciding which technologies to ban and which to allow. Take delivery systems . . .'

'Why are delivery systems hard to negotiate?' Aquinas knitted his momentous brow.

'Because as warheads get smaller, almost anything can be a delivery system. A Wasp-13 manned bomber is obviously a delivery system, but what about a Piper Cub? What about a hot air balloon?'

'So you never eliminated any missiles or bombers because you couldn't tell them from hot air balloons?'

'I'm saying it's a real pain arriving at certain definitions.'

'It's a real pain having your face burned off, too.'

Bonenfant rose. 'Your Honors, might we declare a moratorium on cheap shots?'

'The court was not amused by that last remark, Mr Aquinas,' said Justice Jefferson.

Aquinas made a modest bow and renewed the examination. 'STABLE I dealt with missile launchers, right? Each side was granted eight hundred fifty-six submarine tubes and eleven hundred seventy-five hardened silos.'

'Those were the limits.'

'They don't sound very limiting.'

'If you let the numbers get too Spartan, Mr Aquinas, you increase the temptation to strike first.'

'So it was inconceivable that you would ever negotiate the launchers down to zero?'

'We felt it best to err on the side of safety.'

Aquinas held a seal-oil lamp near his ice slab. Graphs and statistics danced in the spectral glow. 'STABLE II addressed the bombs themselves . . .'

'We put ceilings on fractionation – twelve warheads per missile.'

'According to my arithmetic, the number of warheads on both sides increased dramatically after STABLE II.'

'But each missile carried only a dozen.'

'Mr Overwhite, did you ever tell a *Time* magazine reporter, quote, "We must not saddle the economy with agreements negotiated just to impress the public"?'

'I was thinking of those men who wouldn't be showing up for work if, say, the Omega program were suddenly canceled,' Overwhite knocked frost from his beard. 'We had to keep the arms control process from, you know . . .'

'Escalating?'

'Falling prey to special interests.'

'Let's talk about bargaining chips.'

'Very well.'

'Could you please name three fully developed offensive weapon systems that your team relinquished at the negotiating table in exchange for concessions by the Soviets?'

'We were always retiring bombs and missiles as they became obsolete.'

'That's not the question. I want you to name three systems that were bargained away.'

'I can't think of three off hand.'

'Can you name two?'

'Not two exactly, no.'

'Can you name one?'

'Well, as you can readily imagine, once a new weapon is actually in production, it becomes more valuable as a deterrent than as a chip.'

'Mr Overwhite, it seems to me that, when all is said and done, you and the arms builders were really in the same line of work.'

'Your bitterness is quite understandable, Mr Aquinas. Your conclusion, however, is not.'

The chief prosecutor shuddered theatrically and told the court that he had no more questions.

'That was an excellent point about general and complete disarmament,' said Randstable, tipping over his king to concede defeat to himself.

'He was in charge all the way,' said Wengernook.

From the gallery a red-faced old man called, 'Hey, Overwhite, here's a weapon for you to control!' He stood up and hurled an icicle shaped like an independently targetable warhead. The malicious little cone zoomed through the frosty air, missing the negotiator's head by an inch.

That was uncalled for, George decided.

The next morning the court heard the autobiography of Dr William Randstable, who had worn almost as many hats in his life as there were in Theophilus Carter's inventory. Chess prodigy. Inventor of the popular computer game *Launch on Warning* (the royalties had put him through M.I.T.). Author of the bestselling science fiction novel, *The Dark Side of the Sun*. Youngest whiz kid at the think tank known as Lumen Corporation. Head of the Missile Accuracy Division at Sugar Brook National Laboratory.

'I'm impressed already,' said Wengernook.

'They don't hang guys like this,' said Brat.

'I've always wondered what it's like to be smart,' said George.

Randstable finished explaining how he had checkmated a Russian grand master who was also a KGB agent.

Bonenfant said, 'Now during your early days at the Lumen think tank, you—'

'Think tank – is that a kind of weapon?' asked Justice Yoshinobu.

'No, not a weapon, your Honor,' said Randstable.

'I picture a Sherman tank with a disembodied human brain inside,' said the judge.

'That's actually an interesting idea . . .' Randstable pulled off his horn-rimmed glasses and chewed contemplatively on the ear piece. 'The electroneural interface would be the trickiest—'

'The what?' asked Justice Gioberti.

'Wetware modem,' said Randstable. 'Inter*face* is, now that I think about it, a misnomer, since you'd be removing the cranium and stripping out the eyes, nose, and other material.' He elaborated for several minutes, until Justice Wojciechowski interrupted to remind him that he was on trial for his life. 'Oh, sorry,' said the former whiz kid, 'Excuse me.'

'Tell us something about Lumen,' said Bonenfant.

'Our group analyzed the logical difficulties raised by the superpower arsenals. The epistemological pitfalls of assured destruction, for example, or the tautologies encountered while climbing the ladder of escalation.'

'What did you do about these problems?' asked Justice Gioberti.

'We thought about them.'

'A nerve-wracking job, I imagine,' said Bonenfant.

'God, yes. When Sugar Brook Lab made me an offer, I jumped at it.'

'I believe you directed their Inertial Guidance Project.'

'Whenever a nuclear missile came my way, I made it more accurate.'

'How accurate?'

'Imagine Robin Hood standing in Nottingham Square and shooting the apple off William Tell's kid in Switzerland.'

Bonenfant issued a slow-motion smile. 'What was the ultimate result of inertial guidance?'

'A safer world,' said Randstable.

'A safer world?'

'Sounds paradoxical, huh? But when you know for sure you

can stand on the old pitcher's mound and throw a strike – that is, when you're certain of taking out any given silo or command post – the amount of overkill you need goes way, way down.'

The chief counsel handed his client a large piece of sealskin framed in bone. Two line graphs were painted on one side of the membrane. 'So as missiles become more accurate, they become less destructive?' Bonenfant asked.

'Exactly. Now as you can see, ever since the early sixties, mega-tonnage has steadily decreased in both America and the Soviet Union.'

'How did your guidance device work?'

The years dropped from Randstable like a heavy overcoat. He was Willie the Wunderkind again. 'The basic unit was a beryllium ball chock full of gyros and accelerometers,' he said with the zest of a boy discussing electric trains. 'Now, my idea was to float the thing inside another ball filled with a nonconducting liquid having neutral buoyancy. Presto! All during flight, the gyros keep warm and steady in their hydrocarbon bath. A human embryo is protected in much the same way.'

'You also supervised the Smart Warheads Project.'

'This approach allowed even greater targeting precision. Each warhead got its own personal computer, right? It could then compare, pixel by pixel, a radar picture of the target terrain with a stored reference image.'

George liked the word *pixel*. It sounded like something an elf would use for self-gratification.

'Did Sugar Brook develop the ground-launched Homing Hawk ballistic missile interceptor?' Bonenfant asked.

'Yes,' said Randstable.

George remembered that he had been planning to tell Holly a story about an elf who casts a golden shadow.

'I guess it was a great day when you proved that a Homing Hawk could destroy an incoming warhead,' said Bonenfant.

'We broke out the champagne and got a little bombed.'

'Your Homing Hawk was actually a forerunner of the space-based defenses Mr Seabird praised so lavishly in his testimony on Einstein VI.'

'I guess it was.'

'You must feel good about that.'

'I feel good about all of Sugar Brook's accomplishments.'

'The prosecution, I am sure, will suggest that Sugar Brook was a dealer in the death trade, a cornucopia of demonic devices . . . I apologize if I'm stealing your rhetoric, Mr Aquinas.'

'That's quite all right,' said the chief prosecutor.

'What business were you *really* in, Dr Randstable?'

'The business of making nuclear weapons obsolete.'

'No further questions.'

Bonenfant danced merrily back to the defense table.

'That was good, when he mentioned making them more accurate,' said Brat.

'The part about making them obsolete, that was good too,' said George.

After removing his right glove, Aquinas ran an extended index finger along the comforting decline on the sealskin graph. 'An impressive picture.'

'I think so,' said Randstable.

'Do you truly believe that the megatonnage would have just kept dropping?' the chief prosecutor asked.

'I do.'

'Down past the extinction threshold?'

'That's what our extrapolations suggested.'

'There's another side to this accuracy business, isn't there?'

'What do you mean?'

'As missiles become more accurate, they also become more usable.'

'Yes, but if you ever get to that, it's better to have usable missiles than unusable ones.'

'Dr Randstable, wasn't it rather bizarre to be perfecting all these clever technologies knowing that their purpose was essentially psychological – that if they were actually fired, then the world would be better off if they *didn't* work?'

'Pessimism had no place at Sugar Brook.'

'Tell me honestly, did you ever pretend that a missile had been successfully tested even though it had gone down in flames?'

'No.'

'I mean, so long as the Soviets *believed* the thing worked, its deterrent value remained the same. We could have built our whole arsenal out of uncooked spaghetti, right?'

'My client has already answered that question,' said Bonenfant, rising.

'Let it go, Mr Aquinas,' said Justice Jefferson.

When George glanced toward the gallery, he saw that several spectators had opened their veins with razor blades. The steaming blood spelled out SMART WARHEADS ARE A STUPID IDEA in tall, dripping characters.

'You must have been happy when Sugar Brook became the prime contractor for the Homing Hawk interceptor,' said Aquinas.

'Well, sure. I mean, we were in this life-and-death struggle with Winco Associates and General Heuristics.'

'And then, when you got the Hawks to work, you celebrated with champagne?'

'That's right.'

'*Newsweek* reported that you drank to "a bad night in the Kremlin." '

'To "a sleepless night in the Kremlin," actually.'

'You didn't foresee any sleepless nights in the White House?'

'I can't grasp your logic.'

'Well, each Hawk you deployed would have further blunted Russia's retaliatory capability, until mutual deterrence was virtually nonexistent. Thinking that America was about to strike first, the Soviets might have struck first.'

'When America had a nuclear monopoly, we did not strike first.'

Aquinas pulled a folder from one of the evidence piles and shoved it into Randstable's lap. 'I would refer you to Document 476, the 1951 edition of the SPASM, the Single Plan for Aligning the Services of the Military. As you know, it calls for the complete pulverization of the Soviet Union – the nuclear strip mining of an entire nation – in response to conventional aggression against Western Europe.'

'That was a long time ago.'

'To me, Dr Randstable, everything was a long time ago. No further questions.'

The engineer gangled his way back to the booth and asked, 'Well, what's the verdict?'

'You stood your ground,' said Wengernook.

'I think we're on top of this thing,' said Brat.

'I couldn't follow the part about the embryo,' said George.

During lunch – the defendants could choose between killer whale chowder and cold boiled skua – Randstable showed George some chess openings, then challenged him to a game, offering the tomb inscriber a rook advantage and the first move. George had not played since junior high school, but he thought it might be fun to lose to somebody who had beaten a Russian grand master.

Reverend Sparrow testified next. In a voice that blasted its way into icy nooks and crannies never before visited by human speech, the evangelist told the tribunal how, as an adolescent mired in 'a slimy pit of drugs and fornication,' he had one night reached into his parents' collection of X-rated videocassertes and inadvertently grasped a Bible. He began reading it. He could not put it down. A year later he was attending the Coral Gables Theological Seminary. Before the decade was out, his cable television channel had more subscribers than any except the one sponsored by *Crotch* magazine, and he had become the youngest person ever to chair the celebrated right-wing Committee on the Incipient Evil.

'This guy makes me nervous,' said Wengernook.

'No, no, it's good he's on the team,' said Brat. 'We need a religious component.'

'Your bestselling book,' said Bonenfant, '*Christians Will Come Through the First Strike*, argued that as the millennium approached, certain Biblical prophecies would be fulfilled. How do your interpretations square with the recent Soviet-American exchange?'

'The Hebrew prophets were right on the money.' The evangelist unzipped his scopas gear and pulled his little Bible from the vest of his three-piece suit. 'As you know, that war destroyed the temple at Jerusalem, a prelude to what Christians call the Perfect Exile. In the Perfect Exile, the church – those who have accepted

Jesus – is cleaved into seven segments and transported to the far corners of the earth. Which explains why I'm here. If you look in the North Pole and other remote places, you will find boatloads of Christians.'

'And after the Perfect Exile?'

'More explosions – though of course they cannot touch the church. So destructive are these bombs that the survivors succumb to a man who promises peace. But who is he? The Antichrist, that's who.'

For the first time in his life, George realized what an intrinsically boring religion Unitarianism was.

'I'm not sure where all this is leading us,' said Justice Jefferson.

Sparrow responded by raising his voice. 'For seven years the Antichrist provokes a series of major nuclear conflicts, including the hundred-thousand-megaton Battle of Armageddon! But then the Son of Man returns in time to prevent total annihilation!'

'Is that pretty much it?' asked Justice Jefferson.

'The present world vanishes, the Last Judgment occurs, and a New Heaven and Earth appear!'

'Anything else?'

'Eternity,' said Sparrow quietly.

'Last week,' said Bonenfant, 'former Vice President Mother Mary Catherine accused you of measuring a nation's Christianity by the size of its thermonuclear arsenal.'

'There's no such passage in any of my writings.'

'But you do advocate peace through strength.'

'If you study the Scriptures with an open mind' – Sparrow tapped his Bible – 'you will realize that they urge the United States to regain nuclear superiority over the Soviet Union, a nation that the prophet Ezekiel calls Magog.'

'When I read your books, I saw immediately that you regard nuclear war as a threat that all Christians must work to overcome.'

'Yes, but we shall succeed only through a willingness to bear the sword of God. The Bible teaches that, in a world of fallen men, military force is essential for social order.'

'Well, it shouldn't be a crime to want social order. No further questions.'

'I've never heard that "world of fallen men" hypothesis before,' said Randstable as he inflicted a fool's mate on George. 'Intriguing.'

'We could have used this guy at SAC,' said Brat. 'Our public relations director was a washout.'

Are we going to become fallen men? asked George's spermatids. I don't know, he replied.

Aquinas approached the stand without enthusiasm. The Devil's advocate, the Lord's prosecutor – equally thankless jobs. 'Leafing through your books, I'm struck by all the charts comparing American and Soviet military strength. Don't these statistics take us pretty far afield from theology?'

'I wanted Christians to understand that the enemy had acquired the edge in every category – throw-weight, conventional forces, you name it. We had to save America while there was still time.'

'Given that America's demise had already been revealed to the prophets, wouldn't it be blasphemous to try averting it?'

'God has a plan for us,' the evangelist explained.

'The title of your last book, *Deals With the Devil: A Christian Looks at the STABLE Treaties*, speaks for itself. Obviously you do not believe in arms control.'

'I *do* believe in arms control. What I don't believe in is appeasement.' Sparrow's smile was so sweet it threatened to rot his teeth. 'After all, Mr Aquinas, the Soviet Union is a police state, isn't it? There is no way to tell what agreements they're breaking or what bombs they're building.'

'If it was impossible to know exactly how many weapons the Soviets had, why did you publish charts showing exactly how many weapons the Soviets had?'

'Those statistics were compiled by the Committee on the Incipient Evil.'

Aquinas went to a document pile, fished out two paperback books, and opened the one with the mushroom cloud rising over Golgotha. 'Now, on page one hundred forty-three of *God's Megatons* you say, "The approach of Armageddon should cause not fear but joy. For Armageddon is the Lord's war to cleanse the earth of wickedness." I wonder how many Christians read this passage and found themselves hoping for a nuclear exchange?' He consulted the second book. 'And then, in *Christians Will Come Through the First Strike*, you quote Zephaniah 1:15, "A day of wrath is that day, a day of thick black clouds, a day of battle alarm against fortified cities, against battlements on high." You add, "Doesn't this sound like our second-strike weapons defeating the antiballistic missile system of the Soviet Union?"'

'I wanted to reveal that, if America were wise enough to avoid the disarmament trap, then the Son of Man could use our arsenal to bring violent judgment against those in Magog who reject the free gift of salvation.'

'Jesus would do that?'

'His First Coming was as the Lamb of God, His Second will be as the Lion.'

'Oh,' said Aquinas, rolling his eyes into his huge skull. 'No more questions.'

'Knows his Bible, doesn't he?' said Wengernook.

'I always liked the Sermon on the Mount,' said George. 'Job has some memorable parts too.'

'I thought you were a Unitarian,' said Brat,

'Jesus was ahead of His time,' said Randstable.

At nine o'clock the next morning, Bonenfant called Wengernook to testify.

'Well, men, here we go,' said the assistant defense secretary, nervously saluting his co-defendants.

'Just remember, history is on our side,' said Brat. 'Strength made the Soviets move cautiously.'

'Watch out for Aquinas's left hook,' said Randstable.

Once on the stand, Wengernook pulled cigarettes and matches from his scopas suit. Justice Jefferson gave him permission to light up.

Bonenfant said, 'The prosecution has introduced several documents authored by you, including an address titled "The Soviet Plan for Nuclear Victory" delivered to the Massachusetts Medical Society. Were the Soviets really planning on victory?'

'The evidence was overwhelming,' said Wengernook. He struck a match, missed the cigarette by inches. 'Their arsenal was geared to a protracted nuclear war, and they also had an extensive civil defense program. By the time I joined the current administration, Russia had fully embraced the ugly concept of a winner.'

'So America had to configure her own deterrent accordingly?'

'Not only was mutual assured destruction immoral, it had outlived its usefulness. We needed a policy of damage limitation and force modernization, plus a menu of realistic strategic options. In short, a transition from MAD to MARCH.'

'Some people were troubled that MARCH necessitated a large increase in warheads.'

'Under MAD, you could get away with, oh, I don't know – a couple hundred bombs.' At last Wengernook made match and cigarette connect. 'But when your goal is damage limitation, you require a much larger arsenal.'

'I'm not sure I understand this "damage limitation" business,' said Justice Wojciechowski.

That makes two of us, George thought. That makes four hundred million of us, his spermatids added.

It took Wengernook most of the morning to clarify the various meanings of damage limitation. 'So you see, your Honors,' he concluded, 'in the awful event that deterrence fails, you want to remove targets selectively. Your missiles must send the right message.'

'What message is that?' asked Justice Yoshinobu.

' "We're not trying to annihilate you, we're trying to save ourselves. That's why we're hitting only your silos, bomber fields, submarine pens, and warhead factories." ' Wengernook took a prolonged drag on his latest cigarette. 'Hence, the enemy is inspired to refrain from a massive attack.'

'So in its early phases such a conflict leads to better communication between the superpowers?' asked Justice Gioberti.

'If a war ever started, God forbid, the Soviets would immediately see they had nothing to gain by moving beyond surgical strikes,' answered Wengernook.

'They would be deterred from escalating?'

'Exactly. Their only option would be peace.'

Bonenfant allowed the word *peace* to linger for several beats, then announced that he had no further questions. Justice Jefferson ordered a lunch recess.

'I'm glad he got immorality in there,' said Brat.

'The line about peace was good too,' said George.

His bullet wound throbbed crazily as he tried to recall Victor Seabird's testimony. A complicated test ban, is that what the old man had negotiated? And there was something about weapons-grade material . . .

'Secretary Wengernook,' Aquinas began after the break, 'is it fair to say that the defense of Western Europe lay at the heart of America's involvement with nuclear weapons?'

'Given the superiority of the Warsaw Pact's conventional forces, tactical deployments were essential to NATO's security.'

'Some observers believed that the new intermediate-range missiles in Europe forced the Soviets to adopt a policy of launch-on-warning.'

'You must consider the stabilizing aspects of launch-on-warning.' Wengernook jettisoned his cigarette. 'When a nation puts her missiles on a so-called "hair trigger," her military leaders feel much less threatened.'

'Because they know they won't lose those forces in a pre-emptive strike?'

'Yes.'

'So they're less likely to do something foolish?'

'Right.'

'Like launching on warning?'

'Exactly.'

'Tell the tribunal about no-first-use.'

'This was the proposed doctrine whereby NATO would never be first to fire nuclear weapons, even in the face of a total defeat by the Warsaw Pact's tank divisions.'

Aquinas retrieved several items from one of the document piles. 'Glancing through your writings, I see that you were opposed to a no-first-use pledge.'

'It would have severely eroded deterrence. I much prefer a policy that says, "NATO will never shoot any nuclear missiles unless attacked." '

'By conventional weapons.'

'It also had a credibility problem. The whole thing would have gone out the window as soon as the Soviet blitzkrieg began.'

'Let me get this straight. The problem with no-first-use was that it had just enough credibility to invite a grand scale assault, but not enough credibility to hold up during one?'

'You should never let the enemy know your intentions.'

'Is that why in this issue of *Strategic Doctrine Quarterly*, Document 794, you praised President Truman for introducing something called "The Hiroshima Factor"?'

'Well, Hiroshima certainly gave us an advantage over the Soviets in the ambiguity area,' said Wengernook, leafing through the document in question. 'They never knew just *what* we would do.'

'So by rejecting no-first-use, America could retain its superiority in ambiguity?'

'I'm trying to give a serious interview here.'

'Your 1992 commencement address at the Air Force Academy, Document 613, includes the famous remark that, quote, "In a nuclear war our forces must prevail over the Soviets and achieve an early cessation of hostilities on terms favorable to the United States." Unquote. What does it mean to "prevail" in a nuclear war, Secretary?'

'It means absorbing a first strike and then retaliating decisively.'

'How would you characterize a country that has absorbed a first strike?'

'The industrial base is largely intact, the command structure is functioning, and deterrence has been restored.'

'What about the civilian population?'

'A significant percentage has survived.'

'And a significant percentage hasn't survived. Is this what you people call "acceptable losses"?'

'Occasionally we used that term.'

'Five million people killed, is that acceptable?'

'Well, we had that twenty million figure staring us in the face.'

'What twenty million figure?'

'The casualties Russia suffered in the Second World War.'

'A troubling sum. You were losing the acceptable losses race.'

Justice Wojciechowski asked, 'Mr Wengernook, may I assume that no losses were acceptable to you *personally*?'

'That goes without saying.' The defendant drew a pair of mirrored sunglasses from his scopas suit and put them on. 'Acceptable losses is a very abstract concept. It only comes up in strategic discussions.'

'I hate to be a Monday-morning quarterback,' said Aquinas, 'but the United States didn't "prevail," did it? Your menu got used up, the Soviets neglected to offer favorable terms, the SPASM was implemented, and the human race disappeared. Now, in light of these events, do you still believe your plans were more moral than mutual assured destruction?'

'There is a world of ethical difference between offensive war-fighting plans and preventive war-fighting plans.'

'Is that why winning was an ugly concept when the Soviets thought about it and a realistic option when you did?'

'We had to live in the world as it was, Prosecutor, not as we would have liked it to be.'

Aquinas moved so close to Wengernook that his breath fogged the defendant's sunglasses. 'But you *made* the world as it was! Your strategic menu threatened the Soviets from all sides! Your theater forces menaced them! Your Multiprongs taunted them! Your Omegas—!'

' "If you would have peace, prepare for war," ' Wengernook quoted somberly. 'Appius Claudius the Blind.'

'And if you would have war, you *also* prepare for war!'

George had seen this scene before, on movie screens – the prosecutor trying to break down the defendant.

'I submit that your strategies had the Soviets frightened to death!' Aquinas persisted. 'I submit that the best hope they saw was a quick, unexpected decapitation of the American command structure!'

But this was not the movies. This was the post-exchange environment, where everybody is extinct and assistant defense secretaries are as unyielding as Vermont granite.

'No, you're wrong,' said Wengernook wearily. 'That Soviet Spitball attack was completely unmotivated.'

Aquinas was at the bench, standing before the little frozen missile exhibits. 'When was this arms race supposed to end, Secretary?' He kicked the ice arsenal. 'When?'

'An unmotivated, naive, pointless, reckless, suicidal attack,' said Wengernook. 'Everybody knows that Spitball cruise missiles are not good for first strikes.'

'When?' shouted Mother Mary Catherine from the gallery.

'How many times can you fantasize all these battle plans before wanting to get the whole thing over with?' Aquinas demanded, kicking missiles. 'How many times can you go through the door marked DETERRENCE before you end up in a concrete bunker turning launch keys?'

Wengernook ripped off his sunglasses and said, 'To this day, I don't understand the enemy's reasoning. Spitballs are *second*-strike weapons. Not *first*-strike – *second*-strike. Is that clear?'

For the next ten minutes Aquinas kicked missiles and shouted rhetorical questions, Wengernook patiently explained why Spitballs were useless in first strikes, Mother Mary Catherine released balloons with WHEN? painted on their sides, and Justice Jefferson made halfhearted attempts to restore order. Finally a haggard chief prosecutor announced that he had no further questions.

Back in the booth, Wengernook received warm congratulations and firm handshakes from Brat, Randstable, Overwhite, and Sparrow. He approached George and gave him an amiable slap on the shoulder. 'This sort of testimony must sound awfully technical to you, huh?' asked the defense secretary.

'I didn't hear you say how many times you could go through the door marked DETERRENCE,' George replied. His tone was more acid than he intended, but it sounded right. 'The crowd drowned you out.'

'Defending a country is a damn sight harder than sticking a few words on a tombstone,' said Wengernook between locked teeth. A WHEN? balloon bounced off the booth door. 'You're going to testify tomorrow, aren't you? Just remember, we're with you one hundred percent.'

CHAPTER FIFTEEN

*In Which Our Hero Learns that One
Person on Earth Was Less Guilty than He*

George's spermatids trembled as his advocate left the defense table and walked through the mid-morning darkness. *It won't be that bad,* he told them. *I merely have to explain that I was not involved with smart warheads, damage limitation, any of it.*

Bonenfant said, 'The defense calls George—'

'No!' a familiar voice piped up from the back of the courtroom. 'The defense calls *me*!'

Theophilus Carter ambled forward stomping on WHEN? balloons and carrying a steaming cup of tea. His scopas suit was diamond-patterned like a harlequin's tights, and its utility belt sagged with daggers and pistols from the costume racks of the Mad Tea Party. 'I don't normally arm myself so heavily,' he explained, sipping tea, 'but I understand there are war criminals present. Say, shouldn't somebody ask me to remove my hat?' He darted a blobby finger toward Justice Jefferson. 'Aren't you in charge of that?'

'I don't care what you do with your hat, sir,' she replied, 'Can anyone tell me who this is?'

'Dr Theophilus Carter, unadmitted tailor and inventor,' said Aquinas, rising. 'We hired him to deliver Document 919 to the defendant Paxton.'

'Why did you retain the services of such an unbalanced person?' Justice Jefferson demanded.

'Oh, I'm *highly* balanced,' asserted the MAD Hatter. He set the teacup in the brim of his hat and did a pirouette. 'It's the strategic forces that are unbalanced.'

'We were unaware of his condition at the time,' Aquinas explained.

'You don't *really* want this man testifying, do you, Mr Bonenfant?' asked Justice Jefferson.

'But I have evidence to give,' said the Hatter. 'I can prove that George is innocent.'

Bonenfant uncurled his index finger, aimed it at the client in question, wiggled it. George left the glass booth and joined his advocate in a niche jammed with documents relating to STABLE II.

'Any reason not to hear what this fellow has to say?' whispered Bonenfant.

'He's a madman,' said George. 'Can you put a madman on the stand?'

Swearing in Theophilus Carter was the greatest challenge of the court usher's career. After fifteen minutes of semantic circumlocution, the job was done.

'Are you acquainted with the defendant Paxton?' Bonenfant asked.

'George and I go back a long way,' the Hatter replied. 'I knew him before his secondary spermatocytes were failing to become spermatids. May I give my testimony now?'

'That's what you're doing.'

'This whole thing would go a lot quicker if I told you what to say. Ask me, "When did you first meet the defendant?" '

Bonenfant's upper teeth entered into violent contact with his lower ones. 'Er – when did you first meet—'

'When he came in to get his free scopas suit. Ask me how much the prosecution paid me to make it.'

'How much did the prosecution pay you—'

'Objection!' The Hatter shot up as if attached to a delivery system. 'Leading the witness! The prosecution did not pay me to make the suit. But they did bribe me with a wonderful flying shop.' He flopped back into the stand. 'Ask me what happened after I told George he had to sign a sales contract implicating himself in the arms race.'

'The tribunal will please note that my client was entrapped by the prosecution. Now, Mr Carter, what happened after you told George he had to sign a sales—'

'He signed it, took the suit, and left.'

'What happened next?'

'I became curious. Would *anyone* have behaved as George did – accepting a free suit even after being told that this technology undermined deterrence? So I filled my hat with unsigned contracts and flew off in my shop. I figured that if fifty people refused to sign, then George was an unusually negligent person, and I was obliged to surrender his confession to the prosecution.'

'Did you find fifty such people?'

After removing the teacup from the brim, Theophilus flipped his hat over and reached inside. His hand emerged with a stack of scopas suit sales contracts. 'These are the first two hundred I gave out. Every one is signed. All right, I said to myself. I'll settle for forty-five refusals. No luck. Thirty? Impossible, Ten? Nope. Time was running out. The warheads had started landing. One! If *one* person is less negligent than George Paxton, I'll hand over the evidence of his guilt.'

'And did you find such a person?'

'Ask me if I found such a person.'

'I just did.'

'You did? What a coincidence – I found one too! Ask me whether this person was a man or a woman.'

'Was this person a man or—'

'That's irrelevant! What's relevant is that only one person on earth was willing to worry about the impact of scopas suits on deterrence.'

'Your Honor, I object,' said Aquinas. 'Dr Carter did not approach every person on earth.'

As Justice Jefferson instructed the stenographers to delete the witness's last remark, Theophilus unhooked a pineapple-type fragmentation grenade from his belt and began biting the cast iron case.

'Ask me why I'm insane,' he said.

'Why are you insane?' the advocate responded.

Theophilus pulled the pin from the grenade – nothing happened – and used it to stir his tea. If admitted, he explained, he would have been part of the abolition regime. His job would have been to sit in a rubber room in the Pentagon all day, thinking about strategic doctrine. It was assumed that people who took this job would go crazy. They were the heroes of the twenty-first century. Their madness was their gift to the human species; because of the Hatter and his fellow martyrs, humanity would never forget how close it had come to suicide.

'Ask me what job I have now,' said Theophilus.

'What job—'

'History rehabilitation. Long hours, low pay, bad smells. 'Again he reached into his hat, this time coming up with a stack of computer software disks. 'Now this program here,' he said, 'this is Marcus Aurelius. And this one will go into Mahatma Gandhi's brain. At one time, all of history heartily approved of what this tribunal is trying to do. But then, after George saved my life—'

'Saved your life?' said Bonenfant, pouncing on the testimonial. 'How did he come to save your life?'

'I'm asking the questions around here! Ask me how George came to save my life.'

'How did George—'

'Somebody was going to shoot me. Ask me who.'

'Who?'

'Don't ask! It would not help Tarmac's case one bit.'

'I wasn't really going to shoot him,' Brat explained to his co-defendants. 'I just wanted to scare him into giving me his shop.'

'It flies – is that what he said?' asked Randstable.

'Twenty-first century know-how,' said Brat.

'Love to see the schematics,' said Randstable.

Theophilus took more software from his hat. 'After George saved my life, I realized that the framers of the McMurdo Sound Agreement had been overstepping their authority. He's a fine fellow, old George is. You should see the witnesses I've got lined up.' The Hatter waved a disk around. 'Look! Socrates will testify in his defense! And Saint Francis of Assisi! Joan of Arc! *Jesus Christ Himself* is prepared to take the stand on George's behalf . . . Yes, the same Jesus Christ who said, "But whosoever shall nuke thy capital city, turn to him thy best seaport also." '

George noticed that Reverend Sparrow's face was rapidly shifting toward the purple end of the spectrum.

Aquinas rose and said, 'I move that all of this witness's babblings be stricken.'

'Mr Carter has stated that my client was entrapped,' said Bonenfant. 'That is vital testimony.'

While the president of the court deliberated, Theophilus refilled his hat with software and sales contracts.

'The testimony will stand,' said Justice Jefferson. 'However, we do not wish to hear any more of it. The prosecution may cross-examine.'

'We decline to cross-examine,' said Aquinas.

'Oh? Why?'

'Because life is short, your Honor.'

As when a fever seizes the brain and makes things grotesquely smaller, larger, fatter, or thinner, so did the perspectives afforded by the stand disorient George. The audience, a tame and predictable creature when viewed from within the booth, now looked ferocious. The judges had acquired a terrifying hostility. The court usher was stark and unforgiving.

'What did you do for a living?' Bonenfant asked.

'I inscribed tombstones,' George answered. 'And sold them.'

'Did this work have anything to do with national defense?'

'No.' So far, so good, he thought.

Bonenfant retrieved Document 919 from a nearby evidence pile. 'The prosecution's entire case against you seems to rest on this sales contract. Is that your signature at the bottom?'

'Oh, yes.'

'Did Theophilus Carter insist that you read these statements carefully before signing?'

'No.'

'*Did* you read them carefully?'

'Not really.'

'According to the contract, you believed that scopas suits were encouraging America's leaders to pursue a policy of nuclear brinksmanship.'

'I didn't even know what "nuclear brinksmanship" was. I'm still not sure.'

'Did you believe, as the contract says, that scopas suits were distracting people from the real issues – STABLE talks, the MARCH Plan, no-first-use?'

'Certainly not.'

'This document was putting words in your mouth, wasn't it?'

Commotion at the prosecution table. 'And Mr Bonenfant is putting words in his client's mouth,' Aquinas asserted.

'Ask another question,' said Justice Jefferson.

'To tell you the truth, your Honors' – Bonenfant ambled back to the defense table – 'my client is so palpably innocent that I cannot think of a single additional question to ask him. He's yours, Mr Aquinas.'

As the chief prosecutor charged forward, the butterflies in George's stomach began producing larvae.

'You have told the court that you used to sell tombstones,' Aquinas began.

God, has he nailed me already? No, I did sell tombstones. 'That's right.'

'Was it your practice to have customers sign sales contracts without reading them?'

'No.'

'And yet you are asking the court to believe that you signed a scopas suit contract without reading it?'

'I did read it, sort of. It confused me.'

' "I hearby confess to my complicity in the nuclear arms race." That sounds like plain English to *my* ears.'

A vulture expert. Everything would be fine as long as a vulture expert showed up. 'It was the other parts that confused me.'

'Do you or do you not understand the words, "I hereby confess to my complicity in the nuclear arms race"?'

George knew that his voice was going to sound weak and

defeated. 'I understand them.' Weak, defeated. 'I wanted my little girl to have a scopas suit. Is that so terrible?'

The chief prosecutor placed the contract at arm's length, as if it harbored an infectious disease. 'Can you point to a single action on your part that would lead the tribunal to doubt your negligence?'

'Well, not exactly. No. But if you heard Mr Carter's testimony, then you know that just about everybody else—'

'Just about everybody else is not on trial here.'

Aquinas took a long, deliberate stroll around the prosecution table. George twitched like a skewered moth.

'I'm curious, Mr Paxton,' the chief prosecutor said at last. 'How do you feel about your co-defendants?'

'How do I feel about them?'

'Yes.'

'They're my friends.'

'Good friends?'

'We play poker. Reverend Sparrow once saved me from some dangerous ensigns. Dr Randstable has been showing me the basic chess openings. General Tarmac helped me find a fertility clinic.'

'So you like them?'

'Sure I like them. They certainly aren't war criminals.'

'And how do you feel about their ideas?'

'Their what?' George asked politely.

'Their ideas.'

'If I'd been the one in Washington, I probably couldn't have done any better.'

Aquinas scowled. 'Again I put the question to you. How do you feel about your co-defendants' ideas?'

The high-school students were back in George's mind, merrily kicking off the abolition regime. Plop! went the Soviet SS-90 intermediate-range missile into the glowing magma of Mount Erebus. He thought: our case is going well, my friends did an excellent job of defending themselves, and now I'm about to blow it. Still, this is a court of law. I touched a Bible and swore to give the truth. 'I guess I'd have to say . . .'

His intestines writhed around each other. Overwhite will never speak to me again. Randstable won't teach me any more openings. Sparrow will stop praying for me. Brat will hate me forever . . .

'I guess I'd have to say that my friends' ideas were pretty bad.'

'Pretty bad?'

'Yes. Bad. Bad ideas. Terrible, in fact.'

Aquinas began warming up for a gigantic smile. 'Why do you suppose your co-defendants spent so much time and energy on these bad ideas?'

'That's hard to say.'

The prosecutor's smile grew. 'Can you guess?'

'Well, I suppose that thinking about bad ideas is more interesting and exciting than . . . you know.'

'Than what?'

'You know.'

'Abolishing the weapons?'

'Yes,' sighed George.

Aquinas's smile reached full potential. 'No further questions,' he said, slapping the sales contract on the bench.

A new and particularly bitter layer of frost had infested the glass booth during George's absence. 'I found you very sympathetic,' said Overwhite tonelessly as the tomb inscriber settled back down in the dock.

'Sincerity city,' said Randstable without passion.

'I don't think it was necessary to mention bad ideas,' said Brat.

'Yes, I had trouble with that part too,' said Overwhite.

'Abolition regimes are inherently unworkable,' said Wengernook. 'Seabird admitted as much.'

'You don't need to keep saying that,' George snapped.

Justice Jefferson put on her whalebone glasses, briefly studied the sales contract, and asked, 'Might I assume that the case for the defense is concluded?'

'Our final witness will take the stand tomorrow,' said Bonenfant.

When his advocate glowered at him, George's bullet wound felt as if it were reopening.

*

Thrust into a frigid hell with nothing to sustain him but a glass painting of his unborn child, infused with the feeling that his performance on the stand had been a disaster, sick with the thought that he had betrayed his friends, George was nevertheless as happy as any human has ever been. For walking boldly through the courtroom, eyes dead ahead, was the future mother of Holly's stepsister. His spermatids thrashed with desire. Morning smiled at him quickly, subtly; perhaps she hadn't smiled at all. She changed the world. The palace brightened. Everyone in the gallery, even the old ones with their bleak eyes and crushed postures, had a beauty George had not noticed before.

'Hey, look,' said Wengernook. 'It's the periscope lady.'

'Somebody that frigid should feel right at home around here,' said Brat.

'Why don't you be quiet?' hissed George.

After Morning had been sworn in, Bonenfant asked, 'Are you a war refugee?'

She closed her eyes and said, in a voice George and his spermatids found overwhelmingly sensual, 'I practiced psycho-therapy in Chicago when it existed.'

'Did you treat the six defendants for survivor's guilt aboard the *City of New York*?' Bonenfant asked.

'Yes.'

'Why do you wish to testify?'

'I know something that will help Paxton's case.'

'Something you learned while treating him?'

George grimaced internally. Nothing makes you as self-conscious, he realized – no magnitude of nakedness or public blunder – as the experience of observing others discuss you.

'No, my testimony comes from before that time,' said Morning. 'Mr Bonenfant, members of the tribunal, let me take you back to the day of Paxton's rescue. Our submarine lay in Boston Harbor, waiting for the abduction team to return. I trained one of the periscopes on the defendant's hometown.'

'Why?'

'I was trying to spot my new patient.'

'Did you?'

'No. I became fascinated by the town itself. I realized that it was about to disappear, and I wanted to see how everyone was spending his time. The people's faces were tight and grim. They went about their Saturday morning duties – getting their mail, buying their doughnuts – and I could find no joy. This was seven days before Christmas. But then a little girl and her mother came out of a store. The mother carried a bag of groceries. The child had a small plastic snowman in her hands. She was bubbling about it. Her lips said, "You're going to live on our Christmas tree!" I began feeling much better . . . and much worse.

'The warhead was groundburst, and the mother became trapped under a brick wall. Everything was dark. I had to use the infrared. "I'm thirsty," the woman said. The initial radiation, of course. So the little girl ran into the burning store and came back holding a carton of orange juice. It was hard to tear open. She said – children's lips are easy to read, they put so much into talking – she said, "Look, Mommy, I opened it! Will this make you better, Mommy?" She nursed her mother with orange juice. "Everything will be all right, Mommy," the little girl said. The mother closed her eyes – stopped breathing. Then a man who knew the child came along. I think he worked at the bank. He seemed to be sleepwalking. "Is my mommy dead?" the girl asked. "Is my mommy in heaven now?" she wanted to know. The man fell down. The little girl began to cry. "I want my daddy," she said. A few seconds later, another warhead arrived.

'And then, the following month, while I was treating the defendant, he showed me his daughter's nursery school photograph, and I realized who had given the dying woman the orange juice. The point I wish to make, your Honors, is that George Paxton is much more a victim of this war than a perpetrator. His wife and daughter were innocent civilian casualties, and he would have been one too if the prosecution hadn't pulled his name out of a hat, entrapped him, and brought him to this ridiculous trial. Do you want revenge? Convict him. Justice? Let him go . . . I shall not answer any further questions, nor shall I submit to cross-examination.'

George's sobs were slow and regular, like tympani notes at a funeral. Somebody – Brat? Wengernook? – gave his knee a firm, sympathetic squeeze.

'Mr Aquinas, are you satisfied not to interview this witness?' Justice Jefferson wanted to know.

'I would like to ask her one question,' said the chief prosecutor.

'All right,' said Morning. 'One.'

Aquinas stomped on a WHEN? balloon and approached the stand. 'As I understand your testimony, Dr Valcourt, you were on the *City of New York* during the whole of its seven-week passage from the United States to Antarctica. I also understand that, during this time, you engaged George Paxton in an intimate series of psychoanalytic sessions. Assuming that you do not wish to deny these facts, then my question is this – to what extent are you romantically involved with the defendant?'

The unpregnant expectant mother frowned gently and straightened up. 'I am not now,' she said, 'nor have I ever been, romantically involved with the defendant.'

CHAPTER SIXTEEN

In Which the Essential Question Is Answered and
Something Very Much Like Justice Is Served

'The tribunal will hear the closing argument of the prosecution,' said Shawna Queen Jefferson.

Aquinas rose, approached the bench, and stood silently before the judges.

'Fifteen billion years ago,' he began at last, 'the cosmos came into being. Nobody, even the best of our unadmitted scientists and clerics, quite knows how, or why.' Looping his arms together behind his back, he paced around the pile of frozen missiles. 'Later, some three and a half billion years ago, another miracle occurred. On one particular planet, Earth, organic molecules formed. We do not know whether the same miracle happened elsewhere. The opportunities were overwhelmingly for it, the odds overwhelmingly against it.'

'At this rate he won't get around to us for a week,' said Wengernook.

'Shut up,' said Overwhite.

'The organisms evolved,' said Aquinas. 'Great apes appeared. Some of these apes were carnivorous, perhaps even cannibalistic. It is probable that the human species branched off from bipedal, small-brained, weapon-wielding primates who were stunningly proficient at murder.'

George noticed that Reverend Sparrow appeared to be suffering from apoplexy.

'Are we innately aggressive?' asked Aquinas. 'Was the nuclear predicament symptomatic of a more profound depravity? Nobody knows. But if this is so – and I suspect that it is – then the responsibility for what we are pleased to call our inhumanity still rests squarely in our blood-soaked hands. The killer-ape hypothesis does not specify a fate – it lays out an agenda. Beware, the fable warns. Caution. Trouble ahead. Genocidal weapons in the hands of creatures who are bored by peace.'

'I think I'm going to throw up,' said Brat.

'But the fable went unheeded. And the weapons, unchecked. And then, one cold Christmas season, death came to an admirable species – a species that wrote symphonies and sired Leonardo da Vinci and would have gone to the stars. It did not have to be this way. Three virtues only were needed – creative diplomacy, technical ingenuity, and moral outrage. But the greatest of these is moral outrage.'

'Self-righteous slop, you needed that too,' said Brat.

'You needed a trough of it,' said Wengernook.

'Shut up,' said Overwhite.

'For the past twenty days the walls of this sacred palace have enclosed a curious world,' said Aquinas. 'A world where peril is called security, destruction is called strategy, offense is called defense, enlightened self-interest is called appeasement, and machines of chaos and ecological horror are called weapons.'

'And kangaroo courts are called tribunals,' said Brat.

'It is the world of Major General Roger Tarmac, the MARCH Hare, who believed that his Holy Triad meant salvation for America. In the name of the Bombers, and of the Subs, and of the Land-Based Missiles – Amen! It is the world of Brian Overwhite, the weapons industry's favorite arms controller, who never in his entire career denied the Pentagon a system it really wanted. It is the world of William Randstable, the doomsday doctor, whose smart warhead was just one more bullet in the revolver with which humanity played, you should forgive the expression, Russian roulette. It is the world of Peter Sparrow, the Ezekiel of the airwaves, who wanted America to demonstrate her moral superiority over her adversary by becoming just like her adversary, adopting the economy and mentality of a garrison state. It is the world of Robert Wengernook, the auditor of acceptable losses, who forgot that a species as inquisitive as *Homo sapiens* cannot draw up plans for a war, even a war of extinction, without eventually needing to find out how well they work. And it is the world of George Paxton, citizen, perhaps the most guilty of all. Every night, this man went to bed knowing that the human race was pointing nuclear weapons at itself. Every morning, he woke up knowing that the weapons were still there. And yet he never took a single step to relieve the threat.'

Has Bonenfant's team found that vulture expert? asked George's spermatids. I don't know, he told them.

'Learned justices, you are about to write a verdict in the case. Your opinion will be the final chapter in human history. It will matter. Indeed, it is not unreasonable to speculate that, beyond our solar system, another intelligent species monitors this trial, seeking to learn what nuclear weapons are good for. And so I urge you to fill your pens with your black blood and tell these celestial eavesdroppers that the harvest of nuclear weapons is threefold – spiritual degeneration, self-delusion, and death. Perhaps we should bury your verdict in a capsule beneath the Antarctic ice, so that one day, a year or ten years or a century from now, some wayfarer in the Milky Way might find it and know that, for all our love of violence, at the final moment we were able to say no to fusion bombs and yes to life.'

'Does he make up this crap himself?' said Brat.

'All the greeting card writers are dead,' said Wengernook.

'Shut up,' said George.

'While we cannot know for certain to whom your verdict will speak,' said Aquinas, 'we do know *for* whom it will speak. It will speak for the thousands who sit in this courtroom and for the multitudes who wait on the glacier. It will speak for history – for those who struggled to make this planet a repository of art and learning, and whose achievements have now been laid waste. And it will speak for a population who, in our self-pity as unadmitteds, we sometimes forget. I refer to the five billion men, women, and children who were blasted and burned alive, irradiated and crushed, suffocated and starved and sickened unto death in the recent holocaust.

'Their blood cries to heaven, but their voice cannot be heard.
'Give them a voice, your Honors. Give them a voice.'

AQUINAS DELIVERS ELEGY FOR HUMAN RACE, said Mount Christ-church that afternoon.

'The tribunal will hear the closing argument of the defense,' said Justice Jefferson.

George noticed how barren Bonenfant's table had become – Dennie gone, Parkman gone, all of the papers gone save one.

'Remember what he said on the boat,' muttered Brat. 'He's got a rabbit or two in the hat.'

'I'll take two,' said Wengernook.

'A boy rabbit and a girl rabbit,' said Randstable.

'Honored justices,' Bonenfant began, 'I submit that, beyond the ornate pieties of my learned opponent, the issue you must decide is simple. Did these six men aim to wage a war or to preserve a peace? Their aim, we have seen, was peace. Indeed, no firmer fact has emerged from this long inquest.

'Lest we forget, my clients did not *ask* to have thermonuclear weapons at their disposal. They did not *want* to inherit a world that knew these obscene devices. But inherit it they did, along with the threat to freedom posed by Russian Communism. I ask you, learned judges, would any of you have acted differently in their place?

'We all know that the peace was not preserved. During this hearing the mechanism of peace-preservation – the policy of deterrence through strategic balance – has been characterized as self-defeating. In his cross-examination of Robert Wengernook, the prosecutor even went so far as to suggest that my clients pursued deterrence so vigorously that they forced the Soviet Union into the suicidal action of striking first – and with second-strike weapons, no less.

'Now that is a most improbable scenario. Crazy. Fantastic. Weird . . . Indeed, it simply did not happen that way. *I can prove as much.*'

Gasps rushed through the courtroom like a thousand icy

breezes. The Mount Christchurch reporters leaned over the balustrade of the press box.

'At this point in the hearing it would be most peculiar were I to put anyone else on the stand. And yet, your Honors, that is what I now propose to do. For there is a seventh defendant in this case – a defendant who should have stood trial in place of my clients.'

The gasps faded into the rumble of the question *What?* in fifty languages.

'Legal proceedings against animals have a long history. Plato's *The Laws* includes the directive that "if a beast of burden shall kill anyone, the relatives of the deceased shall prosecute it for murder." The Book of Exodus tells us that "when an ox gores a man to death, the ox must be stoned." However, until today no one has indicted the animal that my assistants will now bring forward.'

A loud, high *skreeee* filled the courtroom – the shrill protestations of wheels turning on axles. Dennie and Parkman were pouring all of their youthful, unadmitted energy into pushing a large wooden cart toward the bench.

On the cart was a metal cage.

In the cage was a gigantic vulture.

'The first day of the war found me on a vulture hunt,' Bonenfant explained, 'chasing this creature from Nova Scotia to Massachusetts. I captured it not far from George Paxton's hometown and then made my rendezvous with the *City of New York.*'

Aquinas boiled over like neglected oatmeal on a hot stove. 'Your Honors, this is a courtroom, not a zoo! Whatever relevance Mr Bonenfant's fat bird may have – and I see none – its arrival comes much too late to be considered admissible.'

'I beg the court's indulgence,' said Bonenfant, gently lifting the solitary document from the defense table and handing it to Dennie. 'Two days ago my chief assistant began an arduous trek up the glacier. She was searching for someone. This morning she found him. Your Honors, the defense is pleased to offer the deposition of one Dr Laslo Prendergorst – resident of Ice Limbo 905, unadmitted ornithologist, hypothetical Nobel laureate, and Antarctica's most illustrious vulture expert.'

'We didn't have time to copy it,' said Dennie, placing the document before Justice Jefferson.

'Dr Prendergorst has examined the specimen in question,' said Bonenfant, 'and he has confirmed our suspicions. During the late Pleistocene era, a swift-flying, migratory species of vulture inhabited North America – the *Teratornis*, one form of which, *Argentavis magnificens*, was the largest bird ever to have lived. Twentieth-century scientists assumed that all the teratorns, including the gargantuan *Argentavis magnificens*, were extinct. The scientists were wrong. A small breeding population of *Argentavis* survived. In his deposition Dr Prendergorst draws an analogy with a fish called the coelacanth, believed to have vanished during the Cretaceous period. In 1938 a live coelacanth was found off the southern coast of Africa. Rumors of its extinction had been greatly exaggerated.'

Justice Wojciechowski smiled. The teratorn chewed the cage bars with its steam-shovel beak, shook them with its chipped and twisted claws.

When Bonenfant snapped his fingers, Parkman pulled some papers from the chief counsel's briefcase and delivered them to the judges.

'Your Honors, we are now offering a fresh copy of the prosecution's own Document 318, a NORAD computer printout indicating the sizes, velocities, radar signatures, and trajectories of the objects that triggered this war. Were these objects heading across Canada on a line with Washington? Yes. Were they shaped like Soviet Spitball cruise missiles? Yes.

'But' – Bonenfant paused, weaving his hand through the air as if it were in flight – 'were they Soviet Spitball cruise missiles?

'*No*! They were a flock of admittedly hideous but completely unarmed vultures pursuing their annual one-day migration from Newfoundland to the Yucatan Peninsula. If you doubt my claim, turn to the last page. You will see one of the satellite photographs taken to corroborate the NORAD sighting. This is not a cruise missile, your Honors. You can even see the bloodstains on its beak.'

Aquinas leaped up. 'Your Honors, how much longer must we endure this ludicrous presentation?'

Justice Jefferson seesawed her glasses on the bridge of her nose, looked at Document 318, and said, 'Your findings are most unusual, Mr Bonenfant, and the court considers them admissible, but what is the *point*?'

'Just this. Armed deterrence did not fail. The war happened through a freak of nature. If the teratorns had taken a slightly different flight path on that particular Saturday morning, they would have eluded the NORAD early warning systems, as they had done so many times in the past, and the nuclear balance would have remained intact. My clients planned no crimes against peace, nor did they carry them out. Armed deterrence worked, your Honors. It worked.'

'It worked,' said Brat.

'It worked,' said Wengernook.

'It worked,' said Overwhite.

'It worked,' said Randstable.

'Amen,' said Reverend Sparrow.

'And that is all I have to say,' Bonenfant concluded.

Justice Jefferson cast a thoughtful glance toward the foul-smelling bird – a glance into which George read vast volumes of wisdom and compassion – and announced that the court would withdraw to write its verdict.

And so the ice continent became a kind of physician's office, humanity's final remnant fidgeting in the anteroom, waiting to learn whether its collective case was terminal.

In George's brain vicious and sadistic memory cells played his testimony over and over, torturing the guilt areas with snatches from speeches he might have made. Should I have spoken of Justine – of how she instinctively knew the suits were no good? Said more about Holly? Mentioned the Giant Ride horse, the Big Dipper, or the Mary Merlin doll back home in the closet? Certainly I could have put more stress on my co-defendants' positive points . . .

He paced his cell, wearing a groove in the ice.

Why doesn't your future wife come to visit you? his spermatids asked.

If word got back to the judges, he explained, they'd know she cared about me.

Of course, said the spermatids. Yes. Naturally. Why doesn't she come anyway?

I don't know, he confessed.

On the witness stand, she said she didn't love you.

That was just to help our case.

JUSTICES STILL DELIBERATING, the slopes of Mount Christchurch declared to the assembled legions.

'This game is seven-card stud,' said Overwhite.

'They're probably hung up on Paxton's testimony,' said Brat. 'All that talk about bad ideas – it must have thrown them.'

'For a loop,' said Wengernook.

'I told the truth,' said George.

'Leave him alone,' said Overwhite. He squeezed George's hand. 'I'm sorry you had to hear that stuff about your kid.'

'It's all right,' said George. 'No, it isn't,' he added.

'War always has its human side,' said Brat.

'Do you suppose Jefferson and company were favorably impressed by that vulture?' asked Overwhite.

'Definitely,' said Wengernook.

'An excellent move by Bonenfant,' said Randstable. 'Very pretty.'

'It proves that you don't get into a war by being too strong,' said Brat.

'Ace bets,' said Randstable.

'One egg,' said Wengernook.

'Two,' said Overwhite.

'We should be glad,' said Brat. 'It's a good sign when a jury is out for a long time.'

'That's just in the movies,' said Wengernook.

'There is no jury,' said Overwhite.

'There are no movies,' said George.

'Raise,' said Brat.

*

JUSTICES TO ANNOUNCE VERDICT TODAY, said Mount Christchurch.

The final week of school, the final day of a summer by the sea, the
final hour of a long train trip – George could recall all of these
experiences. In each case the space in question had changed,
abandoning him even as he attempted to abandon it. For nearly a
month the Ice Palace of Justice had been his home, but now it was
regaining the aloofness and unfamiliarity it had worn on the first
day.

The judges entered slowly, their black robes soaking up the oily
gloom, each wearing a face that could have bluffed its way
through a thousand losing poker hands. Shawna Queen Jefferson,
who carried a ream of paper and a biography of Abraham Lincoln
in her arms, was mumbling to herself. Theresa Gioberti seemed
worried, Jan Wojciechowski bemused, Kamo Yoshinobu sad.

They sat down.

The cold, muffled stillness of a planetarium seeped through
the palace. George scanned the gallery – the faces, the signs. Yes,
there she was, between LET US IN and GIVE THEM A VOICE:
Aubrey's mother. His spermatids longed for the South Pole and
the strength they knew they would find there.

At the defense table Bonenfant, Dennie, and Parkman held
hands.

Justice Jefferson took her whalebone glasses from her scopas
suit and put them on. She spread out the papers, selected one.

'I shall begin by stating that, in the opinion of the tribunal, the
doctrine of armed deterrence remains vigorous, credible, and
intact.'

A vast and spontaneous 'NO!' thundered down from the
gallery. The judge smashed her gavel into the bench, launching a
spray of ice chips.

'Even while undergoing certain disturbing variations during
the last administration, the armed-deterrence doctrine continued
to boast such resilience that it could be used to make as good a
case for expanding America's thermonuclear arsenal as for scaling
it down.'

A smile jumped onto Dennie's impossibly pretty face.

'Hot damn!' said Wengernook.

'Guys, we brought it off,' said Brat.

'All they wanted was an explanation,' said Overwhite.

'We agree with Mr Bonenfant that armed deterrence might have lasted until the nuclear powers grew tired of maintaining their pointless stockpiles, subsequently scrapping them,' said Shawna Queen Jefferson. 'And we agree with the defendant Randstable that the warheads might also have disappeared through a kind of technological evolution.'

When the groans and catcalls finally subsided, the judge continued.

'In his closing argument the chief counsel put a crucial question to us. What would we have done in his clients' place? A fair question. A tormenting question . . .

'Oddly enough, Mr Aquinas miscalculated when he introduced his scale-model weapons as evidence for the prosecution. For we learned that, whether carved from ice or from metal, such technology has a fearsome glamor. We found ourselves saying, "Yes, yes, give us these sensual missiles, these steel boats, these wondrous planes, these high-IQ warheads. Give us these things, and no one will ever *dare* to attack us." So we too would have wanted that Triad, in all its completeness and power.'

Randstable and Wengernook exchanged thumbs-up signals. Transcending their differences over STABLE II, Overwhite and Sparrow embraced. Brat offered his bony right hand to George; the tomb inscriber shook it.

And then, after taking a drink of cocoa, Shawna Queen Jefferson removed her glasses and slammed them *klack* against the bench. 'It is not we four judges who are on trial here, however,' she said swiftly, tersely. 'It is you six defendants,' she added. 'Thank God,' sighed the president of the court.

She opened her Lincoln biography and, moistening her black thumb with a pink tongue, flipped back several pages. 'In a message to Congress on December 1, 1862, Abraham Lincoln wrote, "The dogmas of the quiet past are inadequate to the stormy present. The occasion is piled high with difficulty, and we must rise with the occasion. As our case is new, so we must think anew and act anew. We must disenthrall ourselves . . ." ' She slammed the book shut. 'Gentlemen in the dock, you know as well as I that the vast record assembled in this courtroom admits of but one interpretation. It is true that your crimes had the outward appearance of legality. It is true that you committed them under conditions that made it difficult for you to feel you were doing wrong. It is even true that you tried to limit their essentially illimitable implications.

'*But you did not rise with the occasion.* You did not think anew. You did not disenthral yourselves . . . And you failed to reckon on the vulture.

'There will always be a vulture, gentlemen. History is full of vultures. When you booby-trap an entire planet, you cannot cry "Non mea culpa!" if some faulty computer chip, misfiled war game, nuclear terrorist, would-be Napoleon, unmanageable crisis, or incomprehensible event pulls the tripwire. You cannot say that you were simply obeying your constituents or leaders. To quote Hannah Arendt, "Politics is not like the nursery. In politics, obedience and support are the same." '

Bonenfant was shivering as if his scopas suit had ceased to function. Dennie's exquisite face had turned ugly with anger and frustration.

'Support,' repeated Justice Jefferson. 'There is where your guilt lies. For when all is said and done, what remains is this. Each of you in his own way encouraged his government to cultivate a technology of mass murder, and, by extension, each of you supported a policy of mass murder.'

George looked at Morning and realized that he had never before seen anyone weeping at a distance. He felt his spermatids shaking with dread.

'Speaking personally,' Justice Jefferson continued, 'I would like nothing better than to say, "Gentlemen, there has been enough slaughter already, and we have decided to answer your crimes with love. You are free to leave this courtroom and survive as best you can here in Antarctica." ' She bent her head for a moment. When she looked up, tears were poised on her eyelids. 'But I cannot say that, for the tribunal's duty at this moment is to tell all creation that we loathe what you did, and we know only one way to accomplish this.'

Parkman left the defense table and, throwing up his hands in a gesture of contempt, stalked out of the courtroom.

'The defendant Overwhite will please rise,' said Justice Wojciechowski. 'Mr Brian Overwhite, the court finds you guilty on all four counts and sentences you to be hanged at sunrise tomorrow.'

'I thought you just wanted an explanation,' Overwhite sputtered.

'The defendant Randstable will please rise,' said Justice Yoshinobu. 'Dr William Randstable, the court finds you guilty on all four counts and sentences you to be hanged at sunrise tomorrow.'

'If I may say so, your Honors, that is the poorest decision I have ever heard,' responded the former whiz kid.

'The defendant Sparrow will please rise,' said Justice Gioberti. 'Reverend Peter Sparrow, the court finds you guilty on all four counts and sentences you to be hanged at sunrise tomorrow.'

The evangelist pulled the little Bible from his three-piece suit and kissed it. 'I am with you always,' he said with great dignity, 'even unto the end of the world.'

'The defendant Tarmac will please rise,' said Justice Wojciechowski.

'There's a pattern developing here,' muttered the MARCH Hare.

'Major General Roger Tarmac, the court finds you guilty on all four counts and sentences you to be hanged at sunrise tomorrow.'

Brat pantomimed his opinion that Justice Wojciechowski should be subjected to an involuntary and unpleasant sexual experience.

'The defendant Wengernook will please rise,' said Justice Yoshinobu.

The assistant defense secretary did not move. His eyes looked packed in wax. His hands vibrated like chilly tarantulas. Gila Guizot entered the glass booth and hauled him to his feet.

'Mr Robert Wengernook, the court finds you guilty on all four counts and sentences you to be hanged at sunrise tomorrow.'

Gila repositioned the defendant in his chair.

Brat is right, thought George. A pattern is developing here. But not for me. My luck is too good. *Cancer? Nah, it's only scar tissue*, the family doctor had said. *Yes, 'I'll marry you,* Justine had said. *Sure, I'll give you a job,* Arthur Crippen had said.

'The defendant Paxton will please rise,' said Justice Jefferson.

I'm a survivor, he thought. *Nuclear war, radiation poisoning, human extinction – nothing can touch me.*

George felt himself rising. He realized that he was standing, that Morning was studying him with moist eyes.

It's positive, George! The pregnancy test was positive!

'Mr George Paxton, the court finds you . . .'

Nothing to worry about, folks, every baby gets ear infections.

'Innocent—'

Innocent!

'. . . on Count One, Crimes Against Peace. Innocent on Count Two, War Crimes. Innocent on Count Three, Crimes Against Humanity.'

Aubrey, Morning, we've done it!

'On Count Four, Crimes Against the Future, the court finds you guilty as charged and sentences you to be hanged at sunrise tomorrow.' Justice Jefferson winced violently. 'I am sorry, Mr Paxton. We rather liked you.' Her gavel hit the bench for the last time. 'The International Military and Civilian Tribunal is hereby dissolved.'

CHAPTER SEVENTEEN

*In Which Orange Trees Sprout Nooses and
Our Hero Is Reunited with His Vulture*

Even if George had heard the aphorism that nothing concentrates one's mind so wonderfully as knowing one will be hanged at dawn, his mind would still have been woefully unconcentrated. A tribunal stenographer transcribing his thoughts would have produced only babblings, yipes, and the same chant he had improvised when the warhead was groundburst upon his home town. *This cannot be happening, this cannot be happening, this cannot . . .*

Like a cancer victim scanning a medical dictionary in hopes that the standard definitions have been repealed overnight in favor of good news, George reviewed what Justice Jefferson had said to him, seeking to find alternative meanings for 'guilty' and 'hanged' and 'sunrise' and 'tomorrow.' Futile. He picked up his Leonardo. His tears hit the paint, turning Aubrey's dress to mud. *I must face all this with dignity,* he recited to himself. But where was the audience? In what history book would his courage be recorded? He returned the glass slide to the nightstand.

A discordant jangle of keys reached his ears, and then the door cracked open, sending a burst of torchlight across the cell floor.

'Morning?'

But it was only Juan Ramos, bearing a large, hourglass-shaped object and a plate of food. 'Your last meal, brave extinctionist. Also, if you want it, an ice clock.'

George's last meal was a sumptuous pile of fried skua, boiled sea lion, and corn, the latter harvested 'from the ice-free valleys near McMurdo Sound,' as Ramos explained. There was even a small glass of wine – 'fermented penguin lymph' – and a fresh orange.

'I would like some privacy,' said George.

'My fear is the utensils, Señor.' Ramos set the ice clock next to Aubrey's portrait. 'You might try killing yourself, no?'

The profundity of George's appetite embarrassed and confused him. Didn't his body know what was going on here? He devoured every morsel, scraping the plate with his knife, licking the blade. His wine vanished in three gulps.

Ramos said, 'The clock will tell you when dawn arrives. As we say, "It's always darkest before the dawn in Antarctica, and it's always darkest after that too." ' He demonstrated the device. At the base, a small seal-oil lamp. In the top chamber, a block of ice. As the heat rose, the ice dissolved drop by drop into the lower chamber, which already contained a puddle.

'The design comes from Leonardo da Vinci's notebooks,' the jailor explained. '*Buenos noches*,' he added softly. He collected the utensils and left.

When the clock's lower chamber was half full, so that barely ten thousand drops divided George from the scaffold, another visitor arrived, a person to whom he was certain he had nothing more to say.

The trial had aged Bonenfant, wrinkled him. It was as if his face had been painted on a balloon, and now the air was leaking out. 'Justice has miscarried,' he announced. Zags of white cut through his black hair. 'No – worse. Justice has suffered a back-alley abortion. We've made all the appropriate appeals, of course.'

'Hopeless, right?'

'I thought you'd get a fair trial, I really did. The judges simply couldn't see that most nuclear wars don't end this way. All that high-flying talk about impartiality, and they never once stopped being darkbloods. I'm sorry, George. My best wasn't good enough.'

'See this?' George removed the glass painting from the night-stand, held it before Bonenfant. 'An original Leonardo.'

'Hmm?' The advocate examined the slide from several different distances. 'Impressive. So much detail in such a small space.'

His voice was redolent of rusty hinges. 'Looks a bit like you and Dr Valcourt, doesn't it? Leonardo, you said?'

'Following orders from that famous liar and charlatan, Nostradamus.'

Bonenfant paced around the cell, a subtle limp in his gait, a minor stoop in his posture. 'The tribunal wonders whether you have any final requests,' he said.

George cast a weary eye on the ice clock. 'I would like my family back, my planet restored, and my execution postponed fifty years.'

Bonenfant forced a laugh. When you are about to be hanged, George concluded, you get laughs for your jokes.

'Tarmac asked for a soldier's death.' The advocate enacted a guard raising a rifle. 'Firing squad.'

'I've heard that your bowels let go when they hang you,' said George.

'Request denied.'

'Poor bastard.'

'But they did grant his other wish – he'll be hanged with that man-portable thermonuclear device in his holster. Defused. He told Jefferson, "I still believe that armed missiles served the cause of world peace, and I would be a hypocrite to reject them in my hour of adversity." ' Bonenfant pulled a sealed envelope from the hip pocket of his scopas suit. 'This is for you.'

George tore off his gloves, clawed at the envelope with frozen fingernails. A scrap of paper fell out.

Dearest Darling,

  Some things are too painful.

  Human extinction.

  Reunion with the man I love on the eve of his execution.

  Do you hate me for not coming? I thought of the things we would try saying to each other, and it was unendurable. I shall not abandon you. I shall join you at the end. There is no justice. Forgive me.

                                        All my love,
                                        Morning

Bonenfant touched the ice clock, failed to staunch its flow. 'You're quite a celebrity, George – do you realize that? People are saying your case should never have come to trial. They know you're being hanged for symbolic reasons. Cold comfort, I guess, but—'

'I would like you to leave now.'

With more violence than he had ever brought to anything in his life, George shredded Morning's letter.

'Bad news?'

'I said you should leave.'

'I found a Presbyterian minister for Overwhite. I could try to get you a Unitarian.'

'Mr Bonenfant, in ten seconds I am going to strangle you to death, and my sympathizers out there will realize that I am not so symbolic after all.'

George looked at the ice clock and saw that the lower chamber was two-thirds full. The slam of the cell door dislodged a particularly large and malicious drop.

Latitude: 70 degrees 0 minutes south.

Longitude: 11 degrees 50 minutes east.

Dawn.

Thrusting through the brash-ice that clogged the Princess Astrid Coast, Periscope Number One cast its eye on the frozen beach. The beholder of this panorama, Lieutenant Commander Olaf Sverre of the United States Navy, grinned expansively. The Astrid barrier was as deserted as he had guessed it would be. Not a single ice limbo rose from the sparkling silver cliffs. Home to the stations of Lazarev and Novolazarevskaya, Astrid had become like all other Soviet claims in Antarctica – an antimecca, unholy in the extreme, a land occasioning unspeakable profanities and pilgrimages of avoidance. A most reliable sanctuary, he decided.

He went to the galley, brewed a cup of coffee, sweetened it with gin. Walking down empty passageways and past abandoned quarters, he considered the facts of his triumph: a twelve-day run beneath five thousand miles of harsh, ill-charted ocean, from McMurdo Sound to the open Pacific, then out past the Circle, around the Palmer Peninsula, and on to the Astrid Coast, with not one man to assist him. He entered the periscope room, pushed his good eye against the viewfinder. Aiming toward the base of the Nimrod Glacier, a place called Shackleton Inlet on his chart, he adjusted the zoom control and twisted the focus knob.

A broad, flat hill of stone emerged from the blur. Clustered in the center of the nunatak were six trees – Lieutenant Grass's hydroponic orchard, born and bred in the missile tubes, rocked in the cradles of death. Owing to rigorous applications of killer-whale dung and other indigenous fertilizers, the trees were healthy, oranges glowing beneath shawls of ice, branches bowing pliantly in the breeze, roots seizing stern nourishment from the bedrock.

From each tree dangled a noose of steel cable.

Several platoons from the Antarctic Corps of Guards stood between the orchard and the spectators. The infinite crowd spiraled outward from the nunatak to the glacial tongue, and from there to the plateau above and the Ross Ice Shelf below. Blazing torches grew from the pressure ridges, their jack-o'-lantern glow catching the branches and throwing serpentine shadows on the ground. GUILTY! Mount Christchurch shouted in letters ten feet high.

Walled off from the mob by a brigade of police, a score of dissidents waved banners: FREE PAXTON . . . NO SYMBOLIC EXECUTIONS . . . ANYONE WOULD HAVE SIGNED. Well, well, mused Sverre, Dr Valcourt's lover has a following. A misty image formed in the captain's mind. His bride-never-to-be, Kristin. Where was she now? Attending the executions? In an ice limbo? At what age had she gained the continent?

Under one of the nooses sat a Sno-Cat – a Death-Cat, Sverre decided – bristling with a fresh and lavish coat of black paint. Its windows were smeared with frost; dark flatus poured from its tailpipe. On the roof, a man in a black scopas suit paced anxiously. The eye holes of his black face-mask looked like terrible wounds. A rope ladder spilled from the Death-Cat to the ground.

Surrounded by guards, a second Cat, this one painted a morbid white, rumbled into view, stopping about ten yards from the orchard. Juan Ramos and Gila Guizot leaped from the cab and tromped around to the rear. Prodded by a gun muzzle, Randstable stumbled out, tripping over himself. Ramos guided him to the Death-Cat, ordered him to climb the ladder. As the condemned man reached the roof, the executioner set about his duties, lashing Randstable's wrists together with a leather thong and securing his ankles with a scopas suit utility belt. He eased the metal noose around the ex-Wunderkind's neck.

'You have anything to say?' shouted Ramos.

'The megatonnage had dropped to twenty-five percent of our late fifties arsenal,' Randstable stated evenly, each word unmistakable even to a novice lip reader like Sverre.

The executioner tightened the noose and pulled a black leather hood over the prisoner's head. Turning to the driver of the Death-Cat, Ramos pantomimed a guillotine blade encountering a neck. The vehicle chugged away, taking the executioner with it.

Randstable stayed behind.

Applause erupted from the mob. Some cried, 'Bravo!' Others, 'Encore!' and 'Hooray!' Sverre drank gin and cringed. He had expected better of his race. In the middle of Randstable's second spasm, the front of his suit split and his little magnetic chess set burst out. The wind buckled the spectators' signs: LET US IN . . . SLOW DEATHS FOR EXTINCTIONISTS . . . TARMAC, YOU SHOULD HAVE BASED THEM UP YOUR ASS . . . WHEN?

The Death-Cat stopped beneath the next tree.

Neck broken, consciousness gone, Randstable rotated in the frigid wind, his chess pieces scattered below his feet like fallen fruit. The physician of the court came forward with a stethoscope and listened to the hanged man's heart. Shaking his head, the doctor stepped away. He shuffled, advanced, checked again, retreated. He checked a third time. A fourth. Finally, after twenty minutes in unquiet suspension, Randstable was pronounced dead.

Ramos went back to the white Cat, ordered Overwhite out. Within a minute the author of the STABLE treaties was on the gallows, bound, noosed, ready.

'Have you anything to say?' Ramos called.

'In exchange for your compassionate understanding, I shall

affirm that I see your viewpoint on this war and that I more or less comprehend why you are hanging me.'

His last negotiation.

The executioner lowered the leather hood, tightened the noose. Ramos signaled the Death-Cat. Overwhite's boots bounced along the roof, and then they didn't. Eleven minutes later, the physician declared him gone.

Gila Guizot dragged Reverend Sparrow into the gloomy air. Once atop the Death-Cat, he took out his little Bible, opened it, and recited with considerable majesty, 'Father, forgive them, for they know not what they do.'

There's more truth in that than he realizes, thought Sverre, closing his good eye. When he looked again, the Bible lay in the snow and the evangelist was aloft.

Sverre focused on the white Cat. Had Wengernook, Tarmac, and Paxton seen the executions? What odd sensations were shooting through their red blood? Were they weeping? From the little he had experienced of the admitted mind, Sverre doubted that their thoughts were equal to the cosmic implications of the moment.

America's Assistant Secretary of Defense for International Security Affairs had become protoplasm. Four guards carried his limp and quivering body to the Death-Cat. They hauled him to the roof like a sack of rags, forced him into a standing position. Their muscled shoulders shored him up. Sverre recalled a videocassette that the tribunal had given him as he embarked on Operation Erebus. 'This is the man we want,' they had said, 'You can watch it on the boat.' It was a commercial for scopas suits starring a pious and nervous Robert Wengernook; the assistant defense secretary had explained that the suits were a deterrent, but failed to mention their uncanny powers against Antarctic weather. 'Deterrence is only as good as the people it protects,' he had said.

A guard stuck a cigarette in Wengernook's mouth, where it bobbed around like a compass needle responding to a passing magnet, then fell out. Sverre grimaced. Operation Erebus was a mistake; there was no poetry in this.

'Have you anything to say?' Ramos called.

Wengernook began retching. Once airborne, it took him only two minutes to die.

The blizzard collected its forces. It rattled the trees and spun the four dead men. Branches flew away, crystalline oranges hit the ground. Through whirring snow Brat Tarmac walked to the scaffold – his pace was certain, measured, calm – and climbed.

Gazing through his rubber eye, Sverre directed his thoughts back to the days when he had believed in the tribunal, to the afternoon Tarmac had barged into his cabin demanding a retaliatory strike. He had disliked the general then, but today he noted a trait that he was inclined to call nobility. Admitteds took getting used to. He opened his good eye and saw Tarmac standing quietly on the dark roof, hands and feet bound, neck tethered to the tree. The MARCH Hare grinned at the crowd as the executioner placed the man-portable thermonuclear device in his holster.

'Have you anything to say?' Ramos called.

'I say that I am inno—'

The executioner cinched the noose. It bit into the general's throat, bringing blood. In a gesture at once dignified, insouciant, and vain, Brat refused the hood.

The Death-Cat lurched away, but the general had an iron neck, it would not snap. Briefly he danced amid the squalls of snow, grew tired, stopped. When the physician came forward, Brat planted a hard, icy boot in his face. Immediately Ramos took charge, ordering ten guards to line up. The MARCH Hare smiled crookedly as the rifles were raised. The order came. Bright red blood fountained forth, thick admitted juice rushing down the pristine front of Brat's suit, speckling the ice, and then it was over, a soldier's death after all.

Sverre drank gin, studied the white Cat. Under these circumstances, could Paxton possibly be thinking of sex? Had he and Dr Valcourt managed to make love before their separation? The captain pivoted the scope, fixed on where the future had taken its revenge, five trees fruited with convicted war criminals, the sixth tree empty, waiting.

George's mind was slipping away from him.

Autistically he watched the progress of the ice clock, drops falling noisily to their destination, each as sad and final as a tear. Bang, bang went the drops, and barely an hour remained.

Then half an hour. Twenty minutes. Ten.

On the *City of New York*, Sverre entered the periscope room and scanned the continent in search of Lieutenant Grass's orchard.

Bang, bang went the drops.

George looked up. A great red stain bloomed above his head. His ceiling was bleeding. The stain grew rapidly, extending its wet peninsulas.

He guessed that he was seeing the last unexpected effect of nuclear war.

A dark shape attacked the bloody ceiling from above. A fissure appeared, then a river system of cracks. Bits of ceiling fell inward, striking George's shoulders and chest, panicking his spermatids.

The shape bartered relentlessly, until at last the ceiling split with a sound like a despairing frog. A million ice pellets burst into the cell; red droplets spattered downward, a bloodstorm. The wind entered in raw, razoring gusts, howling like an unadmitted child.

Why the Antarctic Corps of Guards did not simply come through the door was a puzzle George felt no inclination to solve. He picked up the family portrait, zipped it into the hip pocket of his scopas suit. Brat is planning to die with his man-portable thermonuclear device at his side, he thought, and I shall die with my Leonardo.

A gigantic vulture of a type once thought extinct descended through the breach and landed on the floor.

So, thought George, they've changed the mode of my execution. I'm not to be hanged but devoured. Probably quicker, actually.

The teratorn screeched. Blood spilled from its beak like soup slopping out of a tureen. Its ratty feathers were inlaid with jewels of ice.

When George noticed a scopas-suited human astride the

vulture's neck, he realized that something other than an execution was in the making.

'Climb aboard,' called the rider, removing her helmet and releasing a burst of red hair. 'I still believe you're innocent,' said Morning Valcourt. She tossed George a pair of goggles and a parka, its hood rimmed with wolverine fur.

'You've tamed it?' asked George. 'God!'

'Psychology 101 – Operant Conditioning. It's usually done on pigeons, but it also works with teratorns.'

As Morning replaced her helmet, footfalls echoed through the tunnels outside the cell. George heard curses.

Grabbing successive fistfuls of feathers and pulling himself upward, he ascended the vulture's left wing. The bird stank. It regarded him with an eye resembling a volcanic cinder. He straddled its scrawny neck, threw his arms around Morning's waist.

'There was blood on the ceiling,' he said.

'A dead seal, so our friend would cut through the roof. The feeding frenzy, right? Hold tight!'

The door flew open, mashing into the cell wall. George looked down. The guard held a shotgun in one hand, a pistol in the other. A scar ran like a black wadi all the way from his forehead to his mouth, which at the moment gaped in astonishment.

The vulture beat its wings, and the fugitives rose toward the lightless dawn.

Guards scurried across the courtyard, their lanterns and torches darting about like crazed fireflies. Gun metal flashed. Rifleshots ripped through the dark, shattering the teratorn's tail, so that great severed feathers drifted toward the ground. A slug drilled through George's boot heel, another clipped the fur on his parka. The vulture screeched, shook, but stayed aloft. The volley was answered by dozens of shadowy, armed protestors streaming through the gate. FREE PAXTON, their banners said. NO SYMBOLIC EXECUTIONS. The protestors cheered as the fugitives ascended beyond the skirmish. Shots, bright bullets – bodies hit the ice, black blood erupting from their scopas suits, their screams mingling with the vulture's cries. Oh, valuable bird, thought George,

254

carnivorous angel, braver than an eagle, more perfect than a horse, Leonardo need not have feared you. With a great heave of its rudderless body, the teratorn cleared the Ice Palace ramparts. Soaring over a tower, it stretched its legs, opened its talons, and turned the Antarctic national flag into a dozen fluttering ribbons.

She's made good on her scheme, Captain Sverre concluded when Juan Ramos failed to return to the white Cat. He smiled, pleased that his final voyage had not been made in the service of the McMurdo Agreement's framers and their show trial. Pivoting the periscope, he watched a search party swarm across the Nimrod Glacier; their lanterns bobbed among the hummocks like wills-o'-the-wisp. He looked toward the plateau, focused on a black and menacing shape cutting across the southern constellations. A Soviet Spitball cruise missile? No – a teratorn. For unto them a species will be born. Fly, George. Fly, Morning . . .

'Fly, *Teratornis*!' George screamed.

Although he had ample cause to feel that his escape was a mirage, the wish-dream of a man confronting doom, the plausible discomforts of the flight told George that all was real. Bird riding was far less romantic than he would have guessed. Teratorns, it seemed, were flying ecosystems, their feathers clogged with parasites – worms, bugs – and the parasites of parasites. The wind lashed George's face; it bored under his skin and made icy tunnels in his bones. The bird's cervical vertebrae defied the padding of his suit, cutting into his thighs. The oozy odor of vulture sweat, death left in the sun, blew into his nostrils. Yes, this was truly happening.

'Where are we going?' he called above the hysterical wind, certain that at any moment he was going to fall off.

'Across the Pole – to the boat!' Morning called back.

The Pole! His gonads buzzed. In one of his seminiferous tubules, an Aubrey Paxton spermatid lay waiting to be steered into its appropriate duct. He could feel it.

'The boat?'

'She's been at sea! Sverre brought her back into the Pacific, round the Getz Shelf and—'

Her words were claimed by the gale.

CHAPTER EIGHTEEN

In Which Our Hero and His Mate Visit
a Garden of Ice and One of Earthly Delights

By nightfall the fugitives were at the Pole, a stretch of open plateau seamed against the dark sky and heaving with waves of frozen snow. Vents and antennas poked through the sasgruti, evidence of the submerged outpost known as New Amundsen-Scott Station. They hitched their teratorn to a chimney.

Someone had left a mirror ball – the type intended to decorate a garden – at the precise endpoint of the earth's axis. George pressed it to his stomach. Was this how a pregnancy felt?

'I shall regain my fertility here,' he said. 'I've got millions of spermatids now, but unless they are pulled into my epididymis, they will never mature.'

Morning's shrug, her frown, the cant of her eyebrows – yes, there was certainly some skepticism in these gestures, but mainly, he felt, she was expressing curiosity. She wished him luck. Good, he thought, she's keeping an open mind. We have no idea what wisdom the future would have brought, what breakthroughs in mushroom therapy and geomagnetic cures.

He hugged the mirror ball tighter. His lower body trembled. Am I committing the great Unitarian sin of self-delusion? No, something was definitely occurring in his gonads, a grand-scale spermatid migration. Tendrils of light rose from the ice, forming tiny diamond-like satellites that went into orbit around the mirror ball, a thousand sparkling moons following their own reflections. He sensed his spermatids' happiness, the joy of children being chased by an incoming tide. Onward the seedlets marched, driven by the resilient, magnetic earth. They reached the epididymis. Here they would mature, learn to whip their fine, new tails. In time, as he recalled from the biology text he had read on the sub, they would be diluted by the great fluids of the seminal vesicles – what a technician God was! – then move on to new and exciting vistas: *vas deferens*, urethra, vagina, cervix, ovarian duct, uterine wall. While only one of his nascent spermatozoa was destined to sire his child, the others would do their part, bumping against the ovum with their protein-degrading enzymes – knock-knock-knock-knock – thus removing the troublesome outer layers.

Knock-knock.

Who's there?

Aubrey Paxton.

The little moons stopped in their orbits, ceased to exist, and he set the mirror ball back on the ice.

Morning had shot two skuas with the assault rifle from her scopas suit. One corpse protruded from her backpack. The other lay across the *Teratornis's* beak, and then – snap, gulp – the meal was gone, not dead long enough to suit the vulture, perhaps, but it made no complaint.

'I believe I'm cured,' George said. Spermatids were frolicking in his epididymis, home free.

'You are a man of formidable ambition,' Morning replied.

They followed the spray of her flashlight down a sloping wooden ramp and into the heart of the station. Tunnels branched left and right from the central bore, thirty-foot trenches roofed by arching sections of corrugated steel. Turning, they found themselves amid a congestion of radio equipment and meteorological instruments. Here they plucked the skua and cooked it on the primus stove from her suit. It was gone in two minutes. Weary, numb, they pushed their cold lips together, kissed without feeling it, engaged in a bulky Antarctic hug. They slept.

Dawn came, dark, dismal.

'I have hope,' he said.

'Lazarev is fourteen hundred miles away,' she replied.

'Hope for our family.'

Morning fired up the primus stove and began preparing coffee.

'Yes, I know, it's hard to imagine bringing the whole human species back,' he said. 'All that intermarriage – it gets messy, the genes degenerate or something. Still,' he smiled, 'Adam and Eve brought it off.'

'I thought you were a Unitarian.'

'All right, maybe it will be the last family – but it will *be*. Life is not nothing. Sverre can show us how to run the boat. We'll take her out of here, away from all this ice and justice. We'll get to someplace warm.'

Morning poured coffee into her expressionless mouth. She harvested ice flecks from her hair.

'I'd like to know what you think,' he said.

'Do you want some coffee?'

'No.'

She placed her chilled hands over the primus flame, moved them as if they were on a spit. 'I think . . .'

'Yes?'

His fiancée was at the most precise and unambiguous place on earth, yet she looked lost. 'I think that we must get to Lazarev before we get to the Garden of Eden.'

'Yes, but after Lazarev, we can try to become pregnant, and then—'

'Men don't want children, George, men want strategic options. Didn't you lean anything at the trial?'

'I want children. A child. Our child.'

'You want Justine and Holly back.'

'I want you and—'

Morning hurled a fistful of skua bones against the hard snow wall, slicing off his sentence. 'Can't you figure anything out on your own? Must it all be *explained* to you? In two days we'll be flying over Skeidshoven Mountain. Do you know what Skeidshoven Mountain is, idiot?'

'No.'

'Yes, you do.'

I do not know what Skeidshoven Mountain is, he told himself, over and over. His bullet wound had not hurt so much since its inception. I do not know . . .

He knew. Oh, God, he knew. Damn you, Nostradamus, prince of frauds! And damn you as well, Leonardo, painter of lies!

He pulled the magic lantern slide from his breast pocket. His supposed wife smiled up at him, his alleged daughter still wore a merry face. With a quick slapping motion he rammed the glass rectangle against the floor. There was a sound like a nut encountering a nutcracker. It's not everyone who gets to destroy a priceless Leonardo, he thought. And then his tears started, large and cold, as if an ice clock were ticking in his brain.

Morning removed her gloves and picked up a Leonardo sliver. It contained Aubrey's head.

'What is Skeidshoven Mountain?' George asked. He knew.

She rested the sliver against her palm. 'It's where I . . .'

'Yes?'

'Gained the continent.'

She drew the glass across her flesh. Black blood rushed out. Clotting, it acquired the tormented contours and pinched skin of a weeping face.

'On the second of May,' she said, 'a bright winter afternoon. I beheld my memories, and I had nothing. No children, no lovers, just a working knowlege of psychotherapy.'

Squeezing her eyelids together, she bottled up her tears.

Even with the frequent pauses for gulps and sighs, her story did not take long. Stowing away as the submarine left McMurdo Station . . . pretending to come aboard with Randstable . . . going to Sverre and convincing him that his prisoners were threatened with sudden mental collapse . . .

'I wanted a *life*, George, not the dead dreams of those wretches in the limbos.' Her tears escaped, hardening into thin bright glaciers before they could leave her face. 'And I did it. I brought it off. You would never have loved a darkblood, but you loved *me*.'

She opened her eyes. He was gone . . .

I don't understand the first thing about admitteds, Morning thought. I love this man, and I have no idea what matters to him.

She ran through the maze of ice-and-steel tunnels, following the flashlight beam, chasing his crackling footfalls and the shouts that rattled off the frozen surfaces of New Amundsen-Scott

Station – howls of unfathomable sadness, curses targeted against God, and, most of all, over and over, a thousand echoing demands that the universe give him a child.

The sickness began in his spleen. Sverre could feel it corrupting the fat organ, rushing outward, pouring into his lymph, pressing toward the headwaters of his heart. He lay in his bunk for hours, days, powerless to stop the progress of his unadmittance, his mind wandering the foggy border between sleep and oblivion. His brain floated on dark, tarry fluids. Occasionally it showed him snatches of his beloved Kristin, more often an Antarctic crevasse, an ice tunnel to hell.

It was all in the McMurdo Sound Agreement. Sverre had been the first of his race to gain the continent, and so he would be the first to lose it. Ragnarok, he thought. World's End. He was satisfied with his new verse. It did not rhyme; poetry need not rhyme. *Yea, Thor struck Jormungandr the Midgard Serpent as it shot from the sea, and the worm's last breath did blast the god and dry his blood, and next the mortal world itself did crack, locked in endless winter.* Ragnarok – when all debts fall due, all legends climax. And so, pursuant to the legend, an Antarctic storm rushed through the boat, sea dragon's breath prying back the hatches, whooshing down the corridors, crossing Sverre's cabin. He drew his blankets tight, but the dragon's breath still came; it squeezed his bones and turned his gutta-percha eye into a hailstone. His ears throbbed with the detonations of Jormungandr's heart.

He awoke. The heart was a human fist, pounding at his cabin door.

Rolling out of bed, he was hit by the smell of himself, flesh marinated in alcohol and sweat. Gin, he knew, and gin alone, would get him to the door. He limped to his writing desk, found the bottle, shoved its mouth home. His intoxicated hand staggered across the desk, knocking over the ink pot, scattering pages of the *Saga of Thor*.

Behind the door two ghosts in scopas suits waited. They were rimmed with frost. One had an ice storm raging in its beard.

'You're out of uniform,' Morning said, removing her helmet.

'Dr Valcourt?' He took a pull at the bottle.

'From the Pole to Astrid Land by vulture in fifty-one hours,' she said. 'That must be a record, right? They'll put us in *National Geographic*.'

'Morning and I are in love,' said George.

'I know,' said the captain.

Sverre walked forward, tripped. George bear-hugged him, and the gin bottle clattered to the floor. It was shocking how insubstantial the captain had become, his skin like paper, his beard the color and consistency of dead seaweed. The fugitives carried him to the bed, lowered him into the Sverre-shaped mold in his mattress. He asked for his poem and some gin. While Morning gathered up the papers from the writing desk, George retrieved the bottle.

'I saw the executions,' Sverre said. 'Tarmac refused the hood. A real four-ball general . . .' He coughed. 'I would like to hear the *Saga of Thor*.'

Morning read the captain his poem.

'That's not bad, is it?' said Sverre.

'You would have been one heck of an epitaph writer,' answered George.

'Be honest now – is it any good?'

'In your time you became a poet,' Morning replied.

George lifted the white raven from Sverre's writing desk, smoothed its alabaster feathers. Holly would have named it Birdie. 'Sir, you've made certain efforts on my behalf,' he said stiffly, 'and I appreciate them.'

'Your name should never have been in the indictment, Paxton.' Sverre grinned, showing teeth that resembled Indian corn. 'Be fruitful and multiply – both of you.'

Morning fired an unambiguous glance toward George: leave him his illusions. 'My dear Lieutenant Commander Sverre,' she said, 'may I assume that you never mustered yourself out of the Navy? Are you still captain of the *City of New York?*'

The dying man could not stand, and so he sat on the altar, boots dangling against the silk antependium. At one time his voice could have filled the whole chapel, rocking it as would a hellfire sermon from Reverend Sparrow, but now the engaged couple had to lean forward to catch his words.

'Dearly beloved, we are gathered together here in the sight of . . . whatever.' A cough attacked, spinning him around. He flailed at the air, smacked his hand against a candlestick, sent it toppling. 'Something, something. To join together this man and this woman in . . . something. Holy matrimony. Consecrated fornication. Something.'

He took the gin bottle from his coat and drank.

'Do you, Morning Valcourt, take this man to be your lawfully wedded wife . . . husband . . . to have and to hold from this day forward, for better for worse . . . something . . . for richer for poorer, in sickness and in health, to love and to cherish . . . all that. . . till death do you part?'

'I do.'

He coughed, and black blood came up.

'And do you, George Paxton, take this woman to be your lawfully wedded wife, to have and to hold from this day forward, for better for worse, come locusts . . . gammas rays . . . come . . . never mind. Do you?'

'I do.'

'Forasmuch as you have consented together in wedlock, and have witnessed the same before God and the captain of this ship, I now pronounce you husband and wife.'

Husband and wife kissed. Their scopas suits came together, separating a few seconds later with a loud, rubbery *skluck.*

When Sverre smiled, black blood spilled over his teeth. 'Tell your children to respect the Navy.' He collapsed on the altar, muttered, 'Look – she's never been clearer. Look at Kristin, would you, flying up and down on that roller coaster, up and down, so . . . clear . . .'

They laid him out, opened his claw-hammer coat. Like an abused onion Sverre lost his layers, skin, muscle, viscera, veins, nerves, all sloughing from his bones, and then there was dust, and then there was nothing, nothing at all save a solitary gutta-percha eye.

The newlyweds gathered Sverre's vacant coat into a bundle,

brought it on deck, tossed it over the side. An ice floe slapped against the coat, pounding it into the depths of the bay. A flock of penguins watched from their rookeries. Dressed in their finest tuxedos, they had come for a wedding, only to find it superseded by a funeral. They stood dutifully on the cliffs, solemn as professional mourners, until the vulture came and, with fearsome squawks and a tumultuous beating of its wings, chased them away. It was the last George ever saw of the great unextinct beast, his feathered co-defendant, freak, fluke, ender of the world. Exhausted, famished – they had not known deep sleep or a true meal in two days – husband and wife returned to their bower. They went to the galley, a wonderland of kettles, and prepared their wedding feast, eating it on the spot. Apples and pears disappeared into ravenous mouths. Turkey drumsticks were consumed half raw. Corn went down frozen. They devoured their wedding cake in batter form.

Staggering into the corridor, the happy couple realized that they were over a hundred yards from any cabin. They looked at each other. A hundred yards, a hundred miles – no difference. They dropped to the floor and nuzzled. Like a lizard abandoning its skin, George slipped out of his scopas suit. He heard a grinding noise – snores, yes, but these were the snores of Morning Valcourt, hence, pleasing snores, subtle, intelligent. Quietly he studied his new wife, this great unadmitted psychotherapist, this brilliant vulture pilot, gleaning endless delight from her freckled, ice-scarred, beautiful, sleeping face . . .

When he awoke, the world had become an erotic film, the rug soft, the corridor warm, sweat accumulating inside his underwear like sweet balm, and there she was, freshly showered and dressed in silk pajamas emblazoned with the anchor insignia of the United States Navy, displaying herself in a provocative low-angle shot, offering a wet hand. He jumped to his feet and followed her down the corridor, glorying in the fragrance of her soggy hair, his erection moving before him like a bowsprit. He shivered with the hair-trigger sexuality of adolescence. Outside the executive officer's cabin she kissed him with awkward desire.

'I'm sweaty,' he said.

'I don't care,' she replied, leading him over the threshold.

The cabin was ablaze. How many candles? A hundred? A thousand? Candles lovingly arranged on the nightstand, the bureau, the floor, candles stuck in gin bottles and teacups, candles lined up along the headboard like the Constellation Midgard Serpent.

'Are we having a séance?' he asked.

She gasped and lost her smile. George bit his lower lip mercilessly, wincing at the pain.

'I'm sorry. I—'

'I thought you would like them,' she said. Her eyes grew moist. 'They're supposed to be . . . romantic.'

'I like them,' he said hastily. 'They're fine.'

'Look, George, I simply don't know about these things.'

'They're *very* romantic.'

'I've never done this before,' she said.

'Follow my lead.'

He placed his arms around her, massaged her shoulder blades. She did the same to him. He undid her top, working the wonderfully pliant buttons, tossed it onto the bed, the only place in the room where it would not catch fire. She mimicked him; his undershirt flew away. Though not large, her breasts still partook unmistakably of that inscrutable genre of sensuality, that religion of round altars, source of obsessions so intense that the males of his extinct species had been mystified and powerless, the females mystified and annoyed, and so he gawked, feeling that he owed the indulgence not only to himself but also to his dead gender, and then he kissed her nipples, which pushed out like brown shoots from soil, and within seconds she had picked up the cue and was kissing his.

He finished unclothing her. She reciprocated. They stood together in the flaming room.

'You see, I have to put this in you.' Ready to burst, he lowered her onto the bed.

'So I've read.' She laughed. 'Do I put something in you? I forget.'

He entered her, sawed, released his eager sperm. He withdrew instantly.

'Was that it?' she asked.

'The first time you drank coffee – you were probably nine or something – you didn't like it, right?'

'I was never nine.'

He pivoted, put his legs over the bed. A candle flame nipped at his ankle. 'What we really need, I think' – he stood up – 'is for me to wash.'

He went to the adjoining shower, feeling like a general who had lost a battle but still retained high hopes for the war. Morning followed faithfully. They bathed each other, kissed wetly. She was so solid, so gloriously bone-filled – not at all what he expected of her race. He had heard of the psychology experiment in which a male rat is kept endlessly potent through a steady supply of new mates, and when he saw how the water changed her, rolling in glittery pebbles down her impossibly desirable sides, and then, a few moments later, when he saw how the sheets gathered around her thighs changed her yet again, he knew that he had found in Morning Valcourt an infinite source of arousal.

This time it was a screw of which both their sexes would have been proud. She began to grasp the crux of the matter, liquifying, trembling, reveling in the unfamiliar feelings. Memories of her canceled love life flooded back. He touched her with the same appreciative passion he had brought to creviced granite. Her orgasm was florid and long, driving him to analogous spasms. They napped, awoke, met again amid the little flames, Morning improvising now, initiating novelties, using her leased body to deny her unadmittance, and he realized that, when all was said and done, she had a greater aptitude for this than he. His pleasure was fuller than he had ever known it. Around the clock they subsisted on sex – napping, eating, breathing for its sake. They discovered uncharted orifices, claimed them; they invented lewd jokes, some verbal, some enacted with fingers and mouths; they drank each other, rutted, tried to make it dirty, then cosmic, so that on some occasions they fucked, on others they made love, ever mindful of the potential in new locations – the gaming tables,

266

the chapel, the swimming pools, the main mess hall, her office. She got her period. They screwed on sheets soaked with black blood. His cock darkened. Their mutual maneuvers, their thrusts and archings, became gestures of defiance, acts that mocked the bad ideas, and as George's seeds lashed their excellent tails and struggled through Morning's eggless womb, the couple found themselves mentally cheering, thinking: try anyway, you wretched little bastards, be fruitful and multiply, for unto us a child will be born, you can do it, try.

CHAPTER NINETEEN

In Which Information Is Conveyed Suggesting
that Nostradamus Saw the Truth and Leonardo
da Vinci Painted It

April is the crudest month, never stopping, intent on causing May. George's wife grew weak. A cough raged through her. The warm, ebony blood drained from her face, leaving it chalky and dry. Her hair became brittle. Odd noises rose from deep within her, wheezes and scrapings, sounds like burning cellophane.

Sometimes George would find her in the periscope room, hugging one of the machines, pressing it into the shank of her body until her vibrations stopped. She began staying in bed all day, breathing soggily, spitting up ink.

'I want to talk,' she said.

'About what?'

'My life.'

'Won't that make you sad?' Slipping a second pillow under her heavy head, he could not help but notice the stale vapors coming from her mouth.

'Yes.' Black veins pulsed in her eyes.

He kissed his wife. 'Let's talk.'

'Leaves keep occurring to me, autumn leaves, every type, red, yellow. I think I spent some time in Vermont. I would have liked primitive art – this is quite clear – and going into libraries and reading the book spines, so many of them, famous and obscure all jumbled together. Also, I never outgrew stuffed animals.'

Dispassionately she recalled her parents, murdered in their preschool years during the Battle of Corpus Christi. Helen would have been a bowling alley attendant, a cold woman, unhappy, mired in quasi-poverty and a pathological marriage. Hugh would have been a mechanic and also a self-pitying lout who wanted a son, someone he could shoot things with.

Happier thoughts now. Morning, the thoughtful, gushy school-girl, writing meaningful poems about dead birds, creating a craw-daddy farm in Parson's Creek, scholarships piling up, the Jacob Bronowski Award for the Junior Displaying the Most Interest in Science, and other prizes with equally peculiar names, and they were hers – hers! – Hugh couldn't take them away. She flourished in graduate school, taking the clinical psychology department by storm, then converted her Ph.D. into a lucrative practice. Guilt was her speciality.

She told George of her cases – wins, draws, losses. Phillip Cassidy, inhabited till death by seven personalities. Marcie Cremo, debrained by her own revolver. And the triumphs? asked George. Quite a few, answered Morning. (The trick, you see, was to be their friend, though they didn't teach that at the University of Chicago.) Janet Hodges, fat and self-hating, but when they were finished she was a Rubens model, sensually plump, able to have unhappy love affairs just like anyone else. Willie Howard, age six, who didn't talk, not a word, was thought to be brain-damaged, but then Morning got out the puppet with the three eyes, and it taught Willie how to speak Neptunian, and so Willie taught it English.

And now – memory bending back on itself, shards from youth, sacred frivolities: a stuffed octopus, a red bicycle, a stocky ceramic teapot, a clock that looked like a cat, the smell of rain, the caffeine air of fall. My best friend was named Sylvia, I think. I loved major league baseball. Yes, I would have been a fan, can you believe that? I got my first period at a Houston Astros game. I bled for the Astros, red blood.

She described Astros who had never lived. 2003, that was to be their year. Last game of the World Series. Ninth inning. Down a run. Cristobal walks . . . Robin Arcadia comes up and . . . bang!

'Thank you,' she said.

'You've had quite a life,' he said.

'Bet your ass.'

He lay down beside her, shivering from the coldness she gave off and from the thought of what it meant. Sleep came instantly. His dream took him to a moss-muffled forest, all the great women there, Justine, Morning, his mother (SHE WAS BETTER THAN SHE KNEW), the four of them building a house (a cottage actually, on stilts above a lake), and then the children appeared, Holly, Aubrey, and a third child that Justine had gone off and had during the war, a boy.

Waking, he realized that his eyelids were stuck together, and he feared that when he pulled them apart another pair would be lying beneath them, and beyond that, another. My wife is dying. There is nothing I can do. He heard the pops of the little muscles as he opened his eyes. The ceiling lights glowered at him. He turned over, saw the vacant depression in the mattress, and all the ice in Antarctica entered his heart.

But then she limped into the cabin, feverish, shaking. Snow filled the creases of her scopas suit. Scrolls of ice hung from what remained of her hair.

'You frightened me,' he said. 'I thought—'

'No. The second of May. I gained the continent on the second of May.'

'You've been outside? It's crazy for you to go outside.'

'I made a deal.'

'What?'

'Hug me.'

He did.

'I'm going to say something strange,' she rasped. 'No matter what it is, you won't stop hugging me.'

'I promise,' he said.

'You're going to see your daughter again. Holly.'

He hugged her more tightly. 'Holly is dead.'

'I made a deal,' she said. 'It will happen in a week. Sunday. Be ready.'

'I don't understand,' he said.

'You will have half a day with her. Twelve hours. That's not much. You can say no.'

'I want this more than anything.'

'All right. It's done. Sunday. A twelve-hour visit, starting at noon. Remember – be ready.'

'I don't understand.'

'I made a deal.' Ice water drizzled from Morning's body to the carpet.

'The little girl in Leonardo's painting, it wasn't Aubrey?'

'There is no Aubrey. It was—'

'Holly?'

'Yes.'

'It looked just like her,' George said knowingly. 'It *had* to be her.'

'The painting predicted the future,' Morning confirmed. 'Nostradamus saw correctly. Kiss me.'

They went to the periscope room, Morning leaning on him all the way. Periscope Number One gazed unflinchingly across the continent. Up and down the Transantarctic Mountain Range, the McMurdo Sound Agreement took its toll, millions dissolving, deserted by their minds and bodies, leaving behind scopas suits in lieu of corpses.

'I don't want to watch this,' he said.

'You've seen worse,' she said.

He focused on the Ross Ice Shelf. The crater scooped out by the Battle of Wildgrove was but a footprint compared with the central crevasse. And then they came, marching proudly – those who preferred free will to the McMurdo Sound Agreement, friends holding hands, lovers locked together, women clutching children, children cuddling bears made of snow. In a vast white tide they hurled themselves over the ragged edge, platoons of unlived lives returning to the bedrock, generation upon generation losing the continent.

'They were right to indict me,' he muttered.

On a nearby nunatak a great bonfire flourished, flames against the snow, bright and red as an eye from the Midgard serpent. Led by Mother Mary Catherine, a hundred darkbloods moved toward the fire, each bearing an icon of ice. Warhead by warhead, delivery system by delivery system, the prosecution's frozen arsenal was abolished. The Javelin cruise missile melted instantly. Then the Guardian Angel ICBM was salvoed. Next the Multiprong fizzled away, the MacArthur III, the Wasp-13 heavy bomber, the mine, the shell, the depth charge, the free-fall bomb. Cheers shook the glacier, and then the dancing started. Cocoa flooded into frigid throats, smiles brightened tired faces, and he saw that there was nothing like a clear, cold night of security destruction for bringing joy to an unadmitted heart.

'Weaponless deterrence,' said George.

'What?' said Morning.

'A way to get rid of nuclear arsenals. Instead of missile deterring missile, factory deters factory. The Soviet and American strategists all see that any move toward rearmament on one side will be matched by the other side, until the world is back to mutual assured destruction. So nobody rearms.'

'I don't know what you're talking about.'

'The knowledge of how to build them – that's the real deterrent. I'm just beginning to understand.'

'Sounds unstable.'

'Maybe.'

'Did I tell you about my best friend? Sylvia? She had the strangest laugh you ever heard.'

Hour after hour they beheld the deaths, most anonymous, a few with names. Shawna Queen Jefferson evaporated while crossing the courtyard of the Ice Palace of Justice, her robe flapping in the wind like a great black wing. Alexander Aquinas went out attempting to preserve a copy of the verdict in a hole in one of the nunataks. As Gila Guizot began to fade, she grabbed her rifle and shot herself in the heart; liquid shadows rushed down the Antarctic National Police insignia on her breast. Jared Seldin, would-be star voyager, vaporized while crawling across the interior plateau trying to catch and befriend a baby penguin.

And everywhere, the suits. Suits lying in the streets of the ice limbos like massacred Armenians, littering the nunataks like slaughtered Huguenots, piled up in the dry valleys like purged kulaks, suits on hummocks and suits on bergs, clean white fossils of the race that had never known a single warm day.

A young woman stood on a berg calved from the Ross barrier. She paced back and forth, raised a trembling fist toward heaven. George had seen her during the trial, seated in the gallery, her gaze locked longingly on Aquinas. A screaming Antarctic gale whipped across the sea, throwing sub-zero water across the castaway's white boat, slapping her cheeks, salting her eyes. Even during his therapy sessions George had not seen so much misery compacted into one face. It seemed almost a blessing when the McMurdo Sound Agreement finally caught up with this lost and lovesick girl.

'I have never been dancing,' Morning said two days later.

'We'll fix that,' he replied.

'Waltzing is nice, I hear.'

'I can't waltz.'

'Me neither.'

'Put on your waltzing clothes.'

He left. He had no plan, but he was a good husband, and he would think of something.

Silence enveloped the little movie theater, clinging to the walls, sinking into the seats. He entered the projection booth. The 16mm film cans were stacked in three wobbly towers. In the middle of the highest stack, sandwiched between *Panic in the Year Zero* and *The End of August at the Hotel Ozone*, he spotted what he wanted, the English-language version of Sergei Bondarchuk's *War and Peace*, all eight cans' worth. He threaded up one of the middle reels, popped on the amplifier, pushed the lever to Forward. The projector grunted and squealed. Out in the theater, the narrator, golden-throated Norman Rose, declared in a voice that seemed to belong to a doctor whose patients always got well, 'If evil men can work together to get what they want, then so can good men, to get what they want.' Moving to the audio patch panel, he began to experiment, plugging, unplugging, until at last the *War and Peace* sound-track roared through the ship's intercom.

He returned to Morning and said, 'May I have this dance?'

'Delighted,' she said and coughed. Her white silk kimono hung from her failing body.

They went to the main mess hall. The noises and voices of *War and Peace* echoed off the marble columns, clattered amid the crystal chandeliers. After setting her on a velvet sofa, he pushed tables aside, flung chairs away, rolled back the carpet.

Natasha Rostov and Prince Andrei Bolkonsky were waltzing now, Ludmilla Savelyeva as Natasha, Vyacheslav Tikhonov as Andrei, original film score by Vyacheslav Ovchinnikov conducting one of the Moscow symphony orchestras.

George lifted his wife off the sofa and extended her arms. And they danced. A wise, benevolent god entered their blood, instructing them. Adeptly they revolved through the Russian palace, round and round, one two three, Ovchinnikov's melody pouring through them, one two three, notes soaring, gleaming half notes, burnished quarter notes, then came the sixteenth notes, thin and silver, needles weaving airborne tapestries, one two three, and Morning was smiling, and the hall was hot, and now she was laughing, and it seemed as if the autumn-leaf red were back in her hair.

'I'm so glad I married you,' she said.

'Would it have lasted?' he asked.

'Oh, yes,' she said. 'Forever.'

The waltz quickened. Love blossomed between Natasha and Andrei.

'You're good at dancing,' she said.

'So are you,' he said.

'The sex part was good, too.'

'First-rate, I thought.'

The orchestra reached full velocity. The notes burned as they struck the air.

'I once heard that it's great to have a dog jump in bed with you in the morning and lick your face,' she said.

'That's true,' he said.

A dotted half note soared by, trailing fire.

'Good-bye, husband,' she said.

'I'll miss you,' he said.

Her bones turned to balsa wood, and she threw all of her remaining substance into a kiss. Painlessly she quit the world, became dust, less than dust, a mute vibration, a thing never christened, born, or conceived, a notion kept only in the frail memory of a man staggering across a mess hall in an ice-bound nuclear submarine, carrying a silk kimono and weeping like an orphan.

CHAPTER TWENTY

*In Which a Most Unusual Yuletide Is
Celebrated, Including Presents and a Tree*

Each midnight he walked the carpeted corridors of the *City of New York*, master of an empty ship, his ears turned to the sound of his boots, hoping their thumps would lull him to sleep. Sometimes he heard pale whisperings issue from some dark alley or forgotten passageway, but when he investigated there was nothing. In this sunken and deserted city even George's own hallucinations declined to keep him company.

As dawn approached he would rub his eyes, force his face into a yawn, and collapse on the nearest bunk in a parody of exhaustion. Useless – Morpheus was not fooled. George stared at the ceiling, pawed at his blankets. And then, come noon, his teeth would begin grinding so briskly he expected to see sparks, and he knew that a new day was upon him. Did I dream? he would wonder. It pleased him to remember one, for this meant he had actually slept.

'Be ready,' Morning had said.

Monday, the tree. He went to the missile compartment and searched among the remaining specimens from Project Citrus, eventually finding the runt of the orchard, barely four feet high, perfect for his purposes, with frail branches and scrawny fruit – no question why it had not been among those selected for the honor of lynching a war criminal. He cut it down, bore it away, set it up in his cabin.

Tuesday, the ornaments. After securing a hammer from the torpedo room lower deck, he ran through the ship smashing every bright and gaudy object he could find – gyros, compasses, gauges, valves, pumps. He collected the shards in a duffel bag.

Wednesday and Thursday, the presents. His goal was ten. That seemed a substantial number for her to open, whereas twelve or fifteen would have smacked of overindulgence. He went to Sverre's cabin and appropriated the white alabaster raven, the captain's stovepipe hat, the globe, and an empty gin bottle. From the Silver Dollar Casino he took a stack of poker chips and a poster of a harlequin whose word balloon contained the rules for blackjack. He wrote the names of countries on the chips. The main galley yielded an assortment of utensils. He put them in a cardboard box, labeling it SUPER DUPER COOKING SET with a Navy-issue laundry marker. The library was a disappointment – not a single children's book in the stacks. So he made one, transcribing the fable he had once improvised for her in which a bunny with Holly's personality conquered self-doubt, learning to ride a two-wheeler bicycle. He illustrated it with stick figures.

For the ninth gift, George devised a rag doll out of patches and swatches cut from commissioned officers' uniforms. Its eyes were brass buttons.

The final gift had been hanging in his closet for months.

Half a day. So short. Best to trim the tree in advance. After all, she would have all those presents to unwrap and play with. For hooks he used the paper clips that held the pages of Captain Sverre's bad poetry together. By Friday afternoon the former orange tree had become a cheerful mass of glittery, twisted armatures and curled, nameless metal.

He beat the lid from a canned ham into a star. Christmas trees without stars on top were totally unacceptable. He moved the step-ladder into place . . .

Why am I lying on the floor? he wondered. What am I doing staring at the ceiling? He glanced at the rivet-studded walls, the unfinished tree. I am lying on the floor because there is no point to anything. People are extinct.

Midnight came. He stood up. 'The point,' he said aloud, 'is that Holly and I are not extinct.' He placed the star where it belonged.

Saturday, the final preparations. He wrapped the ten gifts in aluminum foil and set them under the tree, stacking and restacking them in an effort to find the perfect arrangement.

Sunday.

Seven AM.

Round and round the Christmas tree he cut a path of nervousness and doubt, periodically stopping to rearrange the presents or reposition an ornament. She wouldn't like the doll. She would start fussing. Something . . .

Eight AM Nine AM Ten AM.

After Chester the cat had died, they had decided to give him a proper burial, complete with a little headstone inscribed CHESTER that George had prepared at the Crippen Monument Works from a stray scrap of granite. Holly hated the whole idea; she refused to attend the funeral and screamed at her parents for dreaming it up. But the very next day, just as George and Justine had predicted, she began telling everyone about the big event – the monument, the grave, the cardboard coffin from the veterinarian – and continued doing so for months . . .

Eleven AM.

Justine had blown up a tarantula. This was really pretty funny when you thought about it . . .

Noon.

Outside the cabin: quick, trundling footsteps. Veins throbbed frantically in George's neck and wrists, seeming almost to break free of his body. His bullet wound ached, and he breathed deeply. Dear God, make this a good day.

A little girl ran into the cabin. Her feet cycled furiously. Her arms opened wide.

'Daddy! Daddy!' Though raspy – a cold coming? – her voice still had the angelic tone that George had never heard in any child except his.

'Holly!'

They embraced, the child giggling and trilling, George weeping. She was warm. He wiped his eyes with his sleeve and blocked his incipient tears, Holly being too young to comprehend why anyone would weep out of happiness.

278

'It's so good to see you,' he said.

'It's so good to see *you*,' she said.

The war had taken its toll. Her hair looked like yarn. Her smile was interrupted by far more missing teeth than the predations of the tooth fairy alone could explain. She moved cringingly, with a slight limp. But her green eyes sparkled, her face was incandescent, she still had her wonderful compactness, and it was her, it was her!

'Ahh – look at the *tree*!' Holly shouted.

'Do you like it? You can actually *eat* those oranges.'

'No thank you. It's beautiful. It has a star on top. That *reminds* me of something.'

'What?'

'Those Halloween trees we used to put up.'

'Yes. We hung rubber bats on them.'

'And little pumpkins. They were so *cute*.'

'I want us to have Christmas,' George said. 'You did not get Christmas this year. This was because of the war.' He was always careful to speak in complete, grammatical sentences around her.

'Daddy, I have something very sad to tell you. This is important.'

'What?'

'This is important. Mommy died.'

'You are right. It's very sad. The war killed her.'

'I *know* that,' she said, mildly annoyed.

'You gave her orange juice, didn't you?'

'She died anyway.'

'Holly, Holly, it's so *good* to have you here. See those presents down there?'

'Are they for *me*?'

'Yes. They're all for you.'

'All of them? All? Oh, Daddy, thank you, thank you. I'm so *excited*.'

'Why don't you start with this one?' he said, handing her the gin bottle. She sheared away the aluminum foil. 'A flower vase,' he explained.

'Later could we pick a flower?' she asked.

'Of course.'

Lunging for the big box, she stripped it bare. 'That says, "Super Duper Cooking Set," ' her father explained.

She pulled back the lid, took out the dishes, cups, saucers, pots, pans, kettles, and tureens. 'Oh, Daddy, I love it, I love it. Will you play cooking with me?'

'I think maybe we should finish the unwrapping.'

'*Then* will you play with me?'

'Of course.' Apprehensively he picked up the doll. 'Try this.' She tore at the foil. 'I know you wanted a Mary Merlin,' he said, 'but I couldn't find any.'

'Couldn't Santa Claus either?'

'The stores were out of them.'

'That's okay.' Holly kissed the doll and stroked its hair. 'I like her so much. Her name is Jennifer.'

She put Jennifer to bed in a roasting pan from the Super Duper Cooking Set, covering her with a blanket of aluminum foil. Next George gave his daughter the white alabaster raven. She unwrapped it, named it Birdie, and laid it next to Jennifer. Soon the doll and the raven were fast asleep.

'Be very quiet, Daddy.'

'Okay.'

'I want to pick out the next one.'

'Sure.'

She yanked the stovepipe hat from the pile, unwrapped it. Making no comment, she put it on and grinned her ragged, episodic grin. Now the bright cylinder caught her eye. Bits of foil took to the air. 'Oh, a clown!' she said, unscrolling the harlequin poster. 'He's funny. I want to hang him up.' They taped the poster to a bulkhead.

'And now you've got this one,' George said. Gleefully she ripped the foil. 'It's a story I once told you,' he explained. 'A bunny wants to ride a two-wheeler bike, and—'

'Read it to me.'

Done.

'Read it again.'

He did.

'Read it again.'

'You've got another present over here.'

'I'll bet it's a beach ball.' She pulled apart the wrapping, continued beaming even after the beach ball proved to be a globe. 'What does it do?'

'It shows us what the world is like. Well, it's really a kind of game.'

'Let's play it.'

'Okay. You need this thing over here.' He handed her the poker chips, and she unwrapped them. 'You see, they have the names of countries on them. Everybody gets ten. Then you spin the globe like this, and you keep your eyes closed, and you put your finger out the way I'm doing. And if your finger stops on a country that's the same as one of your chips, then you—'

'Is that last present for me too?' Holly asked, removing her stovepipe hat and waving it toward the tree.

'Yes. It's from Santa Claus.'

She freed her civil defense gear from its foil. 'Oooh, a *gold* one. Pretty.'

'It's called a scopas suit.'

'I *know* that.'

'I thought you might like to dress up in it.'

'Nice. What's the matter with the glove?'

'Something hit it.'

'Let's play tea party. I'll be the sister. You be the visitor.'

Holly distributed her new cooking things around the coffee table. She set out Sverre's gin bottle, filling it with several tree ornaments that vaguely resembled flowers. The raven was invited, and the doll, and the visitor, and also the scopas suit, which Holly decided was a scarecrow. Everyone had invisible cake and gossamer ice cream. During the course of the afternoon, the scarecrow's name went from Suzy to Margaret to Alfred.

Later she played alone, giving Birdie, Jennifer, and Alfred their bottles, putting them in for their naps. Outside the submarine, the black of day gave way to the black of night.

Father and daughter went to the galley and had Christmas

dinner. The stale pretzels were scrumptious. They sneaked extra sugar into their cocoa.

When they were back in the cabin, George said, 'Holly, would you like a horsey ride?'

'No.'

He was grievously disappointed.

Ten seconds later she said, 'Give me a horsey ride.'

For George it was to be a test. All previous horsey rides had ended with him insisting that he was too tired to continue. In truth he had been too bored. Each time, he had received the impression that there was no point at which Holly herself would end the ride, that she would more likely fall asleep in the saddle.

She climbed atop his big equine shoulders, and he galloped down the corridor. The pressure on his spine was extraordinarily pleasant. Waving her stovepipe hat, she urged him on. 'Turn . . . down here, Horsey . . . go through the door . . . that's the way, Horsey.'

Fifteen minutes passed. Horsey became bored. He thought: how can this be? Yet there it was, boredom. I shall keep going, he told himself. Nothing will stop this horsey ride, nothing.

'This *reminds* me of something,' Holly said.

'What?' Horsey asked.

'That ride you put the money in. Back home. Oh, I wish we were home again, Daddy. I miss my kitty.'

'Horsey is tired now,' he said. The lump in Horsey's throat felt like a stuck walnut. 'Horsey wants to go sleep in the stable.'

'Can we play that *game*? The one with the world in it?'

'Sure, honey.'

Back in the cabin, they made a half-hearted attempt at playing the stupid game. Holly became frustrated and ornery. 'How about another round of *Bicycle Bunny*?' he suggested.

They read it in the bunk, huddled beneath blankets. After it was over, she said, 'This book *reminds* me of something. Long ago, when I was very little, like three or something, you used to read me a book about the beach.'

'*Carrie of Cape Cod*. We read it lots of times last fall.'

'Remember the part about the Big Spoon?'

'The Big Dipper. Yes.'

'Could we go see the Big Dipper? I mean, *now* could we see it?'

'All right,' he said, dragging her scopas suit away from the tea party, 'But you'll have to wear this. It's cold out there.'

'No, no, *that's* Alfred Scarecrow!' she shrieked.

'Here's the deal, honey. If you don't put this on, we can't go see the Big Dipper. I'm going to wear one too.'

'Birdie wants to come.'

'Sure.'

He girded his daughter against the elements. The suit fit perfectly. She looked adorable in it, her round, glowing face popping from the gold collar. To compensate for the bullet-shattered glove, he wrapped her hand in silk strips torn from the bedsheets.

He scooped her up, carried her and Birdie through half a mile of corridor, pausing briefly to remove an electric lantern from a bulkhead and hook it around his wrist. Twenty risers spiraled from the navigation room to the first sail deck. At the door he stopped and said, 'Honey, there's something I want to ask.'

'What?'

'Do you know what's happened to you?'

'Yes, I know.'

'What's happened to you?'

'I don't want to tell you.'

'Please tell me.'

'You *know* what's happened.'

'Tell me.'

'I died.'

A thick stratum of snow covered the outside deck, sealing the missile doors. Ice flowed from the diving planes in silver sheets and drooped from the periscopes like the web of some monstrous Antarctic spider. Ragged bergs squeezed the hull from all sides, locking it tight against the barrier.

'Oh, great!' Holly said. 'It's been snowing! Look, Daddy, it's been snowing!'

He did not want to tell her that it did not snow in Antarctica, that the crystals were simply redistributed by the winds.

She looked up. The stars were sharp and bright. 'Is it there? Can we see the Big Dipper?'

'I'm not sure.'

'I think I see it.'

'Honey, I just realized something. We're in the Southern Hemisphere—'

'Is that it?' she asked, thrusting her stubby, insulated fingers heavenward.

He studied the sky. Amorphous clusters. Meaningless forms. 'Yes, honey, I think that's it.'

'You're just *saying* that! We *can't see* the Big Dipper!'

'I'm sorry, honey. I'm really sorry. We're too far south, and—'

'It's okay, Daddy. Put me down.' He lowered his arms, and she slid into the crusty snow. Groans filled the air as ice and hull ground against each other. 'I love you, Daddy.'

'I love you, too, Holly.'

'Mommy couldn't come,' she said softly.

'Yes. That's very sad.'

'We couldn't see the Big Dipper.'

'Yes. That's sad too.'

A wind blew up, churning the snow, tossing iceballs against the sail. 'Thank you for all the presents,' she said. 'I *love* that doll. This has been a *great* Christmas.'

'It's been the best Christmas ever,' he said.

'I have to go now.'

'No! You can't go!'

'I really like that cooking set, and I had fun playing visitor with you. And thank you for Birdie. And be sure to take care of Jennifer. She gets her bottle at six o'clock midnight.'

'Please stay, Holly! Please! You're not allowed to go yet!' He ripped a gob of wolverine hair out of his parka hood. 'I need to tell you a bedtime story. It's about an elf who casts a golden shadow. Please! So one day the elf's uncle asked him to—'

'Good-bye, Daddy.'

They hugged, squeezing so hard it should have hurt.

'*Please* don't go, Holly! *Please*!'

'Good-bye, Daddy. I love you.'

284

'Good-bye, darling. I love you so much. I love you so much.'

She worked free of his grip, coasted bum-down along the hull as if it were a sliding board. Her stovepipe hat fell off. Now George could hear snow crunching under her little boots. The starlight caught her golden suit, so that a figure made of phosphor moved across the barrier toward Lazarev. She clutched Birdie tighter, ran faster, and was soon swallowed by the darkness and the gale.

Vanity of vanities. George had actually believed he could save his species. And yet, despite the scale of his failure, he had not reverted to his old, unambitious ways. He expected things now. God owed him. Tirelessly, enterprisingly, he dashed across the Lazarev Ice Shelf. I'll go to whomever Morning made that deal with, he thought. They'll let me keep my child. They must.

His lantern was strong, more than equal to an Antarctic blizzard, and he had no trouble keeping Holly in view. She was only four, and unsteady, and burdened with a scopas suit and Birdie. He called her name. The wind threw it back in his face. Bits of ice sailed past, pelting his forehead, slicing his cheeks. He wished that he were unadmitted, so that his memories would be fogged, but instead the images all boasted a brutal clarity: Holly's first trip to the zoo, Holly being a bug for Halloween . . .

The crevasses of Antarctica are predatory, hungry, lying in wait. Holly did not notice the great Novolazarevkaya Crevasse. One second she was running, the next she was gone, falling in a flash of golden scopas threads.

George cursed the crevasse aloud, vowing to defeat it as totally as Sverre's navy had defeated the invalidated past. Already he was at the brink, throwing himself on his stomach, extending his lantern arm. The beam spilled downward, illuminating flying whorls of snow and a child's figure pressed against the wall, her boots frozen to a feeble lip of ice. George saw two frightened green eyes, heard whimpering. His muscles and tendons creaked, nearly tearing apart as he fought for an extra inch of reach.

The tomb inscriber proved stronger than himself. He touched something soft, seized it. He yanked. Her silk-wrapped hand came forward, safe in his, but it was strangely, horribly weightless.

'It wasn't supposed to end this way!' a voice shouted from out of the storm.

George stared at the awful object he was holding. The wrist was cut. A plastic tube poked through the crack. At the fractured elbow, ball bearings and copper wire protruded. The stump of the upper arm was a fountain of yellow hydraulic fluids; the technological blood gushed from rubber veins, spilled around steel bones, and dripped onto the Lazarev Ice Shelf.

Dressed in his diamond-patterned scopas suit, Theophilus Carter ambled into view. Icicles grew from his nostrils like tusks and drooped from the inside brim of his top hat like crystalline hair. His gloves were stuck to a teapot. In the murky distance, the lights of his itinerant shop ('Remarkable Things for Human Bodies') burned through the blizzard.

Again Theophilus said, 'It wasn't supposed to end this way . . .'

George hurled the puppet arm into the dark whistling pit, and when Holly's double looked up at him he lost consciousness and collapsed on the ice.

CHAPTER TWENTY-ONE

In Which Our Hero Crowns a Madman,
Carves an Epitaph, and Sees a Constellation

Smells cut through his brain, forcing him into the world. For-
maldehyde. Viscera. How different from the odorless continent,
how different from the prophylactic *City of New York*. He was
pleased to find himself on the MAD Hatter's hospital gurney.
Good. *He's planning to take me apart. He's going to stuff me with
circuits and pumps. I'll become Plato or Julius Caesar or George
Washington.*

Like a speeding subway car, the laboratory vibrated and
lurched, winds spurting through the cracks in its walls. The
organs trembled in their jars, the severed arms bumped against
the walls of their tanks, and the skeletons flounced on their ceiling
hooks like chandeliers of bone.

Airborne.

The Hatter waddled over with a tea tray. He had shed his
scopas suit, leaving himself attired in his morning coat and vest.

George tried to speak, but his vocal cords were iced up. He
poured himself tea, drank. 'I had no idea there was such cruelty in
the world.'

'Strange words from a convicted war criminal. Your loving
bride wanted to give you a day of happiness, that's all. We
calculated we could sustain the drama for twelve hours. Call it
cruelty if you like, deception, a ruse, though a ruse by any other
name would smell as sweet. I call it a gift.'

'She said she had made a *deal*,' George protested.

'With whom? Extinction? Stop living in a dream world. You

can't make deals with extinction – I told you that back in the city. The deal was with yours truly. Your bride gave me some free therapy, so I gave her a free automaton. The therapy proved useless, as we knew it would. Assured destruction is a hopeless disease.'

Rising from the gurney – his neck was stiff from Holly's horsey ride – George followed the Hatter out of the laboratory and into the shop. A pile of scopas suit sales contracts lay on the counter. The mannequins' shoulders pushed through their rotting costumes like cantaloupes tearing through grocery bags. The two men walked to the bellied window, leaned toward its congestion of hats. Theophilus traded his top hat for a bejeweled crown. George put on a homburg and stared at the birdless sky. Dark, bloated clouds floated by like plumes from the stacks of a weapons factory.

'Ever since the war,' said the Hatter, 'your child has been a lot of random molecules. You knew that. You always knew that. All the King's accountants and all the King's lawyers couldn't put . . . so I built her from scratch. Your wife gave me a nursery school photograph plus relevant data. The Big Dipper, everything. I programmed the reunion well, *n'est-ce pas*?'

The shop began to roll and pitch. The mannequins flapped their arms. Frantic tintinnabulations arose from the bells over the door.

'Admit it, things went swimmingly,' said the Hatter. 'A bit mawkish for my tastes – yours, too, probably – but on the whole, swimmingly.'

George noticed how cadaverous Professor Carter had become. His pink hair was almost white, and his skin looked like stale cheese. The four-in-hand tie surrounded a neck as narrow and coarse as a loaf of French bread. Only one of his rabbit teeth remained, and it was black and cracked.

Stripping himself naked, the Hatter went to a mannequin dressed in royal regalia. 'Help me with this, will you?'

Together they hauled down the coronation mantle, which was as heavy and bulky as an Oriental rug, and placed it around Theophilus's tiny shoulders. Immediately he toppled under the weight. His crown fell off. 'When you're a king,' he gasped, propping himself up on one elbow, 'people are less likely to notice that you're insane.' Through a miracle of effort, he got into a sitting position. 'One more favor.' He petted the ermine on his capelet. 'Crown me.'

George lowered the wonderful sparkling hat over Theophilus's dead hair. 'How do I look?' the Hatter asked.

'Splendid.'

He really did, in a way.

'Off with their heads! Bring on the dancing girls! Turn away those petitioners! Maximize those strategic options!'

For nearly an hour he sat in the corner, raving quietly. George brought him tea.

'Enhance that deterrence! Put Humpty-Dumpty together again! Let them eat cake!'

He motioned George over with his scepter. The tomb inscriber bent low. '*Au revoir*, my friend.' The Hatter drank tea. 'The odds, however, are against it.'

And then, slowly, graciously, as the shop settled onto the ground, Good King Theophilus began his long reign over nothing.

George stepped through the door. He held his lantern high. More immortal than Egypt's pyramids, the Ice Palace of Justice rose against the verbose slopes of Mount Christchurch, pennants shivering, spires skewering black clouds. JUSTICE IS SERVED, the mountain said.

There was no storm here, only a mournful wind bearing the smoky odor of scopas suit insulation. Everywhere he glanced, from the bellied shop window to the limits of his light and beyond, the suits covered the glacial tongue like cocoons abandoned by some huge and over-propagated species of moth. He wanted to have some really profound response to the situation but could not manage it. So, he thought, this is it: no more people, not a one, no admitteds, no unadmitteds, nobody. My, my.

But then, growling mechanically, a Sno-Cat emerged from the gloom, stopping before the Mad Tea Party. An old woman got out, one arm bowed around her scopas suit helmet, the other gripping a cane made of ice. She scuttled forward.

'Hello, George.'

'Mrs Covington?'

'This foolish glacier is almost as cold as your monument works.' Bands of snow flashed through Nadine's gray hair.

'It's good to see you again, ma'am.' Despite the cold, the waves of well-being managed to reach him. 'I was certain your little sailboat would be swamped.'

'The documents barge picked me up.'

'You saw the trial?'

'I caught your part. Don't worry, George, nothing you could have said would have changed the verdict . . . So, tell me, did Leonardo's painting predict the future?'

'I saw my daughter again.' He fixed on the dark effluvium coming from the Cat's tailpipe. 'But it wasn't her – it just seemed like her. You shouldn't have raised my hopes.'

'*You* raised your hopes.'

'I went to that marble city like you said I should, and I found Professor Carter, and he made me fertile, and it didn't matter.'

'That's the way things go in these post-exchange environments. Remember the good old days, when you wrote those epitaphs for me in Massachusetts? "She was better than she knew," remember? "He never found out what he was doing here," right?' She pointed her ice cane toward the Cat. 'It's warm in the cab, and we have work to do.'

They drove past a dozen deserted ice limbos and ten thousand bereft scopas suits. Once the Cat was atop the glacial tongue, Nadine headed for the eastern face of the nunatak and drove up the slope. Five ice-sealed corpses swung on their living gibbets.

The Cat stopped before Brat Tarmac's remains. Drops of frozen blood hung from his bullet wounds like tears leaving blind eyes. George climbed to the roof, a hacksaw wrapped tightly in his glove. He peeled off the belt that held the general's man-portable thermonuclear device, buckled it around his own waist. He went to work on the cable. The grinning blade groaned and shrieked.

Brat tumbled to the roof. George laid him out carefully, as he had seen them do with the deceased at the Montefiore Funeral Home.

Nadine drove to the next tree. Overwhite's beard was a fretwork of icicles and frost. George sawed him down.

Then Randstable. Sparrow. Wengernook, who looked nervous even in death.

After stacking the heavy, rigid bodies in the back of the Cat, he returned to Sparrow's tree. Had his eyes tricked him? No, there it was, a little Bible, frozen solid. He picked it up.

Latitude: 79 degrees 38 minutes south.

Longitude: 169 degrees 15 minutes east.

Pushing up from the ice was a stone reminiscent of the megalith George had inspected at the Snape's Hill Burial Grounds. On this spot, only eleven miles from supplies, Robert Falcon Scott had perished after failing to become the first human to reach the South Pole.

The inscribed monument left George with the impression that Scott felt worse about being bettered by a Norwegian than he did about starving to death.

'Of course, he might just as easily have been born the Norwegian and Amundsen the Britisher,' said Nadine, 'in which case Scott would have been *glad* that Amundsen won.'

'Not if Scott was Norwegian, no.'

'Why?'

'Because then a *Britisher* would have won.'

'I don't understand.'

A pick swayed from the rear door of the Cat. George assaulted the Ross Ice Shelf. Sub-zero winds bore away the sound of metal striking ice; white sparks shot into the air. Gradually the pit expanded until it was large enough to admit all five bodies. With Nadine's help he lowered his friends into the darkness. 'Do you hate them?' he asked.

'I hate their bad ideas,' she replied.

'We should say a few words.'

'Go ahead.'

For ten minutes George struggled with the frozen Bible. Trying to open it was like trying to rip granite. At last he made a fissure slightly beyond the middle – on Ecclesiastes, a set of existential essays that had been included in the Bible by mistake. It was a favorite with Unitarians. Poor Reverend Sparrow would no doubt have preferred something more tumultuous – Ezekiel, Zephaniah, the Revelation – but this would have to do.

'Wisdom is better than strength: nevertheless the poor man's wisdom is despised, and his words are not heard,' George read. 'Wisdom is better than weapons of war: but one sinner destroyeth much good,' he continued. 'Dead flies cause the ointment of the perfumer to send forth a stinking savour: so doth a little folly outweigh wisdom and honor,' he concluded.

'That was very nice,' said Nadine.

The tomb inscriber climbed into the grave, unzipped Reverend Sparrow's suit, and placed the splayed book against his heart.

Once George was back on the surface, they filled in the hole with ice and snow, Nadine all the while reminiscing aloud about her husband Nathaniel, each nugget of memory receiving detailed review, Nathaniel Covington the poet, Nathaniel Covington the great lover.

From the Cat's tool box the old woman procured a hammer and a chisel. It took George an hour to wipe the Scott Monument clean. Nadine held the lantern steady as he laid down his guidelines with chalk. Tongue pressed firmly against his mustache, he began to ply his trade.

The hammer pounded. The chisel danced.

He did a fine, professional job – Nadine said so. The characters all had serifs.

IN LOVING MEMORY

OF

PEOPLE

4,500,000 BC–AD 1995

THEY WERE BETTER THAN THEY KNEW

THEY NEVER FOUND OUT
WHAT THEY WERE DOING HERE

Later, as the old woman lay propped against a hummock, her voice fading, her flesh expiring, George asked, 'Why did you entrap me?'

Nadine attempted to lever herself to her feet using her ice cane, thought better of the idea, settled back against the hummock. 'If they hadn't sent me to Wildgrove,' she said softly, 'they would have sent someone else. When I saw what name the McMurdo framers had picked, I volunteered.' Mischief glinted in her eyes. 'I wanted to see you as you were before the war. I had to meet you, George, touch you. And Holly.' She moved her shriveled head toward him. 'Look at me. Do you see it? My face, your face, my face . . .'

He did.

The old woman's smile was a triumph of determination over materials. Missing teeth, weak face muscles, but still she beamed.

'You're my granddaughter, aren't you?' he said.

They fell into each other's arms.

'Holly was your mother,' he said.

'The only tolerable moments of my unadmittance came when I watched her at nursery school. I wish I'd gotten to baby-sit for her.'

'And your father was . . . ?'

'John Frostig's youngest son.'

'Rickie?'

'Nickie.'

'The hamster killer?'

'He would have grown up.'

'Just like Holly.'

'You would have been proud of her, Grandfather.'

'She always said she wanted to be an artist.'

'She became a teacher. To the first graders she was Socrates and Mother Goose combined. There's no way she could ever see all the good she did – more good than if she'd become an artist. She was better than she knew.'

'I wonder if she ever got to see the Big Dipper.'

Nadine kissed his ragged beard. 'I'm sure she would have.'

'I'll bet you're a hell of a baby-sitter,' he said.

'A world beater.'

'First grade?' he said. 'A worthy profession, don't you think? Honorable. Challenging. Yes, that's perfect. First grade . . . If you were to have an epitaph on your monument, what would it be?'

She coughed. 'I don't want an epitaph, or a monument either. We did not get in. Don't pretend that we did.'

'All right.'

They held hands, scopas glove pressed against scopas glove. Her rough and lovely cheek melted beneath his lips like butter. He saw her suit deflate slightly, felt tissues and bones leaving her glove. He stood up.

The MARCH Hare's little missile clung parasitically to George's waist. He unstrapped it. How did such things work? It needed a code – is that what the deputy prosecutor had said? – and a brass key.

Seizing the buckle, he whipped the belt around as if it were a sling. The bomb whistled. It struck the Scott Monument squarely. A stabilizer broke off, twirled away.

Again he smashed the weapon, and again he smashed it, and again – smashed it in the names of Morning Valcourt and Justine Paxton, smashed it while thinking of the nonexistent first-graders Holly had never taught – until the thing was nothing but springs, detonators, Styrofoam chunks, uranium-238 fragments, and deuterium core pieces strewn across the grave site, not much of a plowshare, but not much of a man-portable thermonuclear device either.

George looked at his granddaughter's empty suit. He thought of Job. Satan lacked imagination. To crack a man's faith, one need not resort to burning his flesh, ruining his finances, or any such obvious afflictions. One need only take a man's species away from him.

There was laughter in Antarctica. Every ice crystal mocked him. The great crevasse of the Ross Ice Shelf spread through his mind. His granddaughter had wanted no monument. Very well, he thought, then I don't want one either. The cold was like a disease. His bowels seemed frozen. There was frost on his bones, sleet in his lungs. He looked up. The sky was dark – dark as

unadmitted blood, dark as the crevasse that was his destination –
and then, as his eyes adjusted, he saw stars, not the Big Dipper but
the crisp hot lights that men had named the Southern Cross.

He got in the Cat, turned on the engine, and started across the
young, disarmed planet.

EPILOGUE

Salon-de-Provence, France, 1554

'Is that all?' Jacob asked.

'What do you mean, "Is that all"?' said Nostradamus. 'How could there be *more*?'

The prophet opened the picture-cannon and blew on the oil lamp. As the tall flame leaned away from the lens, the projected crevasse became blurry and pale. The flame flew into the ether, and with it went the Ross Ice Shelf.

'I thought there might be more,' said the boy.

He marched across the room, pulled back the drapes.

'You don't *live* here,' said Nostradamus.

'Sorry, Monsieur.'

Sunshine pulsed through the window. The boy closed his eyes and felt the rays hitting his lids, turning the world orange-red.

The prophet slammed his palm against the sash, opened the window. They stood together, man and boy, devouring the air, surprisingly hot for so early in the morning. Strings of sweat sparkled on their faces. Finches hopped amid the cherry trees.

'Why did George drive into the crevasse?' asked Jacob.

'Why do you think?'

'I suppose he was getting too cold. Is this truly the way the world will end?'

'I wouldn't be surprised.'

'Then I'm glad I shall be dead first.'

A scream came through the floor. Jacob flinched.

'Her pain will pass,' said Nostradamus, squeezing the boy's arm.

'I know,' Jacob gasped.

'Concentrate on something else. The show – did you like it?'

'Oh, yes, Monsieur.'

'You truly liked it?'

'Very much so.'

'All of it?'

'I might wish for fewer sad scenes, but—'

'Listen to me,' said the prophet quickly. 'You must go downstairs.' With his Malacca cane he pointed toward the door. 'Find your mother. Hold her hand. Kiss her. Say, "I love you, Mother." Say, "You will bring forth a child soon, and Dr Nostradamus has foreseen that it will be strong, and it will never get plague." Say to your mother, "Somehow, with God's help, we shall manage." Tell her, "Spring is upon the earth, a fine time and place for a baby to disembark."' Nostradamus winked. 'When you have done this, return to me, and we shall talk. Are your shoulders strong?'

'I think so.'

'Strong enough to carry our picture-cannon from city to city, sometimes on an empty stomach, and in the rain?'

'Oh, yes.'

'And your wits – are they strong too? Strong enough to focus the cannon for me each evening and to project the paintings in the right order?'

'Most certainly!'

'Don't ever get the order wrong.'

'Not ever!'

'God help you if you drop one. Your wage will be ten *écus* per week. I can envision nothing better at the moment. Naturally you will send them home.'

The boy ran to the picture-cannon, patted the chimney with his fingertips. Hot, but not enough to burn. He lifted the miracle machine off the writing desk, rested it on his shoulder.

'It's not heavy at all, Monsieur.'

A smile broke through the prophet's beard. 'You'll think differently come winter. Remember – the order must always be right.'

The boy set down the machine and ran for the door, his mind aglow with visions of Paris and Toulon. Or, for that matter, he thought, why not Rome, Valencia, Augsburg, London, Athens, Alexandria, Kiev, St Petersburg? Why not any of the glorious, unburned cities of the earth? Why not the City of New York, wherever that was?

'Oh – and one more thing, Jacob,' said Nostradamus.

'Yes, Monsieur?'

The prophet raised his Malacca cane and traced a Southern Cross in the air.

'Tell your mother that it's going to be a girl.'

James Morrow was born in Philadelphia in 1947. He spent much of his teenage life in Hillside Cemetery, where he entertained his passion for 8mm moviemaking by creating numerous short horror and fantasy films with his friends. Having received degrees from both the University of Pennsylvania and Harvard University, he then turned his creative urges to writing. Commonly in his works, Morrow satirises organised religion and elements of humanism and atheism. He is perhaps best known for the Godhead Trilogy, the first of which, *Towing Jehovah*, won the World Fantasy Award in 1995. He currently lives in Pennsylvania with his family.

A full list of SF Masterworks can be found at

www.gollancz.co.uk